Who Loves Ya, Baby?

Who Loves Ya, Baby?

Gemma Bruce

KENSINGTON PUBLISHING CORP.
http://www.kensingtonbooks.com

BRAVA BOOKS are published by

Kensington Publishing Corp.
850 Third Avenue
New York, NY 10022

Copyright © 2005 by Gemma Bruce

All Kensington titles, imprints and distributed lines are available at special quantity discounts for bulk purchases for sales promotion, premiums, fund-raising, educational or institutional use.

Special book excerpts or customized printings can also be created to fit specific needs. For details, write or phone the office of the Kensington Special Sales Manager: Kensington Publishing Corp., 850 Third Avenue, New York, NY 10022. Attn. Special Sales Department. Phone: 1-800-221-2647.

Brava and the B logo Reg. U.S. Pat. & TM Off.

ISBN 0-7582-1249-6

First Kensington Trade Paperback Printing: November 2005
10 9 8 7 6 5 4 3 2 1

Printed in the United States of America

Who
Loves Ya,
Baby?

Chapter 1

The sole heir of a practical joker should always look before sitting down. Not the wisdom of an ancient Confucian proverb. Not a message in a fortune cookie. Just a little warning that Julie Excelsior failed to heed as she sat in Gunther and Gunther's Manhattan law office and heard the terms of her uncle's will.

Now she was sitting in the dark somewhere in the Adirondacks, crammed into her Volkswagen, with suitcases, grocery bags, boxes of linens jumbled on the back seat, and a sixty-pound German shepherd named Smitty, sitting beside her. And it occurred to her that she might have acted a teensy bit too precipitately.

She turned on her headlights again. Yep, still there. And it wasn't going away. Funny. She remembered a sparkling white, board and batten house, with green gingerbread trim, a shady front porch with two big rocking chairs, and a turret, with elegant oval windows, that rose like a church steeple to a pitched roof and an iron finial that pointed to the sky.

"Giving God the bird," Uncle Wes explained to Julie and he would curl her five-year-old fingers into position so the two of them could join the finial in the Excelsior one-finger salute.

That was before lightning struck, twisting the finial into a knot, blowing out the turret's windows, and flooding Wes's bedroom. Proving to his satisfaction that God couldn't take a joke.

But that was then. What Julie saw now was a monstrous old house, looming out of the shadows, its stark angles and dark recesses sending a chill up her spine. The wood siding was dingy gray, the windows were gaping black holes. The porch sagged ominously, and the turret seemed to be—she tilted her head to the left—leaning downhill. She could practically hear the doors creaking on rusted hinges. No wonder they called it American Gothic.

It was a disaster. And it was all hers. The house, the pond, the apple orchard, the gazebo, the twenty acres of woodland. And the thing that brought her back to a place she'd tried to forget—the riddle.

No bank account was mentioned in Wes's will, only the hint of hidden treasure, written on a piece of yellow tablet paper and placed in a sealed envelope, addressed, but never mailed. It had been too tempting. She'd come home, just like her uncle intended. Good old Wes, laughing to the bitter end.

Beyond the house, the headlights picked out chunks of the stone wall that meandered up the hillside, separating the two largest residences in town, Excelsior House and Reynolds Place. It was hard to believe she'd ever crouched beneath it, pulse pounding, fingers crossed, while she waited for Cas to sneak through the dark and silently scale its heights.

Without warning, he'd tumble over the top, scaring the daylights out of her, and land sprawled at her feet, grinning, his hair sticking straight up from the cowlick over his forehead . . .

Yeah. And the rest was history, not her favorite subject.

Julie briefly considered turning around and driving back to Manhattan. Then remembered that she had nothing to return to. She reached into the glove compartment for her flashlight, clipped on Smitty's leash, killed the headlights, and opened her door.

Smitty scrambled over her lap and leapt out of the car, dragging Julie with him.

"Heel," she cried as he plunged toward the scraggly bushes in front of the house. "Heel, you police academy dropout." Smitty stopped and planted his feet. Julie careered past him and tripped over a piece of gingerbread molding that lay on the ground. Damn. She looked around, then upward and found a jagged, empty space along the eave above her head.

She must have been out of her mind. She was a cop—an ex-cop—not Miss Fix-it.

She let Smitty stake his claim to a rhododendron bush, then started up the steps. The floorboards groaned beneath her feet as she cautiously crossed the dark, deep-set porch, Smitty pressed to her side, the flashlight picking out glimmers of the red, blue and amber stained glass windows that flanked the heavy chestnut front door. It also picked out several squares of cardboard that covered sections of missing glass.

Someone had left a pair of work boots by the door and Julie's gut twisted to think of Wes, living and dying alone in the decaying house, with no friends, no family, just his riddles. He'd left her everything and she'd never even sent him a Christmas card.

"Oh hell." She sniffed and reached into her jeans pocket with suddenly clammy fingers, pulled out the key to the front door, and inserted it in the lock. The tumbler creaked. The latch clicked. She turned the knob and pushed the door inward—and was hit by a blast of air so cold and dead that she stepped backwards, her heart clamoring.

Smitty padded past her into the dark.

After a second, Julie followed. Not that she trusted Smitty's sense of self-preservation. But it was either go inside or sleep in the front seat of a bug-sized car with a giant-sized dog.

She groped for the light switch, and praying someone had paid the electric bill, flipped it on. A yellow light shone down from the teardrop chandelier and Julie let out a pent-up breath. Except for a fine layer of dust, the foyer looked just the way it always had: the dark wainscoting beneath pine green walls, the curving walnut staircase, the oriental runner, more thread-bare than she remembered.

Okay. This was better. She turned off the flashlight and looked into the parlor. The same overstuffed, red velvet couch and wing chair were placed around the fireplace. The same case clock and assortment of figurines rested on the mahogany mantel; the round oak table still held its place by the front bay window.

She let Smitty off the leash and stepped inside the room. The ceiling-high bookshelves were stuffed with books: history books, nature books, sailing books, novels, and the cache of erotica that she and Cas had discovered on the top shelf one summer and had read aloud in the obscurity of the gazebo, only half under-standing the words. They had giggled until their sides ached and then Cas had touched her and it was different. And their laughter turned into something else.

Remembered warmth rushed through her. She clamped a lid on it and backed out of the room, away from the past. She had no intention of taking any little trips down memory lane. She was here to sell the house and get on with her life. Whatever it was going to be.

She went out to the car and unloaded the essentials: her suitcase, a six-pack of beer, dog food, a gallon jug of water, and a bag of donuts. The rest could wait until the morning. She left her suitcase in the foyer and carried the rest down the hall.

Smitty was waiting for her by a closed door.

"Didn't have any trouble finding the kitchen, did you?" said Julie. She turned the knob. The door opened; the knob came away in her hand. She looked at it, looked at the brass rod that hung out of the hole in the door.

She sighed and put the knob on the kitchen table. She thought longingly of Manuel, her apartment house super. He could fix anything, and Julie depended on him. She might be able to unload a clip into a bull's-eye at sixty feet, but she didn't know a washer from a bolt nut.

Tomorrow she'd have to find a handy man, a cheap one.

She turned on the kitchen light. A fluorescent tube flickered a few times, then came on with a buzz . . . and kept buzzing.

And an electrician.

She filled Smitty's water dish from the water bottle, and took a beer and donut out to the parlor. She sat down on the windowsill where she could see the lights of Reynolds Place winking in the distance.

For years, she'd passed that house every Friday afternoon, carrying her overnight case for her weekend visit with Uncle Wes, knowing Miriam and Reynolds were watching her from the window, thinking *white trash,* though they would never dare say it out loud. She trudged along, dressed in her Sunday best, like Pip summoned by Miss Havisham. Only at Wes's you were more likely to get a rubber ice cube than a calcified wedding cake.

Julie grinned. Wouldn't they be surprised when they found out their worst nightmare was now their neighbor.

Too bad Cas wasn't here. He'd get a big kick out of how things had turned out. But he must be a banker by now. The Reynolds men were always bankers. And since the local Savings and Loan had gone belly up fifteen years ago, he wouldn't be banking here.

Just as well. Sort of.

Cas was her closest childhood friend. The first boy to look up her dress to see her underwear. The first boy to reach down her T-shirt to cop a feel. The first boy to tie her to a tree. Actually he was the only boy who'd tied her to a *tree,* but it had been a promising beginning. Julie smiled, then frowned. He was also the first man to betray her.

Well, to hell with him and the rest of the Reynoldses. She wouldn't embroil herself with that family ever again. She'd be more than content to smirk at Reynolds and Marian from over the wall.

Suddenly tired, she pushed away from the sill and sank down on the velvet sofa. The cushion emitted a loud raspberry, and Julie jumped to her feet. "Ugh. For once, couldn't I be surprised by an inflatable boy toy instead of a whoopee cushion?"

She looked around for a safer place to sit and saw a piece of yellow tablet paper propped against a stack of books on the table.

The next clue? Maybe this one would lead her to where Wes had hidden his money. She hurried over to read it.

In marble halls as white as milk,
Lined with skin as soft as silk
Within a fountain crystal clear,
A golden apple does appear.

Great. Total nonsense.

P.S. Sleep in your old room. The sheets are clean.

"Right," she muttered. "If someone else hasn't slept in them in the last fifteen years."

P.P.S. Remember who loves you.

She did remember.

P.P.P.S. Get Cas to tell you the one about the chicken, the horse and the Harley.

She frowned at the paper, but couldn't stop the anticipatory shiver that ran over her.

"Dammit, Wes, if this is another one of your pranks." Cas couldn't be here. He was a banker . . . somewhere else.

She sometimes pictured him sitting behind a desk, tall, pot-bellied, and stoop-shouldered, wearing a three-piece suit and rimless glasses, his cowlick supplanted by a shiny bald pate.

She never imagined him tall and hot and tying her up. Not often. Not when she was awake. She looked at her watch. Hmm. Time for bed.

She washed the last of her donut down with a swig of beer. She was not here to get sidetracked by the past, but to follow the clues to her inheritance. Because the past didn't pay the rent.

She didn't have time to think about Cas. She didn't miss him and she certainly didn't need him. She had a dilapidated house, man's best friend, and jokes from the grave.

All in all, life was looking pretty good.

* * *

Life was not so great for Acting Sheriff Cas Reynolds, a job he'd held for four months and for which he had no experience. What had started out as a weekend visit to a dying friend had turned into three months of disaster. He'd been in town for exactly four hours and ten minutes when Hank Jessop, the real sheriff, keeled over at the Fourth of July picnic, practically at Cas's feet. An hour later, Hank was going through double bypass surgery and Cas had agreed to fill in as sheriff until he recovered.

"Don't worry," Wes told him and slapped him on the back." Nothing ever happens in Ex Falls."

And nothing had happened during his first three and a half months.

Then Wes died and the chicken thefts began. Two coops in two weeks, cleaned out right under the noses of the owners. Cas had driven to each place, poked around in the muck looking for God knew what, took depositions, listened to suppositions and he still didn't have one damn lead.

He banged on a spot above the door handle of the police cruiser and the door swung open. He stepped out onto the graveled parking lot of the Roadhouse, tossed his uniform shirt into the back seat, and replaced it with a green sweater. Then he shoved his hands into his pants pockets and sauntered through the cluster of motorcycles, battered pickups and rusty cars to the entrance of the bar and grill.

The place was hopping and Cas had to squeeze through the crowd toward the bar, where the black jackets of the local motorcycle gang took up nearly every seat. Cas settled onto the one free stool. Unfortunately, it was the one next to Henley Baxter, his least favorite person since third grade.

"Hiya, Cas," said Tilda Green as she slid a Foster's draft toward him. Tonight Tilda's hair was red and combed into a beehive, so high and finely teased that the barroom lights created a magenta halo around her head.

"Evening, Tilda. Nice hairdo."

Tilda patted her head. "My Laverne and Shirley look."

Henley leaned into Cas and Cas got a whiff of hair grease.

"Hey sheriff, seen any chickens lately?" Henley grinned and turned back to his beer.

Cas sighed. He needed to take shit from someone who couldn't decide if they were Elvis or The Fonz.

"Yeah, see any chickens lately?" echoed Bo Whitaker, a shorter, stockier version of Henley, including the hair and the sideburns that grew down to his jawline.

Tilda placed a battered plastic menu in front of Cas and turned to the two gang members. "I don't want any business in here tonight. I'm still four chairs short from the last time you broke up the place. If you do it again, you're out of here."

"Cheeseburger, medium, fries, well done," Cas said and pushed the menu back to her.

Tilda slipped it under the counter. "And Cas is in a mood. You wanna spend the night over on Walnut Street?"

"Depends," said Henley. "What're they serving at the jail tonight? Chicken?"

Beside him, Bo let out a nasal snort and said, "Chicken?"

Cas sighed. He was getting a little tired of the chicken jokes. He didn't know why he still stuck around, now that Wes was dead. The county sheriff could do Hank's job. But there was that damn riddle, and he couldn't leave until he figured it out.

"They're just razzing you, Cas," said Tilda. "Cause there's nothing else to do around here. I'll put a piece of lettuce on that burger. Make sure you get a vegetable today."

Henley chewed on his lip and nodded. "Ya know, you should go down to the hotel. I'm sure your sister's got some . . . chicken cooking."

"Yeah, chicken cooking," echoed Bo.

Cas took a swig of beer. All he had ever wanted to do in life was build a boat, marry Julie Excelsior, and sail away. He'd managed to build a few boats. But he hadn't married Julie and he'd never sailed away.

His burger came, a wilted piece of lettuce drooped over

each side. He doused it and the fries with ketchup and concentrated on eating.

Henley stood up. "Well, gotta get going. Gonna find us some . . . chicks." He pulled his jacket collar up and did a couple of shoulder twitches straight out of a fifties movie. "Like maybe your baby sister."

Cas's jaw clenched. He put down his burger and slowly turned to face Henley as the rest of the bar grew silent. Henley grinned back and sucked on his tooth.

"Put a sock in it, Henley," said Tilda. "Or you'll find yourself without a place to drink. And I mean it. Get outta here."

"Aw, Tilda. I was just goofing."

"You're mean as a skunk, always were. Now beat it."

"Thanks, Tilda," Cas said when Henley and Bo had left and the rest of the drinkers had gone back to minding their own business. "I didn't really feel like breaking up a fight tonight."

Tilda pushed another Foster's toward him and grinned. "Especially one you started."

"It's this chicken thing," said Cas.

"You gotta admit, it's funny," said Tilda. "If I didn't know better, I'd say Wes Excelsior was stealing chickens from his grave just to bust your chops."

Cas took a sip of beer. "Believe me, Tilda, the thought has crossed my mind."

Chapter 2

Julie stood outside her old bedroom, wondering how much dust, mold and mildew could build up in fifteen years.

Smitty pushed his nose against the door.

"Okay, but you're sleeping on the floor." Julie opened the door and felt along the wall for the light switch.

Smitty sneezed.

"Dust," she said, her hand going unerringly to the switch. The light popped on and she blinked; then sucked in her breath.

The room wasn't dusty, it wasn't moldy, it wasn't mildewy. It was pink. Everywhere. The wallpaper was flocked with fuzzy pink blossoms on a light pink background. Her sneakers sank into plush pink carpet. Pink ruffled curtains hung from the window, and a pink satin comforter was spread across a new four-poster king-sized bed. Pink pillows were piled high against the headboard; frills, ruffles, ribbons, all pink.

"Good God," exclaimed Julie. "Maybe I shouldn't mix donuts with beer."

Smitty, quicker to realize a good thing when he saw it, jumped onto the bed, circled twice, and stretched out on the comforter.

Shaking her head, Julie dropped her suitcase on the luggage rack at the end of the bed and walked over to a ridiculously small dressing table with a tiny ornate mirror.

"Nice touch, Wes, very nice. I feel just like the effing little princess." She batted her eyelashes at the mirror. Only she didn't look like a little princess. She looked like someone who had quit her job under duress, driven five hours to the back of beyond, and eaten a chocolate donut for dinner. "Please say the bathroom isn't pink."

It was. Dainty pink hand towels hung over brass towel bars. A stack of thick pink bath towels were perfectly folded on an open brass armoire. The walls at least were white and she lifted her eyes toward the ceiling and, by inference, heaven, to thank her wacky uncle for showing such restraint.

"On second thought . . ." She looked down. "Is there a purgatory for bad taste?"

Behind a shower curtain of pink butterflies, she found a huge, spotless, brand-new Jacuzzi tub. Smiling, she turned on the jets and stripped out of her clothes.

When she emerged from the tub a half hour later, her knees were weak, her skin was tingly warm, and she smelled like peaches from the pink bath salts she found in a wicker basket on the armoire. She wrapped herself in a pink towel and padded across the carpet to open her suitcase. The extra large NYPD sweatshirt she slept in was folded on top. Not nearly up to the mark for her new bedroom, but it was comfy and it wasn't like anybody was going to see it.

She tossed it on the bed and put a stack of jeans in the bottom drawer of the bureau. Her T-shirts and sweatshirts went into the next. But when she opened the next drawer, she found it was already filled.

Not with pink, thank goodness, but with a wild array of the tiniest pants and bras she had seen outside a Victoria's Secret Catalogue. All new, tags on. She dumped her underwear on the top of the dresser and lifted out a black lace thong. "They *are* from Victoria's Secret. Thanks, Wes." She dropped the thong back into the drawer and shoved her underwear in after it.

With a sense of trepidation, she opened the remaining drawer. Yep. There they were. Little nylon nighties, mostly pink. But not little-girl pink like the rest of the room. More Mae West on a hormone day. She riffled through them until she found a creamy white nightshirt. It had a plunging vee neck and little cap sleeves, but it wasn't pink. She dropped her towel and slipped it over her head.

The silk fabric caressed her skin as it slid down her body. Too bad there was no one to enjoy it with her. But the closest she'd come to having a boyfriend in the last year was her ex-partner Donald, the bribe taker. She'd blown the whistle on him and been demoted to a desk job for her valor. She wouldn't wear silk for him even if he showed up at the door with expensive champagne and wearing nothing but a G-string.

Which left her only one fantasy. *Nope*, she warned herself. *Pot belly, bald shiny head, respectable three-piece suit. Definitely not for you.* But the image of Cas—the one she ruthlessly squelched even at her loneliest—popped into her mind anyway. That Cas was tall, lean and hard, with a tight ass and a larger-than-life penis. His face had developed character, but he still had the lopsided smile he had at fifteen. And his dark hair still stuck up above his forehead.

She ran her fingertips along the neckline of the nightshirt to where it stopped between her breasts. Pulled them away. Nah. She was better off thinking about the pot belly. And much better off without Cas.

She lifted the last thing out of her suitcase and weighed it in her hand.

A Glock semi-automatic was a little out of place in the Pollyanna bedroom. She'd worked hard to become a cop only to realize that when you're five feet six and built, with a turned-up nose and wide, baby-blue eyes, perps had trouble taking you seriously. Even wearing a uniform, her feet planted in the standard shooting stance as she aimed her Glock at them, they were just as likely to say "Hey, Babe," as to put their hands in the air. Once she'd made detective and gone undercover things got better. A Glock wielded a lot more clout with stiletto heels and a leather mini-skirt behind it. She bet it wielded even more in front of a thong.

She carried it over to the bedside table and opened the drawer. It was already occupied by a box of condoms.

"Jesus, Wes. Did you leave a list of possible prospects, too?"

But there was only the box. She placed her Glock next to it and shut the drawer. She shoved a snoring Smitty aside, crawled between pink satin sheets, and turned off the lamp.

Moonlight streamed in through the window. She pulled the comforter up to her chin and settled down to sleep. Certainly not to wonder if Cas was in Ex Falls or how he would look in a G-string.

Julie was dreaming about crystal fountains and golden apples when she suddenly awoke. It was dark and for a moment she couldn't remember where she was or why. Then she heard the low growl.

She groped for the lamp switch and blinked against the sudden light. Smitty was at the window, paws on the sill, tail lowered and his fur standing erect.

Julie threw off the covers and went to see what was going on. "This better not be some nocturnal animal you want to meet," she told him as she peered out the window. Below them, the yard was dark. But on the hill where the roof of the gazebo stood out in dark silhouette, the beam from a flashlight wove in and out of sight.

"What the hell?" Julie watched as it turned in the direction of the gazebo. Damn, she had prowlers. But what could they be after in the gazebo?

The treasure? Maybe she wasn't the only one looking for Wes's fortune.

She pulled Smitty away from the window, climbed over the bed and reached into the drawer for her Glock. Then stopped. She had no authority here. Her permit might not be legal outside of New York City. But she couldn't let someone steal her fortune. She had to do something, but short of shooting . . .

She glanced around the room, found the princess phone sitting on the dressing table and picked it up. There was a dial tone. She punched in 911 and was only half surprised when someone answered. A woman's voice, sounding like someone's favorite grandma.

"I want to report a five sev—a prowler—in my yard," Julie whispered.

"Oh dear," said granny.

Julie gritted her teeth. "Could you please send a patrol car to—"

Smitty shot across the room and out the bedroom door. Julie stretched the phone cord, trying to see what was happening outside, but it wouldn't reach the window. *Last time I leave my cell downstairs,* she thought.

"Don't panic, dear. Is your door locked?"

Had she locked the door? She couldn't remember. Damn. What if they gave up on the gazebo and came to the house? They might try to rob her. She looked down at the gaping neckline of her nightshirt. She could see all the way to her toes. Rob or worse. She'd have to shoot them.

"What's your address?"

"I'm at the Excelsior House on Hillcrest Drive."

"Oh," said the operator. "Are you sure? No one lives there."

"Of course I'm sure. Could you hurry?"

"Yes. I'm calling the sheriff now."

Julie could hear Smitty scrambling over the wood floor downstairs as he ran from windows to door, looking for a way out.

"Tell him to hurry," said Julie and hung up the phone just as the granny said, "Stay on the . . ."

Sheriff be dammed. Hank Jessop was slower than a snail even after a thermos of coffee. She had property to protect. She unholstered her Glock and raced down the stairs.

"Stay," she commanded Smitty as soon as she reached the front door. Smitty sat down. She eased the door open and he bolted outside. She made a grab for him, but missed, and she found herself alone on the front porch, barefoot and freezing. Hell. If she went back upstairs to dress, they'd probably get away. She felt around for the work boots she'd seen earlier. They'd have to do.

Praying that nothing was living inside, she shoved her feet into the boots and clomped after Smitty, shoe laces flying, the enormous boots flopping on her feet as she crunched across the frost-covered grass.

Smitty was standing in attack mode halfway up the hill. His tail was wagging like a furry windshield wiper. When he was good, Smitty was the best. Unfortunately he had a short attention span and an innate love of people, which made him a great pet, but not prime police dog material.

Julie slipped into the shadow of a newly built shed a few feet away. "Ease off," she called and slapped her palm to her thigh. Smitty broke his stance and trotted toward her.

"Good boy." She wrapped her fingers around his collar and pulled him into the shadows with her. She peered around the corner of the shed. The gazebo was a hundred feet away, a mere outline in the dark. She didn't see any sign of movement.

"Heel," she whispered to Smitty and stepped around the edge of the shed. Smitty kept right beside her as she clung to the shadows and slowly made her way up the hill. She stopped behind a juniper bush and strained her ears to listen for the sound of a patrol car coming up the drive. All she could hear were her teeth chattering.

She leaned forward to get a better look and instead got a whiff of something unpleasant. *A handyman, an electrician— and a yardman*, she thought.

A figure moved away from the gazebo. Julie stepped out into the open, her Glock steadied in both hands. "Halt," she shouted in her gruffest voice. The flashlight turned in her direction, froze on her, then the light snapped off and the interloper began running for the trees.

"Halt." Julie fired over his head. Smitty raced after him.

When her ears stopped ringing, Julie followed, but the slippery ground and the unwieldy work boots slowed her down and by the time she got to the edge of the woods, they had both disappeared. She pressed her back against a pine tree, listened, then slipped into the trees. In an instant, the moonlight was snuffed out, but she could hear them thrashing through the underbrush. Then a high-pitched motor chugged to life and a vehicle roared away.

Smitty came trotting back and brushed up against her legs. Legs that were numb from the cold. "G-good work, S-S-Smitty. We almost had him."

Cas Reynolds drove too fast for safety, too slow to calm his racing pulse. When his phone rang, and Edith said "prowlers," Cas turned over in bed and thought, *Great. I get to chase chicken thieves through the countryside in the middle of the night.* Then Edith said, "Excelsior House." Cas reached for his pants. "A woman called." And Cas promptly lost his mind.

He'd done little rational thinking on the mad ride to The Hill. It couldn't be. She would never come back to Ex Falls. She hadn't even come back for Wes's funeral last week. Probably didn't even know he was dead.

It must be a prank. But Wes was the only prankster in town and unless he had called from the dead . . .

The old police cruiser swerved back and forth across Hillcrest Drive as Cas dodged potholes. He knew them by heart, he'd driven this road so many times. But tonight he passed the family home without a glance and screeched into the Excelsior driveway.

That's when he heard the shot. He stomped on the accelerator; the car careered around the pond, up the drive and came to a stop beside a light-colored Volkswagen.

Cas grabbed his town issued .38 police special from the seat beside him. Now he wished he'd taken time to load it. Not that he planned to shoot anybody. He yanked at the door handle, ready to hit the dirt. Instead he hit a solid wall and bounced back. Panicked, he'd forgotten the handle didn't work.

"Shi-i-t," he yelled and banged on the spot above the handle. The door swung open. He jumped out and ducked down between the VW and the police car. No more shots. A good sign, he hoped.

He peered through the VW window. Tried the door. Locked. Would thieves lock the getaway car? Wait a minute. He wasn't thinking clearly. It must belong to the person—woman—who called Edith.

But then who fired the . . . *Oh, God*. With a shiver of fatality, Cas knew his father must have overdone the martinis again and was taking pot shots at the gazebo from the Reynolds' back door.

He stuck the .38 in his jacket pocket, climbed the porch steps, and knocked on the door. Heard nothing. Knocked again. Ran around to the side door. Knocked. No answer.

It had probably scared the daylights out of—whoever was here. Because it couldn't be who he thought—wanted—it to be. But someone was definitely staying in the house.

She had probably heard shots, thought she was under attack, and called the police. Then she locked herself inside and was afraid to open the door. He should have called out that he was the sheriff, but he didn't have much experience yelling, "Police. Open up."

So Cas stood in the dark feeling like a fool. Not for the first time since returning to Ex Falls.

Now he would have to explain about his father and warn her not to go out to the gazebo at night, and she would think he was a nutcase instead of the law. And he'd have to confiscate another rifle from Reynolds. And listen to another lecture on the crimes of the Excelsiors.

"Only for you, Wes, would I do this," he muttered under his breath. He turned back to the door, knocked louder. "Hello?" he called. He stepped into the yard and looked up to the second floor where light shone through a bedroom window. Julie's old bedroom. His pulse jolted into overdrive. Not possible.

"Hello?" he called out. "Julie?" Still no answer. "See, not possible." Then a worse thought struck him. She had gone outside and—

Cas groaned. "Please say you didn't shoot her!" He turned in a circle, scanning the night, praying he wouldn't find her body lying on the frozen ground. You couldn't kill somebody aiming at a gazebo, could you? Of course not. He'd been watching too much television. People in Ex Falls didn't shoot each other, just deer, gazebos, and their own feet, cleaning their guns while half crocked.

In the distance, an engine fired to life; a single headlight flickered out of the wooded foothills. Cas reached for his police special. Maybe there really were thieves.

He began running up the hill toward the woods. If he could shoot out a tire, he'd catch the damn thieves red-handed, and everybody would lighten up on the chicken jokes. But of course he couldn't shoot out their tire, even if his pistol was loaded. He couldn't hit the side of a barn.

Julie had been a crack shot, but she'd never made fun of him. Just said, "Don't worry, Cas, bankers don't need to carry guns. There's Brinks."

He shook his head clear of Julie thoughts. It probably wasn't thieves anyway, just a bunch of local boys out having some fun. And when he found out who it was, he'd cart their sorry asses off to jail to cool their heels for the night, just for inconveniencing him. *And making his pulse race like a goddamn horny teenager.*

And he'd find them. Because for once he had a clue to follow. A truck with only one headlight.

Feeling much better, he stopped by the shed and peered at the gazebo. All right and tight there. He cautiously made his way to the crest of the hill and looked into the woods; caught sight of movement in the trees. He pressed back into a juniper bush and waited.

The night was suddenly still. He peered into the woods again. He would swear someone was standing just inside the ring of trees, out of the moonlight. He rolled tight shoulders and cracked his neck. What the hell was he doing in Ex Falls, chasing burglars through the woods?

He snorted. His just desserts. He'd chased Julie through these woods more times than he could remember. And caught her. He smiled, forgetting where he was for a moment. He'd been pretty damn good at Cops and Robbers in those days. He'd been even better at Pirates.

A rustle in the trees. *Wind? No wind tonight.* Another rustle. Not a nocturnal animal, but a glimmer of white. All right, time to act, or he might still be standing here when the sun rose, and someone was bound to see him and by tomorrow night, it would be all over town that he had spent the night hiding behind a bush with an empty gun while the thieves got away.

Cas said a quick prayer that he was out of range and stepped away from the bush. He braced his feet in the standard two-handed shooting stance he learned from *NYPD Blue*, and aimed into the darkness. He sucked in his breath.

A figure stepped out to the edge of the trees. There was just enough light for Cas to see the really big handgun that was aimed at him.

The *freeze* he'd been about to yell froze on his lips.

"Freeze," said a deep voice from the darkness.

Hey, that was his line. He froze anyway, then yelped, "Police."

"Yeah. So drop the weapon and put your hands in the air. Slowly."

Cas dropped his gun."No. I mean. Me. I'm the police."

"You're the sheriff?" A sound like strangling. "Why didn't you say so."

"I did. I was going to, but you—who are you?"

"I'm the one who called you." The figure stepped into the moonlight. Not a thief, but an angel. Not an angel, but a vision that was the answer to every man's wet dream. A waterfall of long dark hair fell past slim shoulders and over a shimmering white shift that clung to every curve of a curvaceous body. His eyes followed the curves down to a pair of long, dynamite legs, lovely knees, tapering to . . . a pair of huge, untied work boots. He recognized the boots, they were his, but not the apparition that was wearing them.

He must be dreaming. That was it. It wouldn't be the first time he'd dreamed of Julie coming back to him. Her hair long and soft like this, hair a man could wrap his body in. A body that he could wrap his soul in. Mesmerized, Cas took a step toward her. She stepped back into the cover of the trees, disappearing into the darkness like a wraith. He took another step toward her and was stopped by a warning growl. His testicles climbed up to his rib cage. *Stay calm. It's just a dream.* Strange. He'd imagined Julie as many things—but never as a werewolf.

He barely registered the beast as it leapt through the air, flying toward him as if it had wings. *Time to wake up*, he told himself. *Now.*

He hit the ground and was pinned there by a ton of black fur and bad breath. The animal bared its teeth. Cas squeezed his eyes shut and felt a rough, wet tongue rasp over his face.

"Off, Smitty."

Cas heard the words, felt the beast being hauled off him. He slowly opened his eyes to find himself looking up at six legs: four, muscular and furry; two, muscular and sleek—and definitely female. He had to stop himself from reaching out to caress them.

Her companion growled and Cas yanked his eyes away to stare warily at the dog. He was pretty sure it was a dog. A really big dog.

"Never lower your firearm on a perp who might be armed." She waved the muzzle of her weapon in Cas's direction, then leaned over and picked up his .38 from the ground. She looked at it. "And maybe next time you should try loading this." She dropped it into his lap and heaved a sigh that lifted her shoulders and stretched the fabric of her shirt across her breasts. And Cas forgot about the dog, as he imagined sucking on the hard nipples that showed through the silk.

She stomped past him, shaking her head. The dog trotted after her.

Cas watched them—watched her—walk away, her hair trailing behind her, the work boots adding a hitch to her walk that swung her butt from side to side and set the fabric shifting and sliding against her body. And he wanted to touch her, slide his fingers inside the shift, and feel warm, firm flesh beneath his fingers. But mostly he wanted to touch her hair.

Halfway to the house, she paused and looked over her shoulder. "They're getting away," she said and continued toward the house.

After a stupefied second, he pushed himself off the ground. What was happening to him? He never thought about groping strange women, even magical ones like this one. He licked his lips, stuck his .38 in his jacket pocket and followed after her.

When he reached the porch, she was at the front door. So was the dog.

"Uh, miss . . . Ma'am? If you'd call off the dog, I could take down some information."

He saw a flick of her hand and he had to keep himself from diving for the bushes, but the dog merely padded past her into the house.

"Well, if you're not going to chase the thieves, you may as well come in," she said and turned to go inside.

"Wait," he cried.

She stopped mid-step.

"You might want to leave those boots on the porch."

She looked down at the work boots, sniffed, then wrinkled her nose. "Oh." She leaned over to pull them off.

Her ass tightened beneath the soft nightshirt, and Cas had a tightening response of his own. He shifted uncomfortably and stared at the mailbox until he got himself under control.

This was ridiculous. He should be used to this. For four months, women had called him in all sorts of getups at all hours of the night. He was, after all, the town's most eligible bachelor. Actually he was the town's only eligible bachelor. None of them had the least effect on him. But this one knocked him right out of his socks. Made his dick throb, just looking at her. She might not be Julie, but she looked pretty damn good. He might as well find out who she was and what she was doing here—and how long she planned to stay.

"Coming?" she asked and let the screen door slam behind her.

Oh yeah, thought Cas. *I'm coming.*

Chapter 3

Julie padded barefoot down the hall to the kitchen, thinking, *I am such a dolt for turning my back on this rube. I didn't even ask for his ID.* But unless he stole the police cruiser, he was the local law enforcement.

She heard the door open, then close. And not much enforcement if he was following her instead of the trail of her burglars.

Well, what did she expect from a guy who carried an unloaded gun, then stood out in the open, a perfect full-frontal target for any gun-happy asshole that might be passing by.

"Seriously inept," she said to Smitty, who was waiting alertly by his food bowl. "And it's the middle of the night, so don't look pathetic." She placed her Glock on the counter within reach and tossed him a dog chewy from a box on the counter. He caught it with the efficiency of long practice. It was one of his better skills.

Julie sniffed. "Did you bring that smell back in with you?" She crossed to the sink and searched for a bar of soap.

"It's on the windowsill."

Julie jumped; she hadn't heard him come into the kitchen. She begrudgingly gave him a point for stealth.

"Thanks." She stretched over the sink to reach the bar of soap and her nightshirt crept up the back of her thighs. She remembered that she wasn't wearing underwear. She pulled at the hem, grabbed the soap, and turned on the water.

"Watch—"

"Shit!" she cried as water exploded into the air. "Shit, shit."

She jabbed at the tap, cutting off the spray, then turned around. "I don't suppose you know a good plumb—"The rest of the word stuck in her throat. It was the first good look she'd gotten at the less than enthusiastic sheriff and it took her breath away.

The guy was a hunk, tall and solid, enticing even wearing a pair of holey gray sweats, a ragged windbreaker, and a battered Red Sox baseball cap. She ran her tongue over suddenly dry lips. She'd probably gotten him out of bed and she wouldn't mind getting him back there again.

No. She didn't mean to think that. She was here to solve Wes's riddle, find the rest of her inheritance, and get the hell out. His eyes were fixed on her chest. Julie became aware of the wet silk, clinging to her body. Her nipples tightened and she forgot what she was thinking. She stepped toward him.

"Uh." He pulled out a chair from the table and sat down hard. Then he winced and rolled to one hip.

Oh great, a big hunky sheriff with hemorrhoids. No wonder he didn't want to sprint through the woods after a burglar.

His face was extremely pale.

"Are you going to faint? Put your head between your knees." *Or between mine*, she thought as she stepped toward him to render basic first aid.

He waved her off. "No, I'm fine. Really. Don't come any closer."

Julie stopped. What was wrong with him? Oh right, the hemorrhoids. He was probably embarrassed.

He shifted again, pulled off his cap, and ran a hand through his hair which she noticed was dark brown, thick and slightly wavy. Hair that a woman could get her fingers into. Then his hand moved away; the hair above the right side of his forehead stood straight up. The sheriff had a cowlick. In the same place as Cas's cowlick. She leaned forward and frowned at him over the expanse of formica.

He moved back against the chair and eyed her warily.

Chocolate eyes, chestnut hair, a cowlick. It couldn't be. Julie swallowed. "Cas?"

The sheriff's muscle-tight body lifted off the chair and landed again.

"Yeah?" he said in a choked voice.

"Cas Reynolds?"

He nodded.

"It's Julie." She pointed to herself like a teacher in an ESL class.

"Julie?"

She nodded, while she tried to reconcile the bald, stooped banker Cas of her imagination to this Adonis in sweat pants, sitting at her table.

"Wow." He stood up and reached for her. Julie reached for him, and at the same moment, he sat down again and Julie sprawled across the table top.

Smitty, who was lying next to his chair, jumped to attention.

"Down, Smitty," said Julie and pushed herself back to her feet. "I don't believe it."

"Me neither. Oh shit." He stood up and yanked her into a hug.

Her head snapped back as her body arched forward, then rebounded off his chest before settling against him. And Julie thought, *Home at last.* Home in the figurative sense, since home in Ex Falls had been an old factory shack only two steps away from the local trailer park.

"Oh shit," Cas said again and tangled his fingers in her hair.

He was definitely glad to see her, unless the thing pressing into her stomach was his police special. And she knew for a fact that it was sitting in full view on the kitchen table.

She rubbed against him just for old times' sakes, as payback for all the times he'd tied her up and peeked at her underwear. He groaned and his erection hardened.

This could be fun, she thought. *This could be a disaster*, she reminded herself.

Then Cas pulled away. "I don't know where to start."

Julie knew where she'd like to start. But this was Cas, and although he'd grown up to be everything she could have hoped for, at least physically, it was Cas after all. And she knew better than to expect anything good from him.

"For starters, what are you doing here?" asked Julie.

"You called 911."

"No, I mean what are you doing *here*? In Ex Falls?"

"Uh." His brows knitted.

It seemed like a no-brainer to Julie, but the silence grew. She was beginning to think he had forgotten the question, when Cas said, "Just am."

Oh, well, he may not have grown into a great conversationalist, but he was lovely to look at. "Why don't I put on some coffee and we can catch up," she said, thinking, *I could fuck you brainless and you'd deserve it.* "Unless you have to get home, uh, to your family . . . or something."

"I don't live at home. I mean, with my parents. No other family. Not married. Anymore."

Julie nodded. At least they'd gotten that out of the way right up front.

"You?"

"Me? Married? No."

"Good—I mean, do you think you could put on some clothes? I'm having a hard time thinking here."

"Oh. Sorry," she said, frowning. For someone who'd spent years trying to see under her clothes, he sure was in a hurry to get her dressed again. It didn't make sense. His motor had definitely been revving for her.

"I'll make the coffee, while you're gone. I know my way around."

"Great." Julie hurried toward the door. "Don't go anywhere."

"No," said Cas, casting a glance toward Smitty, who stood between him and the door.

"Smitty, behave," said Julie. Smitty bared his teeth. "Good boy." And she was gone.

"Nice dog," said Cas, inching toward the counter. Smitty stood up. Cas froze. There was a momentary standoff, then Cas tilted his head to crack his neck. Smitty cocked his head, keeping his eyes fixed on Cas. Cas eyed him back, then tilted his head to the other side. So did Smitty.

"You know, Smitty, you scared the shit out of me out there, but you're really just a pushover. Aren't you?"

"Arf," said Smitty and thumped his tail on the floor before heaving to his feet and following Cas over to the counter.

Cas reached into a cabinet and brought out a tin of Maxwell House, then plugged in the coffee maker. He placed the carafe in the sink, turned on the spigot and jumped back. The pipes clanked to life, water exploded into the air, then slowly trickled into the carafe.

"It's a knack," he said to Smitty as he poured the water into the coffee maker.

The dog smiled appreciatively.

While the coffee brewed, Cas began to pace, occasionally stopping to look down at Smitty. "I can't believe this. I never thought—but of course, Wes—she probably thinks I'm an idiot, right? I am an idiot. I haven't seen her since—ugh. I was an idiot then, too. A real idiot. Do you think she remembers? Of course she does. She probably hates me."

Smitty snuffled and lay down with his head on his paws.

"I know, I sound pitiful. She has every right to hate me. And here I am with the biggest boner I've had in years just because she looked at me. Do you think she noticed? God, I'm an idiot. Maybe I should just leave before she gets back."

Smitty's ears pricked up and he bared his teeth.

"Or maybe not," said Cas, taking a step back. He frowned down at Smitty. "I'm not sure. Are you about to attack me or burst out laughing? It's hard to tell."

The door opened and Julie walked in, wearing skintight jeans and a stretchy short T-shirt that exposed her midriff. Cas sucked in his breath, felt his sweatpants start to tent, and turned to pour the coffee, trying to think of something besides the little silver ring that pierced her navel.

He managed to hand her a cup and still keep his back to her. When she sat down at the table, he threw himself into the chair across from her.

"Ugfff," he said as his balls hit the wooden seat and pinned themselves against his thigh, sending a jolt right up to his incisors.

Julie winced. "Preparation H."

"Huh?" asked Cas, his brain fuzzing over with pain.

"All the hook—models use it to reduce swelling. Under their eyes," she added hastily. "I thought it might help with your, uh, problem."

Cas glanced past the table to his lap and shuddered. "I don't think so."

"Just a suggestion," she said and picked up her coffee cup. She took a couple of thoughtful sips and put the mug down. "Are you really the sheriff?"

"Really."

"But what about—"

"The Reynolds banking legacy? I tried it. I hated it. I quit after four years. God, do you know what it's like to wear a suit eight hours a day, five days a week, and never know what the weather is like?"

"No." She got to wear outlandish outfits and go places no one who wasn't being paid would ever go. But Cas giving up banking? Becoming a sheriff? It was a little too much to believe.

"What?"

"Nothing. I'm just surprised, that's all." When they were kids, he'd been the make-believe cop. She had become the real cop. Now, she wasn't and Cas was. Life was weird.

"Yeah. So was Reynolds."

"And you've been here ever since?"

"N-o-o. Only a few months." He paused and looked away. "I went back to school."

"In law enforcement?" Her surprise made her voice rise.

"No." Cas looked down at his untouched coffee. Began to circle the cup on the table. "In boat building—"

"You didn't."

"I did. And I was making a decent living at it."

"Good for you. So . . . what are you doing here?"

Cas shrugged. "Came for a visit. And stuff happened. They needed a sheriff, and my father is . . ."

Nuts, supplied Julie.

"And my mother is . . ."

Living in la-la land, thought Julie.

"Well, you remember my mother."

Julie nodded. *Still in la-la land.*

"Bruce has a job in Chicago, Christine and her husband bought the old Excelsior Hotel and are trying to make a go of it. Melanie's still in high school and at a difficult stage. So . . ." He shrugged.

"You decided to stay and take care of things?"

"Temporarily."

"Not much call for boat building in the Adirondacks."

"No, though I started a new project since I've been here." He looked away. "The job of sheriff isn't too demanding. Usually. And it's just until Hank gets back up to speed from his heart attack. I'm really not cut out for the job."

Julie smiled. "I don't know. You were always good at interrogation."

He blinked at her, then grinned. And Julie felt a zing where she hadn't felt a zing in a long time.

"You were easy."

I'm still easy, she thought. *Just try me.*

"But that's enough about me. What about you?"

"Me? There's not much to tell. Wes left me all this. I just came back to sell it, but it looks like I might be staying longer than I anticipated. It needs a little work."

"Great," said Cas. "I mean, you can leave your job long enough to fix it up?"

Julie nodded. She didn't think it would be wise to tell him about her disaster at the NYPD, and she didn't want him to worry that she might be competing for his job of sheriff. Not to mention that a woman being a cop was a huge turn-off to a lot of men. And she had no intention of turning this one off. "I've got a lot of vacation time due."

"Good. That's good." The case clock gonged in the background. Cas looked at his watch and stood up. "It's after two, and you've got an early morning."

Actually Julie planned to sleep until noon, but Cas probably had to get up, so she let it pass. There was no hurry. She'd be here for a while and she had just added Cas Reynolds to her to-do list. She was due for a little fun. And if it was at Cas's expense, all the better. She smiled at him. *Hot sex and sweet revenge.* She was going to enjoy this.

She followed him out to the porch, stood while he gave her one of those teepee hugs, where the faces come together, but the bodies don't. It had all the warmth of window shopping.

She watched him walk toward his car and wondered when he had turned into such a prig. He opened the driver's door and looked back at her. "Don't go roaming around in the woods anymore."

"Lions, tigers, and bears?" she asked.

"Deer season." He shut the door, started up the engine, and drove away, while she mouthed a silent *oh* into the suddenly lonely night.

Cas drove away without looking back, one hand on the steering wheel, the other pulling the seat belt strap away from his painfully hard erection. If he didn't get his mind off Julie

Excelsior, he'd be cross-eyed by the time he got home. Any way he looked at it, it was going to be a long night.

And for what? The whole time in her kitchen, he'd been announcing his attraction loud and clear, and she stood there asking about his life—an oblivious siren—aloof, tempting, unattainable.

Well, what did he expect? It had been fifteen years since Reynolds had destroyed their friendship. She was just a kid and he was no match for his father. He deserved the reaction he got tonight. Who would still care for someone who deserted her without a word of explanation? How could she know that afterwards was the unhappiest time of his life? Because even then, he knew he loved her and always would.

He had lost Julie and hadn't even managed to please his father. And he knew as sure as he felt the throb in his crotch, that he would be caught between the two of them again. And would lose again.

He turned onto Highland Avenue and drove back down the hill. Not that he would ever have her to lose again. Not after showing up dressed in ratty sweats and a rattier jacket. And then that farce with the pistol.

And what was she doing with a weapon like that? Wes didn't own a handgun, only a couple of hunting rifles.

And he'd been so busy blathering on about his life, his boats, hoping for her approval, that he hadn't asked her about hers. Though now that he thought about it, he did ask her. She just hadn't answered. He probably hadn't given her a chance.

Well, now he had a reason to stick around a while longer. They could get to know each other again. He wouldn't let his father ruin this for him again.

And then he remembered the riddle that Wes had shoved at him, the day he died, and he grew cold. *Thieves break in and steal the gold.*

"What gold? Who stole it?" Cas had asked.

Wes just smiled.

"Was it the old Savings and Loan? Did my father steal something?"

Wes's smile faded and he stopped breathing. And Cas was left without an answer or a friend.

For a few minutes tonight, Julie had made him forget that riddle. Made him feel like everything would turn out all right. Wes had found a way to keep him here until she returned. Cas had no doubt about that. He just didn't know if it was to bring them together or to bring his father down.

Maybe he should just confront Reynolds. Find out once and for all if his father had something to hide. Then he would be free to get back to his life, have the chance to make Julie a part of that life. If she wanted to be a part of it.

He had some time. And the next time they met, he wouldn't act like such a slow-witted idiot. He'd go back in the morning. He had forgotten to fill out a police report. He hadn't questioned her about the burglary. Hadn't looked for clues. Hadn't done much of anything but lust after Julie.

He was still lusting after her. But he knew his duty. And his duty as sheriff was to keep his eye on the inhabitants of Ex Falls, and Julie Excelsior was an inhabitant, if only temporarily. Cas was definitely going to watch her. And with luck, hell, who knew what would happen.

He wound through town and stopped the car in front of his cottage, ablaze with lights. Wes had insisted on furnishing the place for him. It seemed to bring him so much pleasure, that Cas didn't have the heart to say no. Now, he was glad Wes had insisted on the king-size bed.

Chapter 4

Her nightshirt slid down her shoulders, down her hips, her thighs, skimmed along her calves and pooled at her feet. Cas stood before her, his skin golden in the candlelight. His dark eyes, pools of mystery. "I've waited for you," he said and pulled her to him. His body was hard and lean. She could feel the heat of him as he pushed her down on the big four-poster. Could feel the ripple of his muscles as he came down on top of her, capturing her mouth, her body, stoking her desire for him.

His tongue traced her lips, invaded her mouth as his hands began to explore her, tracing curves, following valleys as she writhed beneath him. Closer and closer until finally they slid between her legs, across the spot that made her shiver, and two supple fingers slipped deep inside her. She arched against him, but he held her in place with a kiss.

"I've waited for you." His voice was husky and incredibly arousing. "I'm not waiting any longer."

His fingers withdrew, trailed up her stomach, between her breasts, alive to the heat of his touch. Played across her collar bone, then up her neck to where he took her chin and lifted it for his kiss. As his mouth captured hers, he pushed inside her. She stretched around him, taking him in, every hard, huge inch of him. Capturing him, clinging to him, keeping him this time.

He began to move, slowly at first, grinding his pelvis into hers. She lifted her hips to meet him and he drove into her, again and again, pushing her up the bed. She wrapped her legs around his waist; her arms clung to his powerful shoulders, as they crested the wave of tightening pleasure. Then it uncoiled and Julie broke into a million pieces. She screamed—or he screamed.

Somebody was screaming.

Julie bolted upright in bed as a bloodcurdling cry tore through the night. She shook the sleep from her head. "What the hell?"

Smitty jumped off the bed and leapt toward the window.

Without thinking, Julie rolled over, grabbed her Glock from the bedside table, and dropped to the floor. She scrambled to the window, then carefully peered over the sill.

It was dark outside, but behind the mountains, a dim glow told her that it must be near dawn. Her eyes scanned the yard but could barely distinguish the outlines of shrubs and trees. She followed the slope of the hill to where the gazebo stood black against the lightening sky. Had she imagined movement? She blinked several times and looked again. A shadow moved across the ground, headed toward the gazebo.

Hadn't she done this once already? Didn't these people ever sleep? It was the second time in one night someone had attempted to get in her gazebo. Something worth taking must be out there. And as soon as she got rid of this trespasser she was going to have a good look at the place.

She checked her Glock. "This time we take no prisoners." No firing into the air. No wasting time calling 911 and getting Cas out of bed again. She glanced toward her own bed. Of course it was empty, but what a great dream. Too bad it had to be interrupted.

A higher-pitched scream resounded through the darkness. It brought Julie fully awake.

Smitty gave a short insistent bark and trotted over to the door.

A third scream, this time longer and louder. Smitty bounded back to the window panting in excitement.

Julie rocked back on her heels and shook her head. "I don't believe it." It was a rooster. What jackass would keep roosters on the Hill? He should be shot. But not tonight.

Smitty pranced by the door, looking at her expectantly.

"False alarm, boy." She locked off her Glock and returned it to the drawer. She'd seen more action in the last few hours than she had in weeks. Thanks to Donald, the bent cop. She yawned. She'd deal with that damn bird in the morning. Which, she noticed, was already appearing in the form of a yellow neon line behind the mountain peaks. *Later* in the morning.

She couldn't wake up to that horror every morning. She'd have to go to bed at sunset to get enough sleep—and she was a night person.

There had to be an ordinance against keeping roosters within the town limits. She'd file a complaint. That would give her an excuse to see Cas again and find out if he looked as good in the daylight as he did in the dark—or in her dream.

She climbed into bed. The sheets had lost their warmth and her body had lost all residual arousal caused by her deliciously erotic dream. She nestled under the covers anyway.

"Now where was I?" She closed her eyes. "Oh yes. Ummmm." She sighed and fell asleep.

It took Julie a few seconds to realize that Cas hadn't suddenly developed halitosis in addition to his hemorrhoids, a condition she had conveniently edited out of her dream. Smitty was standing over her, panting his *Get a move on, I've got to take a piss,* wake-up call.

She stretched, yawned, while her body made creaking noises, and wondered how far she would have to drive for a double latte. Light was coming through the window, but Julie could tell it was still early. In the city she'd just be getting off her shift. If she had a shift, which she didn't.

Smitty whined and looked mournful.

"All right, all right." She pushed him away and shoved back the covers. And shivered. She grabbed the comforter and pulled it over her head. She hadn't thought about heat the night before; there had been plenty of that between her and Cas, but this morning was another story.

Smitty grabbed the comforter in his teeth and tugged it away. "Just another teeny minute," she pleaded and grabbed it back. Smitty shook his head and the comforter fell to the floor.

Julie sat up and gooseflesh erupted on every inch of uncovered skin. She slid out of bed and rushed to the dresser, pulled on jeans and a sweat shirt, then added another sweatshirt, one that covered her midsection, for extra warmth. She shoved her feet into a new pair of Timberland boots she'd bought from a street vendor, laced them up, and followed an anxious Smitty downstairs.

She stopped in the hall long enough to turn up the thermostat and was surprised to be met with actual heat and not more clanking pipes. When she reached the kitchen, Smitty was pacing at the back door, and he bolted past her as soon as she cracked it open.

"Don't stray," she called after him as he disappeared around the back of the house. "Do not roll in pond scum. Don't chase anything with rabies. Stay away from early rising roosters. And all things Reynolds." She closed the door on the frigid morning. Pretty damn cold for October.

A few minutes later, having successfully filled the coffee carafe from the exploding tap, Julie leaned her elbows on the counter and listened to the steady drip, drip of liquid caffeine as it played a counterpoint to the bass line buzz of the fluorescent light.

In the background, she could hear Smitty barking. It was early, she was coffee-less and Smitty was communing with the wonders of nature. She wondered if Cas walked dogs; she already knew he could make coffee.

A particularly loud-pitched bark interrupted that train of thought. "Damn it, now what?"

She looked out the window and saw nothing. There was definitely action going down outside, but since she didn't think Smitty had cornered a drug dealer, she merely opened the door and whistled.

But Smitty didn't come bounding around the house. She whistled again, called his name, and finally tramped across the back porch and into the yard to look for him. A gust of wind sent a shiver down her spine, and she crossed her arms to ward off the cold.

Up on the hill, the gazebo glistened white in the early morning sunlight. Julie stared in disbelief. It was surrounded by a mesh fence, at least six feet high. The open arches had been enclosed with whitewashed plywood, leaving only small crescent-shaped windows near the top. Instead of the wooden steps, a ramp ran down from the original door to the ground.

What had happened to her gazebo?

And then she saw Smitty. He was inside the fence, running in circles, cutting in and out of a mass of moving fluff. He stopped with his nose down, rump up, barked, then started up again. Something had triggered an inbred, and for Smitty, never used, herding instinct. Because he was definitely herding. A sudden flurry and frantic squawking rose up as he dove into the quivering mass.

Julie rubbed her eyes, looked again.

Chickens. Dozens of them. Red ones. White ones. Brown and black ones. Running mindlessly in all directions as Smitty's latent sheepherding abilities came to life, while a person, stocky and squat, dressed in a heavy brown jacket, overalls and a wide-brimmed hat, furiously waved both arms at him.

"Smitty," yelled Julie as she ran toward him. "Off, Off! Don't eat anything. Chickens have all sorts of diseases and I don't know where to find a good vet."

Smitty turned to look at her. So did fifty beady chicken eyes. And suddenly as if on some silent command, they began to move away from Smitty and toward her. They squeezed through an opening in the fence and began high-stepping down the hill like a demented poultry regiment.

Jesus. Julie slid to a stop, then took a step backwards as chickens surrounded her.

The rooster was hers. Wes had left her chickens.

"What am I going to do with chickens?" she asked the sky. "What am I going to do with chickens?" she repeated in the direction of hell. "Damn it, Wes, if this is the answer to the riddle, I've got to say, 'Not Funny!!' "

She stood motionless, not knowing what to do, while chickens pecked at her boots, her jeans and anything else they could reach, which thankfully wasn't much. *At least chickens can't fly*, she thought, just as a fat white hen rose several feet into the air. Julie ducked out of the way as a cloud of feathers brushed by her face and settled on the ground a few feet away.

Smitty pounced toward it; the chicken let out a squawk and beat her wings. Undaunted, Smitty nipped at her tail feathers until she hopped back to join the others.

The commotion at Julie's feet suddenly escalated. A black and brown hen pecked at a little speckled one. A red puffed-up monstrosity, whose top thing looked like it had had a bad run-in with a curling iron, joined in and soon there was an out-and-out chicken fight.

"Smitty. Do something. Make them go back to their . . . " What did you call a chicken gazebo? Her mind retrieved every nature program she had tuned into by mistake while looking for the *Daily Show*.

Then it came to her. *Coop*. Wes had turned the intricately ornate gazebo, the place of summer breezes, homemade lemonade and games of dominos, into a chicken coop.

The man in the hat barreled down the hill still flapping his arms as if he, too, were going airborne. Which would be a problem since he was not designed for lift-off, though the hat was wide enough to catch a few wind currents. The chickens made a path for him, then crowded in behind him as he came to a stop in front of Julie.

"Call off your damn dog. This isn't the National Herding Trials. Which is a good thing, because that mutt doesn't have a clue."

Smitty, who'd stopped to sniff the newcomer, barked and poised for attack.

"No-o-o," cried Julie as Smitty leapt through the air, knocking the man against her. Julie fell back and the three of them tumbled to the ground. They were soon surrounded by chickens, which overcome by curiosity or stupidity, began to climb over them.

"Damn it, Smitty," said Julie.

Smitty arfed and thumped his tail in the newcomer's face. His hat fell to the ground.

Julie pushed the roly-poly stranger and a few chickens away, then sprang to her feet as sudden realization dawned. Now she knew what the pond scum odor really was. She quickly checked her clothes for signs of chicken droppings.

The trespasser struggled to his feet and reached for his hat just as Smitty snagged it between his teeth.

"That's my best hat," he said.

Julie stopped and looked at the hat and then at the man.

His silver gray hair was cut in a bowl shape. His crinkly, sun-parched face made Julie wonder about the efficiency of the outlandish hat.

"Drop it," Julie commanded.

Smitty released the hat. It fell at her feet. She handed it back to its owner.

"Thank you." He brushed off the brim, inspected it, then stuffed it back on his head. He slapped his hand across his overalls and stuck it toward Julie. "Maude Clemmons. You must be Julie. Took you long enough to get here."

Julie quickly wiped off her own hand while she readjusted her initial appraisal of the stranger. He was a she named Maude.

"How do you do," Julie said as her hand was taken between strong fingers and a callused palm, and she was given a handshake that threatened to rattle her teeth.

"You seem surprised to see me. Didn't Wes tell you I'd be over to feed the beauties?"

"Wes is dead," Julie blurted out, then bit her lip. "You knew that, didn't you?"

"Damn heart. Never did take care of himself, the old coot. I told him if he didn't cut out that feud with Reynolds he'd have a coronary. But you know Wes. Never did things by halves. Had three in a row. The last one did him in. Should have saved my breath. Damn." Maude stuffed her hand into a deep pocket, pulled out a red handkerchief, and wiped her eyes with it before stuffing it back into the pocket.

"Uh," said Julie.

"Welcome aboard. Where do you want to start?" Maude walked away without waiting for an answer. The chickens, who had settled into a clump some distance away, crowded behind her.

"Come on," she said and started back toward the gazebo.

Since the chickens were following her, Julie felt no need to do the same, until Maude stopped, turned around and said, "Come on."

Julie followed . . . reluctantly. As soon as she was inside the compound, Maude latched the fence. Smitty whined from the other side.

Julie held her breath. The smell was overpowering.

"Yeah, it's getting a little ripe. I'll send the Pliney boys over to cart it away. Twenty bucks. And watch them or they'll leave a trail all the way to the truck. It's a good thing you got here. I'll be out of town next week. You should be able to get along without me by then."

"Me?" Julie squeaked, trying not to breathe.

Maude picked up a tin pan and began tossing little pebbles at the chickens who fell on the particles like they were caviar. "Wes left you instructions. I'll show you through the routine." She handed the now empty pie pan to Julie.

"Wes liked to let them roam. Even let them in the house. A little too laissez-faire for me. I mean, have you ever tried to clean chicken shit out of an Oriental carpet?"

Julie shook her head. Her lungs were bursting.

"Never get rid of the smell. Which reminds me. Be sure to leave your shoes on the porch. You don't want to track anything into the house."

Julie shook her head, then nodded, thinking of the boots she had worn last night. The smell. That's why they'd been left on the porch. And Cas told her to leave them outside. He must have know about the chickens, too. Why didn't he warn her?

Her eyes began to tear from the attempt not to breathe. Her lungs gave up the fight and she gasped for breath. Her stomach rolled over.

"I don't think I'm ready for this." She fumbled with the latch, squeezed through the mesh opening, and sped back to the kitchen and coffee and sanity.

Twenty minutes later, Julie heard two clunks on the porch, followed by a loud rap on the kitchen door. She put down her coffee mug and went to open it. Maude stood on the threshold, holding a basket of multi-sized eggs and a paper grocery bag. She was hatless and bootless, and red, yellow and orange striped socks stuck out from rolled-up overalls.

"You're gonna have to learn to take care of these chickens. I can't be on permanent call. I have my own flock to take care of. Plus I got a thousand chickens to sex over in Plattsburgh next week." Maude marched past her and plunked the basket and bag down on the counter.

Julie blinked. Did she say sex and chickens?

"Oh, don't look like that. It's easy. Wes left you detailed instructions in the ledger. I'm not leaving until Monday and I'll be back by Thursday. If you run into something you can't handle, ask Dan Pliney down at the Hardware and Feed Store." Maude leaned over and disappeared head first into a deep cabinet. She came up a second later, wielding a heavy cast iron frying pan.

"What are you doing?" asked Julie.

"Showing you the right way to fry farm eggs."

Julie grimaced. "I'm not much of a breakfast person."

"You will be. Just takes some gumption. Breakfast is the most important meal of the day. Especially when you have chores to do." Maude reached in the bag and pulled out a cube of butter.

"Chores?" squawked Julie. "I'm not doing any chores. I'm only staying long enough to clean out the house and put it up for sale."

Maude dropped a cholesterol-packed slice of butter into the frying pan and turned on the burner. Then she turned on Julie. "What's your hurry? Take some time. Don't you have things to do here?"

Julie thought about the riddle and her hopes that it would actually turn out to be something that she could use—like money—but was afraid it was only chickens.

Maude did a one-handed egg crack and opened the shell over the pan. The egg sizzled as it oozed into the butter. She cracked another egg and dropped its contents into the pan. "Well? Don't you?"

Julie, who had been distracted by the efficiency with which Maude was dealing with the eggs, started. "What?"

"Don't you have things to do?"

"No," said Julie automatically. "Just dispose of Wes's effects."

Maude whirled around. "What the hell kind of attitude is that? He loved you all his life and he left everything he held dear to you. Dispose of his effects. Of all the—"

"Sorry," said Julie. "It's just a phrase. All of his possessions, his . . . whatever."

Maude took the end of a bag of bread in her teeth and tore it open, while she wrestled with the cord of the toaster that seemed to be stuck under something on the shelf.

The toaster came free and Maude dropped the bread next to it.

"Not *whatever*. Or maybe *whatever*. Because you, girl, are going to do whatever it takes. Wes was counting on you and you're not going to let him down."

"Counting on me for what? What does he want me to do?"

Maude shrugged and dropped two pieces of bread in the toaster slots. She pressed the lever down hard enough to send the toaster sliding across the counter. "How should I know? That's for you to figure out."

She stretched up on tiptoe and pulled two plates down from a cabinet and slid eggs and toast onto them.

Julie watched in amazement. Not one broken yolk. "How did you do that?"

"Practice. Don't worry. You'll get the hang of it in no time. Wes said you were bright." She opened a drawer and took out silverware and paper napkins and began to set the table.

It was obvious that she knew her way around Wes's kitchen. What else did she know?

"Sit down and eat. Even I don't like cold fried eggs."

Julie sat down and looked at the two yellow yolks that stared back at her. She swallowed, took a sip of coffee.

Maude placed the second plate and a mug of coffee across from her and pulled out a chair. She did a little jump and plop to get her butt on the chair seat, then picked up her fork and pointed it at Julie. "Eat."

Julie gingerly cut into her eggs and watched the yellow run across the flowered plate. She lifted the fork to her mouth, knowing Smitty was under the table, if she could just figure out a way to slip it to him. She realized Maude was watching her, so she pushed the egg into her mouth. Waited for the gag reflex to kick in and was surprised when it actually tasted good.

Maude nodded, smiled, and dug into her breakfast. "Told you they were good. No immunized, hormone-pumped, antibiotic-riddled store-boughts here. Just good old natural fertilized eggs."

"They are good," said Julie, surprised. She tore off a corner of toast and dipped it into the yolk. Even better on the second bite.

"Well, enjoy them 'cause there won't be many more this season."

"Why? Is something wrong with the chickens?"

"Nope. But when the days get short, the hens stop laying, unless you set up an artificial light source. You want to do that?"

Julie shook her head. "No," she said vehemently just in case Maude had mistaken the head shake as a nod.

"So enjoy them now." Maude pushed her plate away. It looked like it had just come out of the dishwasher. Julie looked down at her own plate. Pretty close. She threw a sympathetic look toward Smitty, who had quietly crept closer to her feet. He knew better than to beg, but that didn't stop him from keeping an eager eye out for any accidental falling breakfast parts.

Maude leaned back in her chair and placed her hands over her middle. "Well?"

Julie suddenly had so many questions, she didn't know where to begin. Mostly she wanted to know why Wes had left her everything, but had never tried to contact her while he was alive. But she wasn't ready to open up to Maude. She didn't remember her from before. And even though she appeared to be a good friend to her uncle, maybe more than a good friend, Julie knew better than to trust anyone in this town.

"Why did Wes start raising chickens?"

"Cause he liked them. They're good company. You'll find that out."

Julie didn't bother to repeat that she wouldn't be staying long enough to bond with any chickens.

"Was he lonely? Did he suffer? Was he happy?" Julie heard

herself asking the questions and couldn't seem to stop them once they started.

Maude let her carry on for a while, then sighed. "I told him he should just bring you home, but he was a stubborn cuss. Thought you were better off without him and without this town."

"He didn't know where I was," said Julie, then remembered the envelope addressed to her.

"Of course he did, he knew everything about you. Went to the library every week and looked you up on the internet. And he was as proud of you as your no-good father should have been. And he stuck by you, while your father just drank himself to death."

Julie's throat tightened and without warning her eyes began to sting. "My father never got over my mother's death."

"I know. And nobody blames him."

I did, thought Julie. And then a more frightening thought occurred to her. "Wes followed my career?"

Maude nodded.

"He knew I was a . . . a . . ."

"New York detective."

"Oh, God."

Maude narrowed her eyes at Julie. "When he got too sick to go to the library, I went for him. He didn't know about the internal investigation. I didn't want him getting upset." Maude looked away, then said in a shaky voice, "I thought maybe he'd pull through."

"I'm sorry." Julie sniffed and swallowed hard. "I wasn't guilty."

"I know. I kept reading about you even after he died. It just got to be a habit. Kept him closer."

Smitty heaved himself off the floor and put his head in Maude's lap.

"My partner was taking drug money," said Julie. "I blew the whistle on him."

"Good for you."

"It didn't make me very popular with some of the movers and shakers in the department. They should have given me a medal, instead I got desk duty. Shit." She brushed her sleeve across her eyes. "Sorry. I can't believe I just dumped all this on you."

"Well, hell. Why not. We're just a couple of watering pots," said Maude, absently stroking Smitty's head. "And Wes would give us both a swift kick if he were here."

"Yeah," said Julie. "Well, he's dead now, so where does that leave me?"

"That, girl, is up to you."

"Someone tried to break into the chicken coop last night."

"Did they?"

"I called the sheriff." She watched to see what Maude's reaction would be. Got nothing. "Why is Cas Reynolds sheriff?"

"Hank Jessop had a heart attack. They needed someone to fill in for him. Cas was available."

"Why is he even here?"

Maude shrugged. "Better ask Cas about that." She pushed Smitty away and slid off her chair.

Julie stood up, too. "Maude."

Maude lifted both eyebrows at her.

"Did—did anybody else know? About me?"

"Well, I didn't tell." She picked up the bread and butter, put it in the fridge, and slammed the door. "It's about time you stopped worrying about what everybody thinks. You're the last of the Excelsiors. Start living up to it. I gotta get going. I'll be back in the morning. In the meantime, you start learning about chickens." She headed for the door. "I left an egg in the basket for the dog. If you crack it over his kibble, you're on your way to having the glossiest coated mutt in the county."

Smitty sat up and lifted a paw.

"Damn, is that dog smiling at me?"

Chapter 5

Cas didn't believe in fate, usually. But Wes's illness, his strong-arming Cas to take over for Hank Jessop, the riddle, Julie's return, the sailboat he was working on, the furniture Wes had bought for him, were all floating around in his mind, trying to fit into a pattern. He could almost believe that Wes had set this in motion to bring him and Julie together, except for the riddle. That was what had him stumped. And if he admitted it, afraid.

He sat in his police cruiser in front of the station, staring out the front window, gritty-eyed and achy and in no hurry to go inside. It was Saturday and if he had been the real sheriff, he would have the day off. But he wasn't. He was a banker turned boat builder. A boat builder who was pretending to be a sheriff. One who'd overslept and was now late for work.

Well, it was his own fault. If he hadn't stayed awake half the night, thinking about the return of Julie Excelsior, why she was here and how she looked in that slippery night thing. If the other half of the night hadn't been spent in erotic dreams of what would happen if she weren't wearing that slinky night thing. If he wasn't just sitting here in the car, thinking about Julie and getting hot all over again, he wouldn't be late.

He should go inside. Instead, he closed his eyes, humming Randy Newman's *Sail Away* under his breath, and imagined Julie with the sea wind blowing her seductive hair, whipping her windbreaker against her shapely body, the pitch of the sailboat . . .

He jumped when someone tapped on his window, then groaned inwardly when Emily Patterson's face appeared on the other side. She squinted at him and smiled, while she made roll-down-your-window motions at him.

Reluctantly he did.

"Morning, Cas," said Emily. "You're working on a Saturday?" She leaned into the window, emitting a cloud of sweet cologne and displaying an impressive cleavage that threatened to spill out of her tight, pink cardigan, much too skimpy for the chilly fall morning. Cas couldn't help but be mesmerized by two thrusting, hard nipples that had found their way past the glass. But they didn't turn him on.

"No rest for the wic—weary," he quickly amended, not wanting to encourage false hopes. Emily was the town librarian for the three half days the library was open each week. A nice woman, with two ex-husbands and looking for number three. One of several women that Edith informed him, "had their snares out for him."

The single women in town had great hopes for him. His mother had great hopes for him. Christine had great hopes for him. The whole town had been planning his wedding since the day he drove down Main Street last July. All they were waiting for was for him to choose a wife. But after one disastrous, short-lived marriage while he was in college, he hadn't considered repeating the ordeal.

And then Julie Excelsior had come home.

"You're in a brown study this morning," said Emily, blinking several times. "Anything I can do to help?"

"Uh, no thanks, Emily. I'm afraid I'm late for work."

"You work too hard."

Cas smiled. The truth was, he hardly worked at all and it was beginning to really bother him. He banged on the side of the car door. It popped open and Emily hopped out of the way.

"Gotta go. Have a nice day, Emily." He tipped his head at

her and left her standing in the street while he made his way across the sidewalk to the entrance of the station.

The Excelsior Falls Police Station was an old brick storefront. Somewhere in the distant past, bars had been cemented across the wide plate glass windows as if daring the occupants, including the sheriff, to attempt an escape. Cas always felt like he should be wearing a couple of six shooters every time he stepped inside.

The front door opened into a room large enough for two desks, one for the sheriff and one for his secretary-operator-dispatcher, a job that had been shared by the Turnbull twins, Edith and Lou, since the beginning of time. A second narrow room ran along the back of the building and contained two old-fashioned cells that were rarely occupied.

"Good morning, Lou," said Cas as he unbuttoned his jacket.

Lou lowered her copy of *Cosmopolitan* and looked at him over her wing-tipped glasses. She shook her head, her blue tinted perm moving in one piece.

"Not a good morning?"

Lou shook her head again. "Another robbery last night."

"Yeah, I know, Edith called. Excelsior House. It was thwarted."

Lou shook her head, and Cas's stomach went south. Having been chased away, they must have gone on to their second choice, while he sat drinking coffee and ogling Julie. God, he hated chickens.

"At Henry Goethe's," said Lou.

"Henry's? He doesn't keep chickens."

"His stereo, television and his wife's jewelry."

Cas braced his hand on her desk while his world started to spin. Now, what was he supposed to do?

"They just called it in this morning. They spent the night over in Glen Falls and came back to find the place cleaned out." Lou shook her head. "Sure seems like we're having a lot of thefts lately."

"Tell me about it." Cas put his jacket back on. "I guess I'd better drive over there." So much for spending his morning at Excelsior House. "I'll be gone for a while. If you need me and the radio isn't working, call my cell."

"Will do and don't be surprised if an acquaintance offers you a big surprise."

Cas slipped a citation pad into his pocket. "What?"

Lou held up her magazine. "Says so right here. This is a good month for Leos. And you'll be glad to know that your jacket is just the right color for an afternoon stroll through the park."

"We don't have a park," said Cas.

"Just thought you'd want to know," said Lou and went back to her magazine.

Julie watched Maude drive away, the red hen logo on the side of her white paneled truck bouncing down the drive like an arcade target. When the truck disappeared around the edge of the pond, Julie went back into the house.

I'm an Excelsior, she thought as she fixed Smitty's egg and kibble. *An Excelsior*, she repeated as she washed the dishes. An Excelsior. She wasn't sure if that was a good thing or not. But she was an Excelsior, and it was time to put it to the test.

She showered and changed into clean clothes and headed for town.

Excelsior Falls had been a prosperous manufacturing town until the fifties, when the falls dried up, the mill closed and everyone who could moved away and those who couldn't or wouldn't, began calling the town Ex Falls.

Julie slowed down at the yield sign where the road forked around the town's only bar and grill, The Roadhouse, an old stone building dating back to the Civil War with a red clapboard addition and a neon sign perched crookedly on the flat roof.

To its left, the road became Main Street. To the right, Old

Mill Road followed the river to a bridge which led to the "other" side of town, a jumble of deserted cottages, a trailer park, and the abandoned mill. The side where Julie had lived for the first thirteen years of her life. She wasn't going there today or ever again.

That Julie Excelsior, of the "other" Excelsiors, would now be living on The Hill. *Not living*, she quickly reminded herself. But she'd let everybody in town know who owned it, before she dumped it.

She sucked in her breath, lifted her chin and took the left fork downtown.

Her first stop was Pliney's Hardware and Feed.

"Yep. I can get you a handyman," said Dan Pliney. "Plumber, too."

"Great," said Julie, pulling unconsciously on her denim jacket and wishing she'd worn a longer shirt. The three old guys sitting around the wood-burning stove had nearly fallen out of their chairs when she walked in.

"Do you think they could come by today?"

"Today?" Dan frowned. "Not today."

"Tomorrow." Julie was conscious of the attentive ears behind her. She tried to lower her shoulders so that her jacket would cover some of her butt. She could practically hear the drool hitting the wooden floor.

"Not tomorrow, either."

There was a snicker from the three men, whom she'd dubbed Winkin', Blinkin', and Nod when she first arrived. Now they were wide awake and obnoxious and she was about to name them something else.

"Then when?"

"Oh, 'bout six weeks, I'd say."

"Six weeks? You've got to be kidding. They can't all be that busy."

"No, you're right about that, but it's deer season. They'll be back to work when the hunting's over."

"What am I going to do?"

"I 'spect all it needs is to flush the system and replace the washers. I can sell you what you need."

More snickers from the chair-warmers in the corner.

Julie rounded on them. "Do you mind?" She got no response, the three of them had zeroed in on her navel ring. She tugged at her shirt and turned back to the counter.

"Fine," she said and followed Dan to the back of the store.

Half an hour later, she was standing on the sidewalk while Dan put a box on the back seat of her Beetle. It held a variety of wrenches, washers, hammers, screwdrivers, saws, nails, screws, and a few other things that she'd forgotten the names of and uses for. She was holding a paperback titled *How To Be Your Own Handyman* and she was hungry.

"Only two places to eat in town," said Dan. "The Roadhouse and the Excelsior Hotel." He slammed the car door shut. "That should do ya."

"Thanks, Dan."

"My pleasure. Welcome back home, Julie."

Wow. "Thanks, Dan. It's good to be back." *Sort of.*

She stood on the sidewalk and weighed the ogles she'd receive at the bar and grill against the shocked stares at the hotel. She might be inappropriately dressed for either, but they could just get used to it. Julie Excelsior wasn't taking shit from anybody anymore. Not yet anyway.

She turned toward the hotel and caught a glimpse of spiked black hair as it ducked behind the hood of a parked Ford pickup. It was the same black hair that had ducked into the shoe repair shop when Julie had first gone into the Hardware Store.

Must be one of the new generation of crazies that the town seemed intent on producing. But Julie's neck prickled all the same as she made her way down Main Street. She tried to ignore the stares of the people she passed, even tried a smile on a couple of them. Some scurried into stores as she walked by like she was a notorious gunslinger come to town.

You're an Excelsior. They're just curious, she told herself. A new face. They probably didn't recognize her. Hell, they may not even remember her. *You're an Excelsior.* It was all a long time ago. Dan Pliney had been charming. He didn't hold her past against her. Maybe no one else did, either. *You're an Excelsior.*

But she couldn't shake the feeling that she was being judged all over again. She lifted her chin. *I'm an Excelsior.*

And this was Excelsior Falls. It was kind of depressing. Every thing looked smaller, shabbier. The awning across Lily's Yarn Shop was faded. The old drugstore was gone and a laundromat had replaced it. And next to the laundromat was a pawn shop. Things were not looking good for Ex Falls.

The second block of town had faired better. Everyone needed a mortuary, and Gilbert's was freshly painted, with new red indoor-outdoor carpeting running up the front steps. The signs for the law office and CPA's office were still hanging in the windows of the old stone house on the far corner. Across the street, the Excelsior Hotel, a paradigm of Edwardian architecture, had been given a face lift.

She crossed the street toward the hotel and saw someone move away from the window of the dining room. *I'm an Excelsior,* she thought and went inside.

The hostess was waiting for her just inside the door.

"Hi, Julie. Remember me, Christine Reynolds, Cas's sister? I'm Christine Macgregor now. How have you been? I'm so sorry about Wes."

Julie broke into her prattling. "Can I get lunch?"

Christine looked taken aback. "Of course, come this way."

Julie winced. The woman was trying to be nice and Julie was so jumpy that she hadn't even accepted her condolences.

She followed Christine through a double doorway and into a large dining room, empty except for a couple at the window. Christine pulled out a chair for Julie several tables away.

Julie sat down.

"I'll just get you a menu."

"Thank you for asking about Wes. I'm still—getting used to the idea."

"Of course. I understand." She patted Julie's shoulder, then drew it quickly away when Julie looked at her.

"The hotel looks great," Julie said, trying to repair the damage her nerves had done. She had nothing against Christine. She was two years older than Cas and hadn't had much to do with them as children. But she had always been kind enough and never stooped to the rudeness of her parents even when she had the chance. Which predisposed Julie to like her. *So why are you treating her like the enemy?*

Christine blossomed into a smile, looking unexpectedly like a young, feminine Cas. "My husband Ian and I bought it a couple of years ago. Actually, Ian bought it. Just came into town one day looking for a place to open a B and B, and well, what with one thing and another, we ended up getting married and . . ." She looked around, her face glowing with pride. "And here we are."

With two customers at lunch time. Not a good sign. *Not my business.* Julie placed her book on the table and wondered if it would create a scandal to order wine with lunch. If she could even get a glass of wine for lunch.

"Couldn't find a plumber, could you?" said Christine, twisting her head to read the book title. "I'd send Ian over, but he's so busy. Deer season." She made a face and shuddered. "I shouldn't complain. It's our busiest season. Fortunately, they're gone all day and spend most of the night at the Roadhouse. So it isn't so bad." She looked around. "Where is that girl?"

At her words, a girl about seventeen, skinny as a zipper, dressed in unrelieved black including her spiked hair, slinked in through the front door and grabbed a red leather menu off the hostess podium.

I know that hair, thought Julie. It had been following her ever since she'd come into town.

She slouched up to the table.

Christine's lips tightened. "Why don't you take a few minutes to put on your uniform, Mel?" She tugged the menu away from the girl and handed it to Julie, smiling apologetically.

The girl slouched off toward the double doors of the kitchen.

"That was Melanie? She was two the last time I saw her," said Julie, dying to burst out laughing. The town Goth was Charles and Marian Reynolds's youngest daughter.

"I'm afraid so." Christine let her eyes trail after the girl, then turned back to Julie, her smile reaffirming itself. "We've got pot roast today. It's really good. Ian made it. He's a great cook."

"That sounds fine," said Julie and closed the menu.

"Anything to drink? Ice tea? Seltzer? We finally got our liquor license last spring. Took us two years. God, these old farts." She clapped her hand over her mouth and looked toward the other table.

Julie laughed, then realizing she had attracted the attention of the two other diners, she lowered her voice. "I've run into several of them already this morning. I'll have a glass of whatever your house red is."

"Great," said Christine and bustled away.

Julie picked up her book to learn about the finer points of plumbing, while dining on pot roast and what would probably turn out to be pink Zinfandel.

Christine returned with her wine and placed it on the table. "I opened it special," she said. "Sort of a welcome home. It's so good to see you."

"Thanks," said Julie, thinking, *she really must be desperate if she's glad to see me.* Though next to Melanie, Julie felt downright conservative.

The wine was dry and the pot roast, delicious, even though it was served by a sulking Melanie, whose white skin and shadow of quickly removed black lipstick and eyeliner cast a cadaverous pall over the meal.

Julie read and ate and drank, aware that Melanie was never far away. Either Christine had put the fear of God into her or she was just as curious as everybody else. Maybe she was hoping that Julie would turn out to be a kindred spirit.

She was reading the chapter on how to change a corroded washer when the two other diners got up to leave. A man about Wes's age and a much younger woman slowed down as they passed Julie's table.

"Miz Excelsior," the man said and touched his head as if he were wearing a hat, which he wasn't. "Ed Schott. Sorry for your loss. Wes was a fine man."

The Schotts were another family from the Hill. All she needed. "Thank you," she murmured. *Now go away.*

"We missed you at the funeral."

Julie flinched. *Sure you did.* She felt the heat rise to her face and willed it down. Melanie took that moment to step between them and fill Julie's water glass. When she left the Schotts were still there.

"And this is my daughter Isabelle. She was a few years behind you in school."

Isabelle Schott was petite with a sweet face and a peaches and cream complexion, surrounded by white-blond hair. She looked as if she'd stepped out of a fifties Sears catalogue.

Julie smiled. "It's nice to meet you."

"Nice to meet you, too," said Isabelle. "Sorry for your loss."

Julie smiled.

Mr. Schott touched his forehead again and they were gone.

Julie heard Melanie snicker as the door closed behind them, but when she looked up the girl was inspecting her nails.

Julie had a sudden urge to smack her, mainly because she reminded Julie of herself. Not the Goth part, but the hard edge that she guessed hid a vulnerable spirit.

Not your problem, she reminded herself, but she was grateful for the timely interruption with the water, so she left a generous tip, said goodbye to Christine and hurried back to her car before anyone else could stop to chat with the prodigal niece.

* * *

It was mid afternoon by the time Cas finally made it out to Excelsior House. After his fruitless trip to the Goethes, he'd stopped by to see Hank Jessop and ask for advice. All Hank said was, "These things come in cycles. Don't let it worry you, boy, you're doing fine."

Of course he wasn't doing fine. He wasn't doing anything. He'd already told the Goethes the same thing Hank had told him, to call their insurance company and not expect to see the things again.

But for once, he was glad he'd accepted the job of sheriff, because that was the only reason he was still here when Julie returned. And if Wes had planned it that way, Cas was grateful.

Now if he could just redeem himself after the fiasco of last night. The uniform would help. He'd just go in, act professional, and pretend he knew what he was doing. Then he'd have to go out and muck around like he knew what he was looking for and end up smelling like chicken shit, which would definitely put her off.

He parked next to the VW, took his pad and pencil and tried to think cop thoughts. It should be easy. For years whenever they were together, he was either a cop, a cowboy or a pirate. He smiled as he got an image of Julie tied to the old chimney in the woods, while he strode up and down in front of her. Then would come the inevitable tickling to make her confess to whatever, and that secret, tantalizing glimpse of blue flowered underpants. He broke into a grin. Had he ever been that innocent?

Yeah, he had. But that had ended. He banged on the car door and waited for it to open. Then he climbed out and walked up the steps.

He'd just raised his hand to knock when he heard a scream from inside. He wrenched the door open and ran down the hall. The scream had stopped, but there was a burst of obscenities coming from the kitchen. She was a wild woman. Heaven help whoever had broken in.

The kitchen door was ajar, which was a good thing, since the doorknob had come off again. "Police," he yelled and burst into the kitchen, only to slide halfway across the room before banging into the table. Water sprayed into the air, covering everything; the floors, the walls, the counters. Smitty ran from one side of the room to the other, barking and occasionally stopping to shake himself.

Julie stood next to the counter, scowling. Her hair and face were dripping. One long strand was stuck to her cheek; her T-shirt was soaked and plastered to her skin. Cas took a deep breath.

"Well?" she said over the splashing water. "Do something." She pushed her wet hair back with both hands then wiped them on the front of her shirt.

Cas lost his breath. She was going to drive him crazy, and all the Reynoldses would end up in the psych ward together.

"Aaaargh," not from Smitty but Julie, who threw up her hands, dropped to her knees, then fought her way through the spray to stick her head and shoulders into the cabinet beneath the sink. Water sprayed out to either side of her tempting bottom.

Cas watched as it wiggled in response to something she was doing inside the cabinet. His mouth went dry in spite of the fact that he was quickly becoming as wet as the rest of the kitchen.

With an effort, he snapped to. He hurried around the table while Smitty jumped at his legs. He dropped to his knees and taking Julie's butt in both hands, pulled her out of the cabinet. Then he reached in and felt for the water valve. One was turned off, but the other was stuck in the open position.

He came out for breath, water dripping off his face and running down his shirt collar. He wiped his eyes with his now soggy shirt sleeve and looked among the floating cans and bottles for the WD 40. It was lying on its side; he flipped off the top and went back in. A quick spray and he crawled back out, shut the cabinet doors, and sat back on his knees to wait.

Julie was standing over him, her hands on her hips, looking like a demented water nymph. "That really solves the problem. Just shut the damn doors. Why didn't I think of that?"

He counted to ten, waited another twenty seconds, while his trouser legs soaked up water, and crawled back in. A couple of quick twists and the flood slowed down to a stream and finally stopped completely. He crawled back out and got to his feet, picking up a waterlogged, oversized paperback on his way.

He tossed it on the table where it landed with a soggy thud. *How to Be Your Own Handyman.* He shook his head and turned to Julie who was probably still scowling. He wasn't sure because his eyes never got to her face. They jolted to a stop where her wet T-shirt clung to two very full, rounded breasts.

"I turned off the valve, just like it said."

Cas smiled—at her breasts. "You did. But there are two. You only got the hot water."

"There're two?"

He dragged his eyes to her face and her look of chagrin made him want to kiss her.

"Where?"

On your mouth, your tits, everywhere, thought Cas.

She shoved him aside and crawled back into the cabinet.

Or your ass, he added.

"Where," echoed from under the sink.

"Huh?" Where what?

"I see the red one. Where's the other one?"

Taking that for an invitation, he moved her butt aside, feeling the tingle on his fingers long enough to make him see stars, and climbed in beside her. "Right here." He pointed to a blue covered handle that was partially hidden by the hose of the dish sprayer.

She looked at the valve shutoff, then turned her head to look at him. Her lips were close enough to kiss. So he did.

"Umphh," said Julie and collapsed onto one elbow, taking him with her. He managed to twist one arm free and get it around her shoulders, then slid them both out of the cabinet and onto the floor where they lay in the water among the cans of cleanser, dish detergent, and floor wax.

But he didn't stop kissing her.

Julie wrapped her arms around his neck and opened her mouth to him. His tongue slid in, touched hers, and his groin flared to life. Julie fell onto her back and Cas stretched out along her body. He rocked against her and she responded with a sound somewhere between a groan and a laugh and pushed back. He found the edge of her shirt and eased his hand beneath it, sliding over her wet skin to the swell of her bra. He broke the kiss and licked her neck, buried his nose in her skin, and continued to lick downward, his mouth on a mission to rendezvous with his hands.

She twisted beneath him, managed to get her thigh between his legs and moved against him until he began pulsing against her leg, mindless of the water, the cold or anything but the warmth of her—until he felt heavy footsteps on his back.

Then heard the low growl.

"Shit," he said against her breast, afraid to move and have Smitty rip his throat out. Smitty slid off his back onto the floor and pushed his nose between them, snuffled for a few dreaded seconds, then slurped Julie's face.

"Mine," said Cas.

"Go away, Smitty," said Julie.

Cas came to his senses. He was seducing Julie on a wet kitchen floor surrounded by cleaning products and a dog. Not good. Not cool. Not romantic in the least. So much for doing things right. He tried to get up, but Julie held on and he brought her up with him, until they were standing, locked together from chest to toes.

She pulled herself up his body and found his mouth with hers.

Hell. He was lost. He staggered backwards, feet sloshing and slipping until his back hit the wall and the back of his head banged into the cuckoo clock.

"I came to . . ." he began.

"Mmmmm," said Julie.

His hands roamed down her back. "Take your statement."

"Hmmm," said Julie.

He kissed her and his hand slipped around her side until his palm found her breast again.

"Did you see who it was?" His fingers tightened around the curve of her flesh and she rolled to one side so he could reach between them. His hand closed over the luscious weight of her breast.

She gasped. "No."

"Oh. Sorry." He jerked his hand away, but she grabbed it and pushed it back to her breast. His thumb rasped across the tight nipple.

"Yes," she sighed.

His erection hardened while he tried to grasp the thread of his questioning. "You saw them?"

"No, but don't stop."

"No." He rolled them along the wall so that she was against the wall and he was pressing his erection against her stomach. His second hand joined his first and they cupped her breasts, while his groin ground into her.

Then something knocked into his knees and he nearly went down. Smitty whined.

"At ease," Julie said around Cas's tongue.

"Huh?"

The dog whined again and tried to walk between them. Cas pushed him away with his foot. Smitty growled.

"Shit." Cas began sliding Julie along the wall, until they were by the door, then he rolled them out and kicked the door shut. Smitty barked from the other side.

Cas continued to kiss her as he walked down the hall and into the parlor, moving her backward like a clumsy dancing partner, until they reached the couch.

They fell onto the cushions together.

The couch emitted a loud raspberry.

"Damn it, Wes." Cas fished under the cushion and pulled out the whoopee cushion. Threw it on the floor where it gave a half-hearted wheeze.

Then he pushed himself up the length of the couch so that Julie lay on top of him. He broke the kiss long enough to pull her T-shirt over her head. She shivered. The room was warm, but their clothes were wet and clammy. He unfastened her bra and she sat up to let the shiny fabric fall from her shoulders and down her arms.

Cas sucked in his breath, enthralled by the closeness of that creamy skin. She fumbled with the buttons of his uniform and in a deep recess of Cas's mind, he thought of the consequences of . . . then he lost his mind again as Julie's hands pressed to his bare skin.

Her hands were cold and he took them in his and rubbed them against his chest until warmth spread to her fingers and she was rocking against him, breathing hard, smiling a seductress's smile, her eyes never leaving his.

He reached for the button of her jeans. Fumbled. The wet fabric made it hard to navigate. She swung one leg off him and stood up. Unzipped her jeans and pushed them down her legs, keeping her gaze on his face. Then she leaned over, until the tips of wet hair brushed against his abdomen. She licked into his belly button, and his pelvis rose up to her, demanding its share of the same.

She unclasped his belt and unzipped his trousers. He lifted his hips and she pulled them down his legs, tugged off his shoes and socks. The air rushed across his skin. Julie crawled back on the couch and straddled him.

His hands reached for her hips, cupped her butt and rubbed warmth into her cheeks.

She nestled against his erection and began to move. Lightly, sliding up and down his penis until he was slick with her.

"Julie," he said and tried to remember which pocket he kept his condoms in. *Wallet, you fool.* He let go to grope around the floor for his pants.

Julie laughed and leaned over, her breast brushing against his arm as she picked up his pants. He had to wrestle his wallet out of his back pocket. Sweat broke out on his forehead.

Julie continued to rock, like a boat on a quiet lake, he thought, and he finally pulled out the foil square. She took it from him, and just as efficiently as she'd removed his pants, she had the condom out and rolling down his cock.

"Oh, Jesus." He bit his lip. He tried to think of chicken thieves, so he wouldn't come before she got the condom on.

Then she smiled down at him. "Is this cops, cowboys, or pirates?"

God, he couldn't think. He wanted all three at once.

"Cowboys," he blurted.

She laughed and scooped his cock in her hand. "My, what a big saddle horn you have," she said and impaled herself on him.

It nearly pushed him over. He gritted his teeth, gripped his toes. And then she began to ride, a rhythm so perfect that they could have been lovers for ages.

"Relax," she breathed and tweaked his nipples between her fingers.

Cas reared up off the sofa. "It's been awhile," he grunted. "It may be . . . a short ride."

"That's okay . . . I don't have . . . far to go."

He lifted into her. Slid his hands up her thighs until his thumbs opened her to his touch. She shivered, picked up the rhythm again, sliding up and down his cock while his finger slid against her.

And they rode, mindless of the rough couch cushions, of Smitty's whine echoing down the hall, of the whoopee cushion abandoned on the floor. It was fast, furious, and Cas was just reaching the point of no return, when Julie cried, "Yeehaw," and they tumbled over the brink together.

Julie collapsed onto him and he wrapped his arms around her while he floated into a place with no responsibilities, no warring families, no chicken thieves.

Finally he realized that Julie was shaking. Was she cold? Was she crying. Had he hurt her? Was she regretting this already?

"What? Are you okay?"

She rubbed her cheek against his chest and lifted her head just enough so that he could see her face. "I was just thinking. Wasn't that better than peeking at my underwear?"

Cas's arms tightened around her. "You have no idea how much better."

She smiled. "I can hardly wait for pirates. You were always the best at pirates."

Chapter 6

Cas's first thought, when he could think at all, was that his Cass was up the crick. His police car was parked in front of the house, the drapes were open. There was a crazed German shepherd in the kitchen. His parents were next door, possibly with binoculars—or a rifle—aimed at the house. And he was in Julie Excelsior's parlor wearing nothing but Julie and his wristwatch.

He sat up. Julie rolled to one side and snuggled against him.

"I've got to go."

"But what about my pipes?"

"Your pipes are great."

She sat up and smiled at him. "I've got a Jacuzzi upstairs."

"Some other time." He nudged her off him and reached for his pants. They were soggy and wrinkled. Well, hell, if he were lucky, he could get home and change into his other uniform without anyone seeing him. Then Julie's reputation wouldn't suffer and he wouldn't have to face his father's recriminations.

His cell phone rang. So much for luck.

He stood up and Julie flopped back onto the couch.

"Sorry," said Cas, rummaging through his shirt pockets to find the phone. He flipped it open and made the mistake of looking at her. She was sprawled along the cushions like an impressionist painting, curved in all the right places. His eyes rested on hers, then traveled down to her full pouty lips, her dusky nipples to the triangle of dark hair between her legs. His dick stirred.

"Cas. What are you doing at Wes Excelsior's?"

His dick deflated. He turned his back on Julie and pulled his shirt to his crotch. Something about talking to your mother in the nude put him off his game.

"Report of a break-in. I was just leaving."

"She's there, isn't she? It's all over town."

"Someone tried to break into Wes's chicken coop. I'm the sheriff." *And I just had the quickest, greatest sex of my life.*

"Well, your father is at the back door with his .22. And I really think you should come over."

"I'm on my way." He closed the phone, pushed his arm into his sleeve and shuddered. "Shit."

Julie frowned at him, then stood up and yanked the shirt out of his hand. She picked up the rest of his clothes and carried them out of the room, leaving him naked, depressed and on the verge of panic.

He grabbed an afghan off the back of the wing chair and wrapped it around his waist as he watched Julie's round butt disappear around the edge of the doorway.

"Where are you going?" he called after her, then ran after her, the afghan trailing on the floor behind him.

The hallway was empty and with a sinking heart, he knew she and his clothes were in the kitchen with Smitty. "Julie," he called, his voice almost a falsetto. "Come out of there." He expected to hear a shot any minute, and though his father had never managed to hit anything beyond a few pieces of gingerbread molding and the decorative weathervane on top of the gazebo, his balls shrank into peanuts as he ran down the hall.

He stopped at the kitchen door and knocked. "Julie," he called.

The door opened and Julie stood in all her glory, looking a little miffed. Who could blame her?

"If it's an emergency, Wes's clothes are still in his bedroom. I don't think he'll mind if you borrow them."

He heard the tumble of the dryer in the sun porch off the kitchen. "It's my mother."

Emotion flickered across Julie's face. "Figures," she said. She stepped aside. Smitty pounced and Cas instinctively threw his butt back

"Watch the jewels, Smitty," said Julie and turned away as if she didn't care whether Cas was left intact of not.

God. He'd made another hash of what had been an incredible few minutes. He was his father's son, a Reynolds to the bone. Family name always came back to bite him in the ass, when all he wanted was . . . something he couldn't have.

He started to follow her, but Smitty took hold of the afghan and dug in his paws. Cas yanked hard, but managed to do nothing but lose the majority of his covering. Smitty growled and wagged his tail.

"Not now," said Cas.

Smitty looked up at him with a hurt expression, then dropped his mouthful of afghan and docilely followed Cas through the kitchen.

Cas heard the dryer stop and the door open. Clutching the afghan tightly around him, he went into the sun porch. Julie was leaning over the opening. Her butt was covered with goose flesh. Cas opened the afghan, walked into her, and wrapped it around both of them. His dick began rooting around looking for a warm place to stay, but Julie straightened up.

"Your mother's watching. Reynolds, too." She tilted her chin toward the window. And Cas saw two little figures standing on the back steps of Reynolds Place. His first impulse was to pull Julie to the floor out of harm's way, but he doubted if they could see her. His mother was nearsighted and his father couldn't see past his own prejudices.

She reached into the dryer and pulled out his pants. "You really want to wear these? Be my guest." She shoved them at him. He caught them. The afghan dropped to the floor, and they both stood as naked as jaybirds in the sun that filtered through the windows. And suddenly the room was warm, not cold, and Cas couldn't remember why he'd been in such a hurry to leave.

"Go," Julie said, her voice giving nothing away, and left him standing alone, looking at his nutcase parents and wishing he and Julie could sail away.

He hurried after her. "Julie."

She looked over her shoulder and lifted an eyebrow. Her expression was so distant, that he had to swallow twice before he said, "I guess I'll borrow some of Wes's clothes."

Julie lay curled up among the pink pillows, dressed in a pair of sweats and her NYPD sweat shirt. She heard the door to Wes's bedroom open and close, Cas pause in the hallway, then run down the stairs. The front door opened and shut and a minute later the police car drove away.

She pulled the comforter around her, feeling cold now that she was fully dressed and the heat was pumping out of the ancient radiators. He'd done it again. Well, duh, what did she expect? He was a Reynolds, wasn't he?

Julie turned onto her back and threw her arm across her eyes. "Why did I do that?" She groaned, but couldn't keep a smile from creeping across her lips. Because Cas was hot and she hadn't had sex in the last century. Well, at least the last year. It wasn't healthy. If she didn't use them, her washers might corrode. She sucked in a shaky breath. So she got a little carried away. And what did she get for her trouble? He ran off to his mother.

Reynolds and Marian were such idiots, thought Julie. *If they'd just left us alone for another year or two, we'd have gone all the way in the back seat of Reynolds's Cadillac and there would be the end of it.* Instead they had turned it into more fuel for the never-ending feud . . . and been responsible for both Cas and her being sent away. She could forgive them for whatever happened a hundred and fifty years ago, but not for what they'd done to her. She'd lost her home and the only two people who loved her.

Well, to hell with them. Julie curled up again and pulled the comforter under her chin, thinking of Cas's face when that phone rang. It would be funny if it didn't hurt so much.

He'd reacted just like she'd expected him to, but had hoped he wouldn't. Talk about going from hot to cold. Oh hell, maybe he was relieved. Maybe she'd been too forward. He was kind of a prude. Except he was damn good at finding the right buttons, which made her wonder about how prudish he really was. Maybe it was a case of too much too soon.

I came on pretty strong, Julie thought. *I probably scared him. I acted like a hooker. No. Like white trash.* She sighed. Maybe that's why he'd given her up all those years before.

After a few minutes, she chuckled. She had to admit that the whole situation was outrageous. And he started it. He always started it. At least this time he finished it.

"I think it's really finished now." She pushed up to her elbows and threw back the covers. "That's it. I've had my fun and now it's time to flush some other pipes. I should have made him fix the leak before he got sex." She put on her shoes and went downstairs to be her own handyman.

It took a while to clean up the kitchen. She swept water out onto the back porch and into the yard, then she used every dish towel she could find to soak up the rest. She took them, dripping, into the sun room. The top of the dryer was still open and Cas's uniform lay crumpled and wet inside. She shoved the towels in with it and closed the lid. The dryer hummed backed to life.

It took even longer to change the washer, since the book pages had stuck together, and it was nearly impossible to separate them without tearing them. But after a few false starts and banged elbows, the pipes were flushed, the new washers were in place, the thingies were tightened on the pipes, the two valves, red and blue, were turned to the open position, and she was ready for a test run.

"Better stand back," she warned Smitty. She turned on the spigot and jumped back. The pipes clanged but water ran out in a steady stream. Julie held her breath waiting for the explosion and when it didn't come, she stepped cautiously toward the sink. "Hey, cool," she said.

The pipes let out another groan and she jumped back. The water continued to flow smoothly. She turned it off. Waited a couple of seconds and turned it on again. Once again the water flowed out in a steady stream.

"Ha. Who needs men?" Julie lifted her hands in triumph. "I am woman. I am plumber."

The dryer buzzed and the laundry tumbled to a stop.

She dropped her hands. "I am totally fucked."

Cas had no idea what he was going to say to his parents or how he was going to explain the fact that he was wearing Wes Excelsior's dungarees instead of his uniform. *My uniform got wet while Julie and I were rolling on the floor, locked in a torrid embrace.* Language they could understand. It would give them both coronaries.

Better to stick to the story about thieves and go back to Julie's to pick up his clothes. Then maybe they could pick up where they'd left off. After all, she had a Jacuzzi; it was a perfect place to indulge in a game of pirates.

Then he remembered Julie's expression and how he had stolen away without saying goodbye. Well, hell. She'd closed her door. Pretty obvious that she didn't want to see him.

Actually, who could blame her? He mauled her on the floor, had speed sex on the couch, and ran off as soon as they were done. He should have ignored the phone. He'd just go back and apologize. Explain about the rifle. She'd forgive him and they could get on with it. If she'd forgive him.

Because he wouldn't let it end again. He'd been afraid before, years ago. Had let weeks go by, pretending to ignore her, while his heart was trampled; acting like he didn't care, hell, like he didn't even know her, because Reynolds told him if he so much as looked at her again, he would send him away to school. He hadn't looked at her and Reynolds had still sent him away.

When he came back on his first vacation, he rushed to Wes's to explain, but she was gone. She had never come back—until now.

He had to knock twice before the door to his parents' house finally opened. Melanie stood looking at him through raccoon-rimmed eyes, her black painted lips in their perpetual scowl, and Cas thought, *I have to do something to get you away from all this.*

She jerked her head, an invitation to come inside, and opened the door wider.

"They sent Larue to town for more liquor. They're out back. I just got home from the restaurant, but I didn't hear any shots. He didn't kill her, did he?"

"Jesus, Mel." Cas wanted to shake her, she sounded so bored and uncaring. So like Julie, just before she'd shut her bedroom door. Not bored, he thought, but self-protective. "No, he didn't shoot her."

He stepped past her, then turned. "How did you know she was back?"

"She had lunch at the hotel. Christine was treating her like royalty. I thought we all hated her."

"We all don't," said Cas with more edge than he usually used with his Goth sister, even when she was at her most ob-noxious.

"Good, because she has a navel ring."

I know, thought Cas. And his mind wandered away from his responsibilities to settle on Julie's tight stomach, her tight everything.

"Thank God, you're here."

Cas jumped. Melanie shut the door and melted away.

His mother, dressed in a hostess gown of lilac swirls, her hair swept back in a new perm of metallic gold, picked her way into the foyer. She stopped abruptly, teetering on tiny strapped high heels.

"What on earth are you wearing? It's cocktail hour, for heaven's sake." She flurried newly manicured nails at him. "Well, never mind. It's better than that awful uniform. You know how it upsets Reynolds."

Saying her husband's name must have recalled her to her purpose, because her perfectly shaped brows knit together. "He's on the back steps again. Why won't Wes Excelsior just leave us alone? I mean the man's dead, for heaven's sake. Why can't we have one, just one, cocktail hour without Reynolds taking his rifle to the back porch?"

Maybe if you didn't have so many martinis, he wouldn't, thought Cas, but he kept it to himself and let his mother lead him down the hall to the back of the house. She stopped in the great room and motioned him toward the door. "You go ahead. I'll just freshen the drinks."

Left alone in the room, Cas considered how he would relieve his father of the rifle. Right now, he felt like grabbing it and bashing him over the head with it. If it weren't so absurd, it would be tragic. Actually, it was tragic. When Cas left for boarding school, his father had been a formidable, well-respected banker. Within a month, the bank closed and his father became a broken man, and then a lunatic. He still had his moments of lucidity except where Wes Excelsior was concerned. So lucid, that only his family knew exactly how off his rocker he was. And only his children admitted it.

Cas cracked his neck and opened the door to the back steps just as Reynolds took aim. Cas grabbed the rifle and pushed it upward. It discharged into the sky. A low-flying sparrow hawk dropped to the ground.

Charles Reynolds turned on his son, his face ruddy with martinis and outrage. He was wearing a smoking jacket, though he didn't smoke, and dress pants, like the fucking lord of the manor. Cas could smell the sweet vermouth on his breath. He eased the rifle from his father's hands.

"What was your car doing in the Excelsior drive?" Reynolds

asked and Cas unconsciously added, "Young man," without thinking.

His father glared at him. "It's that girl. We saw Edith Turnbull at the bakery and she told us—"

"There was an attempted robbery."

"Then why aren't you in uniform?" Reynolds spit out the word like it was something obscene, and it was to his father, who had angrily told him when he took the job of sheriff that Reynoldses were not, and had never been, civil servants. It never occurred to him to ask why Cas had returned home in the first place. Or why he decided to stay.

"Come inside, Reynolds. Mother's got a new batch of martinis waiting." He took his father by the elbow, much as his mother had taken his, and led him down the hall, while Reynolds muttered under his breath. Outside the parlor, Cas leaned the rifle against the wall so he could take it away with him as soon as he deposited his father in front of the fireplace.

Before stepping into the parlor, Reynolds shook off his grasp, straightened up, and said, "That is no way to dress for cocktails."

"I'm not staying," said Cas.

Marian greeted them at the door and handed Reynolds a fresh martini. She turned to Cas. "Would you like a martini or would you prefer scotch?"

"Neither, thank you. I can't stay."

"Nonsense," said Reynolds from his seat by the fire. "I want to talk to you."

"We can talk tomorrow." At the most dreaded event of Excelsior Falls. Sunday dinner at Reynolds Place. 2:00. Cas, Melanie, Christine, and Ian, sitting in proxy for Bruce who had the good sense to get a job out of commuting distance, posed around the table like dutiful children while Reynolds and Marian sat at head and foot like people out of a thirties movie.

They'd grown up this way, and never thought it odd until

they realized that they were the only family in town living in an alternate universe. Now that Cas thought about it, there were a lot of people in town living in another world, only theirs had to be more interesting than the Reynoldses.

"Cas, your father is talking to you," his mother hinted gently.

"Yes sir?" he said, automatically adding the "sir" because he'd been caught off guard. This evidently pleased Reynolds because he smiled a patriarchal, if not paternal, smile at him and said, "So that's settled. You can drive over on Monday."

Cas opened his mouth and his mother said, "You'll wear a nice gray suit—you have a gray suit, of course. A white shirt, French cuffs. And a blue tie with red stripes; that always looks nice with a gray suit. Thin stripes, you don't want to appear too forward."

"Charles can look as forward as he likes. They need him over there. He'll show them how a Reynolds runs things."

"What are you talking about?" asked Cas.

His mother blinked at him in surprise. "We ran into George Quincy in Henryville the other day." She lowered her voice. "We had a little business with the bank."

Selling off more stocks, thought Cas.

"And Reynolds told him you were back in the area and interested in—"

"No," said Cas. "I'm not interested. I'm only helping out Hank Jessop. I have a job. I build boats."

"Well, really," said his mother.

"Please have the good taste not to mention that folly," said his father.

Cas felt the blood rush up his neck and into his face. *And which of my follies are we talking about now, Dad?*

"Now, now," said Marian. "It's our place as community leaders to help where we're needed. And Hank Jessop needed time to recover from his heart attack. But I'm sure he must be well by now, and so there's no reason not to talk to George Quincy."

She smiled at Cas. And he thought, *I must have been switched at birth*. But that meant Christine and Melanie had been, too. Only Bruce was what their father called, "A chip off the old block," and Bruce had fled to Chicago.

There was no sense in arguing with them. Cas had learned that years ago. He'd just call George Quincy on Monday morning and explain the misunderstanding.

"I have to go."

"Drinks at one-thirty," said his mother.

Cas headed for the door. He grabbed the rifle as he left and caught a glimpse of Melanie standing like Queen Mab at the top of the stairs.

He heard her humming *Sail Away* as he closed the front door.

Chapter 7

Julie folded Cas's uniform and put it in a paper bag, which she left on the front porch. She had no intention of going through any awkward confrontations again. She spent the rest of the evening studying Wes's notes and chicken books. And when she heard a car drive up, she didn't leave her chair, just listened to Cas knock and call her name until he finally gave up and drove away. When she looked later, the bag was gone.

She fell asleep early, exhausted from chickens and emotions, and was surprised when the first rooster crow rent the air on the following morning. She dressed quickly and found Maude waiting for her at the gazebo.

As soon as Julie closed the wire gate, leaving a disgruntled Smitty outside, Maude handed her a flat pan filled with bits of grain and corn and other stuff.

"You just toss out this scratch so they get to know you, while I fill the feeders. Ready?"

Julie nodded. She was ready. How hard could it be?

Maude opened the door to the gazebo and chickens raced past her down the ramp heading for Julie.

"Talk to them," said Maude. "Use a soothing voice."

Right, Julie thought. "Here, chickens. Nice chickens."

"Broadcast the scratch."

"Huh?" Julie looked at Maude and half the contents of the pan fell to the ground. A swarm of chickens crowded around her, taking as many pecks at her boots as they did at the grain. "Stop pushing," said Julie and tried to move her foot away. A little brown and red hen rose in the air and landed in the thick of the crowd. "Christ, I kayoed it," she said, her eyes wide.

Maude bounced down the ramp and took the tin from Julie. "Poor Ernestine," she cooed as she tossed handfuls of grain into the air with the wrist action of a Frisbee player.

"Broadcast, right," said Julie. "I forgot."

"Just got to get the hang of it. And try not to make any sudden movements."

Like drop-kicking Ernestine, thought Julie, truly repentant.

"Well, you're on your own," said Maude, a few minutes later as she climbed into her truck.

Julie smiled and took a deep breath. "Don't worry," she said. "I'll be fine." *I hope.*

"See you Thursday." And Maude drove away.

When she was gone, Julie turned and took a look around, her mind moving from chickens to riddles. Twenty acres on which to hide a clue or two. She'd check their old hiding places first; there were several in the woods and a few in the old apple orchard.

It could take days to find the next clue. A drop of moisture fell on her face, followed by another. She looked up to see a fat, gray cloud swallow up the sun.

"So maybe, I'll start the search inside." She ran toward the house as rain began to fall.

Cas woke up to raindrops pelting his window. He stretched contentedly; grew hard, thinking about Julie. Then he remembered how he'd left without saying goodbye. And how she wouldn't answer the door when he went back to explain.

He rolled over and pulled the pillow over his head. Boy, he had really lived up to her expectation of him. Because he knew she must be comparing yesterday to that day on the river so long ago. And he'd blown it again.

He'd been a kid then, but he was a man now. Right. A real

man would have returned and finished the job, both jobs, the sink and sex with Julie. Hell, a real man wouldn't have panicked and run off to his mother. Except for the rifle, that was a pretty big extenuating circumstance. But Julie didn't know that. And that was his fault, too. What was the matter with him? He became a blithering idiot every time he was near her.

He threw off the pillow and sat up. Fuck it. He'd work on his boat, endure another Sunday dinner, and go back and make her listen to him.

He'd fix the damn sink, and the door, and tell her about Reynolds's penchant for shooting at the gazebo. And if she forgave him for being such an oaf, there was still the Jacuzzi.

Feeling better, he got out of bed, dressed in jeans and sweat shirt and went outside to the boatyard. It was really just a corrugated machine shop, but it was the main reason Cas had rented the cottage. It was long enough to accommodate a sixteen footer, was heated, had plenty of neon lighting and enough electrical outlets to run all his power tools at once.

He was soon lost in the rhythm of sanding the hull. Felt the simple lines of the white cedar slats come to life under his hands. This is what he was meant to do, what he had always wanted to do. *Unrealistic*, his father told him. *The Reynolds are bankers. They don't work with their hands, they use their brains.*

Cas pushed the thought aside. He had good hands, useful hands. Using them made him happy. Gave him a sense of pride when he watched a finished boat launch for its first test run. And using them to follow the contours of Julie's body made him long for more.

His work was the only thing that had kept him sane after hours spent with Wes, watching him slowly drift away. He'd meant to leave after the funeral. Go back to his job at the building yard in Rhode Island. But today he was relishing the old dream of opening his own shop.

He wondered if Julie would like living by the ocean.

But first he had to figure out the damn riddle and make sure his family could survive the answer. He wanted to send Melanie to college, but that would leave him few resources for opening a business. He had to give Christine a chance to make a go of the hotel and her marriage. Ian was a good man, and she deserved to be happy. God knows, there had been little enough of that emotion in the Reynolds household.

And he still had to convince Julie that they had a future together. And he would. Somehow.

He leaned into the boat, concentrated on the feel of the wood beneath his fingers, and immediately remembered the feel of Julie the day before. He gave the same attention to the boat that he would give her, if only she'd give him another chance.

And finally managed to lose himself in his work.

Julie paced back and forth across the parlor carpet, marking off the salient points of her investigation like she was presenting them to a team of detectives. She thought better on her feet.

"First point. Wes leaves me a riddle in his will."

She paused.

"So now I'm here, looking for treasure. The second riddle was easy enough to find, but it makes no sense. We don't have any marble halls." She glanced past Smitty, who was stretched out on the hearth rug before the unlit fire. "Hell, even the mantel is mahogany. The pond is spring fed but that hardly qualifies as a crystal fountain. And when the orchard bothers to produce an apple, they're Romes, not Goldens."

She leaned against the windowsill and looked out at the rain. "It doesn't even sound like a whole riddle. Da-duh-da-duh," she intoned in iambic pentameter. "There must be some lines missing." She looked down at the yellow paper in her hand.

"Eureka," she said. "It *isn't* a whole riddle. It's half a riddle. What use is half—damn it, Wes." She slapped her thigh in frustration.

Smitty lumbered to his feet and padded over to her.

"Sorry, Smitty, that was an exclamation, not a command."

Smitty gave her a look and went back to the hearth to sleep.

Julie began pacing again. When Cas and she got too good at treasure hunting, Wes would jumble up the riddles and they'd have to share their clues, then try to unscramble them before the other one did.

She paused mid-step. "And isn't it interesting that Cas just happens to be here when I come back. I bet he has the other half. He might even know about mine. Might have even seen my half."

She threw herself into the wing chair and stared at the empty fireplace. "Wes would never give him a head start. That wouldn't be fair. The will said 'all my worldly possessions,' so even if Cas found it first, it would still be mine, right?"

Smitty twitched in his sleep.

"You're no help." Julie stood up and walked back toward the window. Hell, if Wes wanted to leave Cas something, he should have just said so. She wouldn't have begrudged it. She didn't think. Well, not much.

"Hmmm," she said, getting a not-so-pleasant idea. What if that seduction scene yesterday was just a ploy to get to her half of the riddle? She shook her head. She could have sworn Cas was just as overwhelmed as she was. Surely he hadn't planned it—not Cas. There must be something else going on here.

Well, enough second-guessing. She'd do a methodical search. Might as well use all that police training for something.

She started with the book shelves, opening books, shaking them and replacing them again. Occasionally, she opened a familiar title and a smile curved her lips.

When she was eleven, she'd had to stand on a chair and a pile of dictionaries to reach the top shelve that held the erotica, with Cas holding her ankles and telling her not to fall. Now she could look right onto the shelf by standing on tip toe. *The Story of O, The Pearl.* They were still here. Dusty. Unread. Their pages crumbling. There would be no more clandestine trips to the gazebo for the forbidden touches that heated their blood and invariably ended in embarrassment and laughter. The gazebo was a chicken coop, Wes was gone, and Cas was someone she didn't know.

But that you just fucked, she reminded herself, and pushed *My Secret Life* back onto the shelf.

She went upstairs and searched the two guest rooms, found nothing close to another clue. At last she opened the door to Wes's room. It was the first time she had actually entered it since she'd returned, merely peeked in that first night to make sure there were no surprises, like the local ax murderer, and closed the door again.

She stood on the threshold, looking in at the shadowed room. Wes's bed seemed smaller than before, though it was still covered by the patchwork quilt that they used for a table cloth for their rainy day turret picnics.

She moved silently across the room, past the curved bureau with its white lace runner and beveled mirror until she reached the far corner where the room ended in a three-walled turret.

It wasn't a real turret, just one of those Victorian additions that held no purpose but was Cas and Julie's crow's nest as they sailed the high seas of their imagination. In those days, the windows were made of amber glass with a row of fruits, flowers and green leaves that ran across the top. They cast a golden glow on everything they saw: the woods, the orchard, and the distant mountains. Sometimes the fog would roll in and they'd sway together and Cas would call, "Batten down the hatches, matey."

On rainy days, Wes would come with lemonade and pickled pig's feet and soda crackers. They would spread out the patchwork quilt on the turret carpet and pretend it was salt pork and hard tack while the rain slashed at the windows. Those were magical days. And then they ended.

One day after Cas was sent away, she and Wes were watching a storm roll in when lightning hit the finial on the turret roof. Two of the beautiful stained glass windows were blown out and they were pelted by shards of glass. Wes carried her out of the room while rain pounded through the opening and flooded the floor. He made her stay outside while he boarded up the windows. When he came downstairs hours later, he was carrying the sodden carpet. He was bloody and soaked and frowning. He threw the carpet out, moved to the guest room, and they never went into his room again.

A few weeks later, Julie was on her way to Yonkers to live with her mother's sister. "Forget Ex Falls," Wes told her through the open window of her father's '87 Chevy. "But don't forget who loves you." And that was the last time she'd seen Wes or her father.

Julie turned from the windows and saw a pair of slippers placed neatly by the bed as if ready to be stepped into.

Wes had loved her. And she hadn't even gotten a chance to say goodbye.

Cas was only a few minutes late when, dressed in suit and tie and the one pair of good shoes he'd kept, he arrived at the family homestead.

Larue answered the door, his short white jacket and black bow tie making him look more like a waiter at the White House than the sole servant of an eccentric family in a dying town.

"Mister Charles," he said gravely and stepped aside to let him enter.

Mister Charles. Jesus. Cas was thirty-one years old, but every time he stepped into this house he became twelve again. And he had to fight the impulse to turn around and run. But he had done that once and where did it get him? Right back here with his life on hold. Except now Julie was here. *God, Wes, I hope you know what you're doing.*

"Charles, you're late," said his father when Larue showed him into the parlor.

"Good afternoon to you, too," said Cas and watched his father's ruddy cheeks deepen a shade. Stupid. Being belligerent wouldn't help what ailed them. He glanced toward Melanie who slouched in a chair, her black spiked hair and makeup an absurd contrast to the yellow twin set and skirt she was wearing.

At least Christine and Ian were making a stab at being sociable. Christine had blossomed during her marriage and she was looking radiant today. At least Reynolds and Marian had accepted Ian. In their minds, he was a real estate developer, when in actuality he'd spent every penny he had to buy the derelict hotel. It was amazing what you could manage not to see if your way of life depended on it.

His collar suddenly felt too tight and his suit coat too confining. He wanted to rip them off. Rip everything off and roll naked with Julie in the spray of the sea.

"Penny for your thoughts, dear," said his mother and motioned him toward a place on the sofa. "And stop fidgeting with your tie."

Cas automatically dropped the hand he didn't know was pulling at his collar. Ian shot him an understanding look and turned back to listen to Reynolds give advice on screening the inn's clientele.

Cas listened, nursing an untouched glass of Glenlivet until Larue announced lunch. They took their places, Cas leading Melanie in on his arm.

She gave him a sour look and whispered, "Is this a reality show?"

"A reality check," he whispered back and elicited the first genuine, if brief, smile he'd seen from his sister in a long time. Reynolds sat down at the head of the table, Marian at the foot. The rest of them sat spread out inbetween, just far enough to make passing the serving bowls a circus act.

Dinner was the same as always. Interminably slow, with terminally mundane food and conversation. Until dessert.

Then his father said, "I suppose that girl is back because she inherited everything?"

Christine and Ian looked at their plates. Mel snorted and covered her mouth with her napkin, and Cas braced himself for the inevitable postprandial tirade against the Excelsiors.

"Dear," said Marian, smiling sweetly at Reynolds. She rang the silver bell at her elbow. When Larue appeared, she said, "We'll have coffee in the parlor," and stood up.

"Well, at least now we can get rid of those damn chickens," said Reynolds, ignoring her. "Selling out, most likely. Take the money and run; just like her kind."

Cas clenched his teeth and pushed his chair back.

Melanie sighed loudly.

"Melanie," Marian warned her from the doorway.

Melanie slouched back in her chair and said, "Well, I like her."

Reynolds and Marian zeroed in on her, while Cas, Ian and Christine froze halfway to their feet.

"You may go to your room," said Reynolds.

"Dad," said Christine, and Ian put his hand on her arm.

"Lucky me," said Melanie. She threw her napkin on her plate and stalked past him to the door. "At least she's alive." She lifted her chin, turned on her heel, and left the room.

Good for you, thought Cas when his initial shock had subsided. *And after only seeing Julie at the restaurant.*

As soon as coffee was passed around and they were sitting uncomfortably around the fireplace, Reynolds took up his train of thought again.

"Call Maude Clemmons and tell her to take them away. Do not go to that house again. You know you have no sense when it comes to that girl."

Marian chimed in. "It will be so nice not to have those smelly birds around anymore. One couldn't even open the windows in the summer for the awful . . . you know. I didn't dare have a party for wondering what people must think."

Cas stood up.

"Cas," said Christine urgently.

"Her name is Julie. Julie Excelsior, not 'that girl.' Surely you haven't forgotten that little bit of information."

"Charles Allyson Reynolds, you forget yourself," roared his father.

Cas tried to quell the nausea brought on by the mushy peas, the overcooked roast beef, and his disgust. He turned to his mother. "Thanks for dinner, I have to go."

"She'll make a fool of you," his father called after him. "Just like she did fifteen years ago."

Cas stopped in the doorway. "No," he said. "You made a fool of me fifteen years ago. And I let you."

He closed the door behind him, gently, to prove to himself that he was under control.

Julie closed the door to Wes's closet and leaned against it. It still smelled like Wes and she was surprised at how familiar it was after all these years, a combination of Old Spice, orange lollipops, and more.

She absently unwrapped the lollipop she'd found in one of Wes's shirt pockets. The wrapper came away clean so it couldn't be very old. And her eyes misted over, thinking of Wes alone with his lollipops, and no one to share them with. Except Maude, she thought. She'd found some pretty interesting toys in one of the drawers of the bureau and a few pieces of Victoria Secret's underwear that were just Maude's size.

She smiled around the lollipop; let the tingle of the sweet-tart flavor take over her tongue and then her mind and she drifted away to happier times. She could see Wes standing at the door as she walked up the driveway, both hands behind his back. And when she'd put down her overnight case, he'd say *pick one*, and she would, though she always got orange because orange was their favorite and it was the only flavor he bought.

Julie took the lollipop from her mouth and looked at it, holding it tight because Wes had held it. *Who loves you?* he'd say.

And she would answer, "You do."

Julie jumped when she realized she'd said the words out loud. "You did." She pushed away from the door. "And I'll take care of your damn chickens just to show you I loved you back. But I'm not going to wallow in the past."

She loped down the stairs and picked up her shoulder bag. "Man the fort, Smitty. I'm taking myself out to dinner."

Cas stopped his truck at the end of the Reynolds Place driveway and loosened his tie. He could turn right, go home, and work on the boat. Or he could turn left and go to Julie's and demand that she talk to him.

But first he needed to be prepared. Just figure out how to get started. He didn't want to take any chances of blowing it again. So-o-o. He'd knock on the door and when she answered, he'd say. . . . *Hi, I came to fix your pipes.* That didn't sound right. *Fix your leak.* Not any better. *I'm sorry I ran off.* Better not to remind her of that. *Listen, the sex was great.* She might be offended. How about just "Hi" and hope she took it from there? What if she still refused to open the door? He'd have to yell at her from outside until she did.

He pulled the tie over his head and tossed it onto the passenger seat. With his luck, someone would see his truck and interrupt them again and the whole mess would be indelibly printed on her mind. He could drive down to First Street, park in Tilda's driveway, and climb the four blocks to Hillcrest Drive. Except that he was wearing dress shoes and he'd look like a tramp by the time he got to Julie's. And someone was bound to see the truck at Tilda's and start rumors that Terrence wouldn't care for. Oh, hell.

He heard a car engine and looked up to see a blue Volkswagen drive past and turn left onto Highland Avenue.

"Shit," said Cas and banged the steering wheel, feeling almost as relieved as he felt frustrated. He pulled out of the driveway and followed Julie down the hill. At Main Street, she turned right. Maybe she was going down to the Roadhouse. That would be good. Neutral territory. But he wasn't dressed for the Roadhouse and he took enough grief from the regulars as it was. He could change clothes and come back.

By then he would have thought of something to say that didn't sound like a come-on or a turnoff. She pulled into the Roadhouse parking lot. He cut back at the yield sign and drove down Old Mill Road. He had a plan—sort of.

Chapter 8

Julie got out of the car and watched the green truck loop back and speed down Old Mill Road. She had been sure it was following her. She must be getting paranoid, and who wouldn't be with the way her life was going.

She looked skeptically at the door of the Roadhouse. Hell, she'd survived her first day in town. And it couldn't be any worse than some of the neighborhood bars she'd frequented back in New York. It might even be fun. She went inside.

The bar and grill smelled like sawdust, spilled beer, and too many men. A jukebox was playing Patsy Cline and the room was pretty dark except for the hanging lamp over the pool table in a far corner. There was a crowd at the bar, but a few empty stools dotted the line of black motorcycle jackets. She could deal with bikers.

She headed toward them even as heads turned and a whistle or two drifted her way. She tugged at her T-shirt and stopped as she got a closer look at the back of the motorcycle jackets. All of them were new with bright red lettering. Julie shook her head and sat down at one of the empty stools.

"Hi," said the bartender, a skinny woman with magenta hair swept up into a beehive.

"The *Hellzapoppins*?" asked Julie, grinning at the row of bikers.

The bartender laughed. "A crate fell off a truck from a road show that was passing through town. The jackets were inside. Hell, we didn't even have a gang before that. What can I get you?"

"What d'you have on tap?" asked Julie.

The bartender didn't answer, but broke into a smile. Then she began to slowly nod her head. "Julie Excelsior, right? I'd know you anywhere. Ain't that a kick."

In the pants, thought Julie and wondered who the hell she was.

"Foster's, Bass, and Michelob on tap. Bud, Heineken, Coors, and Amstel Light in bottles. I'm Tilda Green."

Julie followed her through the beer choices until she came to the name. Tilda Green. Tilda Green. Older than her. Cheerleader at Ex Falls High. Only then she didn't have purple hair. Peroxided, Julie remembered. Skinny. She was still skinny. And the image of Tilda in her uniform popped into her head. Stick legs swallowed by a gold and blue felt skirt, the padded bra making her letter sweater jut straight out in front. She was voted Miss Most Likely to Succeed. Which at the time, Julie thought was a cruel joke, since Tilda lived in the adjacent trailer park. But then being poor if you were a Green wasn't the same thing as being a poor Excelsior.

"Foster's," said Julie and when Tilda's smile wavered, she added, "It's really good to see you, Tilda," thinking, *I am such a hypocrite. I could have spent an eternity without seeing you stuck behind this bar, serving half-soused wombats.* If becoming a bartender in the only bar in town was success, Tilda could have it. And then another memory snagged on her mind. Tilda walking past her house toward the trailer park the week after the "rescue," and tapping on Julie's bedroom window. "Don't let 'em get to you," she said and went on her way.

She smiled at Tilda and wondered how fast she could drink her beer and get out. Because she wasn't up for any more walks down Memory Lane today.

Tilda's smile widened. "I'll just get your Foster's."

"Bet you don't remember me."

Julie turned to face the man sitting on the stool next to her. He was wearing one of the *Hellzapoppin* jackets and had really greasy Elvis hair. "Bet you're right," said Julie.

"Bet you don't remember me, either," said the man on the far side of the first.

"Nope."

Tilda returned with Julie's beer and leaned on the bar. "So are you staying long?"

Julie turned her attention to Tilda. "I'm just here for—"

A beefy hand landed on Julie's back. "Julie Excelsior, huh. We all wondered where you disappeared to."

"Ancient history, bub," said Julie, channeling one of her better undercover personas.

"Name ain't Bub. It's Henley Baxter. Now do you remember me?"

Julie stifled a shiver; she remembered him all right, but wished she didn't. The Bully of Ex Falls High. She shook her head. "'Fraid not." She picked up her beer and Tilda said, "Leave her alone, Henley. You're not my favorite person this week."

Henley smiled. He was missing a right incisor. "I thought that was last week."

"Last week," his companion echoed.

"Every week," said Tilda.

Henley's hand began to creep down Julie's back. "Well, I remember you. And I remember you were real pop'lar with certain people."

She eased her shoulder away.

"Hey, Tilda, three Buds over here."

Tilda moved away to get the beers.

"They said you could be real friendly." Henley moved in closer and Julie got a sickening whiff of hair oil and stale beer.

"They must have meant someone else," said Julie, leaning away from him.

Henley followed her until she was sandwiched between him and the man on the other side of her.

"Back off," she said and nudged him away.

"I can show you a good time."

The man next to her threw some bills on the bar and left. She was about to shift over to his seat when a huge, scruffy bear of a man sat down.

"Hey, babe," he said in a deep booming voice.

Julie groaned. This had been a big mistake. She'd had enough. She turned on the newcomer. "Who are you calling babe, asshole?"

The man's head jerked toward her, his bushy eyebrows making two half circles above deep set eyes.

"Me," said Tilda as she hoisted herself over the bar and planted a kiss somewhere in his beard.

"Oh, sorry," said Julie, wondering if Tilda had actually found his mouth.

"That's okay," the bear said in a voice that sounded like it came from the bottom of a well. "I'm sure you're a babe, too, but Tilda would kill me if I said so. Wouldn't you, babykins?" He began to rumble and it took a second for Julie to realize he was laughing.

"This is Terrence. My significant smoochums," said Tilda, smiling at full wattage.

"Hi, Terrence," Julie said. The guy was the Yeti of the Adirondacks. He towered over Julie and most of the other men at the bar. His shoulder span was incredible and every thickset inch of him was brawn. This was someone Julie would never consider calling smoochums. If she was ever inclined to call anyone smoochums, which she wasn't. "Nice to meet you," she said, feeling an irrational surge of envy as Tilda and Terrence made goofy faces at each other. She took another sip of beer.

"I'll show you significant." Henley leered at her and his fingers started crawling up her spine again.

"In your dreams," said Julie.

She knew better than to incite a belligerent psycho like Henley, but she couldn't help herself. She was on emotional overload. Seeing Tilda and Terrence hadn't helped and being fondled by this jerk made her want to throw up.

"C'mon, Julie. I bet you know how to have a real good time. I heard you used to."

Tilda slapped her hand down on the bar. "Henley, you ignoramus. If you don't stop driving away my female customers, I'm gonna ban you from the bar."

Henley just smiled at her. His fingers reached Julie's shoulder blade and began sneaking around to her front. Julie flicked her shoulder back and dislodged his hand.

It also uncovered her midriff.

"Would you look at that," said Henley. "She's got one of those navel rings."

His companion, a little toad if Julie had ever seen one, said, "Hey, a navel ring."

Henley flicked the ring with his finger before Julie could move away. "C'mon Julie, give it to me the way you used to give it to Cas Reynolds."

"That's it, asshole." Julie swung around; pulled back her fist and let it fly just as Henley was yanked backwards off the stool. Her fist connected to a jaw, but it wasn't Henley's. The impact cracked in the air and the wrong man went down, dragging Henley with him.

Henley's friend slid off his stool and jumped on top of the two men.

Damn, thought Julie. *My second day back and I've started a brawl.* She shoved a five dollar bill across the bar. "I'm sorry," she yelled to Tilda. "And apologize to the other guy for me."

"Don't give it another thought," said Tilda, grinning at the men on the floor.

"You got a great right hook," said Terrence and ducked as someone's beer mug flew by him. "Hey, uncool." Terrence hoisted himself off the bar stool. "Who the hell did that?"

Julie ran for the door as applause burst out around her. Someone yelled, "Nice going, Cas. You just got decked by Barbie."

Julie froze.

"Three cheers for the she-e-e-r . . ." A body flew across the doorway, knocking Julie outside.

She stood in the parking lot, her breath coming out in clouds, wondering if she could pick up Smitty, pack and get out of town before she got arrested. Then she thought of Cas, who had come to her rescue only to have her deck him. And God knew what was happening inside the bar now.

The sound of splintering wood. Then a cheer.

He'll never want to see me again. I've humiliated him in public. She took a step toward her car. *But he might be getting hurt.* She took a step back. *What could she do about it?* She stepped toward the car. *Run in, call out "Police!" and bust a few heads.* She stepped back. *Neither Tilda nor Cas would appreciate that.*

She couldn't keep cha-cha-ing in the parking lot while all hell broke lose in the bar because of her. She started it, she'd finish it. She turned on her heel and pushed back through the door.

The bar was bedlam. A knot of flailing blue jeans and work boots writhed in the center of the floor. An even larger group of spectators crowded around them, taking bets and egging the participants on. Across the room, Terrence had three men up against the wall, and Cas was hauling another to his feet.

Julie pushed through the crowd and stood at the fringe of fighting men. "Hey," she yelled. She stuck two fingers in her mouth and whistled.

Then she reached into the gaggle of fighters and pulled out the first body she could lay her hands on. It was Henley's goon. She dragged him out of the pile, thunked him up against the nearest wall and twisted his arm behind him.

"Ow," he yelled and tried to wriggle free. "You're hurting me. Le' go."

"I'll let go when you call off the fight and apologize to Tilda." Julie twisted his wrist for emphasis.

But it was unnecessary because she had everyone's attention. The onlookers were all looking at her. The fighters disentangled themselves and slowly got up from the floor. Terrence waved at her from across the room, and Cas turned around and stared.

Julie swallowed. He did not look happy. Then he turned away and pushed the miscreant he was holding into Terrence's waiting arms.

When he turned around to face the crowd, Julie could see his shoulders heaving as he got his breath. "If I had a big enough jail . . . I'd lock up every damn one of you. But as it is, clean this place up and Henley . . . you'll turn over a hundred bucks to Tilda for damages and then get out."

"Aw, Cas," griped Henley. "We were just having fun. You got no sense of humor."

"You have no idea," said Cas in a voice that made even Terrence's eyes widen. He crossed a suddenly silent room to where Julie held her captive to the wall. He barely looked at her as he eased the man out of her grasp. "You know, Bo. You want to be so much like Henley. You can pay Tilda a hundred, too."

"I ain't got a hundred."

"Well, get it," said Cas and shoved him toward the bar.

Julie was just thinking, *not bad for a banker*, when Bo said, "You can't even break up a fight without getting a girl to do it for you."

Terrence grabbed him by his jacket collar and lifted him off the ground. "And you're going to be in deep shit if you don't shut up."

Bo shut up. Terrence lowered him to the floor and waited while he reached into his pocket and pulled out a few bills. "All I got."

"Tilda will take an IOU," said Cass. "You too, Henley. And don't come back until you can pay."

Henley glared at him, his fists clenched, his jaw jutting forward. "One day, Cas," he muttered. "One day."

"Yeah, sure," said Cas. "One day."

He waited at the bar while Henley counted out his money and the rest of the patrons cleaned up the fallen tables and chairs. Then he walked Bo and Henley out the door, passing Julie like she didn't exist.

But everyone else was watching her. She caught Tilda's eye and shrugged apologetically. Tilda just shook her head and grinned.

When Julie reached the parking lot, two motorcycles were pulling out onto the highway, and Cas was standing with his back to her, watching them leave.

"Cas?"

"Hm," he said, not turning around.

"I didn't know you were there."

"Hm."

"I'm sorry I caused so much trouble. Are you okay?"

"Mmm."

"I'm really sorry. Say something." Julie took his elbow and turned him around. There was blood on his lip and one eye was partially closed. There was a lump forming on his jaw. She'd seen Smitty look better after a dog fight.

"Which one did I do?" she asked.

"The jaw."

"I'll just ask Tilda for some ice."

He shook his head, winced.

"Can I do anything?"

His mouth twisted in what could have been a smile but probably wasn't.

"Are your teeth okay? Do you need a dentist? Ribs. Anything broken? Can I drive you to the emergency room?"

"I'm fine."

He didn't sound fine. He sounded pissed as hell.

"Good night," he said. And touching his fingers to his eye, he walked away and opened the door to a . . . rusty green pickup truck.

Julie stared, then hurried after him.

Cas pulled himself into the truck. Missed. Tried again. On the third attempt, Julie grabbed his butt and pushed him inside. "I'll follow you home. Just to make sure you're okay. You could have a concussion. Or internal bleeding."

This time she was sure he smiled.

"It was a bar fight, not a car wreck. But you can follow me home." Cas shut the door and started the engine.

Julie raced to the VW and took off after him.

Chapter 9

Julie began to have second thoughts as soon as she realized that Cas was driving down Old Mill Road. She was just deciding not to follow him over the bridge to Mill Town when he pulled into a parking area in front of a two-story cedar shake cottage.

Julie pulled in after him and came to a stop in front of a corrugated machine shop. Strange place for Cas to live, when he had that big house on the Hill.

She reached him just as he was falling out of the front seat. She put an arm around his waist and helped him toward the house. He was heavy and warm and Julie thought, *why can't things just be easy?*

Then his arm went around her and she realized that she wasn't really supporting him. "Overkill, right?"

"Yeah, but it felt good," said Cas. "Come inside."

Julie deliberated. She shouldn't. She'd have to apologize for starting the brawl, he'd apologize for running out on her yesterday, then they'd talk and all sorts of shit would come out. And she'd end up asking him if he had a riddle, too, and he would probably lie to her.

And besides, they were practically opposite her old house. If she really tried, she might be able to see it across the river. Not that she wanted to. She didn't want to be this close to the river at all.

She looked out into the darkness and could almost see them rowing on the water. Cas standing in the bow, a bandanna tied around his head, a black patch over one eye, saying with bravado, "You can't escape me now. You'll bring a good ransom, lassie." And laughing until his voice cracked into a young boy's unchanged tenor. Blushing, he sat down and began to row.

"Julie?"

"What?"

"Do you want to come inside?"

"Uh . . . sure. You need ice on that eye." She followed him up the steps to a wooden deck, waited while he unlocked the door, and then stepped inside. And forgot the past and riddles and everything. One room filled the entire house. The ceiling reached to the rafters. A kitchen was laid out in the back corner, and wooden stairs led up the left side of the room to a sleeping loft that ran along the back wall. The back wall was made entirely of glass, and she was sure it overlooked the river. But it was the fourth wall that drew her attention. It was filled with shelves holding rows of model sailing ships.

She stepped toward them. "I've never seen them all at once." Each time he finished one, Cas had brought it to show her, because she could never go to his house. "I can't believe you kept them all these years."

"Christine salvaged them from the rubbish heap," said Cas in a flat voice.

Julie's mouth dropped open and she turned to look at him. "You threw them out?"

"Reynolds did. Right after he sent me away to boarding school. Christine saw him and saved them. She took them to Wes and he kept them in the spare room until I moved in here." He shrugged. "They're a little battered and some of the parts are missing. But I'm slowly restoring them."

"Ice," she said, ruthlessly suppressing the urge to hug him. "You'd better put some ice on that eye." She walked blindly back to the fridge and pulled the door open.

"Julie."

"Are you sure your teeth don't feel loose?"

Cas tested his jaw. "Where did you learn to hit like that?"

"I didn't," said Julie. This was not the time to tell him she was a cop. Braver men than Cas had been turned off by that confession. "It was just dumb luck. I mean, not luck. I meant to hit Henley, but—I'm sorry."

Cas walked up behind her and shut the refrigerator door. "Forget the fight. Forget the boats. Forget everything."

She couldn't look at him. "I'm afraid there's nothing I can do about your jaw. It's already turning purple."

"There's one thing you can do for me."

She turned to find herself trapped between him and the fridge. "What?" she asked, a little breathless.

He leaned into her, so close that his breath warmed her cheek. "This." His lips touched hers and a voice inside her head said, *no*, but a louder voice said, "Aw, what the hell." And she opened her mouth and his tongue found its way inside.

Her fingers spread against his chest and she broke the kiss. "Are you sure you're okay?"

"Never better." He kissed her eyebrows, her nose, found her mouth again. And this time there was only one voice in her head. And it said, *Me, neither.*

Cas laughed into her mouth. "We seem to have this kitchen thing."

"Yeah."

"I have a king-size bed upstairs."

"You don't want ice? I have Percodan in my bag."

"Later," he said and kissed her over to the wall. He flipped off the lights and when the stairs appeared out of the darkness, they began to climb.

At the top, he turned her to the glass wall. The moon and stars hung like a mobile against a black sky.

Julie looked down and saw the dark, flowing river below them. Only it was smaller now, narrower. Or maybe it just seemed that way, because it couldn't hurt her anymore.

Cas rowed them out into the river, leaving the harbor be-hind, and suddenly the boat shot into the current. One oar was wrenched from Cas's hand and he fought furiously with the other to keep them from overturning, while the river car-ried them away.

And she—his captive princess, wearing a tablecloth cape and tin foil tiara—could only cling to the sides and watch, wide-eyed, as he frantically tried to turn the rowboat against the current.

Julie turned away from the window. From the river and from her memories. "I shouldn't stay. There's Smitty and the chickens and—"

"I might have a concussion."

"Really? Are you dizzy? Do you feel sick? How many fingers do you see?"

He grabbed the fingers she held up and brought them to his lips. "I don't think I should be left alone."

"I think you're goofing on me."

"And I might have a couple of cracked ribs."

"Then you should definitely go to the hospital."

He smiled and wrapped a tendril of hair around his fingers. "Give us a chance, Julie."

Julie pulled away. "Where is this going? Because if you're going to get all weird on me, you'll just have to croak in your sleep and be done with it."

Cas grimaced. "I'm in pain. Would you leave a man who's in pain?"

Julie raised a suspicious eyebrow. "Seriously?"

Cas nodded.

"Where?"

He took her hand, opened her fingers and pressed her palm to his jaw. "Here." He pulled it down his chest. "And here." Moved it again and Julie had an idea where it was going next.

"And here." He pressed it against his erection.

Julie laughed; she couldn't help it. "I'll get some ice."

"No-o-o. This calls for a massage."

"Does it, Dr. Reynolds?" She stroked him through his jeans

and Cas sighed and pushed his fingers through her hair and kissed her, the barest touch of his lips. She nudged his feet open with her knee and fitted her hand between his legs, running her nails along the seam of his jeans and back again. His hands gripped her head and he sucked her bottom lip into his mouth. Julie gave in to him, wondering why she wanted him so much, because she didn't think it had anything to do with payback. And she was afraid to think further than that.

She rubbed her palm up the zipper of his jeans. His hands fell away from her hair, ran down her back until he could lift her shirt. Then his palms were on her skin, moving in circles as if to capture her whole. And she wanted to say something clever or at least something hot, but she couldn't come up with a thing. She squeezed his erection through the fabric.

He pulled his hand out of her shirt and she thought, *Don't go.* But he quickly unbuckled his belt and pulled down his zipper and went back under her shirt. Julie's hand slipped inside his boxers and her fingers closed around him. His erection hardened even more beneath her hand.

They stood toe to toe, their hands inside each other's clothes, with the stars up above and the river flowing by and it seemed so right.

But it was just a game.

Cas eased them down on the bed and rolled her onto her back. He braced himself on his elbows and looked down at her.

"Are you sure you're okay?"

"I am now." He pushed up her shirt, kissed her stomach, drew a line with his tongue down to the edge of her jeans, then licked beneath the denim, leaving a trail of searing heat across her flesh. He tucked his finger inside the waistband and popped the button open.

He moved slowly and she basked in it, reacted to it, and returned his touch. Tonight they would take things slowly. Tonight there would be no banging away like a couple of rodeo contestants.

Each touch was an exploration, a titillation, and Julie thought, *I should knock you silly more often.* And then she stopped thinking and wrapped her arms around his waist. She gently kissed him again and again, each touch of her lips a caress, until her blood ran thick with desire.

The kiss stopped being gentle. Their bodies pressed together, their arms and legs twining and retwining, and they rolled on the bed, pushing the blankets away and knocking the pillows to the floor. Finally Cas stood up on his knees and pulled her jeans down her legs and dropped them on the floor. He gazed down at her, his eyes smoldering in the moonlight, and smiled.

"God, Wes, thank you," he said and pulled the new lace thong down her thighs. His hands followed the curve of her legs until he cupped her butt with both hands and he lifted her to his mouth.

"You're glistening," he said and bent to lick the sweet spot between her legs.

Julie wanted to say, "Not too fast, make it last." But her hips rose up to meet his tongue, and she succumbed to the growing heat as it spread from that one spot to take over the rest of her body. When she felt herself begin to float, she rolled him away and began to unbutton his shirt.

Cas kissed her fingers as she worked her way down until he couldn't reach them anymore. He helped her pull off the shirt, then yanked his T-shirt over his head and tossed it away.

His chest was broad and golden in the pale light. Her fingers ran across the dark diamond of hair until she found the medallions of his nipples and felt their peaks harden at her touch.

Cas sucked in his breath and Julie said, "Shh," and brought her fingers together to trail down the line of hair to his navel and into his boxers. *Banker's underwear*, she thought. So she pushed jeans and underwear down his thighs and continued her journey. His cock jumped as her fingers passed over the swollen head, barely touching the heated, silky skin as they continued south, outlining the shape of his erection. It jumped again when they came together again at the base of his penis.

Cas groaned. He lifted her hands away and pulled off her T-shirt. Found the front catch of her bra and flipped it open.

"Had a lot of practice?" she asked, trying to ignore the pounding in her ears. Trying to slow the meltdown that was pooling between her thighs.

"Hey, I went to college." He grinned at her, then lowered them both to the mattress, catching her between his elbows. He kissed her neck, trailed his tongue across her collar bone and down the cleft between her breasts.

His tongue arced around one breast, moving in concentric circles. Getting smaller and smaller until his teeth nipped her nipple and she whispered, "I can't wait. Take me."

Cas shook his head. "I have to make up for last time."

"Next time," she said.

"And next time and every time."

She sighed as he sucked on the tip of her nipple. "That's good."

"Yeah," said Cas and sucked again.

Julie choked back a cry of pleasure and grasped his head, pulling his mouth closer.

His legs began to thrash, and she realized he was trying to remove his jeans without letting her go. She bent her knees, ran the soles of her feet up his sides until her toes found the open waistband. She hooked them inside and pushed the jeans down his calves and onto the floor. An extra flick of her toes sent his underwear after them.

He lowered himself on top of her and covered her body with his. He rubbed his cock up her abdomen until it touched the navel ring. Cas shuddered.

"Your ribs?"

"Your French tickler." He laughed, the laughter turned into a moan as he circled his groin against her. He slid down the length of her. His tongue flicked into her navel, sending shivers through her. Then he drew a hot wet line down her stomach.

He pushed back to his knees, lifted her thighs over his shoulders and Julie barely had time to think, *Don't puncture a lung*, before his tongue cut a line through her mound of curls, then flicked up in just the right place to make her see stars and forget all body parts except the ones that counted.

"God, you're sweet," said Cas between licks. He pushed her knees higher, cupped her butt in his hands and plunged his tongue into her.

She spiked her fingers through his hair as he withdrew his tongue, flicked up again.

Her thighs began to shake. "Too soon," she said and slid her knees off his shoulders. "I want some, too."

Cas continued to assault her with his tongue while he crawled around and threw a leg over her chest. She wrapped her arms around his thighs, lifted her head and sucked one of his balls into her mouth. Cas shuddered and rolled over so that she was on top, his mouth never leaving her.

She slowly drew her tongue along the ridge of his penis over the tip of the head, across the cleft. Then she sucked him in.

Cas sucked in his breath, went still, then slowly began to pulse into her mouth. Julie tightened her lips around him, and after a minute, he groaned and pushed her away, pulling out so quickly that her lips made a popping sound.

He rolled away and Julie heard the sound of a drawer opening. Cas rummaging inside. "I'm trying . . . to redeem myself. . . . But I don't think . . . I'm going to last. Sorry."

Moonlight outlined his taut body as he ripped the package and unrolled the condom down the length of his penis. And a lovely penis it was, too.

"If we do this enough, I might show some stamina."

She pushed him over. He pulled her down beside him, then rolled on top of her. He fit his hand between them and opened her. Then the head of his cock replaced his fingers. He pushed himself up on his hands and looked down at her. For a moment neither of them moved.

Julie could feel his cock pressing against her but not entering her. And still Cas didn't move, just looked at her. She nudged him with her hips, but he managed to stayed poised just at the entrance.

Julie was about to scream "Hurry, damn it," when he pushed himself into her, tortuously slowly, until he penetrated an inch and waited for her to close around him.

He took two deep breaths and pressed another inch into her. She grabbed his ass and tried to pull him all the way in, but he held himself away. When she was considering bashing him on the head to make him hurry, he slid the rest of the way in and pressed his body against hers.

Julie let out a squawk when he hit something really amazing. He withdrew and hit another spot on his way out. Then in again. And Julie said, "You should . . . get a bumper sticker . . . that says *Bankers do it with interest*. Oh, right there."

Cas laughed into her mouth and hit the spot again. Then the action took on a life of its own, out of his control or hers. She thrust against him as he quickened the pace, until the bed rocked with their movements.

A sense of calm seeped over her. Cas shifted her knee to the side, opening her more, letting him deeper inside her. Julie rose mindlessly to the peak and without warning she shot over the precipice. She contracted around him and Cas shortened his thrusts until they were tiny pulses which drove her on and on until she couldn't catch her breath.

When the orgasm finally released her and she began to float back to earth, Cas sank himself into her and she rose up again, until they were there together.

He pumped himself into her. And she drew him in. Clinging to him until he collapsed on top of her, driving her into the mattress. He rolled to the side. bringing her with him. He blew out his breath like a winded runner while they faced each other and held each other close. And together they drifted into a sweet lethargy.

Julie must have dozed because when her eyes forced their way open, the comforter was lying across them. Cas was breathing deeply. She leaned close to his face and studied him in the moonlight. His eye was swollen and turning blue and his jaw definitely had a bump on it.

Julie winced. His injuries would be nothing compared to the bashing his ego would take when word got around that he'd been decked by a woman. What was he doing here, playing sheriff? What had happened that could bring him back here and what was keeping him here?

With a sinking feeling, Julie thought she knew. He must have a portion of the riddle. He wanted the treasure. That had to be it. Building boats couldn't be all that lucrative. He might need the money.

Well, she needed it, too. She'd have to find it first and leave town before he knew that she had bested him.

Another generation of the Excelsior-Reynolds feud. She smiled sadly; too bad for them.

She and Cas were rescued ten miles down the river, where they were towed to shore. Hank Jessop lifted her out of the boat. Her tiara fell to the ground. There was a whole group of men, come to look for them. Sheriff Jessop, Mr. Dinwiddie, Mr. Baxter and some others, all looking stern.

Then Reynolds broke through the group, yanked the bandana from Cas's head and dragged him away. The crowd parted and Julie saw the big black Cadillac waiting by the road. Reynolds pushed Cas into the back seat, then got in and they drove away. When Julie looked back, the men were frowning.

"I'm sorry," she said, but they didn't hear. They were already walking away.

She sat up, tearing her eyes and herself from Cas. He was a stranger, not the boy who had been her alter ego, her twin, her love. She didn't know anything about him now.

They were merely playing out an interrupted game of pirates

and princess, of cops and robbers, of cowboys and Indians. Cas had deserted her once. He would desert her again.

Old anger and hurt resurfaced. She tried to push it away. It was too late to be angry at Cas. He'd never had a chance against his father and the cursed tradition of the Reynoldses.

And she never had a chance against her mill town upbringing. But still she felt resentful. More against her family than Cas's, strangely enough. Why had Uncle Wes allowed her and her father to live in poverty? Why had she been left to grow up in Mill Town when the Excelsiors had been one of the most prosperous families in the town? Hell, the town was named after them. So why?

And the fear and shame she had struggled so many years to suppress rose up again. She pushed away from Cas.

He mumbled, "Hm?" in his sleep.

"I have to go."

Cas shook his head against the pillow.

"Smitty's been inside all afternoon."

"I'll—" A huge yawn cracked through his words. "Walk you down."

"No, stay here." She kissed him and pulled the comforter up to his chin. Cas settled back to sleep.

When she was dressed and downstairs again, she stopped to look around the room. The ships floated along the wall like a miniature armada, tattered and broken, like both their lives.

She touched one of the sails. If only he could have stood up to Reynolds.

And you? The voice was so real that she turned around. She knew it came from her, but she wanted to smack it anyway. Yeah, she'd become a cop as a talisman against her sense of powerlessness. To help others who were powerless.

She loved her job. And she had walked away from it because she had let herself be bullied. Just like Cas. Let her own insecurities make her an outsider again. She had no one to blame but herself. The thought blindsided her.

Well, no more of that shit. She'd find Wes's money and start over somewhere else. And no one and nothing would drive her away again.

She left the wall of ships and looked at the rest of the room. There was a fireplace with a new couch facing it, and in the space below the stairs, a drafting table and a desk with a laptop computer, and beside it, a stack of neatly arranged folders.

She listened for a minute, and hearing Cas's steady breathing from the loft, she picked up the top file and opened it. Bills. Not just Cas's, but Charles and Marian's, too. And they were pretty damn large. All marked *Paid* in Cas's neat handwriting. He was supporting them. Damn them. Damn them for their inability to change, damn them for what they did to Cas and her. Damn them for what they were doing to Melanie.

She put the folder back and looked in the others. None of them revealed any riddles. The last one contained several pages of detailed sketches, drawn freehand at all angles, not mindless doodles, but sophisticated studies of masts and rigging and keels. She could feel his soul on the page and she had no right to see it. She quickly shut the folder and saw the corner of a piece of yellow tablet paper sticking out from under the ink blotter. She carefully pulled it free.

"What are you doing?"

Julie froze, slowly turned around, shielding the yellow paper with her body. "I, uh, was going to leave you a note."

Cas frowned. His hair was sticking up behind his cowlick. His eye was swollen shut. He was completely nude and his cock was beginning to swell. She might have to fuck him to save her secret, then winced that she could even be thinking of such a thing. It was cheap. It was underhanded. It was such a white trash thing to do.

"Why?" he asked. "Saying what?" He looked at her suspiciously; tried to see around her, but she sat back against the desk and began inching the paper toward the edge of the blotter.

"Thanks for a lovely evening?"

Cas didn't crack a smile.

"And to apologize for starting the brawl."

"Oh." He stepped toward her; she stood up and managed to push the corner of the paper beneath the blotter before wrapping her arms around Cas's waist and giving him a heart-felt kiss.

He fell into it, pulling her hard against him.

"I can't stay."

Reluctantly, he let go and followed her to the door.

"I did have a lovely time," she said, kissed his cheek, and stepped out into the night.

Cas stood in the doorway, watching until the Volkswagen was out of view. Then he went back to the desk and turned on the work lamp. No note begun. All his folders were in place, but Wes's riddle was barely caught under the ink blotter. It was still folded, but she might have had time to read it, before re-placing it. Because she *had* replaced it.

He picked it up. Read it for the hundredth time and still made no sense of it.

No doors there are in this stronghold, yet thieves break in and steal the gold.

A stronghold. A bank vault? It might contain gold. But bank vaults had doors. Thieves. His father? Cold tendrils of fear wrapped around him. How much had Julie read?

It wasn't until she'd let Smitty out, given him a treat, and gotten a beer from the fridge that Julie sat down at the oak table and spread out her riddle before her. She had only man-aged to see a few words of Cas's before he'd interrupted her. Door, stronghold, gold.

Well, at least one thing was clear. The treasure was valuable. Too bad she hadn't been able to read it all. It might have solved her half of the riddle. As it was, it only made it more bizarre.

She added the words to the bottom of her riddle about the Crystal Fountain.

"Jeez, Wes. What are you trying to say?" *Crystal fountain. Golden apple. A stronghold without a door . . .*

"Arrgh," she said, and Smitty looked up from his dog chew. She crossed her arms on the table and lowered her head to them. "I need another clue, Wes. You made this too hard."

Chapter 10

Julie huffed up the hill toward the gazebo in the predawn darkness. It had turned into winter overnight and she'd had to exchange her jeans jacket for Wes's orange plaid quilted coat. The sleeves were rolled up twice and the work gloves she'd found in the pockets swallowed her stiff fingers. But the *pièce de résistance* was the wool cap with ear flaps that she'd laughingly put on in the hallway and was now glad she'd overcome her fashion scruples to wear outside.

Smitty ran back and forth across her path, nose to the ground. He picked up a stick and brought it to her only to snatch it away again. Then he dropped it on the ground and trotted over to the juniper bush and lifted his leg. Steam rose into the cold air.

Smitty might think this was a lark, but for Julie, the novelty of getting up at dawn was beginning to pale. Not to mention that she was nervous as hell.

With Maude in Plattsburgh, she was flying solo, so to speak. But she'd done her homework and she was as ready as she'd ever be.

"You stay out here and behave," she told Smitty as she opened the mesh fence. "After I feed them, I'll let them roam free, uh, free range, or whatever." Not that anyone, even a chicken, in their right mind would want to spend too much time out in this weather.

As she walked up the ramp, she had a horrible image of finding twenty flash-frozen chicken carcasses inside the gazebo. Wes hadn't mentioned heating. "Shit," she said and quickly opened the door to the gazebo, getting a whiff of godawful odor.

Fifteen hungry and very alive chickens surrounded her. It was warm inside, and for the first time, she noticed the quiet whirr of the generator that ran the heater.

Thank God, she thought as the chickens waddled down the ramp. Within seconds, she was the only occupant of the fetid space. She quickly gathered the eggs. Only four today. Which was fine with Julie. She couldn't eat eggs every morning; too much cholesterol.

She followed the chickens out, broke the film of ice on the water dispensers and refilled them with fresh water. Checked the feeders and got a pan of scratch out of the shed.

As she broadcast the kernels of corn and grains, she conjured up Wes's list of names and descriptions of each bird. The roosters were easy. There were only two. Ulysses, a giant leghorn, and Bill, a small red bantam. The females were more difficult. She knew Ernestine, but it would take a few days before she could distinguish the rest. A lot of them looked the same.

Smitty watched obediently from the other side of the fence, panting clouds of vapor into the air, while the sun gradually rose above the foothills behind him, leaving an aureole of gold around his coat.

Gold, thought Julie. *What am I doing feeding chickens when I should be looking for gold . . . for my inheritance?*

She looked past the clearing and into the woods. Thought about treasure and hiding places. Which made her think of Cas's riddle. Which made her think of making love to Cas.

They'd gone at each other twice in the three days she'd been here. Normal people would have taken things slower, gotten to know each other. But not her and Cas. They just banged away like there was no tomorrow.

And for them there probably wasn't. Not here anyway.

A sudden shriek brought her back to the present. Ulysses was flapping at a speckled hen and pushing her away from the feeder.

"Hey, stop that," cried Julie and hurried over to intercede. "That's not polite, you beast. Ladies first." Ulysses spread his wings to their full span and spit at her before turning his attention back to the hen. Julie jumped between them and quickly lifted the hen out of range. She looked her over and said, "Mamie, right?" The hen cocked her little chicken head and Julie smiled, then realized she was holding a chicken. She hurriedly set her down at another feeder.

"Wow. I just picked Mamie up and survived. Am I a natural or what?" She turned back to Ulysses and pointed her finger at him. "Don't mess with me."

Ulysses strutted past her without a look and resumed his inspection of the feeding troughs.

Julie turned to see Smitty watching her. "Okay, so I'm talking to a rooster. I talk to you, don't I? Big deal." She walked over to the fence. "If I let these chickens into the yard, you better mind your manners—no chasing, no herding, no eating. Got it?"

Smitty thumped his tail.

"Good." Julie opened the gate. A little bantam hen, Hilary, hopped past her and high-stepped straight for Smitty.

"Stay," Julie warned him. Then her mouth fell open as Hillary rose in a flurry of wing feathers and settled onto his back. Smitty didn't move, but looked at Julie with such a surprised expression that she laughed out loud.

"That is so cute," she said. "Don't scare her."

Several other chickens cautiously followed Hillary out of the pen. Most just continued to feed, while Ulysses marched up and down the rows, and Bill perched above them observing the proceedings.

Julie took the eggs to the house, poured herself a cup of coffee and returned to the porch steps. She was supposed to let them out twice a day, and she couldn't in good conscience leave them to face the elements alone. There were predators out there.

So she sat on the steps and watched Smitty and Hillary bond. Soon, Bill hopped down from his perch and wandered outside. Julie felt a peck at her boot and looked down. Ernestine rolled in the dirt at her feet. Then she hopped up the steps, cocked her head at Julie and jumped into her lap.

Julie froze. Ernestine puffed out her feathers until her head disappeared and she began to purr. Julie began to absently stroke Ernestine's neck. It was amazingly comforting to have a chicken in your lap—as long as she didn't leave any steaming presents behind when she left.

Don't even think about getting attached, Julie warned herself.

"What am I going to do with you guys, Ernie? I can't really keep you. I have to get a job and I don't think it's going to be raising layers. I'll have to move to a larger town and hope I can get a good reference from the NYPD. I may have really fucked up by leaving. But there it is. Never let people make you feel small, Ernie."

Ernestine cooed; Julie continued to stroke her head. Out in the clearing, Bill joined Hillary on Smitty's back. The sun rose into another clear day, and Julie's coffee grew cold as she sat on the steps and felt contented.

Cas awoke to shining sun and for a moment he thought he was on the water with Julie beside him, the light sparkling off the crests of the waves. But he was alone. And the light was glinting off the dresser mirror.

He rolled over and grunted. His eye hurt, his whole face hurt and his back and a few other parts. Then he remembered why. A fight at the Roadhouse. Julie had decked him in front of half the men in town last night. Of course, she'd more than made up for it later. But he was going to have to take more ribbing from the bar's regulars. *Well,* he thought philosophically. *At least it will take their minds off chicken thieves.*

But he was wrong.

When he walked into the police station twenty minutes later, Lou and Edith were both sitting behind the dispatcher's desk, their blue-curled heads bent over a magazine. Simultaneously, they looked up. Simultaneously, their eyes widened and their mouths opened. Then without a word, they tilted their heads toward the bench that sat along the front wall, their curls moving like identical cotton candy.

Cas slowly turned his head toward the bench where Henry Goethe and Elton Dinwiddie sat with their hats in their hands, scowling at the brims. They stood up and Cas's stomach sank.

"No more robberies, I hope," said Cas as he stepped toward them.

"Not yet," said Henry in a gravely voice. "But Elton and I got to thinking that maybe there's a ring of thieves in this town."

"Chickens and electronics?" asked Cas.

"You got a better explanation?" asked Elton.

Cas considered the possibility as he watched Elton's cheek work on a plug of tobacco. *Do not spit on my floor*, Cas thought and asked them if they'd like coffee.

"We'd like our property back," said Elton, getting ready to spit. Cas nudged the wastepaper basket toward him.

"And we want to know what you're doing about it," said Henry, taking up the demand while Elton hacked into the trash can.

Fortunately, Cas was distracted by Edith, who handed him a mug of steaming black coffee. "Thanks," he said and turned back to the two men.

Elton wiped the sleeve of his jacket across his mouth. "We don't want to make life difficult for you. We know you just took this job 'cause Wes Excelsior conned you into helping Hank out, but dammit, Cas, something needs to be done."

"I realize that," said Cas.

"We're not blaming you, mind, but we got to talking and thought maybe you could use some deputies."

Cas looked at the two men. Elton was pushing eighty, Henry had a bum knee and walked with a cane. "I appreciate the offer, but I'm just a stand-in. I don't think I should be appointing any deputies. You'd better go ask Hank what he thinks."

"Tried that," said Elton, already taking aim at the trash can again.

Cas looked away and concentrated on his coffee.

"Thelma wouldn't let us talk to him. That darn woman. Too damn protective by half."

Henry nodded. "We're not saying we don't think you're doing an okay job, just that these robberies have to stop."

"I agree," said Cas, wondering how he could get them out of the station. "That's why I brought in the county." Except the county sheriff, who'd been on the football team with Cas at Excelsior Falls High, had just wheezed over the phone and said, "Cas, you sucker. I'll be surprised if Hank ever comes back to work. Thelma's been trying to get him to retire for years. She wants to move to Florida." Then he relented. "I'll send someone over to take a look."

He had and they hadn't found a damn clue.

Henry pushed himself to his feet. "Well, if you change your mind, Elton and I are available and so are some of the other men in town."

Elton spit into the wastepaper basket and stood up. "We could set up a neighborhood watch."

"I'll think about it." Cas ushered them toward the door and held it open for them.

"So Julie Excelsior's back, huh," asked Henry, his eyes twinkling as he took in Cas's black eye.

"News travels fast," said Cas, opening the door wider.

"Heard she's got a wicked right hook," said Elton and went out the door to spit on the sidewalk.

Henry pushed his hat back on his head and nodded at Cas. Then went out the door, chuckling to himself.

"So it's true," said Edith as soon as the door shut behind them. "Julie Excelsior *is* staying at Excelsior House."

"And she did *that*," said Lou, pointing to Cas's face.

"It was an accident."

"Good thing she wasn't aiming at you," said Edith and exchanged a wink with her sister.

Cas took his coffee over to his desk and sat down. "Why are you both here?"

"I was just leaving," said Edith and picked up her black clutch purse from the desk. "I have a hair appointment at ten." She paused by the front door. "Do you have a date for the Candy Apple Dance Friday night?"

Cas looked up from a stack of forms that he had yet to fill out. "Are you asking me?" He grinned at her.

Edith tittered. "I'm already going with Ed Schott. But I know his daughter, Isabelle, is planning to be there."

Cas managed to bite back a groan. "I'll be there in my official capacity."

"She's a pretty girl. Prettier than the other two that have been chasing you from one end of town to the other."

Cas cracked his neck and felt pain shoot down his shoulder.

"Edith," said her sister. "You leave the sheriff alone. He's a busy man."

"I'm just saying," said Edith and left the station.

"Thanks, Lou."

Lou shook her head. "She's just angling to get Ed to ask her to marry him. But he won't do that until he gets Isabelle settled."

"Well, she's not settling with me."

"No. She's too straight-laced for you."

"Lou," said Cas. "What makes you think I'm not straight-laced?"

Lou smiled the same smile that Edith had given him. "How long have I lived in this town? Sixty years now?"

Try seventy-one, thought Cas, but decided not to mention it.

"There was a time when we thought the Excelsior-Reynolds feud might come to an end."

"Yeah," said Cas. "Well, it didn't." He picked up a pen and started filling out forms. He heard Lou sigh, then the rustle of paper as she opened her magazine.

"It's not too late. You can look forward to some licks of love around the end of the month."

Cas raised an eyebrow at her.

"It says so right here." Lou lifted her magazine for him to see. The front cover read, *Ten Ways to Make Him Beg for More*. "I wonder if Julie Excelsior will be there," said Lou and turned the page.

When the chickens were back in the gazebo, Julie dressed and went to Henryville. She bought groceries and drove over to the real estate office. But she didn't go in.

"I know," she told Smitty as she unpacked the groceries. "I said we'd only be here a week. I lied." She needed to find Wes's money before she let people start traipsing all over the place. And she needed to get the house in better condition before putting it on the market.

Smitty looked up at her.

"Let me get out of these clothes and we'll take a walk."

Fifteen minutes later, she was dressed in jeans and Wes's coat and hat. She looked into the parlor where Smitty was sleeping on the hearth rug.

"Come on, boy. We're going on a treasure hunt."

They struck off down the driveway toward the pond. A layer of rime covered the surface; sticks and leaves were captured in the ice. Julie picked up a flat stone and tried to skip it across the ice. It broke through and sank.

"Lost my touch," said Julie. Once she'd made a rock skip eight times. It was a record and Wes took Cas and her down Route 28 to the A & W for hot dogs and root beer floats. He had a—green pickup truck. She pushed at the ice with the toe of her boot. Cas was driving Wes's old pickup.

They walked the perimeter of the pond, looked into nooks and crannies, all their old hiding places, and found nothing.

Smitty ran ahead and once she found him digging. But when she rushed to see what he'd found, it was only a chipmunk's hole.

They criss-crossed back toward the house, stopped in the shed where Julie moved supplies, looking for a hiding place. And found nothing.

They walked to the far side of the cleared area and into the orchard. The trees seemed more gnarled than before. Several branches had broken off and lay on the ground. She walked down the rows of trees, looking for a scrap of yellow paper. And found nothing.

Keeping an ear out for hunters, Julie entered the woods. She had heard the report of distant shots ever since her first day back, but none were close enough to make her worry about poachers.

The woods accounted for fifteen of the twenty acres. It was old and overgrown and easy to get lost, and their games never penetrated too far from the clearing.

But there had been a path that led through the woods. She climbed over a fallen log, pushed a low hanging branch out of the way and pressed on. It was much colder without the sun to warm the air. The ground was still saturated from the recent rain, and Julie slipped on wet leaves as she searched for the path.

At last she found it, marked by two large chunks of granite, partially hidden by leaves that had recently been trampled. Julie knelt and peered at the area.

Smitty lifted his nose to the wind.

"Yep. Someone's been here and I bet it was our thief. And they were riding a motorcycle." She just hoped it wasn't Henley or Bo.

Smitty took off, leapt over a mass of leafless blackberry brambles and disappeared into the underbrush. Julie was about to follow him, when a squirrel shot out from the bushes, ran over Julie's feet, and was gone. Smitty came loping toward her, head and tail held high.

"Very brave of you," said Julie and started down the path. Smitty fell in step beside her. She leaned over and began to search the ground; Smitty snuffled through the leaves. After a minute she stopped in front of an old tree stump. Was this the one they had used as a hiding place? She brushed leaves aside and found the tips of two stones they had covered with dirt to mark the place. This *was* it.

She knelt down and touched the stump; the wood fell away in slivers, disturbing a colony of insects. Julie sighed and stood up. Nothing but a bunch of termites. On to number two.

But none of the rocks, fissures, or old trees that had once held their secrets yielded anything but a few scraped knuckles.

They followed the path until they came to a glade deep within the woods. A huge boulder rose out of the forest floor. At least it used to be huge. Today it looked like a big rock. A ray of sun filtered through the trees and lit the surface.

She'd spent a lot of Saturdays on this boulder: tied up as a captive cowgirl, a captive robber, a captive princess.

She found a handhold and climbed up the face. Twice her feet slid on loose dirt and she was out of breath when she reached the top. Smitty was already there waiting for her.

"I used to be better at this," she told him, brushing off her hands. "And anyway, you cheated. The back way's for sissies." She sat down at the top, crossed her legs, and lifted her face to the warmth of the sun.

While Smitty stood guard, Julie's mind drifted into the past. Wes always had an adventure planned; he'd take them fishing or shooting or send them on treasure hunts. On warm sunny days, they'd lay in the grass and count the clouds, while Cass told them about the model ship he was building and where he would sail if it were real.

Or she and Cas would explore the woods and play. Invariably they would end up here, playing cowboys and Indians, cops and robbers, or pirates and captive Princess, Julie tied up and Cas tickling her and sneaking peeks at her underwear. There was something a little kinky about all that bondage. She didn't realize it at the time. And hadn't thought about it since.

Well, she'd thought about it. But not that much. It was all innocent. Sort of. Until that stupid day on the river. Maybe, she and Cas were a little old to be playing make-believe, but she hadn't realized it until Reynolds yanked the bandanna from Cas's head and gave her a look of such contempt that her insides burned.

And there she stood with a tablecloth tied around her shoulders and she felt stupid and small and guilty. It was awful and humiliating then. Now it just seemed ridiculous. She'd felt betrayed when Cas let Reynolds take him away. Then the jokes started at school, and Cas had ignored her, let her face their taunts alone. That was what really hurt. Julie felt her lip tremble. "Actually, it still hurts."

She felt better now that she'd said it out loud, something she had never done before. She felt better, but she wasn't quite ready to forgive.

Chapter 11

*

Cas's day was not going well. His first mistake was to have lunch at the hotel. He thought at least Christine would be tactful about his black eye. She wasn't. Then she proceeded to pick his brain about Julie and what his intentions were. Alice Poole, another marriage hopeful, waylaid him on the street and wouldn't leave until he promised to save her a dance on Friday night.

He spent the afternoon mucking around in the two empty chicken coops, looking for anything that he might have missed the first time, and came away with nothing more than shit-encrusted shoes. And a headache. By mid afternoon, he was considering sick leave when Mel, wearing her usual unrelieved black, poked her head into the station.

"Reynolds wants to see you," she said. "He called the hotel."

Cas groaned. "Why didn't he just call here?"

"Easier to shoot the messenger, I guess. Christine answered. It upset her."

"God damn it," said Cas. Lou looked up from her magazine and tsked at him.

Cas got two aspirin out of his desk and took them dry. "All right." He stood up. "You want a ride?"

"No. I have to work until nine. Ian'll drive me."

He left her at the door, watched her slouch down the side-

walk, beautiful and angry and lonely. Then he got into his police car.

Reynolds was waiting for him in the library, which Cas was
beginning to think of as the interrogation room. He was standing at the French windows, staring out at the stone wall that
separated Reynolds Place from Excelsior House. And Cas
thought, *Why don't you get a job with George Quincy, instead
of sitting around like the lord of the manor, slowly going broke?
It would also do a world of good for your state of mind.*

Cas cleared his throat.

Reynolds turned around and pointed his martini glass to-
ward the decanter on his desk. Liquid sloshed out of his glass.
His cheeks were already flushed and it was only three-thirty.
"Pour yourself a drink, son."

"No thanks. I'm on duty. Mel said you wanted to see me."

"Heard that Excelsior girl gave you that black eye down at
the Roadhouse."

Cas's hand went automatically to eye. "No. She gave me the
bruised jaw. It was an accident."

"Heard her car was seen at your place afterwards."

My life is an open fucking book, thought Cas. "She was
concerned that I might have a concussion."

"She'll make a fool of you."

Cas sighed. "So you've told me."

Reynolds walked over to his desk, weaving slightly. He sat
down heavily in his padded leather chair, knocked back the
rest of his martini, and leaned forward on his elbows. "What's
she doing here?" Reynolds pinned him with rheumy eyes and
Cas felt a stab of pity at what his father had become.

"Wes left her the house in his will," Cas said patiently.
"She's only been here four days. Give her a break." *And me,*
Cas thought. *Give me a break for once.*

"Four days is too long. She's up to something."

"She has things to attend to."

"Wes sent her here to get back at me."

Cas gripped the frayed strands of his control. "Wes is dead. Can't you just leave her alone? She didn't have anything to do with whatever happened between you and Wes. Or what happened a century and a half ago. Just leave her alone."

"I won't have her making up to you. Find a nice girl and settle down. That Isabelle Schott is pretty enough. And her family is respectable."

Cas rubbed his forehead. "I'm not marrying Isabelle Schott. I'm not marrying anybody."

"And you're not going to be seen with Julie Excelsior. Get rid of those chickens and send her packing. This town doesn't need the likes of her."

Cas stood up and braced his hands on the desk, meeting his father's angry eyes with determined ones. "She's an Excelsior. This is Excelsior Falls."

"She's back here to destroy this family. Get rid of her. Or I will."

"Dad," he said, trying to calm his voice. "If you hurt her, you'll answer to me."

Reynolds pushed himself out of his chair and leaned across the desk until his face was inches from Cas. "You were always an idiot when it came to that piece of white trash. And it looks like you still are."

Cas forced himself back from the desk. Took a deep breath. "Leave her alone," he said evenly. "Wes is dead. The feud is over. It's time you started getting on with your life."

"Wes sent her to bring me down. She has to be stopped."

Cas stared at him. His father. The man who gave him life. Whose genes Cas carried and who, Cas realized for the first time, was not just a little crazy, but was afraid.

"This isn't about me or Julie, is it? You're afraid of something she might find out. What are you hiding, Dad? What did you do?"

"How dare you," rumbled Reynolds as his face turned from flushed red to near purple.

"Tell me, I'll help. Is it something between you and Wes?

Something about the Savings and Loan?" *Thieves came in and stole the gold.* "Tell me."

The door opened and his mother fluttered in, a chiffon sash trailing behind her. "Cas. You should have told me you were here. I'll have Larue set another place for dinner."

Cas stood up, too tired to even think straight. He kissed her cheek. "I can't stay."

She smiled vacuously at him. "Of course, you'll stay. I'll just tell—"

"No, really. I can't—"

"Let the boy go, Marian."

Cas started for the door.

"You're a Reynolds. You know what you have to do."

Cas barely looked in his father's direction. Bile was bitter in his throat. "Yeah. I know what I have to do." *But not as a Reynolds.*

When Cas reached the bottom of the drive, he didn't think twice about which way to go. He turned left and then left again into the next driveway. He saw Julie's blue VW parked in front of the house and breathed a sigh of relief. At least she was home.

He stopped his car beside it, turned off his cell phone and left it on the seat. He didn't plan on being interrupted again.

The front door was open, but no one answered his knock. He walked around back. Called her name. No Julie or Smitty. They were probably walking in the woods, like he'd told her not to. The girl was infuriating. No sense of self-preservation at all, even if she did have a good right hook. He started up the hill toward the line of trees.

Julie lay back on the rock, her arms over her eyes. Smitty was warm at her side, and her mind drifted as her body grew drowsy in the sun. Then Smitty jumped to his feet and let out a loud bark. Julie sat up in time to see Cas step out of the trees. He strode straight toward the boulder and stopped below her.

Julie looked down at him and smiled. "Remember this?"

"Didn't I tell you not to go walking in the woods?"

"We were taking a nap."

"Don't equivocate." He scowled at her. Then his mouth curved in a half smile that made him look years younger. "Orange plaid suits you. I especially like the hat."

Julie gave him a look and pulled the earflaps of Wes's hat farther down over her ears. "I like it." She stood up and sank into one hip; her feet shifted on the uneven surface.

"You're cute, but come down before you get shot."

"I'm not going to get shot. But I did find some motorcycle tracks."

"Julie, get down."

"Oh, all right."

He reached up to help her, but she twisted out of his reach. Her foot slipped on a patch of loose dirt. Her weight pitched to the side and her feet slid in opposite directions. Her arms flailed, she flew off the boulder and landed spread-eagle against Cas, while Smitty barked furiously from above their heads.

Cas caught her and staggered backwards. "Are you out to get me?"

"Sorry," said Julie, trying to pull away. "I slipped."

"You sure did." Cas's arms tightened around her.

Julie felt a rush and gave herself a mental shake. There were so many reasons why she shouldn't get involved with Cas. She couldn't afford to let him into her confidence, not to mention her heart. Which, with the way things were going, was becoming a dangerous possibility.

Though standing this close, feeling his heart beating beneath his jacket, she was a little fuzzy on the details of why this was such a bad idea.

Oh right. The riddle, their past history, her recent history. Got it. She attempted to pull away again.

He held her tight against his chest.

Julie felt herself giving in to his warmth, which all things considered, was a lot more enticing than Smitty's. She pushed at his chest before she lost her power to think. "We'd better go."

"What's the matter?" asked Cas, holding onto her.

"You just said we shouldn't be out in the woods."

"Okay, let's go inside. You're shivering. We haven't tried out the Jacuzzi yet."

"Cas, we can't keep doing this."

Cas looked around. "You're right. Let's go inside."

"No. I mean, *this*. Look. It was great to see you. We got to do all those things we never got to do, you know, when we were kids."

"I can think of a few more we haven't tried."

She bet she could think of even more. "And I have to leave soon. And I have to find, deal, take care of stuff, and then your mother's going to call—"

"Nope, turned off my phone."

"Or Reynolds will spy on us."

"We'll close the curtains."

"No."

Cas eased her away and looked at her. "Are you dumping me?"

Julie's mouth dropped open. "What are you talking about? It's not like we're going steady. We just had a couple of one-night stands for old times sakes. But that was all it was. I have things to do. I can't . . . I can't . . ."

"You can't leave until we've played pirates and princess." Cas smiled, a pirate's leer straight from their childhood.

"Cas. Let go."

"No."

She huffed out air and stomped on his foot.

His arms jerked open and she headed for the house.

"What's happened?" he asked, limping after her. "Has my family been harassing you?"

Julie shook her head and kept walking.

"Then who?"

"Nobody. It just won't work." *We'll find the treasure. You'll walk out and I'll get screwed again.*

"You're crazy."

"Crazy maybe, but not stupid."

"Julie, wait."

He grabbed her arm. She wrenched free and broke into a run, not bothering to follow the trail, but slashing through the underbrush until she reached the yard. She sprinted down the hill and flew up the back steps and into the kitchen. She locked the door and leaned against it for good measure.

There, she thought. *Safe.* But not happy.

She was breathing hard, far too hard for a sprint down the hill. She slid down until she was sitting on the floor. Slowly she began to untie her boots. No reason to muck up the linoleum even if her life was falling apart.

"If you're going to shut someone out, you shouldn't leave your front door open."

Julie's head jerked up. Cas stood in the door to the hallway, shoeless, with Smitty leaning against his leg.

"Shit," said Julie.

Cas strode toward her and pulled her to her feet. Then he sat down on a kitchen chair and dragged Julie onto his lap.

"You probably shouldn't sit on hard chairs," she said, sniffing.

"You're the nuttiest girl I have ever known. Why not?"

"Because," she sniffed again, trying to get herself under control, "of your condition."

"What condition?"

"You know, your . . . the . . . hemorrhoids."

Cas took her by the shoulders and looked her in the face. "Are you sure you aren't getting me mixed up with one of your other boyfriends?"

Julie blinked. *Boyfriend? He thought of himself as her boyfriend? Stick to the essentials, dummy.* "No-o-o."

Cas shook his head. "Honey, I don't have that particular condition," he said, fighting a grin.

"But that first night, when you sat down, and . . ." She stammered to a halt.

"Oh," said Cas. "I remember. *That* condition." He pulled her closer until his erection rested against her thigh. "This is the only condition I was suffering from—that night or now."

Julie lowered her forehead to his chest. "I am such an idiot. Why didn't you say so?"

He lifted her chin with his finger. "Honey, I was broadcasting it loud and clear. Now do you want to tell me what's bothering you?"

"No. I mean, nothing. Nothing's bothering me." Except for the hard-on nudging her thigh. She really needed to get out of his lap. Away from all that burning desire.

Unfortunately, half of that desire was hers.

He stroked her hair, then took a fistful and pulled her close. "Tell me." He kissed her, briefly, gently. It was sexy. And way too tempting.

"Tell me." His breath was warm and inviting against her lips. He kissed her again. This time he lingered and she opened her mouth to him in spite of her intention not to. His tongue slid across her teeth and sought out her tongue as his fingers drifted down the front of Wes's coat, undoing buttons as they passed.

Julie was about to pull away, when his hand slipped inside and his fingertips touched her breast. She shuddered.

Cas's tongue drove into her mouth and Julie came to her senses. She wrenched her mouth from his and stood up.

"I can't."

Cas dropped his head to his hands. "Jesus."

Julie took a step back as though distance could keep her resolute. He looked so confused that she longed to throw her arms around him and let him do anything he wanted to do with her. But that could be a disaster.

Maybe, once she solved the riddle . . . *Damn it, Wes. Look what you've done.*

And suddenly she was weak with frustration and heartache.

She missed Wes, even though he was a pain in the butt. She'd give anything to hear him say, "Who loves you, kid?" To touch his hand when she reached for her lollipop.

She yanked a chair out and sat down before her knees gave way. She should never have come back. "Oh God, what am I supposed to do?"

Cas looked over his fingers at her. "You're supposed to love me."

His eyes widened and the color drained out of his face, while his words filled the air and Julie stared back at him. He opened his mouth, shut it again. Looked at Julie. Then he stood up, walked past her and out of the kitchen without another word.

She heard the car roar to life, then drive away. Smitty whined and lay his head in her lap.

"He didn't say what I think he said, did he?"

Smitty sneezed and nuzzled her hand.

The parking lot of the Roadhouse was virtually empty, which was about usual for a Monday night. And for the first time in weeks, Cas was sorry to see that there were no motorcycles parked out front. Because tonight he really felt like busting a few heads.

He pulled an old Yale sweatshirt over his head. It was encrusted with dried paint and frayed at the cuffs, and just putting it on made him feel more himself again. Cas, who built boats, not Cas, the pretend sheriff. Cas who was in control of his life and didn't blurt out things he wasn't ready to say and Julie wasn't ready to hear.

He strode across the gravel and pushed through the door. Terrence was sitting at the bar, talking to Tilda. A couple of tables were occupied, but the only sound in the bar was the snooker balls whacking around the table. He sat down at the bar and Tilda poured out a Foster's and placed it in front of him.

"And a Wild Turkey. Double."

Tilda pursed her lips. Tonight her hair was more purple than red and he wondered if she and Edith and Mel all got their hair done at the same place in Henryville. Color by Crayola.

She slid the whiskey toward him and followed it with her person, leaning over the bar and frowning at him. "I know you don't have a dog. So it didn't die."

Cas gritted his teeth. "Why can't women ever just say what they mean?"

"Then they wouldn't be women," said Terrence.

Tilda leaned over the bar and tugged his beard. "That's right, smoochums. And don't you forget it."

"Ugh," said Cas and knocked back his drink. His breath fled, fire blew out of his ears, and his eyes teared up.

Tilda took the glass out of his hand and set it on the bar. "So. Did that make you feel better?"

"No," Cas wheezed. "Maybe the next one."

"You're gonna feel worse before you feel better if you keep this up." She got out a menu and handed it to him. "Got corned beef and cabbage tonight."

"It's fucking October."

"She's starting early this year," said Terrence. "That way, by the time March comes around, she'll be a pro." His teeth flashed from behind his beard and Tilda planted a kiss on his mouth.

Cas drank more beer and tried to ignore them.

"On second thought . . ." Tilda quickly poured out another Wild Turkey and placed it in front of Cas. "Alice Poole alert at five o'clock."

Cas sighed and prepared for the assault. That was all he needed to put paid to this day.

Alice slipped up beside him. "Buy me a drink, big guy?" she asked as her long pointed nails began to walk up his shirt front.

"Uh." He flashed Tilda an SOS.

Tilda grabbed the roving hand. "I lo-o-ove this color." She pulled Alice's hand closer and peered at her nails. "Who does your manicure? I was using Nails Galore, but I just wasn't happy with how the polish was lasting." She chatted on, never letting go of Alice's hand while Cas and Terrence watched; Cas in amazement and Terrence with pride.

Alice finally retrieved her hand, lifted her hip to the stool next to Cas and smiled at him. She was long and tall, mostly skinny legs in black stretch pants and a sequined top that stretched off one shoulder.

"Have a beer," said Tilda, shoving a mug into Alice's hand. "On the house."

Alice took a sip while she continued to smile at Cas over the rim. He felt a foot slide up his calf. His eyes widened.

"Alice," said Tilda. "Aren't you with Joe? I think he's looking for you." She waved a dishcloth in the air. "Hey, Joe. She's over here."

"Oops, got to go." Alice slid off the stool. "Don't forget to save me a dance Friday night." She winked at Cas and sidled away with her beer.

"Thanks, Tilda," said Cas.

"If you'd just pick one and get married, the rest would leave you alone."

If I just left town and never came back, I'd be better off, he thought, but he said, "I don't think I'm the marrying type."

"Ha. I remember a time back in high school."

"Yeah, well, water under the bridge."

"That's a good one," said Tilda. "Have you looked under the bridge lately? I swear the river's gone down another foot since summer."

"It's the new lake up north," said Terrence. "Now if they had decided to build it here, we'd all be rich instead of them."

Tilda grabbed his beard, pulled him across the bar, and kissed him. "And your front yard would be flooded and you'd have to swim to work everyday."

And I could sail away, thought Cas.

Chapter 12

"You know, Ernestine," said Julie the next morning as she sat on the steps watching Smitty give Bill and Hillary rides around the yard. "If anybody else returned home after fifteen years, they'd at least get a casserole. I come back and not one person has driven up that driveway, not even the mailman. Except Cas. But he doesn't count."

And she was really trying not to think about him and his parting words. How could he expect her to love him after not seeing him for over a decade? Especially with that stupid riddle standing between them. She probably hadn't heard him correctly. And besides, he couldn't mean it. So why did she keep thinking about it?

"It's not that I don't enjoy talking to you and Smitty, but I don't want to turn into one of those potty old ladies—not that I'm going to stay or anything, but you know the type. And if I don't figure out what to do with my life and quick, I'm going to be up the creek. I was sure Wes had left me some money, but maybe he didn't have any. I mean, the house isn't in great shape, but a coat of paint, and a few repairs . . .

"It's not that I'm greedy. I'd really rather have Wes alive." And she knew that if she could trade her treasure for Wes, she'd do it with no regrets.

* * *

Julie spent the next few days feeding chickens, separating Wes's belongings into keep piles and Goodwill piles, then putting them back again because she couldn't bring herself to part with any of his possessions. And she kept looking for another riddle.

By Wednesday, she was going stir crazy. She hadn't found the next clue, she hadn't heard from Cass. And she knew she couldn't put off dealing with the sale of Wes's house any longer. She dressed to go to Henryville, then thought, *Tomorrow, tomorrow's soon enough*. And went for lunch at the hotel instead.

Christine greeted her with a bubbling smile and led her over to a table by the window. "I haven't seen you in town lately," she said as she placed the menu in front of Julie. "I was afraid you'd left."

Julie's eyebrows rose.

"Where is that girl?"

Mel shuffled through the swinging doors to the kitchen, grabbed a pad and pencil off the silverware table and sauntered over to Julie and Christine. She sank into one hip, licked the tip of her pencil and looked at Julie with a bored expression.

Julie saw Christine's look of consternation, and quickly said, "I'll have the roast pork and a house salad, vinaigrette on the side." Mel melted away without writing anything down.

Christine shook her head. "I'm sorry about that. She's going through a rough stage. She was pretty close to Wes, you know."

"No, I didn't," said Julie, suddenly wondering about the young Goth.

"Yeah, but don't let it get out. My parents would ground her for life. Oh, I'm sorry. It's just . . ."

"The feud," Julie finished for her.

Christine didn't answer, just looked broodingly at the tablecloth. "I really am sorry. Would you like something to drink?"

"Thanks, do you still have some of that cabernet I had the other day?"

"Sure. I'll get it."

"Why don't you join me," Julie said on a whim.

Christine looked quickly around the restaurant. Julie was the only patron. "Thanks. I will. The hunters won't be back for a couple of hours yet."

She returned a few minutes later carrying a tray with two wineglasses, one with cabernet and the other with something sparkling. Seltzer?

"It's always quiet during the week," said Christine, taking a sip of her seltzer. "Most people around here only dine out on the weekends. We're hoping to pick up the overflow from the new lake resort up the road. They have skiing and fishing and water skiing and there's a trucked-in beach, but they don't have any really good restaurants. Mainly burgers and stuff."

"These things take time," said Julie, trying to be optimistic.

"So how are things going with you?"

"Uh . . . fine."

"I saw Cas's black eye." Christine bit her lip, then a smile crept across her face.

"That wasn't me," said Julie. "I gave him the bruised jaw."

Christine shrieked with laughter and pretty soon, Julie joined her.

"I didn't mean to do it. There was this doofus hitting on me and I swung and Cas pulled him off the bar stool and . . ." Julie paused, some of the humor dying away. "The rest is history."

"Oh, I hope not. Anyway it serves him right. Sir Galahad. Always coming to the rescue." Christine bit her lip. "I didn't mean that. I'm grateful to him for being here. Between the hotel and Mel and my parents . . ." She shrugged.

"I can imagine," said Julie. "Why is he here?"

Christine frowned at her. "Wes asked him to come. Didn't you know?"

Julie shook her head and sipped some wine.

"I know he'll leave again." She looked at Julie over her seltzer glass. "If something doesn't change his mind."

"Well, maybe something will." Then seeing the spark of interest in Christine's eyes, she quickly added, "Though I won't be around to know. I'm leaving soon, myself."

"Oh, but what about the house?" Christine blushed. "It's none of my business."

"I'm going into Henryville tomorrow to put it on the market." Julie moved back for Mel to put her salad plate on the table. The plate tipped and a few shreds of lettuce fell onto the tablecloth.

Christine sighed and closed her eyes.

Mel picked up the lettuce pieces and shoved them in her uniform pocket. "What about the chickens?"

Christine and Julie both looked up in surprise. Mel stood there, slouched in one hip and scowling. But the question had definitely come from her.

"I think Maude will take them. If not, I'll have to sell them."

Mel narrowed her eyes at Julie. She seemed angry, but Julie had no idea why. Maybe she was just angry in general. Who could blame her, stuck in the middle of nowhere with Reynolds and Marian for parents?

She tested a smile on the Goth and got no reaction. "Do you go to school at Ex Falls, I mean, Excelsior Falls High?"

"Where else would I go?" said Mel without inflection.

"True," said Julie. "Junior?"

"Senior," said Mel, still scowling.

"It's her half day," explained Christine.

Julie nodded, *not playing hooky today*. "Where are you going to college?" She saw immediately from Mel's expression that she shouldn't have asked.

"When?"

Julie blinked. When what? Right, the chickens. "Soon. I . . . soon." Why should a girl wearing black lipstick and nail polish, who looked like she'd never been out in the sun, be concerned about Wes's chickens? "Are you interested in them?"

Mel snorted. "Chickens suck."

"Mel," said Christine.

Mel's eyes snapped at her sister and Julie cut in. "They're pretty stinky, and it's a pain in the butt having to get up so early every day, but I have this one, Ernestine, that actually sits in my lap and lets me pet her." Julie could swear the girl's eyes lightened. "I'll miss her and Bill and Hilary, but I can't exactly take them with me." Hell, she'd even miss Ulysses, though he reminded her of Donald, the bribe-taker.

"Are you going back to the city then?" asked Christine and immediately her cheeks flooded with color. "It's none of my business, it's just—"

"That you talk too much," said Mel and turned her back on them and slouched back to the kitchen.

"Sorry," said Christine. "She's right. But it's not like I get a lot of new people to talk to."

"Innkeepers are supposed to be friendly."

Christine smiled. "Thanks. You're nice."

No, I'm not, thought Julie. *But at least I don't have to live in Ex Falls. It's the least I can do.*

A few minutes later, the kitchen doors swung open. A stocky man with salt-and-pepper hair and wearing a white apron came out, carrying a plate with an aluminum cover.

"Ian," said Christine.

Ian removed Julie's salad plate and replaced it with the entrée plate. He lifted the lid and a whiff of rosemary and garlic rose to Julie's nose.

"This smells wonderful," she said.

"Thank you," he said with a slight bow. "Direct from the chef to you."

"This is my husband, Ian," said Christine, then asked, "Where's Mel?"

"Damned if I know. She came barreling through the kitchen and out the back door without stopping. Didn't know she could move that fast."

"Oh." Christine looked toward the closed doors.

"Don't worry about her. Probably had a date or something." He patted Christine's hand and smiled down at her. She beamed up at him.

Julie felt a pang of envy, then pushed it aside and picked up her fork. The pork was delicious. Too bad they couldn't drum up some more business.

Christine stood up. "I'd better see—"

"Stay off your feet," he told her and dropped a light kiss on her nose, before taking the aluminum top back into the kitchen.

"Do you feel like company?"

"Sure," said Julie. It was more interesting than having to eat staring out the window.

"I'm pregnant," Christine whispered.

Julie looked up to make sure she'd heard correctly.

"I miscarried last year, so we're not saying anything until we're sure this one takes. But I'm so excited, I had to share it with someone. I just found out this morning."

"Congratulations," said Julie. She lifted her glass and thought, *a whole new generation of Reynoldses to carry on the feud*. She could imagine eight or ten little Macgregors, dark haired and kilted, wielding swords as they scaled the wall to Excelsior House. And then she realized that there would be no little Excelsiors to fight with.

"And they won't carry on this ridiculous feud. Hell, nobody even remembers what it was about." Christine peered at Julie. "Yours won't, will they?"

"My what?"

"Your kids? Carry on the feud? I thought maybe we could stop it now that Wes is gone and Reynolds has no one to fight with."

Except me, thought Julie. "Not to worry. I'm not having kids."

Christine frowned. "But you and—you would have beautiful children."

Julie nodded and bit into her pork.

*   *   *

Back at home, Julie put on Wes's jacket and cap and went to let the chickens out. Bill and Hillary immediately fluttered up to Smitty's back and the three of them wandered off to the far end of the clearing.

"Not too far," she warned Smitty and sat down on the steps to wait for Ernestine. Ernestine didn't come.

Jilted, thought Julie and looked around the yard to see what the hen was up to. She didn't see her. Maybe she'd decided it was too cold to leave the cozy, if smelly, roost. *Smart chicken.* Julie climbed up the hill to the gazebo just to make sure she was all right.

The gazebo was empty. Julie walked along the row of nesting boxes, peering into the deepest recesses of straw. She checked the perches and corners and shadows, but didn't find Ernestine.

The first rumble of panic set in. *She'd probably just missed her outside.* Julie hurried down the ramp. But when her excursion through the brood turned up no Ernestine, she really began to worry.

"Ernestine," she called. A few feathered heads looked up but went right back to scratching and rolling in their daily dirt bath. "Ernestine!"

Julie checked the perimeters of the yard, beneath the juniper bush, even in the shed. Ernestine had returned to the gazebo after the morning outing. She couldn't have gotten out.

She quickly counted heads. Everyone accounted for—except Ernestine.

With increasing worry, Julie began to search farther afield, around the front of the house, down the driveway as far as the fishing pond. She called her name, made clucking noises, crawled on her hands and knees to see under shrubs. Finally she ran back up the hill toward the woods.

Smitty, his attention caught by Julie's unusual behavior, came trotting up, Bill and Hillary along for the ride.

"Smitty," said Julie. "Ernestine is missing." She looked at Bill and Hillary. "If only chickens could talk."

She searched the gazebo again, walked farther into the woods, poked under rocks and behind trees until the sun began to set and her fingers were numb from the cold. She herded the others back into the gazebo. Did another head count. And still there was one missing bird. Damn. Ernestine would freeze if left out overnight. Was it possible that she'd gotten into the house?

Julie closed the latch, checked it a second time, and checked the exterior of the gazebo for possible escape routes. Then she went inside. Smitty followed her from room to room, while she looked under beds, behind chairs, even rooted around in closets. And still no Ernestine.

She should call Cas. And say what? "I'd like to report a missing chicken." They didn't even start looking for missing people until forty-eight hours had elapsed.

Had she wandered off? Been stolen? Someone could be sitting down to dinner tonight with a roasted Ernestine on the table.

Julie took a flashlight and went outside to search again. All she got for her trouble were some unhappy hens, a few angry squawks and a couple of pecks that weren't pure affection.

By ten o'clock, she had to concede that Ernestine was truly missing. And though she didn't know all that much about chickens, she did know how to conduct a search. And she'd been thorough.

She opened a beer, sank down on a kitchen chair, and rested her forehead against the cold bottle. Smitty put his paws in her lap and leaned his head against her, while she absently scratched behind his ears.

Finally, Julie stood up, knocking Smitty to the floor. She couldn't interview the witnesses, but she could reconstruct the timeline.

She began pacing, laying out the events of the day. "Ernestine was here this morning. I counted heads when I put them back in the gazebo and everyone was there. Then I came inside and got dressed. Surely one of us would have heard someone in the chicken coop." She stopped in front of Smitty. Smitty tilted his head. "I know. *You* would have heard something and started barking." She started pacing again. "Then I went into town for lunch."

She stopped again. "Arrgh."

"Grrr," echoed Smitty.

"Did something happen while I was gone?"

"Arf," said Smitty and thumped his tail twice.

"Of course, it did. Duh." Because after lunch, she'd come straight into the house, let Smitty out and then went out to the chickens. And Ernestine was gone. "Damn. Double damn." She sank back into a chair. "And I had just told Mel and Christine that I was going to sell the flock. It's instant karma. How could I ever sell Ernestine?"

Her eyes narrowed as she thought about Mel asking her what she was going to do with the chickens. And Christine saying that Mel and Wes had been close. And how Mel left suddenly in the middle of serving her lunch.

"I wonder," said Julie, then immediately dismissed the idea. Melanie stealing chickens? Julie bet the most energy the girl ever used was pressing the remote button from MTV to E!

An hour later, Julie and Smitty climbed the stairs to bed, where Julie spent as much time looking out her bedroom window as she did sleeping, waiting for the return of the wayward hen. She was dressed and outside when Ulysses and Bill began their morning serenade. And there was still no Ernestine.

At least, there was no frozen corpse lying at the door to the gazebo. No scratch marks left on the wood as Ernestine gasped her final chicken breaths before succumbing to the frost.

Maybe she would come running out of the woods or from under the house when she heard the shed open and the sound of scratch rolling against the tin pan. But Julie wasn't surprised that when the pan was empty, Ernestine had still not shown.

She gathered the eggs and returned the chickens to the fenced-in yard early, much to their unhappiness, especially Bill and Hillary who had begun to take their daily rides on Smitty's back as their due.

She took the eggs into the house, but she couldn't eat them. This morning she saw them as little Ernestines in the making. She put them in the fridge and made toast with peanut butter instead.

At ten-thirty she heard a truck coming up the driveway. She jumped up, hoping it was Maude, then remembered that the "Pliney boys" came on Thursday to cart away the chicken manure.

She watched them back the truck up to the growing pile of manure and let down the tail gate. She put on her coat and hat and went out to oversee them, per Wes and Maude's instructions.

Two young, lanky Dan Pliney look-alikes jumped down from each side of the truck's cab, pulling on heavy rubber gloves. They wore green rubber boots that came up to their knees, and bandannas were tied loosely around their necks. To cover their noses while working, Julie supposed.

They introduced themselves as Brian and Doug, not shaking hands, for which she was grateful. Then she said, "I've lost a chicken."

"Dead?" asked Doug, who was the taller of the two.

"I don't know. I hope not. She just disappeared."

Brian nodded. "Foxes." He stuck his shovel in the pile of shit and tossed the frozen bits into the bed of the truck. Steam rose from the uncovered manure and Julie stepped back to a safe distance to watch and think, *Foxes.*

They were halfway through the pile when Doug said, "Shit," and stopped digging.

He ran the tip of his shovel over the top inches of manure, then leaned over and pulled a plastic garbage bag out of the remaining pile. He turned to Julie, holding up the bag. Julie edged back.

"You shouldn't mix regular garbage with manure. Plastic

outgasses and other foreign elements will break down and contaminate the load."

Julie raised her eyebrows. "Well, don't look at me. I didn't put in there."

Doug shrugged, "Well, Old Man Excelsior never would do it, nor Maude Clemmons."

"Probably somebody after the funeral," said Brian.

"Yeah, dumb." Doug tossed the bag off to the side. It hit the ground with a thud. Julie and the two boys looked at each other.

"Doesn't sound like garbage does it?" said Brian.

"No," said Julie taking a cautious step toward it. It sounded like metal. A metal box. She felt her pulse rate kick up. *Wes, so help me, if I go through chicken shit and there is no clue in that bag, I'll search you out when I get to where you are.*

"Want me to see what's inside?" asked Doug.

"No," said Julie as he drove the point of his shovel into the plastic. "Really, just leave it. I'll take it to the dump after it airs out a bit." *After I see what's inside without an audience looking on.*

He went back to his manure pile, the bag forgotten.

Julie shoved her hands in her pockets and rocked back on her heels, yearning to say, "Forget the shit, and get the hell out of here."

At last the boys tossed their shovels into the truck and lifted the tailgate.

Julie pulled out the twenty dollar bill she owed them. She stretched out her hand at the same time Doug stretched out his. He was also holding a twenty.

"What's that for?" asked Julie.

"For the manure. Twenty bucks a load, big or little. It's what we always paid Wes."

"You pay to cart shit away?" asked Julie incredulously as she slowly pocketed both twenties.

"Every month," said Doug, and he and Brian climbed back into the cab.

Julie waited until the truck was out of sight and the sound of its engine had faded away. Then she turned to the garbage bag. "This better be worth it," she said, and minced through the bits of manure to where the bag lay in a heap. She kicked it with her foot. It rattled. Lifted it up with her toe. Lightweight, so no pieces of silver. She took the ends of the bag between her fingers and, holding it at arms length, carried it toward the house.

She left it by the back steps while she got scissors from the kitchen, then cut it open. A metal box showed through the slit in the plastic. Julie gingerly stuck her hand inside and lifted it out.

Then she pulled off her gloves and pressed the catch with trembling fingers. The lid popped open and she nearly dropped the box in her surprise. Inside was a small manila envelope, just the size to hold a safety deposit box key.

Clumsily with anticipation, she tore it open. Pulled out a thin piece of yellow note paper, folded once. She shook it. No key. But maybe the name of a bank was printed inside.

She unfolded it. Scanned it for a name. And found . . . another riddle. "God damn it, Wes."

Half a riddle is better than none, but two clues together will be much more fun. Live and let live, or settle old scores, whichever you choose, the choice will be yours.

PS. Get Cas to tell you the one about the chicken, the horse, and the Harley.

The paper fell from Julie's fingers and her mouth went dry. No doubt about it. Wes expected her to consult Cas. Which meant he knew Cas would still be here. And *that* meant he'd probably planned the whole thing.

"This is my legacy?" She was more confused than ever. What could the treasure have to do with settling old scores? And which old scores did he mean? The feud? Reynolds? Cas? The town?

Hell, she didn't care about old scores. She cared about the treasure and this clue didn't lead her any closer to it. Because she needed the other half of the riddle. Cas's half. She didn't want to need his half. She didn't want to need *him*. But it looked like this was one choice that wasn't hers.

Chapter 13

Cas looked up from his desk when the station door opened. He recognized the orange plaid hunting jacket and the hat with earflaps and his breath caught. Across the room, Edith's mouth opened as Julie pulled off the hat and rich auburn hair tumbled out. Cas stood up.

"I'd like to speak to the sheriff," Julie said.

Edith's look of astonishment changed into a smile. She pointed toward Cas's desk.

Julie turned around. The cold had chafed her cheeks and her hair curled around nearly translucent skin. And Cas thought. *You are the most beautiful woman I have ever seen.*

He glanced at Edith before saying, "What can I do for you?" sounding as close to a civil servant as he ever would. But he couldn't sustain it when Julie's eyes flashed and she stepped toward him.

"Ernestine is missing."

Cas blinked. "Ernestine?"

"My chicken," she said, leaning across the desk and looking exasperated, but very kissable.

Cas pulled his eyes from her mouth and managed to say, "Your chicken."

Julie let lose a huge sigh. Okay, she hadn't forgiven him for whatever had driven her off in the first place, but at least now he had an excuse to be near her. Her coop had been robbed after all. He'd have to go out and investigate, ask questions, finagle a way to get her into the Jacuzzi . . . .

"Are you listening? I can't find Ernestine."

"Uh, right," said Cas, sitting down and reaching for a pencil. "When was the last time you saw her?"

"Yesterday morning. And I counted heads when I put them back in the gazebo—coop. Everyone was there. And now she's gone." She raised her fist and Cas flinched.

She shook a handful of papers at him, then slapped them on the desk. "Wes doesn't have a printer and I left mine in New York. I had to do them by hand."

Reward was hand-printed across the top of each page, with a description of a Rhode Island Red and the offer of fifty dollars for information that led to her return.

"Do I need a permit to post them around town?"

Hell if he knew. He glanced over to Edith who had lost all interest in her magazine and was staring unashamedly at them.

She shook her blue perm. "This is Ex Falls. The only thing you need a permit for is hunting deer."

"Thank you," said Julie, flashing a smile at Edith over her shoulder. She began gathering up the papers.

Cas stood up. "Maybe I should take a look around."

"I already looked. She's gone."

"Oh, dear," said Edith from across the room. "I hope she wasn't stolen. Only the one hen?"

Hey, thought Cas. Who was the goddamn sheriff here? He should be asking the questions. But he couldn't seem to stop smiling.

Julie nodded.

"You're lucky," Edith continued. "We've had two coops robbed in the last three weeks. Near to seventy hens and roosters."

Julie turned back to Cas. "There's a ring of chicken thieves and you didn't warn me? Ugh." She nodded brusquely to Edith. "Thank *you* for the information." She crammed her hat back on her head and started for the door.

Cas jumped up and practically fell over his desk trying to snag his coat off the coat rack. "I'll help you put up the posters, then we'll take a look up at your place." He stuffed his arm in one sleeve while he tried to open the door for Julie. She opened it herself and took off down the street.

"Happy hunting," called Edith as Cas hurried after her.

"I can't believe you didn't tell me about the chicken thieves," Julie grumbled while she held the first paper up and Cas stapled it to a telephone pole.

"I didn't want to worry you." *And I didn't want you to be afraid to stay at Excelsior house.*

"Worry me?" said Julie, moving to the next telephone pole. "Hell, I scared them off the first time they tried, didn't I?"

"Yes," said Cas. He took a sheet of paper from her and stapled it to the pole. *And nearly shot me while you were doing it.* "Thieves don't usually strike a second time in the same place."

Julie stopped in the middle of the sidewalk and stared at him. "That is so much bullshit. You know, you should really stick to banking."

"Boats," said Cas. "I build boats."

He thought her expression softened—for a millisecond—before she let go again.

"Then go build boats. I don't understand why you'd want to be sheriff anyway. Jeez." She stalked off across the street and Cas had to trot to catch up to her.

"I don't want to be the sheriff. I told you. I didn't have a choice."

Julie rounded on him. "Of course you did. People always have a choice. It's what they choose that counts." She lifted another poster to be stapled.

His free hand closed over hers, crumpling the paper. "Julie. What are you mad about?"

She pulled her hand away and lowered her eyes. "I have to find Ernestine." She smoothed the paper against the next pole.

Cas leaned over her and stapled the top of the paper to the wood. "Tell me."

Julie slipped out from under his arm, and by the time Cas finished stapling the bottom, she was walking into Pliney's Hardware, Feed and Grain.

A bell tinkled over his head when Cas opened the door. Julie was at the counter and Dan Pliney was taping the last reward poster to his display case. Henry Goethe, Elton Dinwiddie and two other men were sitting at the woodstove, their eyes riveted on Julie's back, and Cas felt a surge of unwarranted jealousy.

"Gentlemen," he said, and four heads snapped in his direction.

"Julie here's lost a hen," said Dan.

"Damn, uh, pardon me, ma'am." Elton spit into the fire. "But damn, Cas. This has got to stop. You just gonna sit there until there's not a chicken left in the county?"

"Elton, that's not fair," said Dan. "Cas can't help it if he doesn't know jack shit, pardon, Julie, about law enforcement. He's a banker."

"Boats," said Cas. "I build boats."

"Well, we don't need a damn banker. We need a few real men with shotguns," said a third man, who Cas recognized as Arnold Baxter, Henley's father.

Cas sighed. "This—"

Julie overrode him. "This is a job for the local law enforcement. An investigation is in progress. If you'd like to help, keep your eyes open and report any suspicious activity to the sheriff. He's doing an excellent job. Thank you, Dan." She pushed her hat back onto her head, tipped her head toward the seated men, and walked out the door.

Cas forced himself not to run after her. He had just reached the door, when he heard Baxter's lowered voice. "Yeah, I bet he's doing an excellent job. On her, anyway."

Like father, like son, thought Cas. He looked to see if Julie had overheard, but she was already striding down the sidewalk toward the hotel. He dismissed both Baxters from his mind and hurried after her.

"I'm doing an excellent job?"

"You're doing the best you can," she said and kept walking.

"Now where are you going?"

"To the hotel. I want to talk to your sister."

"Christine doesn't know anything about chickens."

"Your other sister."

"Mel? Why?"

She turned on him at the entrance. "Because she lives at Reynolds Place and I thought she could look for Ernestine in case she somehow got over the wall."

"I'll look for you."

Julie sighed. "Cas. I appreciate your concern, but you have a whole town to look after. Ernestine is not your problem. And Reynolds would have a fit if he found out what you were doing."

"And you think he won't have a fit if Mel looks?"

"I don't think Mel will really care."

"And you think I would."

Julie didn't answer but opened the door and went inside.

Christine hurried toward them, smiling. "Lunch?" she said, almost squeaking the words.

"Thanks," said Julie, "but I was hoping to talk to Mel."

"Oh. She's still at school."

Funny, thought Julie, she could have sworn she saw a black spiked head more than once while she and Cas were putting up signs.

"When will she be in?"

"Around three-thirty, give or take a few minutes." Christine sighed. "With Mel you never know."

"Mind if I come back then?"

Christine shook her head, glancing at Cas. "Of course not. Would you like something? Coffee, tea? It's getting cold out there."

"Thanks, but I have errands to do. I'll see you later." Julie nodded to Christine then turned and walked past Cas as if he'd suddenly disappeared. He shrugged at his sister and followed Julie out.

"Now, where are you going?"

"To the library."

"Why? You're out of posters, and hardly anyone goes there anyway."

"Because," she said patiently. "I don't have access to the internet at Wes's. I need to check my e-mail."

"I have a computer with internet access."

"I'm sure the library does, too."

"Theirs is ancient. Mine's new."

"Do they have internet access?"

"Dial up. I have cable."

Julie paused on the sidewalk. "Ex Falls has cable? Wonders of wonders." She started walking again.

"I'll show you."

Julie sighed. "Dial-up is fine."

"Damn it. Julie. Are you going to tell me what's wrong? Was it something I did? I may be dense but I thought—"

She raised an eyebrow and kept walking. He walked beside her, wondering what that meant.

She stopped at the steps of the library and said without looking at him, "Do you realize that the whole damn town is watching you follow me around? It was one thing when we had posters to put up. But the last one was gone two stops ago. You're making a spectacle of yourself."

"You know, Julie," said Cas, speaking loud enough for her and half of Main Street to hear. "You sound just like a Reynolds instead of an Excelsior." Then without waiting to see her reaction, he turned on his heel and strode off down the street.

Julie's mouth fell open as she watched Cas march away. Okay, so maybe she'd been a little harsh. He'd only been trying to help. Well, too bad. It was a day late . . . fifteen years late. She started up the steps. The paint was peeling on the old Memorial Library. The events case hung at an uneven angle, the protective glass was cracked and had been repaired with a piece of duct tape. Behind it, there was only one announcement: a poster for the Candy Apple Dance that weekend.

Julie pushed the door; it rattled but didn't open. She depressed the lever and pushed again. Then she saw the sign taped to the inside of the glass pane.

Mon, Wed, Fri, 10:00-2:00. Damn. It was closed. She whirled around and saw Cas standing at the corner.

"I get off at five," he called. Then he turned and took off down the street.

Julie frowned at him. The jerk. He knew the library was closed. And he'd strung her along. *Arrgh*, she thought. That was just like him. Always talking her into doing stuff. Getting them into trouble. Taking them on flights of fancy that ended in disaster. Cas Reynolds, protégé to the great scamp of life, Wes Excelsior. Shit, how had things gone so wrong?

Julie waited until he was out of sight, then slowly returned to her car, which was parked much too close to the police station. She crept along the sidewalk, feeling like a felon instead of a distinguished citizen.

Right. Well, if Marian Reynolds could play lady of the manor, so could Julie Excelsior. It was time to stop skulking around like she didn't belong here. She did. This was her town. She lifted her chin, but that was about all she could manage. It would take a while before she could feel anything but embarrassment when it came to Ex Falls. But it would happen. She *was* the lady of the manor. Even though the manor had seen better days. It might see better days again.

Not by you, she reminded herself. *Sell and Bail. That's our motto.* But bailing made her think of boats and boats made her think of Cas and she got a little rush because now she *had* to go to his house, because she *had* to retrieve her e-mail. And she might get another peek at his riddle. Maybe even get another peek at him.

It sounded so mercenary. But she knew better than to invest herself in Cas, because she knew where that led. And this time she had no one to drive her to Yonkers.

She climbed into the VW and jacked up the heat. Winter had

set in. Soon it would start snowing and she could be trapped here for weeks, months. But then so would Cas.

Don't think it. She backed out of her spot and drove to the end of town to make a U-turn back toward Highland Avenue. She found herself turning into the Good Shepherd Church parking lot instead.

The church sat slightly higher than the rest of the town. Its old cemetery was enclosed in a wrought iron fence and sloped down toward the river. She hadn't planned to come here; she wanted to remember Wes alive, not lying in the rocky ground.

But she parked and got out of the car, opened the sagging gate, and stepped into the graveyard. A gust of wind rattled the trees overhead. She buttoned up her coat and began to pick her way through the headstones. Each family had its separate little plot except for the two big families and they had big plots, side by side, a little higher than the others, so they could rest in death just as they had lived in life. Both plots were equally grand, and each had a granite mausoleum as well as graves, all of which were now covered with moss and streaked from rain and snow.

She stopped by the mound of freshly dug soil. There was no marker. And she wondered if she was supposed to have ordered it. Of course she was. Who else would do it? She was family.

A dogwood sapling had been planted at the head of the grave. Someone had placed a bouquet of purple violets on the dirt, tied with a ribbon and anchored by a jagged piece of rock. Stuck inside the ribbon was an orange lollipop. Julie stepped back, shocked.

Hell, everybody must know about Wes's penchant for orange. She pushed away the stab of jealousy that the sight had unleashed. They were the only tributes at the grave, and Wes deserved more. He deserved for his niece to have thought to send flowers or visit sooner, but she hadn't been notified of the funeral. No one had even called her to let her know that he was ill.

Not even Wes, though he intended to. Why else have an addressed envelope and a challenge for her to come home?

She dropped to her knees. "Wes," she began. Cleared her throat. "Uncle Wes? It's Julie. I came back like you wanted." And she had to stop because emotion clogged her throat and her eyes were bleary with tears, and she felt sad and deserted and stupid for caring. She took a slow breath. The air shuddered into her lungs and out again. "What do you want me to do? Is it about the treasure? Is it for me or am I supposed to share it with Cas? What is it? I'm out of practice and your clues are too hard."

She dashed tears off her cheeks. "I've lost Ernestine. I don't think it was my fault, but she's gone. Someone's been breaking into chicken houses—coops—I almost caught them the first night I was here." She sighed. "But I didn't. Some police officer, huh.

"Then Cas came. He's the sheriff, but I guess you know that. Or at least knew that before you—before you—" She lifted her hand toward the grave. "Before this. I know you left him a riddle, too. Is it a contest like we used to have? To see who could figure it out first?" She laughed, choked it back before she gave way to blubbering.

"I usually won, didn't I? Cas said it was because I had a devious mind. But I didn't. I'm just a good detective. Well, I was a good detective. That's what I did with my talent. Became a cop. I was going to help people. But things got all screwed up." She swallowed.

Stop whining. Julie flinched because that was not her thought, but Wes's.

"You're right, I don't know what came over me. I'm pretty tough. Like you said I should be. But I sure wish you were here. You'd like Smitty. Bill and Hillary ride on his back. And— oh, shit."

She rubbed her eyes with the heels of both hands. Heard the rustle of leaves and a shiver ran up the back of her neck. She turned around. Swore she saw a black head disappear behind the fence. But that was impossible. Mel was in school, maybe. She turned back to Wes's grave.

"Don't worry. I'll find Ernestine. And I'll find the treasure and I'll make my choice, whatever it's going to be. I have to go now, but I'll come back. I love you." She turned away and stumbled over the edge of a marker that had been uprooted by a tree root. It was old and the chiseled dates were barely readable. Josiah Excelsior. 1822-1884. She turned away, thinking of Scrooge and the Ghost of Christmas yet to come. And wondered if someday there would be a place here for her.

She turned back to Wes's grave. "There's one more thing. I cheated. I found Cas's half of the riddle and I tried to read it. I know I shouldn't have, but Cas didn't tell me about it. Is he trying to beat me to the treasure? Why doesn't he trust me?" She waited, but no response came. "I know. Use my brain."

She stepped away, then ran back to the parking lot. At the gate, she stopped and looked back across the garden of granite and marble, and in the distance, the river where once barges carried rifles from the factory to the New York militia. And later woolens from the converted mill. And beyond that, the mill itself, and the cottages, looking like a set for a model train. And she thought, *One day I'll have to go there, too.*

Quietly, she closed the gate, and with a brief look around to make sure she was alone, got into the car.

She was driving along Main Street, when she saw Melanie, backpack dragging along the pavement. She slowed down and leaned over to unroll the passenger window. "Hi," she said, keeping one eye on the street and one eye on the young Goth.

In spite of the cold, Melanie was only wearing a tight black T-shirt and jeans with a length of chain around her waist. She shifted her backpack to her other hand and kept walking.

"Can't you stop for a minute? I have a favor to ask."

Melanie didn't slow down.

"About Ernestine, the chicken."

At last she stopped and Julie stepped on the brake. There was a skull and crossbones hanging from the ring in her nose, and Julie could imagine how much grief she must give her parents and how much they must give her. But she had to give the girl credit. To choose to be that different in a town like Ex Falls took a lot of guts or a lot of anger. Julie guessed Melanie had a lot of both. And Julie knew just how she felt.

"What about her—the chicken."

"She's disappeared. I've looked everywhere. I even put up signs around town. I didn't know there had been chicken thefts or I would have kept a more careful watch."

"I thought you were going to sell her," said Melanie in a rigid monotone, and Julie thought, *Lighten up, kid. We're on the same side.* "So what do you care if she's gone? You wouldn't get that much for her. She lays lou—" Melanie started walking again.

Julie threw the car into first and followed her. She had to stop short when Melanie stepped in front of the car and began to cross the street. When she reached the opposite sidewalk, Julie called out, "She does lay lousy eggs, but I like her and I don't want anything to hurt her."

This time, Melanie turned and looked at Julie, so long and hard, that Julie began to get spooked. Finally Melanie said, "You're weird."

"Yeah, well. That makes two of us," said Julie. "And that being the case, I thought maybe you could just look around your property for a wayward hen. Just in case she managed to get over the wall."

Melanie shrugged. "I guess." She opened the door to the hotel.

"Thanks. I appreciate it. I'll write down Wes's number." Julie reached into her bag for a pencil and paper.

"I know it." Mel stepped over the threshold and hesitated, "Are you going to the dance tomorrow night?"

Julie gave her a look. "What do you think?"

"I think you should."

"Well, I'm not, how about you?"

"What do you think?"

Julie smiled. "I think you should definitely go." She was almost positive she saw a quirk of Melanie's lips before she closed the door.

Chapter 14

It was after eight when Julie drove up to Cas's cottage and parked between the old green truck and the police car. She tried to convince herself that she was here to check her e-mail and get another look at his clue. But what she really wanted was Cas. Feel his warmth and his strength and every tantalizing inch of him. And she knew she was a fool for wanting him.

She was about to head toward the house, when she heard the sound of drilling coming from the corrugated outbuilding. She walked over to it. A serious padlock hung from the hasp on the door, but it was unlocked, so she pushed the door open and peered inside.

The interior was warm and brightly lit. In the center of the long, narrow room, a boat rested, hull side up, on giant sawhorses. She stepped all the way in and closed the door quietly behind her.

The boat was at least fifteen feet long and nearly as wide as the room. Thin wooden strips overlapped each other lengthwise down the hull. A work table ran along one side of the room and what she could see of the other was filled with tools. The air smelled of cedar and machine oil.

The drilling stopped and the sound of sanding came from the far end of the room, behind the hull.

She eased along the space between the boat and the work

table. "Cas?" she called out softly, not wanting to break the sense of peace that permeated the room.

"Yeah?" Cas's head appeared over the top of the boat, consternation on his face. Consternation that quickly became something else.

Taken off guard by the sudden heat in his eyes, Julie turned away and her gaze fell on a large sheet of white paper rolled out on the work table. Julie leaned over for a closer look.

Cas appeared at her side and whisked it off the table. Turning his back to her, he rolled it up, drew a rubber band around it and tossed it onto a shelf above the table.

He was wearing jeans and a blue plaid shirt and he looked like Mr. Mountain Man instead of clueless sheriff or wimpy banker.

"I didn't mean to interrupt," she said and made a pretense of backing toward the door. But she was mesmerized by the sight of him; dark cowlick sticking up while another lock fell over his forehead, his throat showing at the opening of his shirt. And she wanted to touch him. "Sorry."

He took her hand and pulled her into him. They fit perfectly together. And though Julie knew it was an illusion, it felt so good and right that it took a few seconds for her to summon the strength to move away.

"I came to use your computer."

Cas flashed her a grin and slipped his hands around her waist.

"You don't give up, do you?" said Julie, giving in to his nearness.

He tightened his grip. "Not any more." And he kissed her.

Julie's eyes closed even as she willed them not to. But hell, it was only foreplay, and it felt good. *And it will lead to trouble.* She pulled away. Cas's mouth shifted to her jaw. His hands pulled at her coat, opening the collar, and he kissed his way down her neck to her sweater. Then suddenly he stepped back and frowned at her.

"You make me insane," he said in a strained whisper.

Join the club, thought Julie and wondered how cold the concrete floor was. She shook herself. "My e-mails?"

"Right, better idea." Cas took her hand and led her toward the door. He stopped to fiddle with some dials, then turned out the lights. Outside, he clicked the padlock shut and shivered.

"Leave your jacket inside?" asked Julie, fighting a smile. He only had sex on his mind. Which was not good. But since she only had sex on her mind at the moment, she could hardly complain.

E-mails, she reminded herself as Cas began to pull her toward the house. She was in dangerous waters, a recurring theme when in Cas's presence. Because she knew that she would take more than just sex if he offered. And that wasn't good.

Inside the door, he turned her around and began to unbutton her coat. She placed her hands over his and thought, *these are not banker's hands, these are strong, capable hands*.

She finished the buttons herself, dropped her coat over one of the hooks that were arranged in a row just inside the door.

"Where's your computer?" she asked, as she pulled off her shoes and looked around like she didn't know the room by heart already.

"Over here."

She followed him past the drafting table to the desk. He motioned her into a swivel chair and then leaned over her to boot up the computer.

His shirt was cold as his arm brushed her shoulder, but she could feel his heat through the fabric. She had to force herself not to lay her cheek against his arm. She sat rigidly in the chair, both feet on the floor, eyes on the monitor, until the screen lit up and rows of icons appeared on a blue-and-white swirl of sea spray.

Water again. She smiled in spite of herself, remembering the two of them rolling on the kitchen floor, the open pipe sending geysers of water over them, slicking their skin.

He leaned farther over her to move the mouse to the internet icon. Her gut twisted and heat spread out through her thighs and she thought, *you're doing that on purpose.*

The screen changed again and she was looking at the Netscape home page.

"I'll make coffee," Cas said and moved away.

The air seemed suddenly cold and Julie gritted her teeth. *No. No. No. Think e-mails.* And find that clue. She ran her hands around the edge of the blotter. The paper was gone. She glanced over her shoulder to make sure Cas was making coffee and looked more thoroughly. Definitely gone. Had he become suspicious? Hidden it so she wouldn't be tempted again?

Welcome to AOL appeared on the screen. She typed in her screen name and password.

She had mail. But there wasn't much. Several pieces of spam that had sneaked through her screen and several from friends wondering where she was. She read and deleted until she came to the last message. One from Harriet Andrews from the bomb squad.

Julie clicked it open.

How's it going? Where are you? I've called you a couple of times, but there was no answer. Grimwald said you resigned. Is that true? You were smart if you did. Got a new job? Sitting on a tropical island, drinking pina coladas with some hunky surfer? Let me know.

Julie heard Cas move away from the stove. She moved closer to the computer, shielding the screen with her body.

The shit has really hit. Seems there's more than one AH in the department. But the primo one, Donald, is back at work. Can you believe it? Ratted on the others, so they gave him a desk job. He's badmouthing you to anyone who'll listen. Says you were asked to leave.

"What?" exclaimed Julie.

"Did you say something?"

Julie's head snapped in the direction of the voice.

Cas stood at the fireplace, holding a log and looking at her with concern. "Bad news?"

"No." Julie went back to reading.

"Says you took the bribes and he took the fall. BS. BS. BS. Everyone knows you blew the whistle on him, but they listen anyway, because it's easier than arguing. Grimwald sent around a memo saying you had resigned but were not under suspicion. Don't worry about any of this BS. The only thing you're guilty of is bad luck in partners. You're a heroine among the honest cops, so don't give it another thought. Just wanted you to know. Stay in touch. HA

Julie clicked reply.

That fucking bastard. I can't believe him. If there's any fallout let me know ASAP. I don't want my name associated with that piece of crud. I'm back in my home town. I've inherited a house and stuff. I'll let you know what I'm going to do next. And keep me informed!!! JE

She pressed send just as Cas came over and placed a mug of hot coffee at her elbow.

"No need to hurry," he said. He glanced at the screen. She logged off.

"I'm done," she said, her voice strained with suppressed rage. "I better be going."

"Come over by the fire and drink your coffee first. I could make some dinner. Have you eaten?"

"Thanks, but—"

"Or we could go out. There's a decent restaurant over in Henryville. And we don't even have to dress up."

She couldn't. If they had dinner, she would have to make conversation and she would inevitably tell him about being a cop and that would really turn him off. And they'd be stuck over dessert without anything to talk about. And she wasn't sure if he would applaud her blowing the whistle on a fellow officer. But if they did talk, he might tell her about his half of the riddle. Oh hell, it was just too complicated.

"Thanks, but I can't."

Cas put his coffee mug down next to hers and wrapped his fingers around her arm. He lifted her out of the chair. "Do you know how many times you've said, 'I can't,' in the last few days? Are you having second thoughts about what's happening between us?" He smiled, sort of, but it was that hurt kind of smile that made Julie want to hug him. And she thought, *he's manipulating me so he'll get laid tonight.* But even as she thought it, she knew that wasn't the truth. Cas was after something more and she wasn't sure if it was her or her riddle.

He stepped closer. "We'll just talk, okay? I know everything has been fast and furious." He smiled sheepishly. "Something just comes over me when I'm near you."

Yeah, your hormones, thought Julie as her determination wavered beneath his gaze.

The fire was crackling. The coffee smelled wonderful. And so did Cas, now that she thought about it. A combination of skin, man, smoke and something definitely yummy.

If they just made love—had sex, she amended—just a quickie in front of the fireplace, he might fall asleep and she could search for his clue. And then she'd leave.

Cas's hand shifted from her arm to her back and warmth spread across her. He led her to the fireplace and settled her on a bearskin rug in front of the hearth, then went off to retrieve their coffee mugs.

"Is this rug real?" she asked as he came back and handed her one of the mugs.

He laughed. "No. Just one of We—it came with the house."

"Oh," said Julie, wondering if he'd been about to say "Wes" or "we." Was there a "we" in Cas's life? He hadn't mentioned being involved with anyone. Of course, one didn't usually mention such things when they were busy seducing someone else. He was definitely going solo here. Maybe someone back in Rhode Island?

Julie sipped her coffee and stared into the fire.

Cas sat down beside her.

"Are you going to stay in Ex Falls?" she asked. She thought she saw a faint blush spread across his cheeks, but it was probably just a reflection from the fire.

"Actually I have a place picked out in a little town over on the coast. A marine and boat supply store that's for sale." He fell silent, then said, "You should see it. Ex Falls spiffed up and nestled in a natural cove. There are still families who make their living fishing."

Julie smiled. "It sounds nice."

"It's more than nice," said Cas, looking into the fire, the flames mirrored in his eyes. "Everything is vibrant with life there. The people are tanned and healthy all year round. The water is as blue as the sky. Sometimes it's hard to tell where one ends and the other begins. In the winter, the winds blow in and the waves turn to steel gray and the air is bracing, so heavy with salt, that it can cleanse your soul.

"I keep my catamaran docked at the marina there. I can be on the open sea in less than ten minutes. There's nothing more exhilarating than riding the swells, the wind tearing at the sails."

He stopped, half-embarrassed. "No banker's hours, no suits, no people going bankrupt with me helping them down the road to disaster."

"You always said one day you'd sail away."

"Did I?"

"Yeah. I used to kid you about it, but Wes would say, in that pseudo-stern voice he had," she lowered her voice and said gruffly, " 'Leave the boy alone. If he wants to sail away, he will.' " She returned to her normal voice. "And you did. For a while, anyway."

"Are you trying to get rid of me?" He smiled, making it a joke, but his eyes were serious.

She looked away. *Tell me about your riddle.*

But Cas only gazed into the fire.

Julie rubbed the back of her neck as tension tied her body into knots of disappointment, frustration, and several other emotions she'd rather not name.

Cas put his mug on the hearth and moved her hand away. Gently, he began to rub her neck. His fingers moved in small circles up her spine and she let her head fall forwards. It felt really good.

He shifted to her shoulder and his other hand joined the first, pulling the muscles away from the bone and stroking them into relaxation.

Julie sighed contentedly. "I know you're only trying to butter me up."

"That's right." Cas shifted so that he was sitting behind her. His hand moved between her shoulder blades, and his lips settled on the muscles he'd just left.

Okay, thought Julie, succumbing to pleasure. *I'll let him work his way down, we'll have terrifyingly wonderful sex, then I'll tell him I have to feed Smitty. And I won't have to lie. And he won't have to lie. And we'll be right back where we started. Strangers.*

Cas unfolded his knees and stretched his legs to either side of her. His hands released her long enough to find the ribbing of her sweater and lift it up, then his fingertips pressed into the bare skin of her back, sending sparks up her spine until she figured her hair must have been standing on end.

She exhaled and taking this for acceptance, Cas moved to her hip bones and pulled her into him. Then he slid his hands to her abdomen, circling her ribs with a gentle massaging motion, the same motion that she felt as he pulsed his erection against the small of her back.

Julie lay back against him, let her head rest against his collar bone and when his hands moved from her ribs to her breasts, she arched up to meet him. He unclasped her bra, pushed the pieces of fabric aside, and replaced them with his palms.

She couldn't seem to get enough of him, ever. Especially knowing that it all must end sooner or later. And probably sooner. His thumbs rubbed over her nipples . . . nipples that had been in a permanent state of arousal since she first saw him. This was crazy. It was dangerous. And she wanted more.

"That really feels good," she said and turned off her mind

and gave in to the pleasure, now for the moment. His hands slipped from her breasts and he wrapped his arms around her waist, while he nuzzled the hair away from her neck and he kissed his way to her ear. He bit the lobe, then his tongue invaded her ear, hot, moist, and so erotic that she thought she would come just from the pressure of her jeans between her legs.

She rubbed her hands down his thighs. Made him jump when she squeezed the ticklish place above his knees. Drew her fingernails up the denim to the crease of his hips. Edged her hips away from him so that her hands could slide between them and settle on the fullness in his jeans. Played the denim there until he ground against her.

He slipped his hands down the front of her jeans and she sucked in her stomach to make more room. His chest heaved against her back while his fingers teased her. Then he pulled out his hands, flipped open her jeans, and pulled the zipper down, each action making her rock in anticipation. His fingers dipped beneath the tiny triangle of thong, slid through her slick crease, until he found the center. Julie gulped back a moan.

"On your knees," whispered Cas, the words husky. He nudged her forward with his crotch and pulled her up, rising with her, his hands still cupping her, and the pressure became almost unbearable.

His lips moved to her shoulder. He sucked the skin there, while he unfastened his jeans and pushed them down. Then he pulled hers down until they pooled at her knees. She shifted so that he could tug them the rest of the way down her legs. He tossed them aside, pulled her sweater over her head, and she let her bra slide off her arms to the floor.

His hands explored her neck, caressed her arms, then clasped her hands and held them to her sides, while he licked his way down her back. When she settled back against him, he pulled her up again. He licked down to her tail bone, then across her butt and bit one cheek. It sent a shiver through her. She tried to move her hands, but he held her wrists tight as he trailed a wet line to the other side and bit again.

"Is this a version of cow—" She caught her breath as she felt his cock press against the cleft of her butt, then move its way up her back, warm, hard and silky smooth. He made deep rumbling purrs as he worked himself up and down her backside.

He took her hands and pushed them between her legs. Together they brought her close to climax, while his body pressed against her back, and Julie thought, *This is how it should be*, and gave into whatever was going to happen.

They rocked on their knees, one body, one rhythm, Julie caught between wanting to keep the fragile balance of extended pleasure and desiring to shoot off though the void. Then Cas moved away and she thought, *Not yet*. But his hands slipped between her legs from behind until they met hers in front. He pushed a finger into her, and she lifted her butt to draw him farther inside her.

But his finger pulled out and he spread her cheeks. An instant later, he pushed his cock between her legs. The force of it knocked her off balance and she fell forward onto her hands. Another thrust and he was inside her, his hands beside hers, his chest hot on her back. He withdrew just enough not to slip out and she lifted her butt higher.

He thrust again. "More." The word exploded from him and she lowered herself to her elbows while he straightened up and held her hips to his as he pushed into her again.

She met him push for push, only wishing she could see him. She wanted to see his face when he came, to know that she'd brought him the same kind of pleasure he was bringing her. His hands kneaded her butt as he drove his cock deeper inside her, then his hands moved around to her stomach and downward, until his fingers stretched between her legs. Each time he thrust from behind, his fingers slid back to meet him.

Julie lost track of everything but the sensation spiraling inside her. Winding tighter until she couldn't stand it, and she gave up trying to control the pace. She arched her back and thrust back until lights exploded before her eyes and waves rolled over her, one after the other, so fast and strong that she couldn't catch her breath. She contracted around the thick length of Cas's penis until he went still. She squeezed her thighs together; he cried out and pumped himself into her.

They collapsed onto the bear rug, Julie's back nestled against his front, the heat from the fire warming her face, breasts and knees, Cas warming the rest of her.

And that's when she realized that she hadn't heard him take out a condom.

"What the fuck?"

Cas flinched. "What?"

Julie rolled over to face him, looked down to where a naked penis lay against his thigh. "Did we forget a little something?"

Cas looked at her in that bland self-satisfied look that men got after coming their brains out. His eyebrows knit. "I don't . . . think so."

"Condom?"

"Oh. Oh?" He pushed up to one elbow and ran the tip of his forefinger down her arm, lifting the hairs as he passed and sending gooseflesh across her body. He was too good for safety. Her safety. The thought brought her back to the point.

"I'm safe," said Cas, still basking in postcoital glow.

"Well, that's nice to know. But you don't know that I am."

His eyes widened and she could practically hear his balls shriveling.

"Are you?"

"As it happens, yes. But you didn't know that." Her butt was too close to the fire, in more ways than one. She shifted away from the heat and right into Cas.

He readjusted his arms around her and sighed. "That's nice."

"Damn it, Cas, this is serious."

"I know. It was also stupid, but I just, um, just . . ."

"Felt like living dangerously?"

Cas let go; frowned at her. "No. I always play it safe, don't I? I just wanted . . . something else. It's hard to explain." He lay back down and attempted to pull her close to him. "Can't we just enjoy this and be glad we have—whatever it is we have."

He was right. And she knew even before she asked him, that he would never jeopardize her safety. But that didn't explain why he didn't think to protect himself. He didn't know anything about her. She could be a prostitute for all he knew. Had actually played the part more times than she could count.

She smiled as her sense of humor pushed her exasperation aside. That would be a story that would get his attention. Now that she thought about it, she had plenty of things to tell him about her life for the last fifteen years. She had posed as hookers, drug addicts, unsuspecting women in subways, and salesclerks in department stores to bodegas. That should keep them busy through dinner and a couple of drinks.

And he'd never have to know that she became a cop, only to quit because of someone else's perfidy. The victim again.

"All right," she said.

Cas opened his eyes. "All right, what?"

"All right. We can enjoy this and you can cook dinner." She rolled to her back and stretched, and was amused to see Cas's cock start to respond. "What shall it be this time? Cowboys? Pirates?"

Cas rolled on top of her. "Let's play Julie and Cas." And he stopped any argument she might have by plunging his tongue into her mouth.

Much later, as they lay in each other's arms before the fire, Julie said, "Wes left me a riddle. Actually, a riddle and a half." She felt Cas tense. *Tell me now*, she thought. She waited, gave him one more chance. Ran her fingers up his thigh, tempting him.

He twitched. "He left me the other half."

She sighed with relief. "I'll show you mine if you show me yours," she said playfully. Then held her breath. She was just about to give up, when he said, "Okay."

Chapter 15

Julie pried one eye open when Ulysses let forth with his raucous crow the following morning. She didn't feel like getting out of bed and she didn't feel like waking up alone.

Smitty walked across her and slurped her face. Okay, not exactly alone, but as much as she loved Smitty, he wasn't Cas. And Cas was at home in his own bed. He hadn't asked her to stay, but he had told her his half of the riddle.

Bill answered in his tremolo treble and the morning's dueling cock-a-doodle-doos began in earnest.

"Ugh. Not fair." Julie pushed the covers back and sat up. "Someone should teach you guys to say, 'Good morning, sweetheart,' instead of arky-arky-ark."

Smitty yawned and shook his head.

"I know. They're roosters." And Cas was probably a grouch in the mornings anyway.

The heat was pumping since she'd forgotten to turn it down the night before, and the house was toasty. But even Wes's coat couldn't keep the wind from knifing through her as she and Smitty stepped outside.

The chickens were reluctant to leave the coop and Julie had to bodily remove Hillary from her nest, getting a nasty look and a peck on her finger for her efforts. She dropped the egg, earning further disgust from Hilary. Not one of the brood ventured past the fenced-in yard, not even Bill and Hillary, who had a standing date with Smitty.

Julie hurried through the feeding routine, then carried the three eggs she'd collected back to the kitchen steps, where she sat down, missing Ernestine and thinking about the fire in Cas's cottage the night before.

There wasn't much she could do about Ernie, but she could bring in some logs from the woodpile. Fires were nice, especially when they were the background for riotous, unbridled sex. And that was all it was. Sex. Really good sex, but just sex. And she'd better remember that. Because it was becoming very easy to forget.

Smitty came trotting up, his back empty of his two favorite chickens, and plopped on the ground at her feet.

"I'll just live blissfully in denial, Smitty," she said and leaned over to scratch him behind the ears. "It's the only way to come out of this with my, you know, my heart intact. Let's go inside."

She opened the door just as the telephone rang.

"Ernestine!" she cried and raced into the hall to snatch up the phone.

"Hi. It's Maude. I'm back. I came by yesterday, but you weren't there. How's everything?"

"Ernestine is missing. I think someone stole her."

"I saw the posters in town. I also heard you decked Cas at the Roadhouse, started a brawl, nearly broke Bo Whitaker's arm, and cleaned up after yourself. Nice work."

Julie sighed. "I didn't exactly."

"Also heard you followed Cas home afterwards."

"I was afraid he might have a concussion."

"Uh-huh. I'm calling to ask you to dinner tonight. We'll eat around six. The dance starts at seven, so that'll make us fashionably late."

"What?"

"The Candy Apple Dance. Wear something slinky. I am."

"I'm not going to the dance."

"Of course you are."

"No."

"Julie. You're an Excelsior. It's your duty to put in an appearance. Wes would expect you to claim your place in the community."

"He would?"

"Damn right he would. And he'll haunt me if I don't see that you get there. Not that I'd mind it so much if he did."

Julie felt a stab of contrition. She'd been so caught up in her own problems, her own needs, that she hadn't given much concern toward Maude's, who was Wes's friend and companion. Or even for Cas's, who had been with Wes when he died.

"Okay. I don't know about slinky, but I'll find something."

"Yeah, you will. See you at six. Don't bring anything. I've got plenty."

"But what about Ernestine?"

"Be patient." Julie heard the click of Maude's phone and looked at the receiver. Patient? How could she be patient when Ernestine might be someone's dinner? And now this stupid dance. She could hardly wait to see their faces when the prodigal Excelsior walked in. But not in anything slinky, something sedate. Except that she didn't own anything sedate.

Julie hung up the phone and wandered back to the parlor. This inheritance was turning into more than she bargained for. What happened to *we're so sorry for your loss and here's the check?* Maybe this was a trial by fire kind of thing. A quest. Go through all the hazards; raise chickens, meet Cas again, go to the dance for everyone to gape and speculate.

If I complete my tasks, will I get the treasure? Then I can go about finding a life. One that I won't run from when things get rough.

And Cas would go back to building boats without her.

It was after six when Julie drove up to Maude's house. Her chores had taken longer than usual due to the cold, the sluggishness of the chickens, Smitty's insistence that he shouldn't be left at home, and the fact that her knit dress had serious static cling.

She managed to get the chickens bedded down and Smitty pushed inside with a dog biscuit; there was nothing she could do about the dress but give the town a thrill.

Maude, wearing blue jeans and a checked wool shirt, was standing in the yard by her white-paneled truck. She was talking to someone sitting inside, and Julie got just a glimpse of black spiked hair before the truck backed up and went roaring down the drive.

"Was that Melanie Reynolds?" she asked as she got out of the car and checked the ground for anything that wouldn't look good on the bottom of three-inch heels.

"Yep. Wanted to borrow my truck. She does that sometimes. Reynolds won't buy her a car until she stops with the witch routine, and she won't stop. She usually gets around on that old moped."

Maude pointed to an old, rusted bike leaning against the house. And Julie thought about the motorcycle tracks in her woods.

"Is she going to the dance?"

"Beats me. You never know with Melanie." Maude shook her head. "She really ought to get out of this town. She's trouble waiting to happen."

"I saw her at the hotel and asked if she was planning on going to college. She said no."

"I'm not surprised," said Maude. "She skips too much school to keep her grades up. And the Reynoldses are broke. They can't afford to send her. But we pretend that we don't know."

"Jeez," said Julie. "I thought they were rich."

"They think so, too. Unfortunately it's all in their past, but still in their minds." Maude shook her head and gestured toward the white frame house. "Come on in."

"I hope you're not planning to wear that to the dance," said

Julie as she followed her inside. "Because that would make me seriously overdressed."

"Nope, but I didn't want to get my outfit wrinkled." Maude waggled her eyebrows. "Plus it's a little drafty for feeding chickens."

"I can hardly wait." Julie shrugged off her coat, a black wool Albert Nipon she'd bought off a clearance rack, and handed it to Maude.

Maude whistled. "Now that's a dress."

Julie looked down at the straight black sheath. It clung to her hips and thighs and she succumbed to second thoughts about it being Candy Apple appropriate. "Too much?"

Maude hung up her coat and said, "Fabulous." She ushered Julie through an archway and into a large living room. Julie had imagined Maude's house filled with overstuffed, comfy chairs, needlepoint samplers, and braided rugs, everything smelling slightly of chickens. But Maude's living room was chrome and leather with a berber carpet and recessed lighting. A stainless steel wet bar was set up in one corner and an open bottle of wine stood on the top between two crystal glasses.

"Would you like a cocktail or wine?"

"Wine's fine," said Julie. It wouldn't do to get to the dance already plotzed.

Maude stepped behind the bar, whose height concealed everything but her head and shoulders. She grinned and Julie thought of the Cheshire cat gradually disappearing, except for his smile.

"Wine's red and French. Wes was a stickler for proper vintages and we're having . . . veal. Thought I was going to say chicken, didn't you?"

"I'm glad you didn't."

"I eat chicken. And you will, too, once you get over thinking of them as part of the family. That's what you're doing, right?"

Julie frowned at her. "God, you're right. How weird is that?"

"Not weird at all," said Maude. "It happens. For a while, you'd just as soon eat old Aunt Ida as one of your brood, but you have to, unless you're planning on setting up a little chicken cemetery in the back yard." She handed Julie a glass and lifted hers in a toast. "That would really get Reynolds's blood pressure up. And Marian would call out the bad taste brigade. All two of them."

"I've been meaning to talk to you about the chickens." Julie sipped her wine. It was full bodied and dry.

"Well, have a seat and shoot. We have a few minutes before dinner's ready." Maude hoisted herself onto the overlarge sofa, and stuck a pillow behind her back. "Wes's idea. The man couldn't be stopped once he got started. You'd think Martha Stewart had commissioned him to take her place while she was in the slammer. Would have redone my whole house, if I hadn't threatened to leave town. And poor Ca—and your pink wallpaper."

"He did Cas's house, too?"

Maude widened her eyes. "Oops."

"It wasn't you. The bearskin rug gave him away."

"Saw that, did you?"

Julie blushed in spite of herself. "About the chickens."

"What about them?"

"I'll need to find them a home. If you're interested, you can have them. If you aren't, I guess I'll have to sell them, but I hate to think about breaking up the . . . the . . ."

"Family? Early days yet. Was that the timer going off?" Maude slid off the couch and bustled out of the room. Julie leaned back in her chair and thought about Wes choosing this huge furniture and she smiled. Because she understood. Maude did seem larger than life, even when you were standing next to her, looking down. And Cas needed some softness in his life. And she needed to be pampered. Julie's throat tightened. She breathed out slowly, refusing to give in to stupid regret.

"Ready," called Maude.

Julie followed her voice down the hall and into a dining room. An oval table was set with a white linen tablecloth. A vase of dried wildflowers adorned the center, and two place settings of white china were laid across from each other.

"Have a seat," said Maude as she placed a covered serving bowl on the table. "I meant to dress for dinner, but hell, I'll surprise you afterwards."

Julie was surprised all right. She nearly dropped her coffee cup when Maude reappeared from her bedroom, shrouded in veils of crimson chiffon. They trailed from her shoulders, were cinched in at the waist with a wide rhinestone belt, then flowed out again until ending at her calves, above red Mary Jane shoes. Maude twirled around and the pointed tips wisped about her legs.

"Wow," said Julie on an intake of breath.

Maude lifted her skirts and tapped her heels together. "There's no place like Ex Falls," she said. "Let's get a move on."

They took Julie's car and pulled up to the VFW Hall at exactly seven-thirty. The parking lot was crowded and a really bad dance band blared from inside. Julie tried to let Maude off at the entrance while she found a place to park, but Maude merely said, "And let you get away?" And stayed put.

They opened the door several minutes later and stopped in the hall to hang up their coats. Maude immediately headed for the entrance, but Julie hung back, suddenly wishing she were any place but here. She could feel sweat rolling down her back. Maude grabbed her by the arm and pushed her through the double doors just as the band broke into a tune that sounded something like "Feelings."

Julie froze in place and stared at the floor. Maude's grip tightened on her arm. "Think Audrey Hepburn in *My Fair Lady*," she said and began nodding greetings in all directions.

Right. Julie lifted her chin and got her first look at the dance hall. Red crepe paper garlands hung from the ceiling, festooned every doorway and window. Red cardboard apples were taped to the mint green walls, surrounded by more crepe paper. Several couples moved around the dance floor. A crowd stood around the refreshment table.

"Ain't it grand?" said Maude, and still gripping Julie by the arm, she swooped into the room, trailing flames of chiffon.

No one noticed them at first. But as they walked along the edge of the dance floor, heads began to turn their way and Julie felt her skirt begin to creep up her thighs. She surreptitiously tugged it down and got a shock that made her fingers tingle.

Each time Maude stopped to say hello to friends, Julie stopped too. She missed the first few introductions from concentrating on trying to breathe. Chills ran up and down her neck. She could feel everyone watching her.

"And you know Elton already from Pliney's," Maude said. "And this is May, his wife."

Julie jerked her attention back to the introductions.

May Dinwiddie was taller than her husband and twice his girth. "Julie Excelsior," she said, looking Julie up and down with barely concealed curiosity. "I wouldn't have recognized you. You've grown up."

Julie smiled and wished May wasn't staring quite so pointedly at her hemline, which she knew headed farther north each time she moved.

"Elton had his whole flock stolen a couple of weeks ago," said Maude.

"I heard," said Julie. "No leads?"

Elton slowly shook his head. "Goldurn thieves just walked in and took them out from under our noses. And Cas Reynolds doesn't have a clue. And won't accept any help. The boy's outta his league. Don't know what possessed him to take over for Hank Jessop."

"His sense of community, maybe?" said Julie and Maude widened her eyes at her.

"Actually," said Maude, "we can blame that one on Hank and Wes. They railroaded him so fast that he was swearing on the bible before he knew what he was doing."

Elton twirled a strand of hair that grew from the center of his bald spot. "Well, it was a dirty trick to play and the rest of us are gonna suffer for it."

May whacked him on the back. "Leave the boy alone. Nobody else was stepping forward to help out, and he don't even live here anymore. Count your blessings, Elton Dinwiddie."

"I'd rather be counting my chickens," said Elton.

"I'm sure they'll turn up," said Maude and led Julie away.

"Will they turn up?" asked Julie as Maude scuttled her across the floor, dodging the dancers who seemed to be doing some kind of Texas two-step, and toward another group of people standing at the other side of the dance floor.

"Think so. Hi, Emily. I want you to meet Julie Excelsior. Emily's the town librarian."

Julie and Emily shook hands.

"I came by yesterday, but you were closed," said Julie, trying to ignore Emily's impressive cleavage. Emily smiled coolly and began reciting the library hours until Maude interrupted to introduce Julie to the rest of the group.

She recognized some of the names; others were unfamiliar. But it was pretty obvious from the reactions she got that they all remembered her or at least had heard about her. And she had to force herself not to run screaming from the room.

Soon Maude was trundling her away again. "Your patrician air is beginning to slip."

"I feel like a sideshow freak," said Julie, but lifted her chin higher and smiled at the people they passed. Halfway down the room she put on the brakes. Cas was standing near the band, dressed in his uniform and talking to Christine and Ian and—

"It's Charles Reynolds," said Julie and dug in her heels, which did absolutely no good since Maude outweighed her and still had a death grip on her arm.

"Think of Wes and out-grand him. Hiya, Cas. Christine, Ian, Reynolds."

Christine and Ian both said hello. Cas flashed a smile that

broadcast to the farthest corner of the room and Julie could have kicked him. Reynolds's expression was just as clear, and just the opposite. It could have turned the dancers, or her, to salt.

Cas stepped toward her and kissed her cheek. "You look wonderful," he said under his breath.

"What are you doing?" she whispered as she watched Reynolds's eyes bug.

"You remember Julie Excelsior, don't you, Reynolds?" Maude purred the words.

Christine and Ian took the opportunity to slip off to the dance floor. Cas kept grinning like an idiot, and Julie didn't know which man she wanted to deck more.

"Hello, Mr. Reynolds," said Julie, trying to ignore Cas's proximity.

Maude frowned. And Julie recognized her mistake. Too deferential. She breathed out. "I met Christine and Melanie in town, but I haven't had the pleasure of seeing you and Mrs. Reynolds."

Maude gave her the slightest nod of approval. She'd manage just the right amount of hauteur. And she suddenly realized how much all that role-playing as un undercover detective might come in handy. She began to relax. But Cas was standing way too close and his father's eyes were shifting between the two of them so rapidly that watching them made her dizzy.

"Would you like to dance?" asked Cas.

"What?" Julie squeaked.

"Dance," he repeated, leaning into her.

"Aren't you on duty, son?"

"Great idea," said Maude. "I'll just stay here and talk to Reynolds." She slipped her arm in his.

"Jesus, Cas," said Julie, her smile frozen into place as he led her to the dance floor. "Are you nuts? You'll have the whole town talking."

"So? If I'm expected to dance with every unmarried woman in town, I may as well start with you."

Julie raised both eyebrows. "Thank you very much."

Cas grinned. "But I'm only going to *dance* with the others."

"Cas, stop it." Julie quickly looked around. She wasn't surprised to see the entire room watching them. Even the dancing couples were twisting their necks to get a better look.

Another spectacle. I'm doomed, thought Julie. Then she swore she could hear Wes's voice. *You are an Excelsior. You should be leading the dance.*

He was asking a lot. People were going to talk, to wonder, but as long as Reynolds didn't rush across the floor and drag Cas bodily out of the room, she could pull it off. And she was confident that Maude wouldn't let him anywhere near the dance floor.

Cas reached around her waist. She resisted as he pulled her close. "Julie," he said.

"Let's try to get through this without making a spectacle of ourselves," she said and felt him flinch. Well damn it, it was his own fault. She couldn't help it if he'd walked away from her all those years ago. Made her the object of gossip. She still didn't trust him, she realized with a jolt of sorrow. And she wanted to. She wanted things to be good between them. And they never could.

"What are you thinking?" he asked, lowering his head to hers.

"Nothing. It's just weird being back here."

"I won't let you down, Julie. I promise."

She pulled away to look at him and almost tripped. "Don't make promises you can't keep." Then she took a proper ballroom stance, looking past his shoulder and not at him, and they finished the dance in silence.

When the music stopped and they were walking back to where Maude and Reynolds waited, Julie saw Melanie enter the hall. She was dressed in black as usual. The only compromise she'd made for the dance was an extra length of chain around her hips and a black leather vest decorated with silver studs and foot-long leather fringe.

Reynolds must have seen her, too, because he strode away from Maude just as Cas and Julie returned.

"Melanie's here," said Maude. "Reynolds just went to say hello."

"Shit," said Cas and followed his father through the crowd.

"I saw her," said Julie when they were alone. "Full Goth glory. Is Reynolds going to cause a scene?"

"Not if Cas can get there first. How was your dance?"

"Okay."

"Hmmm," said Maude.

A tall man in a dark blue turtleneck took Maude away to dance and Julie stood staring at the dance floor so she wouldn't catch anyone's eye. Terrence and Tilda danced by, then seeing her, reversed their steps and danced back to her.

"Hi," said Tilda. "You remember Terrence." Tonight her hair was bright red, maybe in honor of the Candy Apple Dance, and Terrence was poured into a black suit, white shirt and necktie that looked like it was choking him. Terrence stretched his neck, reminding Julie of Smitty when he was trying to escape his leash.

Julie smiled at him in sympathy. "Of course I do. How are you?"

Tilda beamed up at Terrence and he beamed down at her. And Julie thought, *I like them.*

"Just hunky-dory," said Tilda, giving Terrence a squeeze. "Oh, shit."

Terrence and Julie turned to look where she was looking. Two men dressed in motorcycle jackets stood in the entrance. It didn't take much to recognize them as the dolts from the Roadhouse.

"Damnation," said Tilda. "They said they weren't coming. And they were already two sheets to the wind when they left the Roadhouse an hour ago."

"You want me to show them the door, honey?" said Terrence, his voice even deeper than usual.

Tilda shook her head. "It's open to the public. If they get rowdy, you can help Cas get rid of them."

Henley and Bo swaggered onto the dance floor, causing a pile-up, before couples began redirecting their steps around them.

Tilda began tapping her toe, not to the music, but in consternation. "No good. Either one of them. And up to no good if I know anything at all."

"I'll fix it for you, sugar," said Terrence.

"Thanks, smoochums, but I don't want you to mess up your new suit. Isn't he handsome?"

"Huh? Oh, yes," said Julie. She'd just seen Cas and Reynolds at the other side of the room, but no Melanie.

"Well, we're off to tear up the dance floor. See ya later." And they started off, Terrence pushing Tilda along, oblivious to the music or the steps, and both having the time of their lives.

Julie began to skirt the room, smiling at people but not stopping until she caught sight of Melanie's black spikes. She must have survived any diatribe by Reynolds because she was alone and still at the dance. *We're two of a kind,* thought Julie as she threaded her way toward the girl. *A couple of misfits.*

But before she reached Melanie, Julie saw her slip out a side door, followed by Henley and Bo. Up to no good was right. Julie picked up her pace.

She stepped through a door into a hallway that led to storerooms and bathrooms. Halfway down, she saw them. Melanie was standing between the two men. Henley had his arm around her shoulders and Melanie squirmed to free herself, while she called him every name Julie had ever heard and some she hadn't. Bo looked on and laughed. Julie began to run.

"Hey," she called.

Henley turned around. "Here's another one wants a good time." Julie got a whiff of whiskey as she stepped past Bo, grabbed Henley's wrist, and bent it downward at a right angle. The action brought him to his knees.

"Ow-w-w," he yelled and Julie clipped him with her high heel. He sprawled on his butt.

"Random," said Melanie and rubbed her shoulder.

"What's the big idea?" said Bo and grabbed for Julie. Julie stepped to the side and gave him a push. He fell over Henley just as Cas and Terrence reached them.

"Guess Julie's got it covered," rumbled Terrence; white teeth appeared in his beard and disappeared again. "I'll just show these bozos outside if that's okay with you, Sheriff."

"Fine," said Cas, not taking his eyes off Julie. "What happened?" When Julie didn't answer, he turned to Melanie. "You're not encouraging those two, are you?"

Melanie rolled her eyes.

"Cas."

"Stay out of this, Julie. Are you? Because those two are trouble."

Melanie sank into one hip. "Christ, you sound just like Reynolds."

"She wasn't encouraging them," said Julie. "They followed her out and accosted her."

Cas frowned at her. "So you came rushing to the rescue."

Julie blinked, unreasonably hurt by his sarcasm. "Us girls have to stick together."

"Did it ever occur to you that they might be dangerous? That you might want to call on the local law enforcement to take care of the situation? Or do you think you can do a better job?"

Melanie smacked him on the shoulder. "What the fuck's wrong with you? She was trying to help. And she did fine without you; brought Henley to his knees in a second, then kicked the shit out of him."

Julie winced. "I didn't really kick him."

"It was some weird judo move," said Melanie. "It was so uptown. So random." Her enthusiasm was so not Melanie.

Cas continued to frown until Julie felt like she had to offer an explanation or give herself away. "I learned it in self-defense class."

Cas's frown deepened and she hurried on.

"All women in the city know self defense. It comes with the territory." She widened her eyes innocently. "Gee, it really works."

Cas's face relaxed a fraction. "Well, don't count on it working again. People get hurt trying to use that stuff." His lips tightened and Julie knew he must be thinking of her kayoing him in the Roundhouse. It wouldn't do if he started asking himself why she was so fluent in defense techniques.

"You're right," she said meekly and saw Melanie scowl at her.

He ushered them back into the hall where the dance continued unawares and Henley and Bo were nowhere to be seen.

Julie danced a few dances with people she barely remembered, ate a few hors d'oeuvres, and drank a glass of punch that tasted like cough syrup. She'd heard the word "heiress" several times as she passed through the hall, and wondered if they could really be talking about her. She didn't see Melanie again. She'd probably gotten bored and gone home, which is where Julie wished she were. Her feet hurt and Cas had been kept busy dancing with other women of the town, making the rounds, being friendly and authoritative, and never once glancing in her direction. His lack of attention irked her as much as his attention had earlier in the evening.

Reynolds must have put it to him, thought Julie. So what else was new?

Maude was constantly on the dance floor or at the punch bowl, a hit in her crimson dress. But her apparent rebound after Wes's death didn't fool Julie. Maude was a trouper.

At last the band wound down and Julie breathed a heartfelt sigh of relief.

"Not over yet," said Maude, coming up beside her.

The band cranked up one last time with a fanfare that rivaled a fire alarm.

Julie looked at Maude.

"The crowning of the Candy Apple Queen."

"You're kidding."

Maude just smiled.

The room became quiet as Marian and Charles Reynolds climbed up the front steps to the stage; Charles, a little unsteady on his feet; Marian nodding over the crowd like the Queen Mother. She was dressed in a red silk suit in honor of the occasion.

She ran her fingers over her frosted French twist and took the envelope from Mayor Felix Baumgarten, who had been mayor when Julie was a girl. Five names were called out and five eager young women climbed the steps to take their places next to Marian and Charles and the mayor.

Two men, one of whom was Dan Pliney, came forward holding a red cape, a third man carried a tiara on a red cushion.

"That could be you up there," said Maude, giving Julie a wicked grin.

"Oh, please. Though I wish Melanie had been picked. Now that would be something to see."

"And this year's Candy Apple Queen is ..." Marian paused.

"The suspense is killing me," said Maude.

"Isabelle Schott."

"Oh surprise," said Maude. "She's Marian's protégée."

"I met her at the hotel restaurant," said Julie.

Isabel lifted her hands to her face as two of her court pushed her none too gently forward. Reynolds took the cape from the cape bearers and settled it around Isabel's shoulders, while Isabel smiled happily at the crowd.

"Lives with her father, a widower," whispered Maude. "He's trying to get her married off, so he can get it on with Edith Turnbull." Maude nodded to where a man clapped harder and louder than the others. The woman from the police station stood next to him, looking every bit as appreciative at Isabelle. "And guess who's the prime candidate?"

"Cas?"

Maude nodded.

"And he?"

"Give me a break. Haven't you figured out anything since you came back?"

Julie turned back to watch Marian Reynolds place the crown on Isabel's head. Reynolds smiled down at her and Julie thought, *Shit. They're planning for Cas to marry her.*

"And now, Isabelle, it's time to name your escort," said Reynolds in a voice that rang across the hall. Isabelle, Reynolds, Marian, and the mayor looked out into the crowd. All but the mayor zeroed in on the same spot and Julie knew that they had found Cas.

Isabel smiled out at the crowd. "I choose for my Escort," she began.

And that's when Julie saw the chicken.

Chapter 16

It seemed to materialize in front of the stage, a huge white leghorn with a red wattle and comb. It shivered and shimmied and high-stepped right toward the crowd, its head jutting forward with each step.

Someone sniggered. The people in front stepped back as the hen strutted her stuff across the floor.

"Hey, that's my Rowena!" Elton Dinwiddie pushed through the crowd. "Here, Rowena. Come here, baby. Pluck. Pluck."

Isabelle looked down, horrified. Marian gaped at the chicken, then frowned at the crowd as if looking for someone to blame. Reynolds yelled, "Get that chicken out of here," just as the crowd broke into laughter. Elton leaned over to pick up Rowena and two more chickens strutted out from under the stage.

And then the room was filled with chickens. Leghorns, Rhode Island reds, bantams, Wyandottes, Minorcans appeared in front of the stage like a magician's trick.

They kept coming, pushing the ones in front closer to the crowd. Soon the floor around the stage was filled with chickens. They began pecking at the floor and at each other.

Three roosters entered last, one after the other.

"That's my rooster," said the man in the blue turtleneck. He pushed out of the crowd, scattering chickens and people as he hurried to claim his fowl.

The largest rooster leaned over and took a bite out of the smallest one. The victim spread his wings and dove at his attacker, and the third rooster quickly joined in.

A roar went out among the men and someone yelled, "Cock fight. Twenty bucks on the bantam."

"Not with my rooster, you don't." The owner grabbed for his rooster, but fell over a hen who'd sat down in the middle of the floor. Startled, the hen airlifted right into Edith Turnbull's mohair sweater. Edith shrieked and tried to bat it away. The hen scrabbled at her sweater and fell to the floor, leaving a trail of chicken shit down the row of mother-of-pearl buttons, before disappearing among the feet of the crowd.

The whole floor was beginning to fill up with chicken droppings as they panicked and ran mindlessly in all directions.

"My God," said Julie. "There must be fifty or more."

"Who are going to get hurt if we don't contain them soon." Maude pushed the onlookers aside and began giving directions, grabbing chickens and shoving them at anybody who would take them.

"Somebody get a box," yelled Elton over the noise of chickens and crowd. "My whole flock is here."

"So's mine," said the rooster owner, who held the giant bird under one elbow and a hen in the crook of his other arm.

"Get these chickens out of here," commanded Reynolds and ran down the steps from the stage, alarming the chickens even more. His foot skidded and he went down on his ass. The chickens squawked and scurried into the crowd. Someone tripped and fell back into two ladies, who screamed and stumbled into the people behind them, setting off a domino effect across the room.

Everywhere people were chasing chickens as the noise level rose amid plucks and yelps, and squawks and laughter.

Marian put her arm around Isabel, who had started to cry.

A group of teenage boys began chasing the bantam rooster who suddenly turned on them and attacked. They leapt out of his path. One of them fell against the refreshment table; sandwiches and brownies flew into the air. The punch bowl wobbled, then turned over. Red punch and melting sherbet ran off the table and onto the floor. The boy's feet flew out from under him. He went down, taking three other people with him.

Cas and Terrence burst into the crowd, pushing people out of the way and ordering them toward the back of the room.

"Dan Pliney's gone to get crates," Cas told several men, who had overturned tables to make holding pens and were throwing chickens inside.

After her initial shock, Julie tossed her heels aside and pitched in, scooping up hens and dropping them into the makeshift pens. She kept one eye out for Ernestine, but with no luck.

As she was attempting to capture a speckled hen, Julie noticed an open panel at the base of the stage. She hiked up her dress and knelt down to take a look. The space underneath was occupied by a ladder and pieces of scenery. A path had been cleared through them and Julie could see light on the other side. Someone had herded the chickens under the stage and into the room.

She crawled inside to make sure there were no chickens lurking among the cardboard palm trees. The smell was overwhelming; nothing like a few hysterical hens to really stink up a place. She backed out on all fours and stood up.

Dan and his sons were carrying stacks of mesh crates into the room. Cas and Terrence and a few other men were loading them up with chickens.

Isabelle's red cape lay on the stage, its train flowing off the edge and onto the floor. Julie picked it up and carefully folded it before depositing it on a folding chair at the edge of the stage. There was no sign of Isabelle or Marian or Charles Reynolds.

Poor Isabelle, thought Julie, *she'll never be able to forget this night*. What should have been her moment of glory had turned into a fiasco, and Julie's heart went out to her. She knew how that felt. And she wouldn't wish the feeling on her worst enemy. Well, maybe on Marian and Reynolds. No, not even them, she realized. They couldn't hurt her anymore.

Maude stood with her feet apart, supervising the crating of the fowl. Her crimson chiffon was torn by hundreds of chicken scratches. A white downy feather floated on her hair.

"You haven't seen Ernestine by any chance?" asked Julie.

"No," said Maude, "But she might turn up."

"Damn," said Elton Dinwiddie as he carried a crate filled with chickens toward the back door. "If I didn't know better, I'd say that Wes Excelsior was up to his old tricks." He stopped, looked at Julie, then shook his head and walked away.

"He doesn't think I did it, does he?" asked Julie, alarmed.

"Nah. He's just talking off the top of his head. Why don't you go home? I'll hitch a ride when we get finished here."

"I'll just take another quick look around for Ernestine, then I'll go," said Julie, and looked up to see several of the towns-people looking at her. A sickening jolt of insecurity zapped through her. Why were they staring? Surely they didn't think she was responsible for disruption of the dance.

Pretending to ignore them, she rechecked each makeshift pen and finally had to accept the fact that Ernestine had not been returned. And if she wasn't with the others, it must mean that she hadn't been stolen, but had run away or become lost and was dead.

Julie swallowed the lump that rose to her throat. Stupid to get upset over a chicken, but she couldn't help it. Maude was right. Ernestine was like family.

She began searching for her shoes, stepping over chicken droppings and trampled foodstuffs. She remembered tossing them under a chair near the stage, but they weren't there now. She finally found one shoved into a far corner beneath a paper tablecloth. The other was as lost as Ernestine.

To hell with it. Someone would find it during cleanup. The car wasn't so far away; she'd just have to hoof it.

She was buttoning her coat when Cas came through the

door, carrying a crate of chickens. She stepped back and he passed by without seeing her.

Lucky him, she thought unsympathetically. His chicken problem was solved.

She stepped out into the night and the pavement shot searing cold up through her feet to her calves. She sprinted past a group of teenagers who were loitering in the parking lot.

Melanie stepped away from them as she passed by. "Where are your shoes?"

Julie held up her one shoe. "L-lost the other. G-goodnight." She broke into a trot and got a whiff of chicken. God, they must all smell like chickens, she knew she did. But she'd been carrying chickens for the last half hour, and she hadn't seen Melanie since before the crowning of the Queen began. She hesitated, then dismissing the thought, climbed into the Volkswagen.

She turned the heat to high, then sat, thinking, while the car warmed up. What kind of person would go to such trouble for a prank? Wes would, but they couldn't blame him for this night's work. Someone stole the chickens, hid them, fed them for weeks just to release them at the high point of the Candy Apple Dance.

That was a lot of work for a few minutes of fun. Or was there a more sinister intent? Was someone out to make Cas appear incompetent? Bo and Henley were the only ones who seemed to hold a grudge against him and they weren't smart enough to pull this off. They would be more likely to use their fists, like they had at the Roadhouse, and like they used to do in school.

There might be a few people in town who would like to see Marian and Charles Reynolds brought down a peg, but there had to be better ways than this.

One of the other Candy Apple Queen hopefuls might be jealous of Isabelle, but none of those girls looked like they'd ever seen a chicken outside a fast food container.

Not your problem, she reminded herself. *Not your job.*

Everyone had their chickens back but her, and that was her problem. Hers alone.

She shoved the car into gear and backed out of her parking place. As she left the parking lot, she glanced in her rear view mirror and saw Melanie, standing apart from the group, her hands shoved in her pockets, watching Julie drive away.

"And a good time was had by all," Julie told Smitty when he met her at the door. "And everyone got their chickens back but us." She yanked up the skirt of her dress and pulled off her panty hose, dirty and torn beyond hope. She'd lost her shoe and her feet were freezing. Some great time.

She threw her coat into the closet and ran up the stairs, Smitty loping after her. She went straight into the bathroom, turned on the tub, and stripped out of her clothes. She climbed in and grimaced as hot water rushed over her feet and set them on fire.

When they began to warm, she cautiously lowered herself into the water and turned on the Jacuzzi jets. She stretched out and rested her head against the side of the long tub.

So much for staking her place in the community. The night had been ridiculous from start to finish.

It was past midnight when Cas parked his truck in Tilda's driveway on First Street and handed her his keys.

"Going for a midnight hike?" she asked, grinning.

"A man's gotta do what a man's gotta do," said Terrence from the living room over the laughter of a late night talk show. "I'll cover for you tomorrow. Sleep late." Terrence rumbled down to silence.

"I'll call Edith and tell her to transfer any calls here," said Tilda. "Sweet dreams."

"Thanks," said Cas.

Tilda closed the door; Cas buttoned up his sheepskin jacket and pulled up the collar. The air smelled and felt like snow. Winter was setting in early this year, and it was time to think about leaving and taking Julie with him. If he could convince her to go.

He walked up the driveway to the back of the house, wishing he had a hat. He'd spent a good hour returning chickens and listening to complaints. Wasn't it enough that they had the damn things back, without demanding he find out who stole them in the first place?

As soon as he could, he'd sped back to his cottage to shower and change into clean clothes, anxious to find Julie, to feel her warmth, just to feel her and know there was a place for him in the world.

Now, trekking up the hill, he wondered if there was a place for him, and if Julie would want to live in that place with him. The lights in the houses on Second Street were out and he passed quietly between the houses and across the street. If someone saw him, he would just say he was following a lead. One that led right to Julie Excelsior and a chance at happiness.

He was just passing the Neville's backyard, when a dog barked and lurched against the fence. Floodlights popped on, bathing Cas in their light, and Ken Neville appeared at the back door.

"It's Cas Reynolds," Cas called out. "Just following a lead."

Ken laughed. "Good for you, boy." He whistled for his dog and closed the door. The lights popped off again, leaving Cas in darkness. He wasn't fooling anybody. Not that he wanted to. He just wanted to spend a whole night with Julie without his family going berserk.

He was shivering from the cold by the time he climbed up to Hillcrest and crossed to Wes's driveway. And it occurred to him that Julie might already be asleep, that she wouldn't hear him knock. Or worse, she wouldn't let him stay. And then he'd have to climb down again, like the fool he was.

He stumbled, barely catching himself before he hit the ground. The damn driveway was filled with as many potholes as the street. The town was dying inch by inch, taking its inhabitants with it. He could feel it himself, wringing the life out of him, even though he'd only been here for a few months. What it was doing to the others, he could only guess.

And he refused to let himself care. His only goal was Julie. He'd resign as sheriff. He should never have let Wes bully him into taking the job in the first place. But at least he now understood why. Wes must have known that death was close and that Julie would come back, so he'd found a way to keep Cas in Ex Falls. And to hedge his odds, he'd handed him that damn riddle. My legacy to you, he'd said, and thrust it into Cas's hand.

It was such a Wes tactic that Cas was about to call him on it, when he realized that Wes's hand had really gone limp. That his eyes wouldn't be opening again, that he would never again hear him say, "Gotcha!" Because true to form, Wes had died with a joke on his lips.

If it was a joke, thought Cas, starting up again and walking faster now that he was almost there. *Almost there.* A thrill of anticipation rushed through him. Almost there. He could see the lights on in Julie's room.

They could have a whole night together of making love and . . . talking. They hadn't had much of a chance to get to know each other, except physically. Julie kept running off or someone would interrupt them. But not tonight. He crossed his fingers and began to hum.

Julie fluffed the pink pillows behind her back and turned the page of Wes's notebook. Even bundled up in Wes's old paisley bathrobe with the comforter pulled tightly around her, she still felt cold, which made her wonder if Cas was in bed or if he was still out returning chickens.

She turned past the chicken notes to a section with Wes's various ramblings, and began to read them for the umpteenth time. There had to be a clue she was missing, because even with Cas's half, she was no closer to finding the treasure. No closer than she was to ever belonging in Ex Falls.

Well, it didn't matter. She'd held up her head, kept her spine straight and looked the town in the eye. For all the good it did. She wasn't even sure if she wanted to belong here. She certainly didn't want to take up the feud and spend her life fighting with Charles Reynolds. She would miss her chickens, but there was no future in chickens. So best to get it over with before she became any more attached to the house or the chickens—or to Cas.

She closed the notebook as tendrils of anxiety wrapped around her. But where would she go? Did she have the energy to start over again? Without an income, unless she found Wes's money, she wouldn't be able to start over. Should she return to the city and ask for her job back? Face the colleagues she hadn't been able to face just two weeks ago? Look them in the eye and say, *I won't be run off again? This is my beat, and you'll have to drag me away before I leave again.*

Or was it too late? Would they always look at her, remembering, wondering. Even if there were no truth in it, there would always be that stigma, Julie Excelsior, mill town trash.

"Whoa," she said out loud. "My colleagues don't know a thing about Ex Falls." It was in *her* mind, not theirs. "Shit, Wes. Is it me? Am I perpetuating my own insecurity?" She pushed herself into the pillows. She never asked herself questions like that, and she wasn't ready to start asking them now.

She reached over to turn off the bedside lamp. Smitty jumped from the bed, nosed the door open and ran down the stairs, barking. Julie reached for her Glock and heard the knock on the door. She hadn't heard a car drive up, but she'd been lost in thought. Maude must have found her shoe and had come to return it. Or maybe she'd found Ernestine after all.

Julie returned the Glock to the drawer, hiked up Wes's robe and ran downstairs. She could see someone standing on the other side of the stained glass windows. Too tall for Maude. She only hesitated for a second, then opened the door.

It was Cas, looking tired and cold. He'd changed from his uniform to jeans and a suede coat with a sheepskin collar. His hair was wet and slicked back from his forehead. And Julie was suddenly warmer than she'd been all night.

"Hi," she said.

"Found your shoe." He lifted his hand. A single strapped high heel swung from his finger.

She stepped aside so he could come in, then looked past him into an empty yard. "Where's your car?"

"Down at Tilda's. I walked up the hill." He pushed off his shoes and left them by the door.

"Afraid you might get caught?"

"Didn't want to be interrupted."

"Oh. You want coffee, a beer?"

Cas shook his head. "Just you."

Julie closed the door and leaned against the knob. "I think that can be arranged." She looked at Cas and thought about him climbing the hill in the dark and her lying in her pink, frilly bed, and thought, *here we go again. We'll call it sheriff and saloon girl.* She wasn't sure she liked her part. It was a little too close to mill town trash.

"What?" asked Cas, eyeing her warily.

"Nothing."

Cas raised his eyebrows.

"Just thinking about . . ." She sighed. "Cowboys and Indians."

Cowboys and Indians. Damn, thought Cas. Julie was still determined to play games. He hadn't been kidding when he told her he wanted to play Julie and Cas. He wanted them to *be* Julie and Cas.

She was going to run again. He could feel it in the air between them. He pulled her close and wrapped his arms around her as if he could keep her.

"What's wrong?" she asked, looking up at him. Her hair tumbled around her face, and he released one hand long enough to smooth it away. He ran his thumb down her cheek, her skin so clear, soft as silk. And wondered where that had come from. It wasn't like him to be poetic, especially when his dick was saying, "Just fuck her." But it *was* soft as silk and his hand lingered on her face as he looked down into the deep pools of her eyes.

"Cas?"

"Don't run from me," he said, though he could hardly form the words. He wanted her so much, not just for tonight—

She pulled away. "What are you talking about? I'm not going anywhere. This is *my* house."

He pulled her head back to his chest and lay his cheek against her hair. It tickled his nose, and he was content for a moment with her nearness, while he silently willed her to trust him, when he knew he'd never done anything to deserve her trust.

It was time they talked. Got out what had happened all those years ago, so they could go forward. He would try to explain, try to make her see his side and get her to forgive him.

Because without that, they had no chance of being anything but casual bedmates. And, Cas, at least, was too far gone for that. "We need to talk."

"Ah, jeez," said Julie, pulling away again. He could feel her trembling beneath his fingers. Then she smiled up at him with enormous eyes and laughed flirtatiously. "No, we don't. We just need to have fun."

"No." He wanted her so badly, he had to fight both her and himself, but it was time. It was past time. "Why did you leave Ex Falls?"

And why did you walk away from me and then pretend like you didn't know me. You were my best friend. "Does it matter?"

"Yes."

She sighed heavily, like she was bored with the question. But she didn't stop trembling. "Wes sent me away. He told me to forget Ex Falls. My dad drove me to my aunt in Yonkers. He left me there. I never saw him again. I never saw Wes again. So now you know."

"He left you?"

She nodded.

"Why?"

"Why does anything happen? It's old news. Do you want to stay?"

I want to know everything about you. "Sure," he said and followed her up the stairs.

Chapter 17

*O*kay, thought Cas. *Sex first, then we'll talk. You won't escape me tonight, my pretty.* He stumbled on the step and Julie looked around with a frown.

"Missed the step," said Cas.

"Then keep your eyes on your feet and not on my ass."

When they reached the top of the stairs, Julie slipped in between him and her bedroom door. "There's something I should warn you about," she said.

Cas's eyes narrowed. *Now what.* "Okay," he said slowly, thinking, *Please don't let this be some earth-shattering confession.* His dick was already hard against his zipper and he didn't think he could hold out much longer. He wanted to know all about her, but he had all night and he was having a hard time not grabbing her and taking her against the door.

"Wes decorated my room."

"Ah," he said. "Hit me with the worst."

She opened the door.

Cas looked inside and shook his head in dismay as he took in the pink rug, the pink walls, the pink monstrosity of a bed. *Thanks for stopping at the bearskin rug,* he silently messaged to Wes. "It's, um, pink," he said.

"I warned you."

He followed Julie inside and closed the door in Smitty's face. Smitty whined, barked, then Cas heard his nails clicking down the stairs. He let out a sigh of contentment. Pink wasn't so bad. Hell, any color was palatable if Julie was naked in it. He set about making it so.

He snared the end of the tie belt she'd wrapped around the huge robe. When she stepped back, the bow fell free. He pulled off the tie and the robe opened to reveal a rose-colored satin negligee. Her nipples were taut against the creamy fabric. His dick stirred again and fought its way upward. Cas shifted to give it room, then thought, *to hell with it*, and opened his jeans.

Julie's hand slipped past his and dipped into his underwear, freeing him. He swelled in her hand.

"My dick thanks you," he said and slipped the robe from her shoulders. It stopped at her bent elbows as her hands slid around his hips to clasp his butt. Everything in him tightened. The robe spilled over her arms and spread out behind her like exotic plumage.

His fingers pulled the band from the braid of hair that hung down her back, then he slowly unplaited it and wrapped it in his fingers. He leaned forward and kissed her neck, then pulled her hair to his lips and kissed it, too.

He could feel her shudder. This is where she belonged, where he belonged. He felt a stab of remorse that they had lost so many years. But she pulled his ass to her and he forgot about everything but the present.

She rubbed against him and he had to get closer. Feel the silky fabric on his skin. But Julie was already pushing his jeans and boxers down. He released her hair long enough to pull off his sweater and T-shirt.

She opened her arms, a high priestess, invoking the gods of hot sex, and the robe slid to the floor.

Cas groaned and pushed his jeans off his feet without taking his eyes from hers. Then he stood before her and waited for her to come to him. It was the hardest thing he could remember ever doing.

She seemed to hover before him. Like the first night when she appeared like an apparition out of the woods. Then, arms at her side, she stepped forward until the length of her night-gown caressed the front of him. She swayed on her feet. The cool, smooth fabric brushed across him and set his skin tingling.

He reached for her, but she shook her head, continuing her seductive dance, using the negligee like fingers to set him on fire. He wanted to snatch it off her *and* keep it sliding against his flesh; indecision held him powerless. And he realized he was moving against her movement. Not the grinding, unchained foreplay they'd indulged in before. But slow, sensuous, and ten times as arousing.

"Julie," he whispered.

She shook her head and continued to drift across him, slowly lowering herself until her breasts hovered near his erection. He reached for her hair, but she shook her head, and he dropped his hands again, reluctantly, because he wanted to take her in his arms and brand her with his embrace.

Her hands slid up her body, lifting the fabric against his erection, sending him perilously close to the edge. Then her hands moved to her breasts. His knees buckled and it was all he could do to stay on his feet as she rubbed them against his dick, making a passage as sweet and hot as any other.

He wondered if a man had ever fainted from the ecstasy of foreplay, because he felt like he might. He was barely hanging onto his sanity. His world was swathed in a pink aura as she continued to work him; the satin gliding along his heated skin; the tiny edging of lace adding an extra titillation each time it passed over the head of his penis.

He was probably leaking all over her negligee and he just hoped he could hold on long enough not to spew come all over her.

She looked up at him with heavy-lidded eyes, a siren's smile hovering on her lips, and a part of his mind thought, *she's playing me*, and another part said, *let her play.*

Just when he thought he couldn't stand it another second,

she moved away, seeming to float backward until she stopped with her back against the big four-poster bed. Mesmerized by the action, he followed her.

She held his eyes with hers and her fingers began to inch the negligee up her thighs until it stopped right below the dark shadow between her legs. Cas tried to swallow as he waited for it to go higher. But Julie just continued to torment him, lifting the satin just enough to make him think she was going to reveal that hidden, mysterious spot, then just as he got a glimpse of her dark curls, she lowered it again.

He was swaying on his feet, swamped by his own desire and Julie's magnetism. And he let her seduce him. But he was nearly undone when she pushed herself up on the bed and opened her knees, the pink satin draped over her lap, and her hand went to that place where his tongue belonged and she stroked herself.

He was caught between wanting to take her and longing to watch her. Her fingers found a place that made her sigh. And she slowly closed her eyes only to open them and let her gaze travel from his face to his cock.

He could feel it reaching toward her, and he thought it might drag him like a giant magnet until it drove its way home, but he fought the impulse as he watched her finger slide through her groove of hair, circle, and disappear only to re-appear again. When she was breathing hard and rocking against her own movements, she pulled her hand away and held her finger out to him.

He fell into her and he took her hand and sucked her finger into his mouth, tasting the salt of her, the tang of desire that filled his senses and while he sucked, his other hand reached out to her and she took his hand and placed it in the warmth of her sex.

His finger entered her and she squeezed her thighs around his hand and pushed against him as he sucked on her finger and his dick pulsed harder and harder.

God, he was going to explode. He pulled his hand from Julie and spread her knees wider. She pressed them shut and he looked up, puzzled.

She shook her head at him and looked down at his erection, then back up to his face. She wanted it now. He stepped forward and she shook her head again.

"What?" he said. And realized that she hadn't spoken since they'd begun this dance.

She looked down at his cock again and nodded. Then she ran a finger lightly up the ridge of sensitive skin. Chills ran over his body. He reached for her but she grabbed his hand and pressed it back onto his erection. Against his will, his fingers closed around it and he could feel the throbbing against his palm.

Julie smiled. She opened her knees again, wider this time, and placed her finger in the crease of her folds and slid it inside her. Then she lifted her chin toward him, all the time looking at his hand on his dick. She wanted him to jerk off in front of her.

He shook his head.

She smiled wider and nodded, while her hand began to move against her crotch. His hand moved against his cock in response and he shuddered down to his toes. She brought her fingers out to where he could see them, then slid them out of sight again. His hand pressed down to the base of his erection, then back to the tip. He pushed up against his hand as it pushed down again. Julie's hand began to move faster.

She breathed out, her lips parted, but she didn't take her eyes off what he was doing. They moved as one, Cas forgetting his inhibitions of a minute before. He opened his feet wider and his other hand found his scrotum, the balls hard and tight against his body. He held them as he pulled his hand up again, circled around the head of his penis, spreading the fluid there over the tip as he stroked his balls.

He forgot that he'd never done this mutual masturbation

thing before because Julie held him in her power. His head fell back and his neck cracked. And he thrust into his hand again. She was rocking on the bed now, her teeth looking incredible as she bit her bottom lip. He was going to come any second now and he wanted to do it in Julie, not explode into the air. But he couldn't seem to stop; his hand moved faster, holding himself tighter and tighter.

Then Julie gasped, "Now."

He lunged forward, grabbed her ass and pulled it to the edge of the mattress. She braced her feet on the side board, and tilted her hips toward him for better entry. Still he had to use his hand to guide his cock inside her.

She was tight and he was afraid he might rocket off before he could get inside. He braced his knees against the side of the bed and took a deep breath, then he pushed into her, so hard that he pushed her away from the edge of the bed. She grabbed the spread and pulled herself back to him. He grabbed her ass and sank into her again. And then he couldn't stop, only rush headlong to release.

He heard growling, and thought it was Smitty, until he realized it was his own voice. So he let it out and pushed harder until Julie cried out and he followed her to oblivion.

"U-u-u-uh," said Cas, when he could finally talk again. Talk, but not move. He was collapsed over Julie, halfway on the bed and halfway off. Julie was smashed into the mattress, but she wasn't complaining.

"Yeah," she said. "Me, too."

He heaved himself up on his elbows and she wriggled to a better position beneath him. He smiled at her. "What do you say to spending the rest of the night under the covers like normal people?"

"The rest? You're staying?"

"You want me to go?"

"No, but—"

"Good, because I'm staying and I have the weekend off." Except the dreaded Sunday dinner, and maybe he could call in sick.

"The weekend?"

He pushed away from the bed and stood up, then pulled her to her feet, so he could turn back the covers. "Yep. And by Monday, I expect to be seeing the world through rose-colored glasses." He climbed into bed, fluffed up a pink ruffled pillow and leaned back.

He patted the place beside him. "Might as well get in. You're stuck with me."

She frowned at him; he could practically see the wheels turning. She liked the foreplay, but not the pillow talk. Maybe her complete abandonment during sex embarrassed her afterwards. He hoped not. Because he wanted to make it a habit.

She climbed into bed, not looking at him and pulled the covers up to her chin, then nestled down against the pillow and closed her eyes.

He pulled her up again. "Oh, no you don't. We have some catching up to do." He made a place for her next to him and put his arm around her, pulling her back until she was lying against him, his arm around her. She was stiff as a board.

He stroked her arm. "I'm not going to hurt you. I just want to be with you. Get to know you." He pulled her closer.

Aw, jeez, thought Julie as she lay uncomfortably against Cas's shoulder. He wanted to talk. *This is what you get for playing with fire, stupid.* And what fire. She couldn't remember a time when sex had felt like this. An out-of-body experience—no, an in-body experience. Wow. And now he wanted to talk. Why couldn't he have grown up to be like other men who started snoring before their dick shriveled and fell out?

But no-o-o. He wanted to talk. She could see it now. "I'm a cop." And he'd be dressed and out the door before she could say, "Really, it's no big deal." So now, instead of basking in total repletion, and slowly drifting into satisfied sleep, she was going to have to come up with stories about her life since Ex Falls—and make them sound believable.

She yawned a jaw-cracking yawn.

Cas shook his head.

Julie sat up and drew up her knees until she could wrap her arms around them. It felt safer that way, though she missed the warmth of Cas's body. "Okay, what do you want to talk about?"

He pulled her back down. "Haven't you ever heard of pillow talk?"

She tried her last tactic. She snuggled against him and let her hand creep under the comforter, headed south.

He stopped it at his navel. "Later," he said, pulled her hand back to the air and kissed the knuckles before letting it go.

The two of them sat against the pillows, legs stretched out, looking ahead like strangers on a train. Finally Julie said, "You first."

He was silent for a moment, then said, "Reynolds sent me to prep school. When I came back for vacation, you were gone." Cas raised an eyebrow at her.

"What?" asked Julie, feeling her skin begin to crawl.

"Your turn."

"Oh. Well, I left and went to live with my aunt in Yonkers. You know that."

Cas nodded. "Then what?"

"Nope. Your turn."

"Okay. Then I went to Yale and became a banker and hated it and quit. Now I build boats, wooden ones, fiberglass ones. My last job was on the coast of Rhode Island. I love what I do. I—your turn."

Suddenly she saw her way out. He had rushed through his life to hear about hers; now she could do the same.

"Well," she said slowly." "I went to City College and studied . . . um, hard and then did a bunch of different jobs. And then Wes died and I came here." She smiled at him and tried to climb under the covers.

Cas pulled her up again. "What kind of jobs?"

"Stupid stuff." She pulled out a few of her least odious undercover jobs and hit him with them. "And that's about it."

Cas was quiet for a minute, which was alright with Julie. Then he sighed. "We just summed up our lives of the last fifteen years in less than three minutes. That can't be good."

Julie turned to look at him and wished she hadn't. His eyes were dark, darker than usual, and his look seemed to burn a hole through her. She swallowed, wanting to tell him everything, like when they were kids. But she couldn't. It was one thing to lie beneath the sky and dream their dreams, but a different thing to say, *I became a cop. I was good. And then shit happened and I was on the outside again.*

And to her mortification she felt a tear slide past her eyelid and down her cheek. She froze, not knowing what to do. Try to hide it or to brazen her way through.

Cas's finger brushed it away. He pulled her across him and held her and said, "I'm sorry, Julie. So sorry."

And he held her until she fell asleep.

Ulysses crowed through the darkness. Bill's treble warble quickly followed. Julie stirred. She was warm and comfy. Cas was stretched out alongside her, warm and muscular. He'd stayed the whole night. The thought made her ridiculously cheerful for so early in the morning. She was tempted to wake him and make love to him, but she had chickens to see to.

Something was heavy on her feet. She sat up and squinted into the darkness.

Smitty was stretched out along the end of the bed. Cas must have let him in during the night. "Come on, boy," she whispered. She dressed quickly and they went downstairs.

The days were getting shorter. It was completely dark outside and she wondered how long it would take for Ulysses and Bill to reset their internal clocks. An extra half hour of sleep would be welcome, especially if she were sleeping with Cas.

She hurried through her chores, planning to be back under

the covers before he woke up. A little morning exercise and she'd send him on his way. The thought brought her up short. She didn't want to send him away.

But she couldn't spend the day with him. It would give them too much time to rehash the past and she didn't want to go there, not even the recent past. She should have told him she was a cop the first night they met. He must have wondered why she was carrying a Glock. Maybe he didn't recognize it as a police special; his was years out of date. She wasn't even sure it worked.

She should have told him then; now it was too late. It would look like she'd been hiding it from him. And she had. Only now, she couldn't remember why it had been so important to keep it from him.

"Aw, shit." Startled by her outburst, the chickens squawked and scattered in a flurry of feathers. "Sorry," she cooed. "Didn't mean to scare you. And I've learned my lesson," she told them. "Next time, don't procrastinate. Just say it and get it over with and face the consequences." Because hiding the truth was just too damn hard.

Insistent pecking at her feet reminded her that she was holding a full pan of scratch and they were hungry. She broadcast the grains. The chickens spread out to capture the seeds, except for one who continued to peck at her boot.

She looked down. Her eyes widened, then she leaned over to get a better look. It was dark, but she could swear . . . "Ernestine!" She squatted down and the little hen strutted between her knees and lifted her head for a pet.

"Where have you been? How did you get back in the coop? I can't believe it." She threw out the rest of the scratch and picked her up. "I can't believe you're home."

Ernestine began to coo, and Julie thought, *How can I be so happy over a chicken?* An inkling of a suspicion crept into her mind. Maybe Wes hadn't meant a monetary treasure, after all. *More precious than silver, finer than gold.* But chicken love didn't exactly pay the rent.

Then she thought of Cas, asleep in her bed and she thought, *Oh no. Not that. Not here. Wes, you wouldn't. Would you? It won't work. I may have dreamed about it often enough, but you know it won't work. And I can't stay here.*

But she held Ernestine closer, standing in the cold, while her cheeks turned numb and her toes lost their feeling.

Smitty trotted up a few minutes later; he was alone.

"Where are Bill and Hil?" she asked. She'd heard Bill this morning, but now that she thought about it, she hadn't seen him . . . or Hilary. "Oh, no," she cried. She tipped Ernestine onto the ground and hurried over to the feeders. No Bill and Hilary. She climbed up the ramp and went into the coop. Walked to the far end of the nesting boxes.

And there was Hilary, sitting in her box, and Bill, perched on the plank that ran along the back of the nesting boxes. Julie couldn't help smiling. "Sleeping in? I know just how you feel." And suddenly she was in a hurry to get back inside. She went outside for the egg basket and collected only three. Pretty soon, she'd have to start buying them at the Buy and Bag.

"Excuse me, miss," she said and tried to nudge the hen aside. Bill made a guttural sound. Hillary pecked at her hand. "Hey, what's with you this morning?" She reached back to move Hilary. Bill spread his wings in what she had come to recognize as fighting posture. She dropped her hand and cocked her head at him.

"Let me get this straight. There's an egg in there and you want to start a family."

Bill settled back on his perch. Hillary began to peck at her neck feathers. Julie looked at the three eggs in her basket. How many eggs did a person need? But what was she going to do with a baby chick? She had no incubator, and no idea of how to care for it. Wes hadn't left instructions for starting a family. How long did it take for a chicken to hatch anyway? She might not even be here to see it happen.

And she would really miss not being a part of that. "Oh

hell," she said. "You have a reprieve until I consult with Maude." She took her three eggs and walked back down the aisle. At the door she turned back for a final look. Bill had hopped off the perch and was sitting beside Hilary, his wing draped protectively over her.

"No way," said Julie. She was definitely spending too much time with chickens.

She sent everyone else inside a few minutes later. She had to carry Ernestine up the ramp, protesting. "I'm sorry, Ernie, but it's too cold for either of us to be outside, and you're not, I repeat, not coming into the house. I'll see you this evening."

She closed up the gazebo, double-checked the door, shut the mesh fence and called to Smitty who came loping out of the woods.

"Breakfast," she said.

Smitty bounded up the steps and into the house. *The way to a man's heart*, she thought, then looked down at the basket of eggs. "Hmmm," she said and closed the door.

The bedroom door opened and Cas smelled coffee. He smiled and opened his eyes. Julie carried a tray of dishes and a coffeepot into the room and set it on the bedside table.

Cas grabbed her wrist, pulled her down on the bed, and kissed her long and sweet.

"Is that because I made breakfast?" she asked, her eyes twinkling.

"One of the reasons," said Cas. "But I brought dessert." He placed her hand on the sheet above his growing erection. Her fingers closed around it and he lifted into her.

"Eat up," said Julie. "I have a sweet tooth this morning." She placed the tray on the bed and went into the bathroom. "And Ernestine is back," she said over the sound of rushing water. "It's like a miracle. She was there with all the others. I can hardly believe it."

"That's great," said Cas. All back and accounted for and his ass was off the line. Feeling infinitely relieved, not to mention randy as hell, he poured coffee and listened expectantly as the tub filled with water.

"You'd better be planning for both of us to be in there," he said.

She poked her head around the door. "I do."

Cas sighed. If he could only figure out how to get her to say those two little words in front of a minister.

They ate while Julie talked about Ernestine and a hen called Hillary, who was hatching an egg. When Cas couldn't wait any longer, he poked a piece of toast in Julie's mouth and said, "Come on."

The tub was filled to the top. Julie turned on the Jacuzzi jets and climbed in. Water splashed onto the floor. Cas climbed in after her, easing himself down into the water. Instead of relaxing his erection, a jet of water pushed against it and sent it into ready mode. He eased Julie over and lay down beside her.

"Wes sure knew how to buy a Jacuzzi," said Julie, trailing her hand down his chest to his navel.

He captured her hand and brought it to his lips. "And you sure know how to use one." He released her hand. It floated back down his body until it found home.

Cas turned into her, pulled her close. Her body slid against him as the water churned around them. And Cas thought about how it would be when Julie was his wife and they lived on the shore. Then he stopped thinking and he and Julie sailed away.

It was past noon when they bundled up and went for a walk in the woods.

"Don't you have to check in at the station or something?" Julie asked when Cas suggested some exercise besides the kind they'd engaged in all morning.

"Already did," he said and held up his cell phone before slipping it into his jacket pocket. "Are you trying to get rid of me?"

"Of course not," said Julie. Just the opposite. She'd like him to stay—forever.

That kind of thinking, she told herself, *leads to heartbreak, so don't even go there.*

They fell in step together, Smitty trotting happily beside them, venturing off to explore and coming back again. He seemed so content that Julie hated to think of him living in a city apartment again. Actually she was feeling a little sorry for herself for the same reasons.

But the magic of the woods soon made her forget the future as the past rose up to meet them everywhere they looked. They stopped at the same places and remembered the same things from their childhood and as they walked deeper into the woods, Julie felt closer to Cas than ever. Now was the time to tell him about being a cop.

She took a deep breath, but Cas suddenly let go of her hand and disappeared through the trees. Soon his voice echoed back to her. "Come here, look at this."

She stepped into the woods, looking for a path and only found more trees and a lot of underbrush. "Cas?"

"Over here."

She followed the sound of his voice, but before she reached him, she knew where he'd be. The old chimney, the only thing left standing of an ancient barbecue and where Cas and she had spent many happy hours talking, dreaming and playing cowboys and Indians.

Sure enough, she stepped out into a small opening and Cas met her, grinning. "Remember this?"

"I was a captive Indian maiden here more times than I can remember."

"Yeah," said Cas, reminiscently.

"You used to look up my shorts and peek at my underwear."

"Yeah," said Cas, his grin broadening. "Too bad we don't have a rope. We could go back to the house and get one."

"I don't think so." Julie looked around at the wobbly brick

chimney, leafless vines entwining it like Cas had entwined her so many years before. She shivered, thinking it must be symbolic of something, but she wasn't sure what.

She stepped closer and frozen leaves crunched beneath her feet. He grabbed her as she neared him, pulled her up against the chimney, and pressed his body into hers. "But this is what I should have been doing instead." He kissed her. It was slow and thorough and lasted until their cold lips warmed and heat surrounded them.

"That would have been a little perverse," she said, breathless from the kiss and from the thought of being tied up and made love to. "The first time you tied me up, I think you were eight and I was six."

"Foreplay," he said. "A really long foreplay. Come on."

He held her hand and they crashed through the trees and came to another spot where they had played, the old smokehouse. It had been falling down then, now only the foundation remained.

"It looks like there was a fire," said Cas.

"Hmmm," said Julie. She was remembering Wes telling them how during the Civil War, when Ex Falls had been a thriving town, manufacturing rifles for the Union army, all the families would bring hams to the smokehouse for curing. Then they'd load them onto a wagon and drive to Gettysburg, so their boys would have food to eat. She always felt sad to think of how many of those men and boys never returned.

She'd imagined herself walking among the troops, handing out slices of ham, like Florence Nightingale or Clara Barton, only she would be giving a gift of home. Maybe Cas would have been one of the soldiers, and he'd see her and say, "Julie, you're a godsend," because that's how they talked in those days.

So much waste. No one even remembered the names of the dead. The monument in the square had fallen over years before and had broken into smithereens. The pieces had been sitting in the basement of the library ever since. And if the bodies made it home to the Good Shepherd Cemetery, they were long forgotten. Like Josiah Excelsior. Maybe Wes was in heaven entertaining the troops with his jokes.

"What?" asked Cas.

Julie shook her head. "I was just thinking about how things change. The smokehouse left to crumble when it should be a landmark. With a little bronze plaque that says, *This smoke-house fed the Union army.*"

"Where did that come from?"

"I was just remembering the story Wes used to tell us."

"Oh, right. About the hams. I remember. I guess it's a case of 'to every season,' et cetera."

Julie sighed. "Yeah." They stood looking at the ruins and Julie thought, this is the perfect time to tell him about your life.

But Cas said, "Come on. It's kind of depressing here."

They circled back through the woods and across the orchard, pausing now and then to try to remember which tree Cas had fallen out of. On the other side they slid down the incline to the dirt path that would become Hillcrest Drive.

As they reached the asphalt, an old black Buick turned right out of the Reynolds's driveway. Julie stepped back.

Cas laughed. "It's only Larue. Going for more vermouth, probably."

They turned up Wes's driveway and stopped at the pond, now completely frozen over. "It will snow soon," said Cas. He sat down on one of the rocks where they'd once fished and pulled her down to sit beside him.

"I know. I'll have to get going before I get snowed in."

Cas frowned at her, then his expression cleared. "The county owns a snow plow these days. They keep the roads pretty clear."

"Oh." Julie looked out across the pond.

"When do you have to go back to work?"

This was the time to come clean. She swallowed. "W-e-l-l . . ."

Chapter 18

She told him about being a department store clerk. It wasn't entirely a lie. She had sold cosmetics in Lord and Taylor her junior year at CUNY.

"But that seemed like a dead end, so I, uh, enrolled in school, took the test and . . . went to work for the city."

Cas smiled.

"What?"

"I'm trying to picture you as a civil servant."

"What's wrong with that?" asked Julie, bristling.

"Nothing. I'm one myself for the moment. Is that why you have that big—"

"I'm freezing. Let's go back to the house." Julie stood up. At least she was getting closer to the truth.

They returned to the house, hand in hand, and it felt so right, that Julie convinced herself that it didn't matter that she'd not been totally forthcoming. It was a start.

They fed and watered the chickens early, then went inside. Julie put water on for spaghetti and shredded lettuce for a salad, while Cas replaced the kitchen light, refitted the door knob, and built a fire in the parlor fireplace.

They ate dinner on the hearth rug, watching the flames. Then they played scrabble while Smitty snored beside them, and when it was time for bed, Cas was still there.

When the fire was banked, the doors locked, the lights

turned off, they went upstairs. And Julie thought, *I could get used to this. This is the way it should be.*

They stopped at the door to the bedroom and Cas kissed her, and for a moment Julie panicked, thinking he'd changed his mind about staying.

But before she could smack herself for being so pathetic, he opened the door and guided her through. She heard Smitty hunker down outside. He was already used to the routine and that made a flutter pass over her heart. Not a good thing. She was going to get hurt again. All it would take was a phone call to shatter everything. He would run off again and it would be her own damn fault for letting it get started in the first place.

But when Cas's fingers begin to pull up the waistband of her sweater, she forgot about the future, good or bad, and gave in to the sensation of his fingers on her skin. Chills ran up her arms and back as he pulled the sweater over her head. She closed her eyes and arched her back, waiting for that incredible moment when he touched her breasts, breasts that were already tingling in anticipation. But his hands moved to her waist and held her lightly in his grasp.

She opened her eyes to see him standing at arm's length, looking at her. She smiled, tentatively. "What?" Her voice was breathy and expectant. She wanted him. Really, really wanted him.

He shook his head, not answering, but continued to gaze at her, her face, her neck, her breasts. His hands slid up her back and unclasped her bra. Then he slowly pulled the straps down her arms with the tips of his fingers, barely touching her skin.

Her bra fell to the floor and he looked his fill. Julie's mouth felt dry and she ran her tongue along her lower lip to moisten it.

"Okay, that does it," said Cas and yanked his sweater off. "I wanted to go slow, savor the moment, but hell, when you do that with your tongue . . ." He tore open his jeans and pushed them down his legs. His cock sprang into the air, dusky and hard and ready.

Julie feasted on the sight, then gave a quiet laugh.

"What?" asked Cas.

Julie unbuttoned her jeans and wriggled them down her hips. Cas's erection jumped to attention. "I was thinking that your cock goes so well with the décor."

He grinned, then groaned, and pulled her onto the bed.

"I might say the same for you," he said moments later, his mouth poised between her legs. He opened her with his fingers. "*This* is pink." And he licked the spot that made her gasp, then he circled it with his tongue, then took it between his lips and sucked.

"Oh God, Cas." She felt his breath on her and it felt too good. He circled her again and drove his tongue inside her, then came back to circle her again. She came before she could stop herself, bucking with the violence of her contractions. Cas gripped her butt and sucked her while she rocked and cried out, again and again.

Finally, she became aware of Smitty whining in the hall and pawing the door. She fell back. Cas turned his cheek to rest on her stomach. "He thinks I'm molesting you," he said, breathing hard.

"You are." She lifted her shoulders until she could pull him up by his armpits. "Now I'm going to molest you."

Cas was jolted out of a deep sleep by the ringing of a phone. His cell phone. He moved Julie aside and crawled over her to reach his jeans. He flipped his phone open and saw Terrence's number. Damn.

"Cas here."

"Edith just called me," rumbled Terrence. "There's a robbery in progress at the Vales, 20 Halbeck Lane. I'm heading over there now. Thought you'd want to know."

"I'm on my way," said Cas and flipped his phone off. Then he remembered his car was parked four long, steep blocks away. Damn.

Julie sat up. "Whatisit?" She sounded groggy and sated.

Cas had to make himself not crawl back into bed and keep her that way.

"A robbery in progress," he said, pulling on his T-shirt and looking for his socks.

"Robbery?" She jolted upright, propelled herself across the bed, and reached for him. Cas automatically stepped back.

But she wasn't reaching for him. She pulled out the drawer of the bedside table and brought out her gun. At the same time, she dropped her feet to the floor and stood up.

"What are you doing?" said Cas, staring at the weapon.

Julie looked down at it like she'd never seen it before, then she looked at him. "I—uh—"

And Cas got a weird sinking feeling in the pit of his stomach. Their eyes met. Hers shifted away and suspicion wrapped around his heart. She slept with a gun next to her pillow and her first reaction was to reach for it. Even groggy with sleep, she was prepared to use it. Was she afraid? Had someone hurt her? He wouldn't let anyone hurt her again. He shook himself. He had to go.

"I—thought—that you might need this." She slowly handed it toward him. "You don't have yours here."

"No, but I do need your car." He headed for the door.

"Keys on the kitchen table."

He looked over his shoulder at her. She was still holding the gun but now she was holding her jeans in her free hand. "Put the gun away," he said firmly.

"I'm coming with you." She stepped into her jeans, while still holding the gun.

"No, you're not. Put it away."

"What? Oh." She dropped it back into the drawer and shoved the drawer shut.

"I'll be back." He opened the door, turned and tripped over Smitty who was still sleeping in the doorway. "Dammit," he said, as he regained his balance and ran down the hall to the stairs. Smitty lumbered to his feet and followed him downstairs.

"Take Smitty with you." Julie called after him.

He found the keys and when he reached the front door, Smitty was waiting for him.

"No, Smitty," he said, pushing the dog aside. "You stay here and protect Julie."

He eased out the door into the night. A minute later, he was chugging down the hill toward Halbeck Lane. His fingers gripped the steering wheel. His jaw was clenched so hard that his teeth hurt. Not from tension or adrenaline, but because of Julie's reaction. There was something major she hadn't told him.

And here he'd been, congratulating himself on finally getting her to open up. Yesterday had seemed so perfect that he'd actually begun to think . . . what was she hiding? What was she afraid of? An old boyfriend, or was it part of her job? The thought sent a chill through his bloodstream. When she said she worked for the city, he'd just assumed she meant as a stenographer or clerk. But she might—no, it was too preposterous. Then again she was pretty damn good at self-defense.

He downshifted at the yield sign and pulled onto the highway just as a van sped toward him, then veered to the right and shot down Old Mill Road. He looked at the clock on the dashboard. 3:26. Too late for the residents of Ex Falls. There were only four houses by the river and no one lived in the boarded-up mill town. Definitely suspicious behavior.

Any other time he would have followed it, but tonight, he had a more serious priority. He pushed the VW up to sixty, and a few minutes later he turned onto Halbeck Lane. He could see the portable blue light whirling on top of Terrence's SUV half way down the block.

Cas pulled in behind it and banged on the car door, then remembered he was in Julie's Volkswagen. He opened the door and unfolded himself from the seat.

Roy Nesbitt and his wife, Nanette, stood on the stoop of their redwood ranch house, talking to Terrence. Nanette's arms were crossed over a purple terrycloth robe. The curlers in her hair were a lighter shade of lavender. Roy had pulled his over-alls on over his striped pajamas and was pointing across the street toward the darkened Vale house.

Terrence looked up when Cas reached them. "Roy here said he was up going to the bathroom, when he saw a light bobbing around through the window. Since the Vales are in Saranac Lake visiting with their new grandbaby, he called Edith."

"Good thinking," said Cas, gazing at the house in question as if he could conjure up the thieves and cuff them. "Are they still in there?"

"I don't think so," said Roy. "When I came out to let Terrence in, we heard a truck drive away. Or maybe it was a souped-up car. There wasn't anything parked in the driveway, so they must have parked it a ways off. If it was them."

"It was them," said Terrence.

"Thanks, Roy," said Cas. "You've been a great help. I'll come back and take a written statement on Monday if that's okay."

"No need," said Roy. "I've gotta be in town anyway. I'll just stop by the station. Save you a trip."

"Thanks," Cas repeated, then turned to Terrence. "Shall we take a look?"

Terrence already had the flashlight off his utility belt.

"New car?" asked Roy, nodding at the Volkswagen.

Like the whole town didn't know it was Julie's. And they would all know who was driving it tonight before he even got to work on Monday. "No. I, uh, borrowed it."

Nanette's lips pursed together. She'd be on the phone to his mother first thing in the morning. Shit was going to hit. But in the meantime, he had thieves to catch.

"Looks like a good little car," said Roy. "If you don't need us anymore, we'll be getting back to bed. Goodnight." He winked at Cas, then ushered his wife back into the house.

Terrence and Cas walked across the street and peered in the front windows. Everything looked normal until they got to the back yard. The kitchen door was flung open. The robbers must have beat a hasty retreat when they heard Terrence arrive. Cas should have thought to tell him not to drive up to the house.

"I shoulda thought not to drive right up to the house and risk scaring them away," rumbled Terrence. "I sure would like to have caught those assholes. I mean, if you gotta get dragged out of bed in the middle of the night when you got a fine woman keeping you warm, you at least ought to catch the offenders."

"Yeah," said Cas. He was thinking the same damn thing.

"Hey, look over here," said Terrence, shining the flashlight at the kitchen window. "It's been pried open with a chisel or something. They must have climbed in here, but taken the stuff out through the back door. Guess they were in too big of a hurry to lock up after themselves."

Cas scowled at the window. "Two robberies, if you exclude the chickens, and both took place while the occupants were out of town. Someone must have known they would be gone."

"Yeah," said Terrence. "Like the whole damn town." He aimed his flashlight beam into the kitchen. "Jolene's been showing pictures of her grandbaby to anyone who'll look. And A.J. was down at the Roadhouse a few nights ago, talking about how they were going to stay at the Holiday Inn because after raising six of his own, he wasn't getting up in the middle of the night for a baby ever again."

The Roadhouse, thought Cas and wondered if Henry Goethe had been there talking about his trip before he was robbed.

"Think we ought to go in?"

"I guess," said Cas. "But don't touch anything. I'll see if the county will send someone over tomorrow and dust for prints, but any fool who watches television knows to wear gloves."

"Yeah," said Terrence and led the way inside.

The entertainment unit in the living room had been emptied out. "Damn, A.J.'s going to be pissed off," said Terrence. "He just bought a big screen TV and put up an extra satellite dish since this side of town doesn't have cable yet."

"Plus a stereo and who knows what else," said Cas, nodding to where a tangle of wires lay on the shelf.

None of the other rooms seemed touched. "You probably scared them away before they could get anything else," said Cas.

"Woulda rather caught the bastards. There had to be at least two to pick up that television and they couldn't carry it very far."

They stopped in the kitchen. Terrence closed the window using a big red handkerchief, then locked the door.

They stood in the backyard while Terrence ran his flashlight over the yard and into the trees behind it.

"What's back there?" asked Cas.

"Railroad tracks from when the Erie local used to come through. Not used anymore."

They walked to the edge of yard and found the broken branches of the rhododendron bushes. They looked at each other, then stepped through the opening.

Up a graded incline, railroad tracks ran parallel to Halbeck Lane.

"And I bet those are the tracks that cut across the road down by the package store," said Cas.

"Yep," said Terrence. "Drove the getaway vehicle right along the tracks, loaded it up and backed out onto the road. Damn. You could have passed them on your way here."

"I think I might have. And if I did, it was a dark van. Let me drop off Julie's car and we'll go for a ride."

Julie heard the VW's engine long before she saw the lights bouncing over the rutted drive. She watched from the upstairs window as two cars stopped at the front of the house. Cas got out, but instead of coming inside, he got in the other car and they drove away.

He wasn't coming back after all. And she'd thought they would have another night and day together, but she shouldn't have. She shouldn't start expecting things. That's what got you into trouble. Hoping she could outrun her past and make a go of a new life, thinking she could change her feelings about the town, meeting Cas again and thinking . . . hoping . . . but she shouldn't. Hell, she didn't even want to admit what she was hoping.

But she could no more stop it than she could stop the river that flowed through town, though maybe that wasn't a good analogy. It was a pretty piss-poor river. She loved Cas. She'd probably always loved him. He'd been her best friend from the day they met. In her child's mind, he would always be a part of her world, like Wes. As an adolescent, she'd never questioned his loyalty; they were a team, like twins. Then they were torn apart. And he walked away, tearing her in half.

I love him, she thought. And she was rapidly falling *in love* with him. *Is this what you wanted, Wes? Did you lure me back because Cas was here?*

But Cas wasn't here, she reminded herself. He was here and then he drove away. She sighed. At least she knew he was safe and now she wouldn't have to endure the third degree over that slip with the Glock.

The telephone rang.

"It's me," said Cas. "Terrence and I are out investigating. Leave the door unlocked. I'll be back."

Julie hung up and smiled. So maybe things weren't so complicated. He wasn't suspicious about the Glock and she'd tell him the truth before he had a chance to figure it out on his own.

It was getting light when Cas and Terrence cruised slowly down Old Mill Road, looking into driveways for trucks that didn't belong to the inhabitants.

"None of these people would break and enter," said Cas.

"You'd be amazed at what people will do," said Terrence. "I'll come back tomorrow and ask if anybody saw an unfamiliar van in the middle of the night." He grinned through his beard. "And poke my head in just for a look-see while I'm asking."

"Have you ever thought about being sheriff?" asked Cas.

"Nope. The garage is doing good, and if the Roadhouse keeps doing as well as it has been, Tilda and I are getting married."

"No shit," said Cas. "Congratulations."

"Thanks. What about you and Julie? Let's take a quick look-see over at the mill." Terrence turned off the road and the SUV rattled over the bridge.

"Jesus," said Cas. "I haven't been on this thing since I came back. Are you sure it's safe?"

"Yeah, but the retaining wall is beginning to crumble. One day some kid's going to be walking along it, and it'll fall down right under him. Then where will we be? The water probably won't be higher than his head, but he could get hurt."

Cas leaned over to look at the two-hundred-year-old wall. It didn't look like it could hold itself up, much less the water that had been diverted to make a harbor for the river barges that once carried goods down to the Hudson. "Why don't they tear it down?"

"So why didn't you answer my question?"

Cas made a pretense of looking out the window, although if anyone had driven over here, they'd be long gone by now. It would take days to search the abandoned houses and the vast interior of the mill for hidden contraband.

Terrence was silent and Cas finally said, "Because I don't quite know what's going on."

"Shit, you're kidding, right?"

Cas frowned at him. "I . . . no, I'm not."

"They used to call it courting, I'm not sure what they call it now."

Try great head-banging, libido-freeing sex, thought Cas, but he wasn't about to share that with Terrence or anyone else. "We're not exactly doing that, courting. She's going to be leaving soon, and I don't know what the hell I'm doing."

"She going back to New York City? Why somebody would want to live there is beyond me. It's a dangerous place. But I gotta say, that girl can look after herself."

Yeah, thought Cas. *She certainly doesn't need me to take care of her.*

"Even so, I wouldn't want any woman I loved living alone down there."

"Love?" Cas yelped the word and then felt the heat rush to his face. "Who said anything about love?" And who was he kidding? He loved her, alright. No doubt about it. "Obvious, huh?"

Terrence pulled on his beard as he guided the truck up a narrow, crooked lane. "Not to me. But Tilda says so and she knows these things."

"And did the all-knowing Ms. Green happen to say whether Julie loves me back?"

"Tilda says she does, but that she just hasn't figured it out yet. She's blocked. That's what Tilda says."

"Blocked?"

"Yeah, something she read in one of those magazines she and the girls are always passing around at the beauty parlor. You know the ones at the grocery store that say things like, Give Him What He Wants, But Won't Ask For. Well, I guess there was an article on how to know if your significant other is in love."

"And how do you know?"

"Aw hell, I don't know. I just know that Tilda loves me and that's enough for me."

An hour later, Cas backed his truck out of Tilda's driveway, tired, frustrated, and wanting only to return to Julie's warm bed, her warm body. But it was after six and she'd be up dealing with her chickens. Cas was too exhausted to help her out and too much of a gentleman to sit while she worked. Besides, he'd be dead to the world by the time she was ready for him.

He flipped open his cell and punched in Wes's number. It rang ten times before he hung up. *Outside with the chickens*, he told himself. He passed Highland Avenue and headed for home.

He needed sleep before he could face the Sunday dinner. They would know all about his weekend by this afternoon, and he'd need plenty of patience to deal with their reaction.

Hell, he and Julie were consenting adults, but he couldn't tell them to mind their own business. Or ask them to accept her as the woman he loved. Reynolds would have a coronary.

He wasn't even sure what he wanted to say, even if they were willing to listen. He couldn't tell if Julie felt as deeply about him as he did about her. Everything seemed to be a game with her.

And the thing with the gun had him worried.

Hell, his life couldn't get much more complicated and he had Wes Excelsior to thank for it, and himself to blame. Wes hadn't really talked about Julie before he died, except reminiscing about the past. Cas let him talk. It seemed to ease the dying man's final days. Now he realized that maybe Wes wasn't just comforting himself, but preparing Cas to meet Julie again. Because somehow, Wes had managed to get her to return to Excelsior Falls.

Maybe that's why she had the gun. She might be afraid to stay in the house by herself. It was pretty isolated. But it didn't explain why she had been roaming the woods that first night, searching for thieves. Or why she had jumped up when she heard there was a robbery in progress.

Cas's insides tightened. Julie Excelsior had a few questions to answer—he yawned—as soon as he slept and confronted his family over dinner.

Chapter 19

Julie sat on the kitchen steps, absently stroking Ernestine's head as she tried to quell her sense of impending doom.

She snorted, her breath making a cloud in front of her. *Doom.* Wasn't she her own woman? Hadn't she handled worse situations than having to explain to Cas that she was a cop? Or at least had been a cop. It wasn't that big of a deal. She'd let the whole thing get out of proportion. She'd been a good detective and she was proud of it. And if Cas felt inferior because she could hit a target and he couldn't, well to hell with him.

Instead of moping on the steps, she should be looking for the treasure, looking for a new job. Hell. She should have never left the old one.

And she should definitely stop rehashing her past and start getting on with her future. Right. If that future had any chance of being with Cas, she needed to come clean about everything. Swallow the chagrin she felt every time she thought about being demoted for being honest. Hell. That's why she didn't tell him. She'd done the right thing and been given the shaft. *Stop beating that dead horse. Let it go and tell Cas.*

And where was Cas? You'd think he'd call to let her know he was all right. He must have called and she'd been outside and not heard the phone.

She stood up and went into the house. Spent the morning with one ear listening for the phone.

It finally rang at twelve-forty, Cas letting her know that he was having lunch with his parents and would come over afterwards. "Two hours, three hours max. You get to see me in a suit."

See, she knew he'd call. And she almost envied his family dinner, except that the family was Marian and Charles Reynolds. So she made herself a bowl of soup and practiced her coming-clean speech while she ate.

Cas knew as soon as Larue showed him into the parlor that he was walking into a full-blown gale. Mel looked up from where she sat on the window seat and frowned a warning at him. Marian perched on the edge of one of the wing chairs as if she were getting ready to pounce—or flee.

Reynolds stood at the fireplace, which today held a blazing fire. He was holding his martini glass tight enough to snap the stem. His face was flushed and Cas guessed that pre-dinner drinks had started early that day.

Christine and Ian were conspicuously missing.

"Where are the Macgregors?" Cas asked, leaning over to give his mother a kiss on the cheek.

Her cheek was cool and her posture unyielding and Cas thought, *why can't you show some emotion toward your children?*

"Christine isn't feeling well," she answered. "I'm sure she's working too hard. One would think they would hire help."

"They did—me," volunteered Melanie with an evil glint in her eye.

"And you know how your father feels on that subject."

"Well, if I got an allowance, I wouldn't have to soil my hands with honest labor." Melanie held up her hands to show them, purposefully turning them so that her black fingernail polish was in full view.

Marian's look could have frozen her to her seat.

Mel smiled coolly back at her parents, and Cas realized that she was provoking them on purpose. That's all he needed, to have Reynolds primed for a fight before they even sat down to lunch. Then he wondered if Mel was drawing their fire to keep it from him. It was going to be a long afternoon without Christine and Ian running interference.

He went to the drinks cart and poured himself a Scotch that he didn't intend to drink but thought he might need just to have something to do to pass the time until Larue rang them in. He would eat and leave—back to Julie.

It seemed to Cas that Larue announced dinner earlier than usual. Maybe because they'd started happy hour early. *Happy hour*, he thought sardonically. *If only.*

He walked Melanie into the dining room.

She lagged behind until Reynolds had left the room. "They know about Julie," she whispered to him. "Watch your back."

Cas nodded, aware that his mother's radar was on full alert.

Dinner passed as always, except that it went more quickly without the full complement of guests. He could be at Julie's in less than two hours if after-dinner coffee went as quickly.

But as they were returning to the parlor, his father motioned him back toward the library instead. As Cas followed him down the hall, he wondered, not for the first time, why he never stood up to his father. He wasn't a coward. But it had always been easier to put up with Reynolds's bouts of ill humor than it was to deal with them. Because Reynolds never listened to reason.

Cas was surprised to see his mother step into the library behind him. Reynolds gave her a look so cold that Cas almost felt sorry for her. "There are a few things I need to discuss with Charles. We'll join you in the parlor in a few minutes."

Marian's long fingers touched her helmet of hair. She hesitated, then lifting her chin, a gesture that marked her as Melanie's mother, she left the room.

Cas watched the door long after it closed behind her. Years ago, she would never have put up with such a dismissal. He unconsciously put a hand to his forehead.

"Sit down."

Cas turned at the peremptory tone in his father's voice. He took a deep breath. "You might *ask* me to sit," he said, continuing to stand.

"It's that woman."

Cas clung to his temper. He should have known Reynolds would find a way to blame Melanie's fingernails, Cas's disobedience, his wife's presumption, on Julie. He sank into the chair out of sheer weariness.

"The whole goddamn town knows you're sleeping with her. Just because you park down at Tilda Green's and skulk up the hill for your liaisons, doesn't mean you're fooling anybody. Do you know how that makes us look?"

"It makes me look happy," said Cas and mentally kicked himself for not thinking before he spoke. Melanie must be rubbing off on him. "And I'm sure most of the town is happy for me, too."

"And then," Reynolds continued as if Cas hadn't spoken. "To have Nanette Nesbitt call your mother this morning and tell her you're driving her car all over creation and in the middle of the night. It's disgusting."

Cas didn't bother to defend himself. It just didn't matter anymore.

"I saved you from her once. You were too young to know what she was up to then, but you could at least have the good sense to stay away from her now."

"She wasn't up to anything then or now. It's all in your mind."

Reynolds shook his head, slowly, a look of pity in his eyes. "She tried to ruin you."

Cas's fist came down on the desk. He looked at it, almost as surprised as Reynolds. "We were kids, playing a kid's game. You turned it into something dirty. Your reaction led the town; they got over it. But I didn't and Julie didn't. You drove her away. You won't do it again."

"Wes threw her at you to corrupt you and get back at me."

"Oh god, Dad. Stop it. Wes took us both in when no one

else cared about us. Not her father, not you, not my mother. He taught us about life, taught us how to laugh and to dream. We were children." Cas wound down, feeling sicker than he had ever felt in his life. He took a breath that seared his lungs. "You've let this thing with Wes take control of your life. He's dead now. Let it go. The feud is over."

He leaned across the desk and was dismayed to see his father edge back in his seat.

"Dad," he said in a calmer voice that took all his strength. "You're sixty-three years old. You have years ahead of you. You need to find something to do with your life. Go back to work, get a hobby, take mother on a cruise. I'll pay for it. Volunteer at the Henryville Y and do some good. But don't try to carry on the feud.

"Because Julie won't be here to fight with you. We're leaving. So anything you say or do to hurt her, we won't know about it. And we won't care."

"We? What do you mean, we?" Reynolds had reached an unhealthy shade of red, but it was too late for Cas to stop.

"We. I'm going to marry her, if she'll have me." He stopped, shocked at his own admission. "I wouldn't blame her if she refused me, but I'm going to ask."

"Over my dead body. If you run off with that woman, I'll disinherit you."

"There's nothing to inherit, but hatred."

"You'll no longer be a Reynolds. I'll disown you."

Cas threw up his hands. "Listen to yourself. You're like some character in an old novel. Give it up." He stood up and started toward the door.

"There's something you don't know about her," said Reynolds. "I knew you'd end up doing something stupid like this, so I had her investigated."

Cas stopped, his hand on the door knob.

"She's a police detective."

"I—I know." Or at least he suspected. Slowly he turned

back to face his father. "Is that why you're frightened? Was Wes holding something over your head? Are you afraid Julie will find out? What did you do?"

"How. Dare. You."

"If I'm wrong, I apologize," said Cas, trying to keep the tremor from his voice. "But Wes left me a . . . message. About thieves stealing gold. Is that why the Savings and Loan closed?"

Reynolds clutched the edge of the desk. "After you were caught on the river, Wes Excelsior took his money out of the Savings and Loan. Every red cent of it. Paying me back for stopping that little piece of white trash from seducing you. It ruined the bank."

Cas lowered his head to his hand, rubbed his eyes. "Everything is Wes's fault."

"Yes, godamn it, it is. Even when he was dying, he had the effrontery to bring that—that—"

"Don't," Cas warned.

"His niece back here. And you, Mr. Hot Shot, let yourself be taken in by a couple of swindlers."

"Enough." If he stayed they would run on this treadmill forever. There was nothing he could do for his father. "I have to go."

Reynolds stood and jabbed his finger at Cas. "She was fired for misconduct." He spit out the words. "She was taking bribes from drug dealers. What do you think about your Ms. Excelsior now? Ah, yes. She'd be an addition anyone would be proud of to a family tree."

Cas's world went dark for a moment. "I don't believe it," he said. He opened the door.

"Drug money," his father yelled.

Cas shut the door on his words. The hallway was empty. No Marian, no Melanie. Not even Larue to see him out. He walked toward the front door, each footfall echoing off the marble floor.

Outside, the air was still. Cas cranked up the old truck and headed down the drive. He'd never felt more alone in his life.

*   *   *

Julie stood at the window looking out. It was nice to have someone to expect, but it was kind of pitiful that she was so eager for Cas to return. The sky grew dark, first with clouds, then with the onset of night, and still she watched.

"I guess we've been stood up," she said finally and stepped away from the window. She looked at the clock on the mantel. "Six-thirty. He isn't coming."

Well, to hell with him. She checked the phone, just to make sure it was working, and got a big healthy dial tone. Maybe there had been an emergency and he didn't have time to call.

But by nine o'clock, she had to admit that something else had prevented him from coming and that something had to be Charles Reynolds.

"Fuck it. I'm not sitting here like I had nothing to do but wait for him." She gathered up her keys and drove down to the Roadhouse.

Terrence stood up when Julie got to the bar. "Take my seat," he said, then turned to Tilda. "I'll pick you up after closing."

"Where's he going?" asked Julie as she sat down.

"To the garage to hitch up his snow plow," said Tilda, setting a Foster's in front of her.

"We're expecting snow?"

"End of the week, but it pays to be ready."

The door opened, bringing in a draft of cold air and several men. "Buds all around," one of them called to Tilda.

"Coming up." Tilda went off to serve them their beers.

The door opened again, and again, and soon the Roadhouse was filled with people.

"Business is hopping tonight," said Julie.

"Yeah. Everybody's coming in for the final fuel-up before getting stuck at home."

"Stuck? Exactly how much snow are we talking about?"

"A couple of feet toward the end of the week. Then it'll all melt and we'll live knee deep in mud til the next freeze."

"Shit," said Julie.

Tilda dipped two glasses into sudsy water and put them on the drain to dry. "That about covers it. I wouldn't mind having a couple of days off, except that Terrence will be busy plowing people out, so I might as well be working." She washed two more glasses. "What are you gonna do?"

"Huh?" Then Julie realized it was a rhetorical question. But what *was* she going to do? She'd meant to be gone by the first snow, and here she was sitting at the Roadhouse like a regular. So much for Sell and Bail. She hadn't even approached a realtor.

"You know," said Tilda. "Maybe you should stay down at Cas's until it's over. He'll get plowed out first and Terrence won't make it up the hill for days."

"I have my chickens," said Julie. She decided not to mention that after two nights of the best sex of her life, Cas had dropped off the radar.

"Yeah, I forgot about your chickens. Where is Cas anyway?"

"Beats me," said Julie trying to keep the bitterness out of her voice.

The door opened, bringing in another gust of wind. Henley and Bo squeezed up to the bar between Julie and the next bar stool.

"I told you two not to came back in here," said Tilda.

Henley slapped his hand on the bar. "That ain't no way to treat a good customer. I'll have a Bud and a bourbon."

"Not from my bar, you won't." Tilda leaned over the bar until their noses almost touched. "Now, get out."

"Shit, my money's good as anybody else's." Henley reached in his back pocket and brought out a money clip with a huge wad of bills in it. Tilda's eyes widened. He pulled a fifty off the top and dropped it on the bar. "Now can I have my beer?"

Bo pulled out an identical money clip with a slightly smaller roll of bills. "Yeah, beer."

Tilda pushed the fifty back at Henley. "I don't want your

money—or yours either, Bo. I don't want to see your sorry asses in here. Go over to Henryville and have a blast."

"The hell I will." Henley picked up Julie's mug and drained it. "She'll have another."

"I was just leaving," said Julie.

Henley stepped closer and stuck a beefy thigh between her knees. "No you're not. You were just going to order another beer. You can afford it from what I hear."

Julie eased her legs away. She didn't want to cause any more trouble for Tilda. Henley moved with her, crowding her space until she thought she might throw up.

"We all wondered why Cas was sniffing around you like you was a bitch in heat. Of course, then we didn't know that old man Excelsior had left you a bundle."

Julie stared at him. "You don't know jack shit."

Henley leaned closer, pushing her back against the bar. "Your money's wasted on him. Come with me and I'll show you what a real man can do."

"Gee," said Julie. "Think you can find one?"

Henley snarled and reached for her.

Julie knocked his hand away. "Ease off, bulldog. If I have to swing at you again, I won't miss." Out of the corner of her eye, she saw Tilda reach under the counter.

Henley laughed. Bo snickered.

Tilda straightened up and aimed a sawed-off shotgun at his chest. "Out," she said and jerked the shotgun in the direction of the door.

Henley eased away from Julie. "Guess money talks if you're an Excelsior,"

"Now." Tilda waved the shotgun again. Several people ducked.

"Don't get crazy, Tilda. We're leaving." Henley stepped back and bumped into Bo. He shoved past him, and Bo was left looking at Tilda's shotgun. Without a word, he scrambled after Henley.

"And good riddance," said someone from the other side of the bar.

Tilda uncocked the shotgun and slid it beneath the counter. "It only shoots salt," she said, pouring out another beer for Julie. "Won't do any real harm if you don't aim at the face. But it stings like the devil. Makes them remember why they don't want to mess with Tilda Green."

Julie let out her breath. "Pretty impressive."

Tilda handed her a fresh beer. "Hear you carry some pretty hefty hardware yourself."

Julie nearly dropped the beer mug.

"Cas told Terrence and Terrence told me. Don't ever tell a man a secret unless you want the whole world to know it. And they talk about women. Sheesh." She beetled her eyebrows and her face took on a demonic expression. Her maroon hair framed her face like the flames of hell. "Makes you wonder."

"Wonder what?" asked Julie apprehensively.

Tilda leaned over the bar and lowered her voice. "A Glock is standard police issue."

Julie's stomach turned over and went into freefall.

"Don't worry. I won't tell. Are you here undercover? Does Cas know?"

Julie laughed and knew it rang false. "You've got some kind of imagination, Tilda."

Tilda looked hurt. "I won't tell."

Impulsively, Julie reached out and touched her wrist. "I'm not undercover. I'm here because of Wes. That's all. But I'd rather people didn't know. I'm enough of a freak show already."

"That's a kick," said Tilda. "Half the men in this bar start drooling into their beer the minute you walk in, and the other half would, but their wives would kill them. And it isn't because you're a freak."

Julie laughed, this time for real. "I'm waiting for a man who wants me for my mind."

"That's a good one," said Tilda. "Honey, men are like hound

dogs, they only want one thing. And I'm not talking about kibble." She propped herself on her elbows and settled in for a talk. "But with good training and a gentle hand, you got a companion for life."

"I think I'll stick to chickens."

"You and Cas have a fight? Cause his truck has been parked in my driveway all weekend, and I was beginning to think that the Reynolds-Excelsior feud was finally gonna end."

So had Julie. She shrugged. "I think we have . . . issues."

"Man oh man. Stay away from anything that goes inside quotation marks. Trip you up every time. Just be happy. That's what I say."

Julie sipped her beer while she thought about that one. "Are you happy?"

Tilda pulled in her chin and looked hard at Julie. "Well, hell yeah. I own my own house, my own business. I've got Terrence half trained. Not bad for a girl who started life in a trailer park. And besides, what's the alternative?"

"Hmm," said Julie. "I hadn't thought of it that way."

"Well, think about it. You want another beer?"

Several beers later, Julie brought the Volkswagen to a stop in front of Excelsior House. She shouldn't have been driving. If she had pulled herself over, she would have given herself a breathalyzer test. And she would have failed it.

She rolled out of the car and nearly jumped out of her skin when Smitty barreled out of the dark and nearly knocked her down.

"What are you doing out?" Julie looked around, disoriented. She would never leave him outside while she was gone.

Smitty jumped at her, then trotted toward the house. He turned to look back at her when he reached the front porch. And Julie began to run.

She raced past him and threw herself against the wall next to the door. Listened but heard nothing from inside the house.

Her keys were still in her hand, but she had a feeling she wouldn't need them.

She turned the doorknob and the door opened. Smitty bolted past her and ran inside. She followed more cautiously. The parlor had been ransacked. Pillows were cut open and feathers spewed out of them. Books were thrown everywhere, their spines broken, the pages bent. But the only thing that was missing was Wes's riddle.

"Goddamn it," yelled Julie. "We've been robbed."

Chapter 20

The burglar had jimmied the kitchen window to get in and had left by the front door. She deliberated for a long time about calling Cas, but since the riddle was the only thing stolen, she decided against it. He'd stood her up and she didn't want him to think she was chasing him.

And she knew that he wouldn't be able to find any clues she might have missed, so she cleaned up the mess and went to bed.

The first thing she did the next morning was call the police station. Lou Turnbull answered the phone. "That's just awful," she said when Julie told her about the break in. "Are you all right? The sheriff is on another call right now, but I'll get him over there as soon as he's finished."

"No," said Julie. "Nothing was taken and I'm fine. I just wanted to file the report. Really, there's no reason for the sheriff to make the trip. He has more serious thefts to investigate."

"Well, he does have that. So many all at once. It doesn't seem right. If you're sure . . ."

"I'm sure. Thanks, Lou."

"You looked real nice at the dance Friday night. Everybody said so."

Julie looked at the phone. "Uh, thank you."

"It's awfully nice to have an Excelsior show an interest in the town again. You take care."

Julie hung up, wondering why Lou was always so nice. And then she thought of all the people she'd met since returning. *Shit, I'm making friends here.*

Which was not good, because she was planning to leave again. But first . . . She grabbed her car keys and drove into town.

Dan Pliney looked up when she walked into the Hardware and Feed Store. "Morning, Julie. Don't tell me. You're here to buy a shovel."

"What?" asked Julie, frowning at him. "I need a new lock for my kitchen window."

"Oh." Dan scratched his head. "That's good, 'cause I'm almost out of shovels. Oddest thing. Seems like everybody that's been in here today needed one." He stepped out from behind the counter. "Come on over here and let's see what kind of lock I can fix you up with."

Julie was paying for the lock when Elton Dinwiddie strode in. He hesitated when he saw Julie, then said, "Good morning, Julie," and stood shifting from one foot to the other until she had finished making her purchase.

She was just closing the door, when she heard him say, "Dan, I need a shovel."

There had been another robbery during the night, this time a mile from town. Cas and Terrence went out to investigate even though it was in the county's jurisdiction. It had the same MO as their robberies and they had no intention of being left out.

When Cas finally made it home that afternoon, depressed and moody from lack of sleep and no leads, his computer was still connected to the internet where he'd been looking up mentions of Julie Excelsior, when the call came in.

Now, he sat down and stared at the screen with gritty eyes. He'd torture himself with a few more hits and then go over to Hank Jessop's and turn in his resignation. The county would have to handle this fresh spate of robberies. He was out of his league and he was leaving.

He clicked on the *New York Times* website and continued to read about the scandal that had broken at Julie's precinct.

Julie was a cop; not just a cop, a detective. And a good one. He'd read articles about the arrests she'd made, the cases she'd cracked, about her heroism, before he got to the series of articles concerning the bribery charges brought against her partner and several of his associates. But not against Julie. Nowhere did it even mention her in relation to the bribery charges.

He already knew that she would never do anything dishonest, but that was hardly the point.

She must have been laughing at him since the first night he showed up with his unloaded antique .38, incompetent as all hell, and wanting to protect her.

Yeah. It left his ego pretty bruised. That he could take, but if his father was really guilty of a crime, he'd almost led Julie right to his door. Thank God he'd chickened out at the last minute and fudged the last part of his riddle. If he'd told her the bit about thieves, she might be arresting his father this very minute.

But he didn't really believe that either. Reynolds was a lot of things, many of them not nice, but he wasn't a crook.

What really hurt was that Julie hadn't told him the truth. Hadn't trusted him. Hadn't cared enough about him to be honest with him. That's what had left him feeling so battered. He loved her and she didn't love him, at least not enough.

So he read until the words swam before his eyes and he was filled with self-loathing and anger at Julie. He shut down his computer just as Melanie walked in the door.

"I knocked—twice. You didn't answer."

"Why aren't you in school?"

"Why aren't you at Julie's?" Melanie crossed her arms and glared at him.

"Why should I be?"

Melanie gave him a look. "Besides the fact that you're fucking her, her house was broken into last night."

Cas's stomach clenched. He had to stop himself from jumping out of his chair and rushing over to Excelsior House. "Where did you hear that?"

"The whole town knows. And knows you're not doing one damn thing about it."

"She can do fine without me."

"That's not what I hear."

"Have you heard she was a cop?"

Melanie's expression didn't change, but Cas knew he had surprised her and he doubted if Mel would like the idea, but *she* surprised *him*.

"I figured it must be something like that. She's pretty good at all that self-defense shit." She uncrossed her arms and took a step toward him. "So she's a cop. Are you going to let that fuck up everything?"

"I don't know what you mean."

"Stop acting like such a dickhead. It's obvious you got it bad for her. And she's got it bad for you. I don't know why. You are such a dweeb."

"Thank you. I'm sure Julie shares your sentiment." He walked over to the kitchen, where he started making coffee. What he really needed was sleep, but he knew that would be impossible.

Melanie followed him. "Just swallow it and go see her."

Ignoring her, Cas poured water into the coffee maker. He reached across her and took a mug from the cupboard. He placed it on the counter.

"She'll never forgive you if you run out on her again."

Cas stopped with his hand on the sugar bowl. "You don't know what you're talking about."

"Do so."

He turned so fast that he caught her smiling. Any other time, he would have felt gratified; today he just felt pissed off.

"I know all about it. Wes told me."

"Wes. Told you."

"Sure. He knew you were probably going to act like a dick-head, so he filled me in on the background."

"If he weren't dead, I'd kill him," said Cas.

"Not funny."

"I know. I'm sorry. I keep forgetting you were his friend, too."

Melanie quirked one shoulder, brushing his concern away. "No big deal. I gotta go. Just stop acting like an idiot, okay?"

"I'll try," said Cas.

She slouched off toward the door. When she got there, she said, "Hey."

Cas looked up. She tossed something at him; he caught it automatically. When she was gone, he looked down. He was holding an orange lollipop.

"Great," he said and tossed it in the trash.

Julie sat in the Beetle outside the library. It was still an hour before closing and she had some serious research to do. If Cas wouldn't help her figure out the riddle, then the Web would. She scribbled in her notebook, trying to reconstruct the exact words Wes had written. "In marble halls . . . soft as silk . . ." She tapped her pen on the page. "A golden apple lies within." And then Cas's part. Something about no door or was it a lock . . . something . . . gold. . . . Something.

She closed her notebook and returned it to her purse. That ought to be enough to get a few hits. She got out of the car and went up the library steps.

Inside, the air was cold except for a halo of warmth cast by a space heater around the circulation desk. Emily Patterson looked up from a copy of the Ex Falls *Gazette* and smiled. Then she saw Julie and the smile dimmed.

"May I help you?"

Guess I'm not her favorite person. No surprise there. Julie had seen the way Emily looked at Cas the night of the Dance.

Her and quite a few others. The town Don Juan. The jerk. "Yes," said Julie. "So they're still printing the *Gazette*."

The librarian blinked several times. "Every two weeks. More or less. This is the library copy. Would you like to see it?" She began to fold the newspaper.

"No thanks, I came to use your internet connection."

"The computer's over there." Emily stood up, leaned over the top of the circulation desk, and pointed to an ancient Compaq. "Do you need help getting connected?"

"Thanks, Emily," said Julie. "I think I know what to do."

The librarian nodded, looked as if she were going to speak, then sat down. "Just ask if you need help."

Julie nodded and headed for the computer.

After what seemed an eon, she was finally connected. She typed in the first line of the riddle. She got over three hundred hits. She clicked on the first. And there was her riddle on a Victorian parlor games and conundrums site.

In marble halls as white as milk, lined with skin as soft as silk, within a fountain crystal clear, a golden apple does appear. Eureka. She grabbed her pencil to write Cas's part of the riddle. *No doors there are in this stronghold, yet thieves break in and steal the gold.* What? She peered at the lines. Cas hadn't said anything about thieves. She would have remembered that.

Julie stared at the screen. *Thieves.* And just where was Cas while she had been at the Roadhouse? Doing a little B and E at Excelsior House? Because he thought she was holding out on him?

Julie clicked on the Answer icon. It took another eternity for the page to appear. And at last the words: *An egg.*

Julie leaned back in her chair. The answer was an egg. A fucking egg. She'd eaten a dozen since she'd been here. And they weren't holding any treasure.

She fed coins into the printer and printed out the page. Then she went back to the desk. "Thanks, Emily. I'm finished."

Emily nodded, then looked up. "There's something in here about you."

Julie looked at the *Gazette*. "Me?"

"Yeah. It's in the *Excelsior Examiner,* the gossip column." She pushed the paper toward Julie and pointed to a place halfway down the page.

A description of the Candy Apple Dance naming all the Queen hopefuls and a full description of the decorations. A few arcane sentences about people that made no sense to Julie, and then: "Julie Excelsior, only living relative of Wesley Excelsior, was looking sophisticated in a black knit sheath."

Hmmm, thought Julie, feeling more kindly toward the writer. "She is the sole heir to what is believed to be an extensive estate. She and Cas Reynolds were looking very happy together. Could the Reynolds-Excelsior feud be ending at last?"

Julie pushed the paper away. *Extensive estate.* That's all she needed: to be hit on for contributions by everyone in town. And when Reynolds read the part about Cas and her—she shuddered to think what he might do.

She handed the paper back to Emily. "I'm glad they liked my dress, but they got it really wrong about the inheritance."

"Aren't you rich?"

"'Fraid not," said Julie.

"What about you and Cas?"

"Just friends."

"Oh," said Emily, looking brighter.

Julie left the library on a slow seethe. She didn't know whether to be angrier over the speculation that she was rich or the innuendo that she was going to marry Cas. God, the men in her life. Donald, the bribe taker; Cas, the cheater.

It wouldn't hurt her reputation to be thought of as rich. It would serve the town right for being mistaken about her so many years before. But Cas. . . .

"He cheated," she told Smitty as she marched into the parlor and threw herself in the wing chair. Smitty sat attentively at her feet while she quoted the new lines. She frowned. *Thieves.*

Was it a warning? Or an incentive? Or something that had already happened? An idea slowly began to take shape.

She jumped up, walked to the window, and looked out. Then she turned and leaned against the windowsill. "Listen to this. Wes leaves me everything, but there's no money. Maybe he didn't hide it. Maybe someone stole it." She started pacing. "So he poses a riddle that will bring me back here and what? Find the perps? Bring them to justice? He knew I was a cop. Hmmmm. And he gave Cas half because . . . he wanted him to help me? Unless it was a warning to Cas, and not me. Wes told me revenge was mine. Did he mean against Cas?"

Cas had arrived in Ex Falls four months before her. He might have stolen Wes's money. Or at least decided to look for it himself. Hell, he might have even prevented Wes from sending her the letter before he died.

She sank back down in the wing chair. "We don't know anything about him, do we, Smitty? Except that he's good in bed."

Smitty whined.

"Okay. Irrelevant." She sighed. "Hell, he might be a crook, but I don't want to exact revenge, and I don't want to carry on the feud. I just want . . ." She lapsed into silence. What she thought she wanted and what she could have were two different things and it was beginning to look like they always would be.

She felt Smitty nudge her leg, then he dropped something in her lap. She looked down; the deflated whoopee cushion lay across her thigh. She picked it up. "Sort of like my ego," she said and hugged it to her chest. "Okay, Wes. Whatever you want. Though you could have just said so instead of sending me on this wild goose chase. I might be finished by now and on my way . . . home."

Right. She had no home. Unless home was here.

When Julie finished feeding the chickens that evening, she stood in the yard, studying the house. It looked different today, just a dilapidated old house. The turret was crooked and the windows were just plain glass. The yard was pockmarked and the shrubs spindly. And Julie realized she had begun to see the house as it once had been. Bright with fresh paint, the yard surrounded by flowering shrubs. the stained glass windows bathing the rooms in prisms of color.

No color there now. No Wes. No future. It was time to go.

The back of her neck prickled and she turned around. She could have sworn someone was watching her, but there was no one there. She stood for a few more minutes scanning the yard and the trees in the distance.

"I'm going nuts," she told Smitty and went inside. But she kept making spot checks through the window during the evening and watched at her bedroom window long after she turned out the lights that night. She couldn't shake the feeling that someone was out there. Watching her, waiting for something.

Cas inspected the Roadhouse parking lot for Julie's car. When he didn't see it, he parked his truck and went inside.

Tilda shook her head when she saw him coming. Tonight her hair had a pink streak through the maroon.

"What?" asked Cas as he sat down.

"It's like Miss Lonelyhearts around here," she said and handed him a beer.

"What?" said Cas.

"What are you doing here? Can't you get a date?" She leaned on her elbows and rested her chin on her fists. "Huh?"

"Lay off, Tilda. I've had a rough day."

"Let's see. Alice Poole should be in soon. They usually come here after the bowling league finishes. Want me to ask her for you?"

Cas picked up his beer; considered throwing it at her, but drank instead. "You know, Tilda, there's a bar over in Henryville that serves microbrewery beer."

Tilda laughed. "Then you could keep Henley and Bo company."

"Finally kicked them out?"

"Yep. Me and trusty Rusty." She glanced down under the bar.

"Do not bring that thing out. I don't want to know about it. What inspired you to finally get rid of them?"

"Henley was hitting on Julie again the other night."

"Oh. Did she deck him?" asked Cas sourly.

Tilda leaned back. "So that's it. Feeling a little threatened, are we? Worried that she's tougher than you are?"

"She's a goddamn cop, Tilda."

"So?"

Cas looked up from his beer and frowned at her. "You knew?"

"Yeah."

"How come I just figured it out?"

Tilda winked at him. "Love is blind, I guess."

Chapter 21

Julie awoke several times during the night to find Smitty at the window, looking out. And as soon as she opened the kitchen door the next morning, he raced up the hill, pissed on the juniper bush and began to snuffle around the shed. He barked. Julie veered over to take a look.

A hole had been started and abandoned.

"Not yours, I take it," she said and received a look of disdain. "Just stay away from it. You do not want to tangle with a skunk or raccoon."

She lifted the latch of the mesh gate to the henhouse and Smitty shot past her to begin sniffing around the base of the gazebo.

"Now what?" Julie followed him over and found another hole, bigger and deeper than the first. And she remembered the Pliney boys saying a fox might have gotten Ernestine. A fox hadn't gotten her, but something was definitely trying to get to her chickens. Fortunately the ground was hard around the building and it thwarted his efforts. But he'd be back.

She counted heads as the chickens filed out of the gazebo, checked on Bill and Hilary, then went outside to stand vigil over the rest of the flock, though she was pretty sure foxes only came out at night.

As soon as they returned to the coop, she put in a call to Maude. "I think I have a fox," Julie told her.

"I'll be right over."

Maude showed up twenty minutes later and Julie took her up to show her the holes.

"Doesn't look like fox to me," said Maude. "Don't know what it looks like." She began checking the perimeter of the mesh fence; Julie followed behind her. "Didn't get in this way. You didn't leave the gate open?"

Julie shook her head.

"Didn't think so. Weird. I brought some sheets of tin to cover the ground around the gazebo, it should keep whatever it is out." Maude shook her head and Julie followed her back down the hill.

It took both of them to carry each unwieldy sheet up the hill. They laid them around the foundation of the henhouse and weighted them down with stones.

"That should do it," said Maude, brushing off her hands. "If you have any more problems let me know."

"Thanks," said Julie. "Would you like some coffee?"

"Love to, but I've got chores at home. They're predicting a snow storm for the end of the week. Make sure to keep the generator clear. You don't want the chickens to suffocate or freeze."

Julie walked her back to the truck.

"Haven't seen Cas lately," said Maude. "How's he doing?"

Julie looked past her toward the orchard. "I don't know. He seems to have lost the need for my companionship."

"What you mean is you two had a fight."

"Not exactly, but he cheated on our deal to share Wes's riddles. I found out about it. He must be staying away so he won't have to confess."

Maude, who had just climbed into her truck, climbed out again. "Why would he cheat?"

"I don't know."

"So did you have any success?"

"Solving the riddle? The answer is an egg."

Maude smiled.

"I don't guess you have any ideas about what Wes really meant."

"Not me," said Maude. "That's one thing I refused to share with him."

Julie flashed on the drawer in Wes's bedroom and bit back a smile.

"Told him I didn't want to be tempted to tell anybody the answer or be accused of anything nefarious."

Julie stopped smiling. "You mean like I just accused Cas."

"Yep. So what are you going to do?"

"Give up I guess. I called Henryville after I talked to you. The realtor's coming out tomorrow to look at the house and give me an estimate on its selling value. Then it will go on the market." She glanced up at the gazebo and had to swallow twice before she asked, "Would you be willing to take the chickens?"

Maude frowned at her. Scratched her head. "Well, yeah, but you can't move Hillary while she's brooding."

"Oh. How much longer is that?"

"Another two weeks. Of course, you could always just force her off the nest. Kill the little chick. Hillary will probably go into a decline. It happens with chickens sometimes. Then if she dies, I don't know what will happen to Bill."

"Okay. Okay. I'll stay until the chick is hatched. Then can you take them?"

Maude smiled. "Sure. If you still want me to. See ya." She hoisted herself into the panel truck and drove away.

That afternoon the weather turned dismal and cold. That night Smitty woke her again with his trips to the window. At last she joined him and they sat watching the darkness. Occasionally, Julie thought she saw the wink of lights in the woods and apple orchard, but dismissed them as optical illusions brought on by lack of sleep.

There were no new holes around the gazebo the next morning, but the temperature continued to drop and heavy dark clouds rolled in and seemed to sit above the old Gothic house. There was definitely a storm on the way and Julie alternated between wanting to leave before it started and kicking herself for her lack of loyalty to Wes and his chickens.

The real estate agent came and was not encouraging. The house needed work, the market was slow. Cas didn't come out to investigate her break-in. And even though she'd told Lou not to tell him, she was pissed at him anyway.

Things were looking bleak. She needed an income and she needed to get back to work for her psyche as well as for her bank account. What she didn't need was to get trapped here in the snow. But what was she going to do with Hilary?

Julie began to prepare for the storm. She moved the feed barrel into the mesh enclosure, rounded up snow shovels and checked the gazebo for chinks that would let in the snow.

And still no word from Cas. She considered going down to the Roadhouse for company, but Cas might be there, and she'd be damned if she would act like she was chasing him. She'd leave those tactics to Isabelle Schott and Emily Patterson.

She called to Smitty and took him for a walk in the woods. But just as they reached the trees, Smitty stopped and growled. Julie stopped too. And listened. Then Smitty bounded off through the woods.

She hurried after him and found him standing over another freshly dug hole. She knelt down and looked at it more closely. Not an animal's hole; this one bore the marks of a tool, and Julie remembered Dan Pliney telling her about the rush for shovels. Someone had been digging on her land.

Not Cas; he would have started at their old hiding places. This hole was in the middle of nothing, just trees. No fountain, no silk, no reason to be dug here. And for the first time since discovering the break-in, Julie thought it might not be Cas who was after her inheritance.

They found several more holes along the path and two around the base of the boulder where she had fallen into Cas's arms a few days before.

Julie erased that image from her mind. Cas might be exonerated from some things, but he was still a cheat. And Julie Excelsior didn't put up with cheats. If she did, she'd still be at work in the NYPD.

She walked along the path until they came out into the orchard. There were holes everywhere. Smitty ran from hole to hole, sniffing and lifting his nose to the wind. Several times he ran a few yards into the woods, but came back a minute later.

"Whoever was here," she told him, "is long gone. And if you ask me, there were a lot of them. Come on. It's time we did something about keeping them from coming back."

She started toward the house, but Smitty ran toward the woods and looked back at her. He barked and took off through the trees. A minute later, she heard a sharp preemptory bark. *More holes*, she thought, and went to check it out. But Smitty hadn't just found a hole, he'd cornered two men at the ruins of the old smokehouse. Their shovels were raised over their heads, ready to fend Smitty off.

"Hey," she cried and ran toward them. They looked up, threw their shovels at Smitty and ran into the trees. Smitty yelped as one hit him on the flank.

"Damn you," yelled Julie and ran after them. Smitty soon passed her and when Julie caught up to him, a rusty red Jeep was bumping down the path back to Hillcrest Drive. She considered trying to cut through the orchard and beat them to it, but knew she would never make it. At least she had a description of the Jeep.

Smitty trotted back to her. A piece of blue denim hung from his mouth.

"Good boy, I hope you got a big piece of flesh, too."

As soon as she got back to the house, she put in a call to the police station. Cas could just start earning his pay for a change and go after the Jeep owner.

Lou answered.

Julie cut across her good morning and said, "Is the sheriff there?"

"Why yes," said Lou, sounding a little hurt. "I'll just put him on."

Cas came on the line. "Cas Reynolds," he said.

Julie rolled her eyes. She didn't know what had happened to make him act like a stranger, but it was fine with her. Once a fair-weather friend, always a fair-weather friend. She'd learned her lesson.

"There are people digging up my land," she said without even bothering to tell him who was calling. He'd recognize her voice soon enough. There was silence on the other end. "I just discovered two men digging a hole at the smokehouse. They got away, but they were driving a rusty red Jeep and one of them has a hole in his jeans where Smitty nipped him."

There was silence on the other end of the line.

"Are you planning to do something about it or are you going to sit there letting moss grow?"

"I'm sure you're much better equipped to handle it than I am."

"What? You're the—" And then it hit her. He knew she was a cop and he was reacting just like she knew he would. Men and their fragile egos. "Fine," she said and hung up. Once she caught herself a few bad guys, she was going to let Tilda have it, because she was the only person who could have ratted her out to Cas.

She went upstairs and got her Glock out of the drawer. But when she turned to leave, Smitty was sitting in the doorway, blocking her way out.

"Don't worry. I'm not going to shoot anybody. But I'll scare the hell out of them if I can. And if I can capture them, I'll take them down to the station and see how Cas's ego survives that." She climbed over Smitty and headed down the hall. Smitty padded after her and they were soon back in the woods, look-ing for Glock fodder.

Cas slammed the phone down. "Don't say it," he warned Lou as she started to speak.

She said it anyway. "According to your Glamourscope, this is not the day to alienate friends. And if you ask me, you were doing a whole lot of alienating on the phone just now." She pursed her lips at him, reminding him of a malevolent teacher he'd had at boarding school.

"Cut me a break, Lou." He lifted his jacket off the coat rack and put it on. "I'm going out there. She just took me by surprise."

Lou grinned at him from behind her magazine. "She sure as hell did." She was chuckling to herself when he left the station.

He was just about to get into the police car when he saw Dan Pliney running up the street, waving him down.

Dan stopped at the car, took a couple of deep breaths, then said, "I don't know if this means anything, Cas. But the Hardware and Feed's had a run on shovels and picks and any other tool that'll dig. And there's a rumor going around town that there's treasure buried on the Excelsior land. Julie was just in yesterday getting a lock to replace one on her kitchen window. She didn't say why, but Wes just replaced all the locks last year. I sold them to him, and there wasn't a defective one in the batch." He stopped to take a breath. "Are you taking this all in, Cas? Are you all right? You're looking a little funny."

"Yeah," said Cas, feeling anything but all right.

"And Roy Nesbitt was in today and he said someone broke into the Vale's and they went through the window. So what I'm thinking is—"

"Thanks, Dan, I'm on my way there now."

He made it to Excelsior House in record time. He was an idiot. Telling her to handle it herself. She'd probably kill somebody and then where would he be? He raced up the driveway, screeched around the pond, and jolted to a stop just as a gunshot rang out from the woods.

"Not again," he yelled, banged on the door and ran toward the woods without any thought but preventing Julie from being killed or doing something stupid.

* * *

Julie crouched below the boulder, holding Smitty with all her might. "Stay," she whispered. "Stay." Somebody had shot at her. They'd missed by a mile, but she could feel the sting on her cheek where the bullet had chipped off a piece of granite and sent it flying into her face.

She'd had it with these people. Was Julie Excelsior fair game for every greedy, crazy asshole in town? Smitty growled low in his throat.

"Quiet." She could hear them coming. Checking to see whether they had succeeded in killing her? She'd give them a surprise they'd never forget. Too bad she didn't have Tilda's shotgun. Now that would give her some real satisfaction.

She eased away from Smitty and crouched, ready to spring. She still held her Glock, but if she could catch them off guard, she could bring them down without firepower.

She saw a flash of brown jacket. She leaned forward on the balls of her feet. *Just a little closer, come on. Come to Julie.*

The shooter stepped out of the trees. Julie sprang from her hiding place. Smitty leapt past her. The man fell back under their impact. As soon as they hit the ground, Julie turned him face down and locked his arm behind him.

"Good work, Smitty. Now, you son of a—" She knew that jacket. She knew that body. "It's you," she said, anger and hurt boiling over.

"Mrrghph," said Cas Reynolds. Her lover. Her nemesis. The man who had just tried to kill her.

Julie felt tears of rage, of hurt, of disappointment clog her throat. "Guard him, Smitty." She ground her knee into Cas's back as she crawled off him.

"Jul—"

Smitty growled and he shut up. Julie stood over him, aiming her Glock. It was shaking in her hand, so she eased her finger from the trigger. She didn't want to shoot him by mistake. She didn't want to shoot him at all. He was her Cas. Her best friend. And even though he'd just tried to kill her, she still loved him. *You are sick,* she told herself. "Get up."

Cas slowly rolled over and sat up. He was staring at the Glock. "Haven't we been here before?" He gave her a crooked smile. Julie didn't react. "Oh, hell," he said. "Go ahead. I deserve it."

"Don't be such a baby," she said, drawing on all her training to brazen this out without bursting into tears. "You know. You should have thought of another way to get rid of me. You still can't shoot worth shit."

"Me?" said Cas, looking genuinely startled. "You think I shot at you? Are you nuts? You called me, for Chrissakes."

"And since you're here, how about answering a few questions? Like what are you after? I know you held out on me about the thieves. Were you planning to steal the treasure? Do you know what it is? Did you already steal it?"

"What?"

"I looked up the poem on the internet. *No locks are there on this stronghold, but thieves break in and steal the gold?* Sound familiar?"

Cas lowered his eyes.

"God, and to think I—" Julie sniffed. "I fucked you. You could have killed me in my sleep."

"Would you shut up and let me try to explain?"

"No."

Cas lifted his hands and Julie's gun hand tightened. But he just scrubbed his fingers through his hair. "Just—"

"No!" She motioned for him to get up. He pushed himself to his feet. Took a step toward her.

"Stop right there."

He stopped. "You didn't fire that shot?" he asked.

Julie scowled at him. "Oh, puh-lease. If I had, I wouldn't have missed my target. And do you see a wounded man here anywhere? I don't. I just see a stupid one."

Cas flinched and Julie felt miserable. "Now, get going."

She followed him back to the house. Every time he tried to speak, she shut him up with a poke in the back. She stopped him by the police car. "Get in. Don't come back here again.

Don't call. Don't try to kill me because I won't be responsible for what I do the next time. You can have the damn treasure, whatever it is. I'm leaving as soon as I get the chickens over to Maude's. I don't want to see you again. I'm not going to try to solve the riddle, so you don't have to worry about me getting in your way."

"Julie, be—"

"Get in the car, now."

He opened the door, looked at her before getting in.

"Now," said Julie, fighting so hard for control, that she could feel her jaw quivering.

He got in the car and turned on the engine. Then she watched as he drove away. The tears began to fall before he even reached the pond. And so did the snow.

Someone had shot at Julie. And she thought it was him. She actually thought he tried to kill her. When all he wanted was to love her. And have her love him in return.

Another dream killed here on the hill. She was leaving. And Cas guessed he should be leaving, too. He thought of the *Julie E.* lying upside down in the machine shop. No reason to finish her now.

The only thing he could do now was go to Reynolds Place, tell his father that he'd won again, and confiscate another rifle. He'd nearly killed her today. Cas had seen blood on her cheek. Well, she'd be gone soon, and Reynolds could shoot away to his heart's content. Because Cas wouldn't be here to stop him. Wouldn't know. Wouldn't care.

He turned into the drive. Fat snowflakes began to drop on the windshield and slowly melt. He stopped the car and entered the house without knocking.

His father was in the library, looking dapper and lordly, not like a man who had just nearly committed murder.

Cas walked in and closed the door. "No. More. Shooting."

Reynolds looked up, stared at him through horn-rimmed glasses, then quickly took them off.

"I didn't hear you knock."

"You have to stop shooting at the Excelsiors."

"It's bad times when a son talks to his father this way."

"No more," said Cas through clenched teeth.

His father drew himself up. "They started it."

"Oh Christ," said Cas, exasperated beyond coping. "That was over a century ago. It was the goddam Civil War, for Chrissakes."

"Josiah Excelsior killed your great-great-grandfather."

Cas sank into the chair across from Reynolds. "You don't know that. He didn't confess. It was never proven."

"He inherited the factory, didn't he?"

"And the factory closed when the war ended and nobody needed rifles anymore." Except the Reynoldses, who couldn't seem to stop reliving the past.

"They made a fortune."

"And our family made a fortune banking it for them. What's to fight about?"

"Josiah—"

"Oh, hell." Cas stood up, placed his hands on the desk and leaned toward Reynolds. "You've gotten your way. Julie's leaving. It's over between us. You win. Are you satisfied? *You win*. But I'm finished with you. You won't see me again."

The door opened. Marian swept in wearing a yellow floral dress.

"Cas, dear. I didn't know you were here. I'll just have Larue—"

"Thanks, no," said Cas, his eyes riveted on Reynolds. He pushed away from the desk. "Goodbye, mother." He kissed her cheek, then strode out of Reynolds Place, out of their lives, into a darker world.

Julie cruised the Roadhouse parking lot and not seeing a green truck or police car, she went inside. She marched over to the bar and said, "Did you tell Cas I was a cop?"

Tilda looked up. "No, but he knew. Sit that angry little butt down and I'll get you a beer."

Suddenly deflated, Julie sat down. "He tried to kill me," she said when Tilda returned with a mug of Foster's. "He can't shoot worth shit and he tried to kill me."

"Whoa, girl. What are you talking about?"

Julie took a long drink of beer, a deep breath, then proceeded to tell Tilda about the riddle, about Cas holding out on her, how someone had broken into her house, and everything else, including her run-in with Cas that afternoon.

"Shit," said Tilda when Julie finally wound down. "There's been some speculation about Wes's fortune; there was bound to be. But digging up your land? That's wild."

"And against the law," said Julie. "Though the law here doesn't give a shit."

"Oh, he gives a shit all right. He's just a little fuzzy on what to do about it. I figure you've got two choices."

"And those would be?"

"Give him time to figure it out on his own. Or hold him at gunpoint until you get what you want from him."

Julie sighed. "It's more complicated than that."

"It always is with men," said Tilda. "What *do* you want from him?"

Julie finished off her beer. "Nothing," she said. "Nothing at all."

Tilda shook her head. "You are the two most skittish people I know. Give yourselves a break and have some fun."

"Yeah," said Julie. "I'll see you later. I don't want to leave Smitty alone with all the traffic at home."

"You be careful. Call me and Terrence if you feel uncomfortable. You can always stay in my spare bedroom."

Julie scuffed through the parking lot, digging in her purse for her keys and thinking, *What do I want from Cas?* Because *nothing* was a lie. She wanted a lot. But she wasn't going to get it. You needed trust to offer love. And she just didn't trust him.

Damn, where were her keys? In the city she would have them in one hand and her mace in the other before she even left the bar. But things were lax in the country and she was getting soft. Then she remembered that she'd stuck them in her coat pocket so she wouldn't have to search for them when she left.

She unlocked the door. A van rumbled to a stop behind her. *Typical*, thought Julie. The idiot had a whole damn parking lot, and he had to park next to her. What was wrong with these people?

She heard the door of the van slide open; something was thrown over her head and she was snatched off the ground. The van took off and she and her assailant were thrown to the floor. Julie ground her elbow into his gut as she fought to free her head and shoulders from the sacking that covered them. The van swerved out of the parking lot.

Julie rolled across the metal floor; her head whacked against the tire well and she went down for the count.

Chapter 22

Cas put his shoulder into sanding the hull of the *Julie E.* and tried not to think about Julie. He'd come home, intending to write his resignation and take it to Hank Jessop. Instead he'd wandered out to the shop to look at his boat.

At first he'd wanted to smash it into a thousand pieces, but he'd spent a lot of hours building it, and his better judgment won out. He told himself that if he couldn't have Julie, at least he could sail the *Julie E.*

And some tiny part of him was still hoping that they would see their way clear of this mess.

He knew she wouldn't take a bribe. He should never have doubted her.

And she should never have doubted him. She was mad as hell right now, but once she calmed down, she would know that he'd never shoot at her. Jesus. Why would she even think that? Probably because he'd showed up right after someone fired at her. Because he never told her about Reynolds and the rifle. Because even after all they'd been to each other, she didn't trust him.

Of course, he hadn't trusted her either. God, what a mess. And he didn't know how to fix it.

So he began sanding the prow, trying to lose himself in the feel of the wood. It curved beneath his hands like a finely formed woman and made him think of Julie. Julie, who hadn't trusted him with the truth.

His cell phone rang. He snatched it out of his pocket. Not Julie. Terrence. He sighed and flipped it open.

"Cas. We need you at the Roadhouse. Immediately. One of the bikers found Julie's purse in the parking lot. Her car door was open and her keys were in the lock. I think someone's kidnapped her."

"On my way." Cas grabbed his jacket and ran for his car.

When Julie roused, her hands were tied behind her back, the bag, smelling of grain, was still over her head, only now it was also tied around her shoulders. She tugged at the ropes that bound her wrists and inanely thought of Cas. But this was not a variation on pirates and captive princess. Cas would never be so rough. And he would never frighten her, even for fun. She held perfectly still, trying to orient herself.

Then she heard the furtive whisper of one of her kidnappers. "What are we gonna do with her?"

"Leave her in the back while we search," said the driver.

Damn, they were after her treasure. *Jeez, Wes, look at all the trouble you're causing.*

"The back of the van? We can't do that. What if somebody sees her?"

"Nobody's gonna see her."

"What if Cas stops us for having that broken headlight?"

"Aw shit," said the driver. "I forgot about that."

"Cause you know he's gonna look for her and he's gonna kill us when he finds her. What if—"

"Would you quit with the what ifs."

The van came to a stop, then started off again. *Stop sign?* It turned to the right.

"Hey, where are we going?"

"You just gave me a better idea."

The van lurched, then slowed down. Julie could hear the

thump-thump of a flat tire. She smiled in spite of her situation. The idiots had kidnapped her with a broken headlight and a flat tire.

"Shit, what's that?" asked the first voice.

"Damn tire must have finally blown." The van slowed and pulled to the side of the road, or street.

"What are you doing?"

"Changing the tire. I don't want to wreck the rim." The sound of the driver's door opening.

"We can't just stop . . ." The sound of the other door opening.

Then the side door slid open. Julie kept her breath steady, while her pulse kicked into overdrive. She lay perfectly still, but gently tested the ropes that tied her wrists together. It just made them tighter. Then she was shoved out of the way.

"Dang, she's still out. I hope she's not dead."

"You nitwit, she's not dead."

"Not dead."

And Julie suddenly knew who they were. Henley and Bo. What a couple of dolts.

She listened to them change the tire, with much cursing and clanging of tools. Once the car slipped off the jack and they had to start over again.

And all the while, Julie tried to free her hands. Then the car was jacked down, the flat tire was thrown in the back with her, and the van started out again.

Damn, thought Julie, *you can never find a policeman when you need one.*

An instant of fear sliced through her. They were idiots, but they were mean. She took a slow breath and gathered her wits. *Think. Listen and wait.*

It seemed like only a minute or two went by, when the van slowed, turned, and stopped again. Julie tensed. Had they pulled into a parking space? They couldn't be leaving her in a van parked in the middle of Ex Falls, could they?

The doors opened and shut again. She waited. And waited. Maybe they had decided to leave her in the van after all. She kept working at the knots.

The side door slid open. Julie froze. The van dipped as one of her assailants climbed inside. Only this time it was Julie and not a tire that was dragged across the floor.

She went limp, making it as difficult as she could to move her. She was hoisted up and tossed over one of the men's shoulders. *Bo*, she thought. What a dumb fuck to let Henley make him do all the dirty work. Probably had to change the tire, too.

His shoulder dug into her stomach and she had to concentrate not to throw up.

"Hurry up."

Definitely Henley and Bo, thought Julie.

"I'm hurrying; she weighs a ton." He shifted her across his shoulder. Julie was bumped through a doorway. It closed behind them. Bo was panting with exertion. Damn, she could probably take them even with her hands tied if she could just see.

She was banged through another doorway. Heard the clank of metal and then she was dumped on a mattress. The springs gave under her weight. Their footsteps moved away. The door closed and a lock clicked.

Julie rolled off the bed and walked right into a wall of metal bars. Damn them. She was in jail.

A knot of people stood in the Roadhouse parking lot, the snow falling around them, making them look like a tableau in a snow globe. Cas slammed to a stop, banged on the door, and jumped out of the police car. "What happened?"

Terrence had his arm around Tilda, whose face was stricken. "Larry," he called, looking over the crowd.

A tall skinny guy wearing a *Hellzapoppin* jacket turned around.

"Tell the sheriff what you told me."

Larry looked over at the VW, then at Cas. "I was coming

out of the bar, when I saw the interior light on in the bug. So I went over to close the door, figuring somebody hadn't closed it right. Only I found this purse on the ground and the keys in the door, so I took 'em in to Tilda."

"And Tilda called me," said Terrence. "I've already alerted the county. They're setting up roadblocks on the two main routes out of here. That's about all they can do since we don't have a description of the getaway vehicle. And they're pissed 'cause we mucked up the crime scene."

"I didn't know it was a crime scene," said Larry. "I was just trying to help."

"Nobody's blaming you, you did right. It was the rest of everybody tramping outside for a look-see. And I'm not blaming them, neither. It's a natural thing to do. And the snow took care of any prints they might have found." He turned to Cas. "What do you want us to do?"

Cas's mind was a dead blank. Julie had been kidnapped. And suddenly all the other stuff didn't matter. He looked around the crowd. "None of you saw anything?"

There was general headshaking and sympathetic looks.

Tilda took his elbow. "Come inside. We'll make a plan."

Cas let her lead him into the Roadhouse. He was not equipped to deal with this. He needed help, and the only real cop around had just been kidnapped. How could she have let herself be nabbed out of a parking lot?

"What's our next move?" Terrence's voice came from far away. The smell of coffee was much closer.

Tilda placed a mug in his hands. "Well, I think you should start by looking for Henley and Bo. Henley's been hitting on Julie every night she's been here until I finally kicked him out."

Henley and Bo. Of course, thought Cas, holding his mug in both hands and looking at it, but not drinking. She'd gotten the upper hand with them twice. If they were drunk enough, they might pull a stunt like this. And if they were drunk enough, they might do worse. A shudder went through him and Tilda put a hand on his shoulder.

"What kind of cars do they have, beside the bikes?" asked Cas.

"Bo has an old Ford Escort," said Terrence. "Henley has a pickup and a van."

"Van," said Cas.

"Yep," said Terrence.

"Damn them," said Larry, who was standing at the front of the crowd that had gathered around Cas. "We've been talking about kicking them out of the club for months now. Jerks like them give bikers a bad name. But since they were the ones that found the jackets, we just sorta let it slide. Shit."

A husky man pushed through the crowd and grabbed Larry by his collar. "You better shut your damn mouth about my boy. He ain't no kidnapper."

Terrence pulled him away from Larry. "You're breaking the law, Arnold."

Henley's father shook him off. "If that girl went with Henley, it's because she wanted to. She mighta dropped her purse without knowing it. I mean, hell, she's been strutting her wares since she was a kid, hasn't she, Cas?"

The coffee mug hit the floor and broke as Cas lunged for Arnold Baxter. Arnold fell into the crowd.

"Damn it, Cas," said Terrence, dragging him back to the bar stool. "We got us a situation here. And we don't have time for fist-fighting over Julie's virtue, when we oughta be worrying about her person."

Cas blew out his breath. "You're right, Terrence. I'm just a little crazy."

Terrence slapped him on the back, nearly knocking him off his feet. "To be expected."

"We could form a search party," volunteered Henry Goethe. "Wouldn't be the first time we had to go out looking for that girl."

A search party, thought Cas, still dazed. Julie would just love that. History repeating itself. But he couldn't see any other options.

"Saved her for you once. For all the thanks we got. But we don't hold it against you." Henry smiled. "We don't mind doing it again."

"As long as you don't let her get away again," added Dan Pliney, coming up beside Henry. "We had great hopes that the two of you would end that damn feud. When you got older, that is."

"And now you're older," agreed Henry. "So let's go find her. Deputize us."

Oh shit, thought Cas. "No deputizing." He was trying to think, but all the television in the world couldn't help him now. He just hoped it was Henley and Bo and not some drug lord from the city.

Terrence turned to Arnold Baxter. "Now, don't take this the wrong way, but give me a description of Henley's van. You might be right and they're just out for a good time—" This was met with several groans from the crowd and one very pointed, "Julie wouldn't touch Henley with a stick," from Tilda.

"And," Terrence continued, ignoring the responses. "Henley and Bo might be peacefully drinking over in Henryville."

"That'll be the day," said someone in the back and Arnold turned to scowl at them.

"But it's the only lead we've got."

"Right," said Cas and stood up. His knees were wobbly. "If it's okay with Tilda we'll make the Roadhouse our command center."

Tilda nodded.

"Call Edith and Lou and tell them to forward any calls to you or my cell. The rest of us will start at a five mile radius and work our way back here. If you see anything suspicious, anything, call here and Tilda will pass it on to Terrence or me."

"What about us?" asked Henry. "We want to be in on the arrest."

"Do not try to apprehend anyone on your own. Just report what you've seen."

Terrence began dividing everyone into teams. They left in one great migration.

Cas started to follow them out.

"Where are you going?" asked Terrence.

"To the police station."

"For what?"

"I left my .38 there."

"Cas, you son of a bitch. You'd better not shoot anybody."

Cas's mouth twisted. "I couldn't if I wanted to. But I can scare the shit out of them long enough to kill them with my bare hands." And he strode out the door.

The police cruiser was covered with a layer of snow and he couldn't have been in the bar for more than a few minutes. The storm would be in full gear before long, and it would be impossible to find Julie once the roads were closed. He drove with one hand while he attached his cell phone to the car charger, and searched the roadside for any sign of a suspicious vehicle—or a body.

At least if Henley and Bo had taken her, she might come out of this alive. If drug lords had come to silence her, it would already be too late to save her.

Cas sped up and the car fishtailed before straightening out again. The whole feud had started over a killing, thought Cas. Please don't let it end because the last Excelsior was dead. He dismissed that as a possibility. He had to find her. Her life—and his—depended on it.

He turned onto Main Street in time to see a vehicle slipping and sliding down the street toward the river. He peered through the falling snow. A van. A goddamn van. He swerved to the curb in front of the station, banged on the door and jumped out, fingering his key chain for the key to the station door. He could still catch them if he hurried.

But when he reached the door, it was open. Someone had used a crow bar to break the lock. Christ. What if they had his gun?

Cas rushed inside. He barely registered movement at his

back, before his skull cracked and fireworks exploded in front of his eyes.

Before Julie even had time to start working the sack over her head, the door opened again. She threw herself down on the cot. Now what? Maybe, they'd changed their minds and decided to take her with them. By now she had a pretty good idea where they were headed, and if she could somehow get to Smitty, they would be up the creek. But they only dumped something on the floor and went out again, locking the outer door.

She waited, listened, heard nothing. What was on the floor just a few feet away?

She rolled her shoulders, shimmied and twisted until she worked the opening of the sack to her neck. Then she bent over and the sack slipped off her head. She stood up; the world grew dark and her senses spun. She closed her eyes and quickly sat down again, breathing slowly, drawing the oxygen deep into her lungs.

She opened her eyes. It was still dark.

No surprise. It was night. But light was coming through a window high above the bed. She'd guessed right. She was in the Ex Falls jail.

A man was lying on the floor. He was wearing Cas's sheepskin jacket.

At first all she could do was stare. Then she sprang off the cot and banged her shoulder on the bars of the open door, in her haste to get to him.

He was still breathing; she could see his jacket rising and falling, but she couldn't tell how badly he was hurt. "Cas, can you hear me?" She nudged him with the toe of her boot.

He groaned.

"Cas, wake up. Are you all right?" A stupid question. Of course he wasn't all right.

He stirred. Tried to lift himself up on one forearm but collapsed again.

"Dammit, tell me how bad you're hurt."

"Ugggh."

Exasperated, Julie flipped him over with her foot. His head cracked back on the floor.

"Sorry," she said and knelt beside him.

His head lolled to the side.

"Answer me, dammit."

His eyes flitted open. He winced and closed them again. "Don't yell."

Julie gritted her teeth. "I'm not yelling. Just tell me where you're hurt."

"My head."

"I can't hold up my fingers because my hands are tied behind me, but can you see me okay?"

"Only if I open my eyes."

"That is not funny."

His eyelids opened and his eyes rolled until the irises settled into place. "I can see you. Where are we?"

"The jail."

"Oh, right." Cas smiled, the same crooked smile he'd had when he fell out of the apple tree.

Concussed, thought Julie.

He struggled to one elbow and peered around. "We're in the jail?"

"Finally," said Julie. She sank down on the concrete and turned her back to him. "Do you think you could untie me?" She lifted her hands so that he could reach them.

"Cute," said Cas. "I love it when you're tied up."

This time she yelled. "Cas, please untie me!"

Cas sat up. "Ow." He looked at her like he had forgotten who she was. "How do you do that thing with your head?"

Julie was close to tears. "Cas, you're concussed. I'm just looking over my shoulder at you. Please try to untie me so I can see how bad you are."

"They tied you up?"

"Yes," Julie said through gritted teeth and jiggled her bound hands for him to see.

He leaned forward, and muttering to himself, he began to pick at the knots. After an eternity, the rope loosened and Julie pulled her hands free. She rubbed them together, forcing the circulation back into her fingers. Then she turned to take Cas's head between her palms. She gazed into his eyes. He blinked back.

"Pupils seem okay."

"Well, they're the only thing that's okay," said Cas and listed to the side.

Julie grabbed him by his jacket and pulled him upright again. She held him in place with one hand while the other roved over his scalp. It didn't take long to find the bump midway down the back.

"Ouch," said Cas.

"You're going to live," Julie pronounced. *Long enough for me to kill you for scaring me like that, and for not showing up, and for tricking me, and not calling, and letting me get kidnapped.*

"Those sons of bitches." Cas heaved to his feet and fell into Julie's expectant arms. She dragged him over to the narrow cot and dumped him onto it.

"Just stay there. I'll go get help."

But he wrapped his arms around her and held her tight. "Thank God you're safe."

She let herself indulge in his warmth. This is how it should be, not fighting and lying. But that would have to come later. She pushed away and peered at him through the dark. "It was Henley and Bo and they're on their way to search my house for the treasure. They stole the riddle, not you."

"Me? Why would I steal your riddle?"

"Gee, Cas, I don't know. Why did you withhold part of your riddle from me?"

"I, uh . . ."

"Later. Right now we've got to get out of here." She felt her way to the door, grabbed the handle and pushed down. Nothing happened. She tried again. Pushed against the door as she held the lock down. Still nothing. "It's locked. Do you have your keys?"

Cas stood up. Swayed. "Julie. It's a jail. It doesn't unlock from the inside."

She knew that.

He fumbled in his pockets. "Damn, my cell is in the car. Do you have yours?"

"I was kidnapped. I didn't think to say, 'just a minute, please. Let me pick up my purse.' "

"Okay. Calm down. Let me think."

Julie fought the urge to tap her foot while he thought. Fought the urge to bang on the door and scream. *Okay. Stay calm.* Someone was bound to come eventually. And would find them together . . . again. She shuddered; she could practically hear their laughter.

Forget them. Henley and Bo had to be stopped from ransacking her house, maybe even hurting Smitty or her chickens. She went back to the cell, climbed over Cas and stood on the cot to reach the window.

"It backs onto a blind alley. Sit down. We'll just have to wait. The important thing is that you're safe. Half the town is out looking for you. Terrence knew I was coming here. When I don't answer my phone, he'll figure it out."

"You were looking for me?"

"Yes."

"So why did you come here?"

"To get my gun."

Julie went weak in the knees. She dropped to the cot beside him. "Cas, promise me you will never pull that antique on anybody. I want you to keep all your vital parts."

He leaned back against the wall. "I figure I won't have to. You can be the sheriff from now on."

Julie glared at him.

"I know you're a cop." He laughed, but not with humor. "Reynolds had you investigated."

"Of course. That's really low. Even for Reynolds."

"Would you ever have told me, if he hadn't? Or were you just going to let me blunder around looking like a fool, while you had a big laugh."

"I wasn't laughing at you and I would have told you. It just never came up."

"Bullshit. It wasn't because you took a bribe, was it? Reynolds said you did. Tell me you didn't."

Julie's mouth opened but she couldn't speak. She could only feel all-consuming rage. Reynolds had her investigated and twisted the truth to suit himself. Just what you'd expect from Charles Reynolds. And Cas believed him. Just like the Reynolds he was.

"Well?"

"Well, what do you think? Do I look like a bent cop to you?"

Cas shook his head, then pressed his hand to his forehead.

Julie stalked back to the door, gave it a vicious rattle.

"For once you can't get away from me," said Cas. "They might not find us for hours. You might as well sit down and tell me everything."

"Why bother? You've already passed judgment, haven't you? It is so typical."

"Hey. Give me a break. You waltz into town like the mystery woman. Refuse to talk about yourself. Then get pissy when I ask a simple question."

"Simple question? You had me investigated. Arggh." Julie started pacing. It was the only thing she could do to keep from smacking him or banging her head against the bars.

"I didn't have you investigated. That was Reynolds. And anyway I had most of it figured out. The thing with the gun in the bedside table spoke volumes." He looked away. "I just didn't have a clue about the other thing."

"I don't have to defend myself against Reynolds's accusations."

"No, you don't."

"And I don't care what you think."

"You've made that perfectly clear."

If that was what he'd been reading from her, he was a bigger idiot than he was acting like.

He drew his knees up, wrapped his arms around them, and rested his head on his forearms, effectively shutting her out.

That hurt. He was giving up. Giving her up. Again. *Why the hell does it matter so much?* Just one more unresolved issue in her life. She stopped in front of the cell and looked in at him. A man behind bars. Trapped by his family, as much as she was trapped by her past. The two of them separated by more than just bars. And she didn't see any way to get free.

To get to the future, you start with the old. She gripped the bars to keep from sinking onto the floor. *Jesus, Wes. I thought that just meant I had to come back. Wasn't that enough? Do I have to confront the past before I can move on? I don't think I can do it.*

You have no choice. She heard the words. Wasn't sure if it was Wes's voice or Cas's or her own heart. But she knew it was true. She released the bars and stepped into the cell. She sat down next to Cas, her back against the wall, not looking at him but at a spot on the floor where the concrete had chipped and been painted over.

"Okay. I was a cop. An undercover detective. But Reynolds is wrong. I caught my partner taking a bribe. I blew the whistle on him and instead of a commendation, I was demoted to a desk job. A desk job, after being on the streets where the action was. Do you know what that's like? It's like . . . like being a banker."

Cas lifted his head and Julie thought she saw a spark of understanding before he lowered it again.

Julie sighed, suddenly tired. Tired of the secrets, tired of running, tired of trying to make up for a past she didn't understand. For a father she didn't know. She leaned her head against the wall and shut her eyes. "I was going to tell you."

"Then why didn't you?"

"Because." She stopped.

Cas looked up.

"Because I was having such a good time. And men usually find it such a turn-off when you tell them you're a cop." She shrugged. "By the time I decided to tell you, I knew that it would look like I'd kept it from you on purpose. So I just didn't say anything."

"I don't find it a turn-off." He turned his head to look at her. "In fact, I think it's really hot. Did you bring your hand-cuffs with you?"

"Cas," she said, exasperated. "I don't get you. One minute you're accusing me of being bent and the next you're seducing me. Make up your mind."

"I kept the other part of the riddle because I think Reynolds did something wrong at the Savings and Loan and that's why he's turned into what he is. I know he's not a good person, but I just couldn't—"

She put her hand on his arm. "Jesus, Cas. I don't care what Reynolds did. If he broke the law, the statute of limitations has probably run out on it. And I'm certainly not doing anything to prolong the feud." She took a breath. "And I wouldn't do anything to hurt you."

"You wouldn't?"

Julie punched his shoulder. "You are so fucking infuriating. Half the time, I don't know whether to smack you or just—"

"Kiss me." He wrapped his arm around her and pulled her into him. His mouth was hot, and Julie forgot for a moment that they might be rescued any minute. For a minute. Then she tried to push away. "Cas, someone might come."

He stilled, then pushed away to look at her. His eyes said it all. He looked away. "I'm sorry. I didn't think. I owe you an explanation . . . about that day . . . on the river—"

"Forget it. It doesn't matter."

"It does. I was young and embarrassed and I felt like a fool. I should have stayed instead of letting Reynolds drag me away."

"So he could drag you kicking and screaming to the car? He was bigger than you then." She took a breath. "It was after that. You ignored me. Acted like you didn't even know me. That's what hurt, Cas. That really hurt."

"I know. It was lousy, but Reynolds threatened to send me to boarding school if I so much as looked at you again."

"Then why did he send you? You certainly didn't look at me."

"Because his life was going down the tubes and he blamed it all on Wes."

Julie put her hand over his. "So he punished you and me. The son of a bitch. I didn't know."

"How could you? I came to Wes's the minute I got home at vacation, but it was too late. I thought I had lost you forever. Have I lost you, Julie?"

"Lost me?" she shook her head. "Henley must have hit you harder than I thought."

He looked confused.

"Aw, hell," said Julie. She leaned over him and brushed her lips against his, licked his bottom lip then gently bit it. Cas sighed and their tongues met. The feeling was sweeter because for the first time, they didn't have to withhold anything from each other.

They broke the kiss at the same time, looked at each other and kissed again. And one kiss became another and another. Cleansing kisses. Barrier-dropping kisses, Hopeful kisses. Until they became something more and they pulled Julie and Cas to a place they needed to be, drawing them in and holding them there while their blood ignited and the world fell away.

Cas lifted her onto his lap. Julie slipped her hands inside his jacket. He was warm and strong, and as long as he stayed away from handguns, he was just the right man for her. She pulled her hands back and wriggled out of her jacket, then pushed his off his shoulders. He shrugged it off and they held each other as if they meant to never let go.

"I love you," Cas said.

"Don't ever leave me like that again."

"You can handcuff me to your wrist," he said.

Julie's blood zinged and she pressed against him. She felt his heart pounding as his erection thicken against her thigh. "Can we hear when someone comes?" she asked, barely finding the breath to speak.

"I'll keep one ear open," said Cas.

"I want you now."

"You've got me." His hands roved over her back, down to her butt. He lifted her so she could straddle his lap and drew her against him. He rocked into her and she rocked back and the cot creaked beneath them. He pulled her in tighter and Julie felt the tingle all the way down to her toes.

Cas grabbed the bottom of her T-shirt and pulled it up. Then he held her shoulders back, looking at her breasts as they moved together. Julie circled against him, riding the bulge in his jeans. His eyes closed and his lips parted.

Julie leaned forward and licked into his mouth. He un-hooked her bra.

"Someone will come," she said against his mouth.

"Just . . . for a . . ." He slipped the bra down and cupped her breasts in each hand, lifting them so that he could take a nipple into his mouth. Julie speared her fingers through his hair and lifted herself against his erection. She could feel the liquid heat beneath her jeans and she wanted his touch there.

He released her nipple, slid his tongue to the other one and sucked until Julie moaned his name. Then he looked at her with smoldering eyes while he pulled her bra straps up and re-clasped the back. He shifted her weight off his lap and gently rolled her down on the cot. He followed her down, his weight braced on his hands and his legs laying heavy and solid between her thighs.

She trailed her fingers down his chest, then reached for the buttons of his shirt. When it was open she ran her hands over the crisp hair of his chest, captured his nipples with her palms, circled them until they tightened into beads.

He sucked in his breath and shifted so that he straddled her on hands and knees. "Free me," he said.

Her hands left his chest and stroked down his abdomen. A sense of power flared in her as she unbuttoned his fly. She slipped one hand inside his jeans and lifted out his cock. It was thick and hot in her hand and she wanted more. She pushed his jeans down over his butt, freeing him completely. She slid down between his knees and he lowered himself so that she could touch her tongue to his skin.

Slowly she licked up the length of him and felt his blood surge against her tongue. His whole body jerked in response, then he shifted his weight so that she could take him into her mouth.

Her hand moved from the base of his cock to take his balls, while she sucked him in and released only to swirl her tongue around him and sucked again.

His jeans were stretched around his thighs and she wanted them off, but she couldn't stop and she knew they might be discovered at any minute. And suddenly, instead of feeling cold fear at the thought, she felt a rush of excitement.

Cas pulled out, breathing hard. "My god, you're, you're—"

"So are you," said Julie, pushing him down beside her and finding him again with her hand and feeling him pulse into it, while he fought to unzip her jeans.

"Next time you get kidnapped—oh God." He surged against her. "You better wear sweatpants."

Julie smiled. She knew she could make him come with a shift of her fingers but she wanted him inside her. She grasped his balls in one hand and the base of his penis with the other, and held them tight while he fumbled with her jeans. He groaned and she felt her zipper open. He pushed his hand past it and cupped her, while he slid his middle finger inside her.

She rose to meet him. He thrust his finger farther into her, then pulled it out and dragged it up her crease, slowing down when she shuddered.

"And then," he said, "we're going to start getting completely undressed. So nothing holds us back." He passed over the spot again, and she nearly screamed. She pushed his hand away. He yanked her jeans down to her knees and she pulled him on top of her. It took a moment of fumbling past jeans and knees and she had to finally guide his cock inside her.

"Definitely no clothes," she breathed and bit his ear.

He grunted. "And more teeth." He drove inside her. Pulled back. "And handcuffs." He plunged again. He slid his hand between them and opened her so that she felt the full force of his rhythm.

Julie moaned and he thrust harder. She grabbed his butt and held on, driving herself even closer to him. "I definitely need my legs around you. No more jeans after tonight. Faster."

The cot began to move away from the wall. And when they came together, the cot was in the middle of the cell.

They collapsed in a heap, arms and legs hanging off the narrow cot, jeans halfway down their legs and sweaters pulled up to their chests.

"And a big bed," Cas said on a sigh of contentment.

"Yes," said Julie and nestled against him. Julie lay half dressed, sprawled on Cas, thinking contented thoughts.

In the following silence, they heard the faint snick of the outside door opening. And Terrence saying, "What the hell?"

Chapter 23

Cas went to the door, pulling up his jeans. Julie quickly rearranged her clothes and pushed the cot back to the wall.

"In here," Cas called.

They heard keys in the lock, and a moment later, Terrence was standing in the open doorway. "What the hell happened?"

"Long story," said Cas and led Julie through the door into a crowd of curious searchers. He tightened his fingers around her arm, trying to tell her he would take care of her because it suddenly struck him, what had no doubt already occurred to her. Not drifting in a boat this time, but locked in a jail cell. Together.

"Julie," gasped Tilda as she pushed through the group. "Thank God. We've been looking everywhere for you. Are you okay?"

"Well, if that don't beat all," said Elton. "Right here under our noses the whole time. And us out traipsing all over the countryside looking for you. How did you two get locked in there?"

"Seems like we been here before," said a disgusted voice from the crowd.

Tilda put her arm around Julie's shoulders and eased her away from Cas.

"No call for that attitude," said Henry Goethe, shouldering Arnold Baxter out of the way. "Tell us what happened."

Cas cleared his throat. "Someone nabbed Julie out of the parking lot and brought her here. She says it sounded like Henley and Bo, but her head was covered so she never saw them." He felt the heat rising to his face. "And they hit me over the head when I walked in. I never saw them, either."

"That's a crock," said Arnold Baxter, stepping out of the crowd. "And it ain't evidence. If you ask me, it was you and her that planned this whole thing. Up to your old tricks."

Terrence grabbed his arm. "You better go on home, Arnold. And you can tell Henley that we'll be out to talk to him in the morning."

"Hey, you got nothing on my boy."

"That isn't true," said Larry, the biker. "Henley's been making a nuisance of himself, and everybody, including Ms. Excelsior, has had enough."

"Well, shit," said Arnold. "Ms. Excelsior. Guess you're too young to remember her last escapade. But we remember it, don't we, boys?"

He was met with silence and unfriendly stares. He snorted. "Seems like everybody's got a short memory." He pushed through the crowd and went out the door, slamming it behind him.

Terrence turned to Cas. "We found Henley's van abandoned up on Highland Avenue. It had skidded off the road and hit a tree. But they won't get far. There's already four inches of snow on the ground. We'll pick them up for questioning as soon as it lets up."

"We can go out looking for those no-good scoundrels right now," said Elton Dinwiddie. "We can organize a posse."

"Yeah," agreed several others.

Cas shook his head. "Thanks, Elton, but at this point, it's Julie's word against theirs. I'll take her out tomorrow and see if she can identify Henley's van."

"Won't be tomorrow," said Henry. "The storm's moved in. So if you want us to go, we gotta go now."

Cas looked at the group of men crowded into the little waiting room. Old and out of shape, the younger ones didn't even know Julie, and yet they'd all come to help. You didn't find people like that just anywhere. He looked at Julie to make sure she realized how they felt. Julie was gone.

"Julie?" He looked over the group again. "Where is she?"

"She and Tilda left," said Larry. "She seemed upset."

"Well, hell, who wouldn't be," said Elton. "They've probably gone back to the Roadhouse. What do you say we all go join them?"

Julie sat in the passenger seat of Tilda's pickup, watching the snow fall through the swish-swish of the windshield wipers, as Tilda drove slowly up the middle of Main Street.

"Why don't I just take you to my house? We can build a fire, pour us a couple of brandies and have a sleepover. This is gonna be a big one, maybe more than two feet."

"Thanks, but . . ."

"Look, hon. I know what you're thinking. Don't pay any attention to Arnold Baxter. The men in that family are born mean and spend their whole lives getting meaner." Tilda reached over and patted her knee. "Everyone else was real concerned. They offered to go out and look for you. And Elton and Henry were champing at the bit to go arrest Henley and Bo."

"I know. And I appreciate it. I overreacted. A moment of . . ." Julie shrugged.

"Déjà vu?" Tilda supplied.

Julie nodded. "Oh hell, it was just like last time." She dashed an escaped tear from her cheek.

"Would you stop it? Do you think you're the only person ever humiliated by this town? Shit happens everywhere. We're no worse than the next place. And you'd know that if you hadn't left." Tilda waved her hand before Julie could form a reply. "The rest of us had to swallow it and get on with it. I'm not saying that leaving was wrong, but it was probably the worst way to deal with something like that. Hell, they forgot about it a week later, when a new scandal came along. But since you weren't around to know that, you just carried it with you all these years."

"I didn't."

"Sure you did. It's like grieving. You gotta go through it sooner or later. And the longer you wait, the harder it gets. You're as prickly as a cactus on the desert. The first night you came into the Roadhouse, your chin was stuck out so far, I thought you were gonna trip on it. I know that look. Hell, don't you think I felt it often enough? Tilda Green, trailer park cheerleader. It was a miracle they even let me on the squad. And let me tell you, they didn't let me forget it for a minute."

Julie frowned at her. "They were mean to you?"

"Oh honey. But I just rah-rahed my little heart out and studied hard and went to community college and look at me today." She slowed down and turned into the Roadhouse parking lot. "And if all the women in town don't love their husbands hanging down at the Roadhouse, well, that's their problem."

Tilda parked in front of the bar. "At least come in for a drink."

Julie opened the door. "Thanks, but I really have to go see to Smitty and the chickens."

She scuffed through the snow toward her car and realized she didn't have her keys. Tears of frustration welled up and she didn't even bother to stop them.

Tilda rolled down her window. "Need this?" She held up Julie's bag. Julie hurried back and reached for it, but Tilda held on. "How long are you gonna keep running, girl? The bear stopped chasing you years ago."

Julie pulled the bag out of Tilda's hand. "I'll be fine."

"You can have a place here," called Tilda. "There's plenty of room."

Julie waved without turning around, then got into the Volkswagen and drove away just as the first truck pulled into the parking lot.

*   *   *

"I got work to do," said Terrence, when only he and Cas were left at the station. "And you better get home, before it gets any worse."

There was nothing Cas would rather do than go home, except go to Julie's, but he did have a responsibility to the town and he wouldn't shirk it.

She's going to leave me, he thought. *She's going to walk out.* Just when they had reached a new place of trust.

"Uh, Cas?"

"Right—thanks, but I'll stay here for the rest of the night. Take whatever calls are coming in. Edith and Lou won't make it in if this keeps up."

Terrence nodded and left to start plowing.

Cas sat in his chair and stewed. What he really wanted to do was go after Julie, but she probably needed a little space. Hell, she hadn't even waited around to thank all those people for trying to find her and so hadn't heard their real concern for her. She was probably already back at Excelsior House, fuming, and blaming it all on him and packing to leave.

Damn. Wes had depended on him to see things through this time, and instead of arriving like a knight on a white horse, he had managed to bungle the job.

All this time, he'd been building a new fantasy. Not from the past but for their future. From the moment she'd stepped out of the woods, even before he recognized her, he'd known her. Felt it down to his bones. He'd embarked on a new journey right there, sitting on the cold ground. A fantasy of finding his missing half, his home.

He slapped his forehead, waves of pain reverberated through his skull. A fantasy. Was that all it could ever be?

She'd never said she loved him. Not even in the midst of incredible sex. But he couldn't be mistaken about those moments when he felt so connected, could he? Had it all been one way? No. He was sure of that at least. There had been moments. But moments didn't make a life together.

Hell, they did if you had enough of them.

He wasn't going to give up yet. He picked up the phone. The line was dead. He stood up and looked out the window. At least six inches of snow already. If it kept up, he wouldn't be able to make it up the hill for days. But she wouldn't be able to make it down.

It was close to three when Julie finally tumbled into bed. She'd meant to start packing, but fatigue washed over her in a giant tidal wave. *First thing in the morning after the chickens,* she told herself, and crawled into bed.

She missed Ulysses' wake-up call, missed Bill's echoing warble. When she finally awoke, the sun was pouring through her window, so bright that she closed her eyes against it. She rolled her head to look at the clock. Nine-thirty. Damn. Her beauties would be in a foul temper. She smiled at her little joke, then dragged her ass out of bed.

She was stiff and had several bruises from her run-in with the van floor. And the night came flooding back, wrecking what was at best a decent mood. She pulled on her clothes, brushed her teeth, and went downstairs to feed the chickens.

She opened the kitchen door. Smitty ran out and promptly disappeared. Julie looked out onto a world of white and she blinked against the glare. White. Everywhere. In the trees, on the ground; her car was a mound of white, the shed something from *A Space Odyssey.* At least two feet of snow had fallen while she slept. Smitty waded out of the snowdrift and barked.

"Shit. The exhaust pipes!" Julie leapt off the porch and sank up to her knees. There was no way she could make it to the gazebo without shoveling. She staggered as she turned around in the snow. Slipped and slid up the steps and grabbed a snow shovel off the back porch.

It only took a few minutes for her to realize that it would take too long to shovel a path to the hen house. If the snow had covered the generator valves, her chickens could be dead. Would be dead if she didn't get to them now. She began dragging herself through the snow, dragging the shovel behind her. Smitty waded ahead, doing little to break the trail, but doing his best.

He barked at her from the mesh fence and pawed at the latch. He backed up a few feet, and sending out sprays of white, he sailed over the mesh fence.

Julie watched in amazement as he disappeared into the snow bank on the other side. Slowly he reemerged and began swimming his way toward the ramp which appeared only as a triangle of snow along the surface of the winter wonderland.

Julie trudged after him, the snow seeping into her shoes and freezing her pants legs. It seemed to take forever for her to reach the gate. And of course, there was no way to open it.

She threw the shovel over, then grabbed the top of the fence. The metal cut into her work gloves, but it began to give, and little by little, she pulled the fence down and herself up until she could roll across it to the other side. She had to crawl to the ramp and by the time she got there, she was breathing hard, and everything hurt: her lungs, her legs, her fingers.

Smitty had cleaned off the top of the ramp but he couldn't unlock the door. Julie clambered up and yanked it open.

She smelled it before she even entered the coop and a little piece of her died. Gas, which meant the generator had been suffocated by the snow. Which meant the carbon monoxide had been building up for a long time before that.

No chickens ran to peck at her, demanding food. *Please*, she prayed. *Please*. A battery-operated emergency light had come on, and she could see hens asleep in their nesting boxes. Others were on the floor where they had fallen from their perches. Julie stumbled back to the door and pushed it back and forth trying to circulate fresh air.

Then she heard a week peep at her feet. She looked down in time to see Ernestine tumble onto the floor. Julie picked her up and rushed her outside, warming her in her arms and willing her to live.

Ernestine flapped once and was still.

"No!" cried Julie. And shook the hen. "Wake up. Please." Ernestine lay inert and after a few moments, Julie lay her down in the snow. She had other chickens that might be saved.

"I'm sorry," Julie murmured, almost choking on the words. Her throat burned and she steeled herself to go back inside. Ernestine twitched. Julie peered at her. No, it was her imagination. Her hope. Then Ernestine shivered, ruffled her feathers, and let out a weak squawk.

"Ernie!" Julie scooped her up and hugged her, tears blinding her even more than the sun's reflection. She stuck her inside Wes's jacket and turned to see Smitty herding several very groggy chickens down the ramp.

"Good boy," she said as she passed him. She lifted up two more hens and took them outside, where they immediately sank into the snow.

They were going to freeze if she didn't get the heat going again, and she had no idea what to do.

"Just wing it," she said out loud. She grabbed the snow shovel and waded around to the side of the gazebo where the generator was housed. It was completely covered by snow. She started digging. Soon she was sweating with exertion and shivering from the drying sweat. She stopped to stretch her aching back; she needed help, but she was afraid to take the time to wade back to the phone and call Maude.

And then she saw a figure emerging over the wall. At first she thought it must be Maude, but this figure, though bundled in coat, scarf, hat and gloves, was much slighter than Maude. Someone had come to help. And whoever it was had come from Reynolds Place. She didn't care who it was. At this point, she'd be happy to see Marian if she knew how to start a generator.

Julie watched in awe as the figure lumbered awkwardly down the hill. It took her several seconds before she understood why. The person was wearing snow shoes.

She went back to shoveling until a shadow blocked out the sun. She straightened up and was only mildly surprised to see Melanie standing over her.

"The generator's out, right? It always does that in bad weather."

Julie grinned at her. "Chickens suck, huh?"

"Give me that," said Melanie. She wrenched the shovel from Julie and in a few minutes the generator casing was clear. "I'll need tools. They're in the shed." Melanie tossed Julie the shovel and pried the top off the generator.

Julie slogged down the hill, dug an opening around the shed door and squeezed inside. A moment later, she was lugging the toolbox back up the hill.

Several engine parts were lying on the engine cover. Melanie opened the tool box, took out a screwdriver, and stuck her head into the opening of the generator. "You can start putting the hens back in," she said, her voice echoing from inside.

Julie saluted and grabbed the first two chickens she came to. Most were huddled together on the ramp and were only too happy to follow her back inside. A few minutes later, the generator whirred to life. *Thank you for small favors,* said Julie.

Then she remembered Hillary. She hurried to the back of the gazebo and found her alive and sitting on her nest. Bill was standing nearby, looking woozy but alert. Smitty lay between the wall and the nest, curved around the two birds like a woolly blanket.

"Generator's fixed," said Melanie, maneuvering her snow shoes through the open door. "Are they all in?" She clomped over to Julie. "What the hell?"

"The happy couple," said Julie. "Hillary's nesting. That's Smitty."

Melanie just rolled her eyes and went outside again.

It took a while to convince Smitty to leave the love birds, but he finally padded out into the snow. When Julie came out behind him, Melanie was standing on the ramp looking up. Julie looked up, too. Ulysses was perched on the roof of the gazebo.

"How did he get up there?" asked Julie, keeping her voice low so she wouldn't scare him.

"Flew," said Melanie, keeping her eyes on the rooster. "But now the dumb shit is afraid to come down. Come here, you stupid bird," she said in a gentle, cooing voice. "Do you want your wattle to freeze? Not to mention your teeny-tiny rooster dick. Get down off the goddamn roof."

Ulysses spat at her.

"You dumb fuck," she sang softly.

Julie had to bite her lip to keep from laughing.

In the same soothing voice, Mel said, "You'll have to go around to the other side and frighten him."

It took Julie a second to realize that Melanie was talking to her and not Ulysses.

"Just make a lot of noise and rush at him. He should come down on my side. If he turns on you, cover your eyes. He'll be vicious."

Julie swallowed. Oh great, she was going to play Oedipus to his Ulysses. And if she did get him to move, he would head straight for Melanie. "You too," she said and waded to the back of the gazebo.

Melanie nodded. "Now."

Julie rushed at the rooster. At first he didn't move, just turned his head in her direction and looked at her with contempt. At least it looked like contempt to Julie.

Then Melanie put her hands to her mouth and shrieked, a sound so dreadful that Julie almost fell backwards. Smitty started barking. Ulysses stretched his wings, ready for a fight. He rose off the roof, and Julie instinctively covered her eyes. When she opened them again, Ulysses was gone.

She couldn't see Melanie, either. Then Melanie shrieked and Julie ran back to help. Ulysses was standing on the ramp. Melanie stood between him and the door. Her arms were spread out like a Valkyrie. Ulysses shrieked back. Melanie held her ground.

It was amazing to watch. Where had she learned to do this?

From Wes, of course. And a big piece of the puzzle fell into place.

"Come on, you dickhead," screamed Melanie and feinted toward him. It was all that Ulysses needed. He charged her. Julie screamed. At the last second, Melanie ducked aside and Ulysses flew through the door. Melanie slammed it behind him.

"Nyah-nyah," she called through the door. To Julie she said, "He'll calm down in a minute and be thankful his sorry ass is inside where it's warm."

"Good," said Julie. "Why don't we get our sorry asses inside and have something warm to drink."

Melanie looked down at the house. "I gotta go."

"Come on," coaxed Julie. "I'd enjoy the company."

Melanie shrugged and tramped slowly across the surface of the snow while Julie trudged through the drifts to the back porch.

Julie opened the door and held it for her. Melanie hesitated, then leaned over and released her snow shoes.

"I haven't changed anything," said Julie, guessing this was Melanie's first visit since Wes's death. And for some reason it was really important to Julie that she came in now.

"I know I saw a tin of cocoa here someplace." She nudged the girl inside, then began to rummage through a cabinet, giving Melanie time to get used to things.

"It's in the cabinet above the cutlery drawer," said Melanie.

Julie got the tin down and heated milk on the stove top. Then she stripped out of her wet outerwear; waited for Melanie to reluctantly peel off her coat and hat. She wore no makeup and the winter hat had pressed her hair to her face. She scrubbed it with her fingers as if knowing what Julie was thinking. All it did was make it curl softly around her face.

Julie carried her things into the sun porch, savvy enough not to say something stupid, like how pretty she looked.

But she was more than pretty. She was beautiful.

When the cocoa was made and they both sat at the table with steaming mugs, too tired and wet to move from the kitchen, Julie said, "Thanks for helping me out."

Melanie shrugged, back in full Goth mode except for the mustache of chocolate on her upper lip. "I didn't do it for you. I did it for the chickens."

"And for Wes?"

Melanie shrugged, looked away.

Everything was getting much clearer now. Julie and Cas hadn't been the only kids Wes had mentored. He'd also taken Melanie under his proverbial and literal wing. No wonder the girl was so remote. She was in mourning, and she had no one to share it with.

Tilda was right, thought Julie. *You did need to share your grief.* She sipped her cocoa and said, "Tell me about Wes."

Her words were met with silence. Melanie didn't look up, just blew on her cocoa.

"I mean," said Julie, trying not to sound too sappy and turn the girl completely off. "I hadn't seen him since I was thirteen, and now . . ." She shrugged, hoping Melanie would fill in the blank. She did.

"He's dead."

Not exactly what Julie had in mind, and she didn't say anything else. They drank their cocoa in silence.

"He was lonely." Melanie put down her mug. "Is that what you're trying to find out? You and Cas deep-sixed him and he was lonely."

"He had you."

"Oh, yeah. That's a consolation."

The bitterness in her voice made Julie wince. Melanie put down her mug and began tracing the squares of the blue and white checked table cloth.

"I'm sure it was . . . to Wes," said Julie.

Melanie lifted one shoulder, dismissing the topic. And Julie longed to say something. Anything to lessen her alienation. Because she knew just how it felt and she had responded in much the same way except there had been no Goths when she was thirteen. She had been so lonely down in Yonkers, with everybody going about their lives and her wondering what hers was going to be. And she missed Wes so much that she thought her heart would break. And now she was watching Melanie go through the same feelings and was helpless to soothe her pain.

"What's going to happen with you and my brother?"

Taken aback, Julie blurted out, "Nothing."

"Try again," said Melanie. "And if you say, I'll understand when I'm older, I'll think you're as big a dickhead as he is."

"Really," said Julie, trying to be honest with herself as well as with Melanie. "I don't think there's any future there, if that's what you mean."

Melanie frowned and her hard façade seemed to fall away. "He's not so bad. Actually, for an ex-suit, he's pretty okay. But he's a dumb fuck when it comes to some things. He's screwing this up, isn't he?"

To her amazement, Julie found herself wanting to tell her everything.

"Once," said Julie. "We were best friends. Wes nurtured us and loved us like we were his own children. And we, I at least, took it for granted that it would always be that way. But then stuff happened and it was over. And then Cas went away to school and Wes sent me away. And that put an end to everything.

"When I first came back here." It had only been a couple of weeks, Julie realized. She felt as if she'd been here forever. "I thought—well, let's just say that I thought maybe we could be friends again. It worked at first. But it can't last."

"Because of Reynolds? Or because of Cas?"

Julie shook her head. This girl was way too astute for her own good. "Both, I guess. And because of me. It's too complicated to explain."

"Yeah, right," said Melanie and stood up. "You're too dumb to figure it out, so you're leaving again."

"Well, I do have a life to get on with."

"No, you don't." Melanie hesitated, then said, "I don't know if you know this, but Reynolds sicced a detective on you. He told Cas what happened with your job. But he didn't tell him the truth. I read the report." She shook her head. "I can't believe you were a cop. That is so lame."

"No, it isn't. I was a good cop."

"Big deal. I have to go." She put her cup in the sink and stopped by the back door to put on her boots. "If you and Cas let Reynolds fuck this up, you're both pretty fucking stupid. Thanks for the cocoa."

She stood in the doorway and looked around like it would be her last, then she was gone. Julie sat at the table, hurt and confused and wondering why this girl got to her the way she did. When she finally looked out the window, she could see Mel's silhouette mushing up the hill toward Reynolds Place.

Chapter 24

It was dark and Julie was putting a log on the fire, which she had built herself, without a book, and she was feeling pretty smug, when her cell phone rang.

She snatched it up and pressed talk.

"Hey," said Maude. "The phone lines are down. I'm at the Roadhouse using Tilda's cell phone. I've been calling you all day and I'm drunk as a skunk. Where were you?"

"Shoveling snow. And clearing the generator. It went out."

"Damn. I was afraid of that. The avenue is closed and I couldn't get to you. Did you lose them all?"

"No. The weirdest thing. Melanie came over and fixed it. You wouldn't believe it, Maude. She knew exactly what to do. She was incredible." *And really unhappy.*

"Good for her. Thought she might come through. That girl needs a mother."

The same thing Wes had once said to her. "Yeah, she does. One that lives in this century."

"You managed to save them all?"

"Yes. Though it was touch and go for a while there."

"Fine. Fine. Just keep the generator clear, and you should be okay. Are you going to be all right up there by yourself? Tilda's been telling me about all the excitement you've been having."

"I'll be fine. I've got Smitty and food."

"Then I'll see you when the road gets plowed or the snow melts, whichever comes first. Call if you need help."

"Thanks. And Maude, don't drive home."

"Not me. I've had several offers already. Hell, I should get out more often."

Julie was smiling when she hung up. She'd like to be down at the Roadhouse, too. With her . . . friends. Shit. She had friends. *Wasn't that a kick?* as Tilda would say.

She sat back down in front of the fire. Smitty jumped up and ran to the door.

Maybe she had spoken too soon when she told Maude she'd be fine. She grabbed the poker and followed him to the door.

His tail was wagging, which didn't mean shit. The Boston Strangler could be on the other side, and Smitty would be glad to see him.

Julie raised the poker and cautiously opened the door, ready to brain Henley or Bo or anybody else up to no good.

Cas was kneeling on the porch. He looked up. "Don't!" he yelled.

Julie lowered the poker. "How did you get here?"

He stood up and picked up a pair of mesh snow shoes. "It took me two hours from the police station to here. Do I get to come inside?"

"Sure." She opened the door. "What is it with the Reynoldses and snow shoes?"

"Mel's idea. They seem to be the Goth travel mode of choice."

He stood in the foyer, shivering. He was wearing bright blue nylon pants and jacket. He began shucking off the pants. Underneath were a pair of snow pants and underneath that, a pair of sweat pants.

"Interesting ensemble," said Julie, thinking, *just take it all off. I'll get you warm.*

"The blue is my sailing gear. I didn't want to die of exposure on my way to apologize."

Julie helped him out of his jacket. "Apologize? For what?"

"For everything. For fifteen years ago and for putting you through the same thing again last night."

Julie shook her head. "Cas, you don't—"

"Have to? Yeah, I do. I know I fucked up."

"You were a child then, and last night was nothing. I overreacted. I saw all those people and freaked."

"They were concerned."

"I know and I'll thank them. Tilda explained a few things and I've done a lot of thinking since then. And none of this was your fault." Julie reached up and kissed him. "You're just juggling too many damn things at once."

"I can juggle one more." He smile at her, tentatively.

She smiled at him. "I was counting on that. Come sit by the fire. I made it myself."

He followed her into the parlor, sat down on the sofa, and pulled her down next to him. Smitty stretched out at their feet.

"The county's taking charge of everything until the snow melts," he said. "Maybe it'll last until spring. Then we can sail away."

Julie looked up at him. "Where would you sail?"

"Wherever you want."

Julie laughed. "You're awfully mushy tonight."

"Do you mind?"

She snuggled against him. "Not in the least."

They sat watching the fire. Just sitting, no longer in a hurry. Growing drowsy as the night wore on. When the fire had burned to embers, Cas kissed her. "Do you care if we never find the answer to the riddle?"

Julie shrugged. "I'm curious, but I think I already know a lot about it."

"What's that?"

"I'll explain it to you over breakfast. Let's go to bed."

Upstairs, Julie pushed Cas into her bedroom and closed the door. "Take off your clothes. I'll be right back." She hurried to Wes's room.

She came back a minute later and stopped in the doorway, her hands behind her. "Are you naked yet?"

"Yes, ma'am."

She looked over to where he was propped up against the pillows, one arm resting on his raised knee, everything laid out for her like a grand buffet. His eyes widened. "Do you have lollipops hidden behind your back?"

She shook her head. "Something better." She lifted up the coil of braided rope she'd found in Wes's bureau.

Cas slowly began to grin. "Let me guess. Pirates."

"Oh, no," said Julie, walking slowly toward the bed. She stretched the rope taut between her hands. "I have a new game." She stopped to grin at him. "Put your hands over your head."

Cas's arms lifted in the air and so did another very vital part of him. "What's this game about?"

His voice had grown husky and Julie basked in the warmth of his desire. "One I thought up not too long ago." She took a step toward him. "I think you'll like it." Another step.

Cas gripped the headboard and shifted his hips, ready for her.

Julie snapped the rope and Cas's cock jumped.

Julie smiled. "It's called. . ." She crawled on the bed and straddled him. "The Amazon and her slave." And she wrapped the rope around his wrists.

The next day another storm blew in, but the temperature rose and in the afternoon, the snow turned to rain. The trees whipped in the wind and drops pounded against the windows.

"So much for being snowbound," said Julie, looking out.

Cas came up behind her and put his arms around her waist. He rested his chin on her head and said, "With any luck, it will ice over."

A fire was blazing, the house was cozy, and except for the time she had to spend outside with the chickens, Julie was feeling pretty damn comfortable. She knew it wouldn't last. Life did go on after all. But she felt so content, so secure after all the craziness of the few weeks before, that she had a hard time remembering that it would soon end.

Sometimes she would turn around and think she saw Wes where he should be—with her and Cas in the old house. Like the old times. And she grew melancholy.

"It's the weather," she said. "It makes me miss him."

"I know," he said. "Probably because he always came up with something fun to do when we were stuck in the house." He laughed softly. "We could play Parcheesi, or Amazon and her slave again. I liked that a lot."

"Me, too," said Julie. "I have an idea."

"I love it when you have ideas," said Cas and gave her a squeeze.

A few minutes later, they were walking up the stairs with a hamper of sandwiches, and a bottle of wine. On the second floor, Cas opened the door to Wes's room and flipped on the overhead chandelier.

When they stepped into the room, Cas stopped and looked around. "So that's what the picnic is for. I haven't been up here since we were kids. Wes had moved down to Maude's by the time I got back. She didn't like him climbing the stairs."

Julie walked to the windows. "Those were good days, weren't they?"

"Yeah," said Cas and joined her at the window. "All those rainy days, when this was our ship and the turret was the crow's nest. Well, shiver me timbers," Cas said in a dreamy voice, and put his arm around her.

"And remember how when the sun came out, you could see the patterns of the window on the floor?"

"Yeah," said Cas. "Fruit or something? What happened to them?"

"One day lightning hit the finial and two of the windows shattered. The whole room got flooded. Wrecked the carpet and warped some of the floorboards. It was a mess. Wes had to move to the back bedroom. He replaced the windows with plain glass. See?" Only one still had the border of fruit and vines. She sighed. "I never came in here again until the other day when I was looking for clues."

Cas tightened his arm around her and they stood together, watching the clouds scud across the sky while raindrops pelted the house. Then they spread out the patchwork quilt, pulled pillows off the bed, and sat down to their picnic.

"I like the new rug," said Cas, handing her a glass of wine. "I remember the old one was so thin, your butt went to sleep sitting on it."

After they ate, they lay on the pillows, drowsy with food and memory and love.

"Look, sun's coming out," said Cas.

Julie looked out at the sky. "With the old windows you could sit in the center of the room and the fruit in the windows would reflect on your lap."

"Hmmm," said Cas and pulled her close.

"I miss those old windows. They were like magic." Julie sat up, looked back at the windows. "My God, it's a golden apple."

"Where?"

"In the old window. Look."

Cas sat up. "It is a golden apple. Do you think . . ."

Julie pushed the leftovers away and sat down cross-legged in the center of the cloth, her hands palm up in her lap. A beam of sunlight fell on her knees, but no fruit appeared. She sighed with disappointment. "Damn. And I really thought. Oh, well."

She stood up and they gathered up leftovers and put them back in the basket. Julie folded up the quilt. "Dessert in my room?" she asked and smiled at Cas.

Cas didn't even look back. He was staring down at the carpet. "Look," he said, pointing at a place on the floor.

Julie looked. The carpet was moss green, and in the center, a medallion of fruit and leaves. In the center of the medallion was a huge, fat . . .

"Golden apple," they said together.

Cas folded the rug back and looked underneath. Most of the floorboards were still warped from the flood. He took out a pocket knife, knelt down and ran it along the seams between the boards. He shook his head. Tried another seam. And another. "Nothing," he said finally and stood up, closing his knife.

"Oh, well," said Julie. "No matter."

They replaced the rug. Then stood looking at it.

"A golden apple does appear." Julie shook her head, picked up the picnic basket and carried it to the door. She took a last look at the rug before Cas flipped the light switch. The apple disappeared into the dark.

"Cas."

"Huh?"

"Turn on the light again."

He turned it on.

"Now off."

Cas frowned at her, but he turned off the light.

"On."

"Julie, what are you doing?"

She dropped the picnic basket and strode back to the rug. She looked down at the apple. Out to the turret windows. Then up to the chandelier above the rug. "How would you like to climb a ladder?" she asked.

They found it hanging between the crystal drops of the chandelier. One small, silver key. With four numbers etched on its surface.

"But which bank?" asked Julie, vibrating with excitement.

"There are only two in Henryville. We'll try both." Cas looked out the window. "When Terrence finally gets around to plowing us out."

Julie sat back on her heels. "I hope it doesn't take long. The suspense is killing me."

It was late morning on the following day when they heard the sound of Terrence's plow. By one o'clock they were driving

the Volkswagen to Henryville. The safety deposit box was at
the Henryville Mercantile. George Quincy put his key in the
one slot and Julie put hers in the other, the safe opened. The
banker pulled the safety deposit box out, carried it to a small
room and placed it on the table.

"I'll leave you now. Take your time." He turned to Cas. "If
you're really interested in a position . . ."

"No thanks, but my father needs to come out of retirement."

"Reynolds? Driving everybody crazy, is he? Don't believe in
retirement myself. Tell him to come over and talk to me."

"I will. Thank you."

When he was gone, Julie and Cas sat down at the table and
opened the box. The first thing they saw was a note in Wes's
scrawling hand.

> *Dear Julie.*
>
> *Inside you'll find two bank books. One is for
> Melanie. It should be enough to send her to college
> and get her started in life. She's quite a kid, reminds
> me of you sometimes. She just needs some nurtur-
> ing.*
>
> *The other is for you. Hopefully, you and Cas
> have bumbled though your differences. I've done as
> much as I could to set you in the right direction.
> Reynolds and I both made a mistake by sending the
> two of you away. But you're back now, aren't you?*
>
> *You can stay or you can sail away together or go
> your separate ways. But I think you are meant to
> join the houses of Reynolds and Excelsior at last.
> It's up to you.*
>
> *There is also a letter that I depend upon you to
> deliver to Reynolds, Sr. I'll have the last say, after
> all.*
>
> *The last envelope will make all things clear.*
>
> *If you decide to leave, please see that Maude gets*

*my beauties. She'll take good care of them as she
took good care of me. Nimble fingers, our Maude.*

Wes Excelsior.

*P.S. Get Cas to tell you about the horse, the
chicken and the Harley.*

P.P.S. Remember who loves you.

Julie put her hand to her mouth as her eyes filled with tears.
Cas slipped his arm around her shoulders. "Open the envelope."

She moved the bank books and Reynolds's envelope aside.
Then she lifted the flap of the last envelope and extracted three
sheets of folded, aged paper. Her fingers trembled and she set
the papers on the table to read. At the top of the first page,
written in ink, faded brown, were the words: The Confession
of Josiah Excelsior—1868.

*On the night of September 14, 1863, William
Reynolds was mortally wounded by a gunshot to
his chest. This is the true account of what happened
on that fatal night. William and I were dining at the
Roadhouse Inn when we noticed several men going
into the private dining room. Two of them, we had
reason to suspect, were members of the Knights of
the Golden Order. Our suspicions raised, we went
outside and crept beneath the window to overhear
their conversation. We were appalled to find that
they were planning to raid the factory that very
night in order to steal rifles meant for our brave
Union army and use them in conjunction with Con-
federate spies to capture New York City.*

*The meeting broke up in due course and we fol-
lowed them across the river. We took a position in
the trees to watch the proceedings, with a mind toward thwarting them if we could by alerting the*

head of the New York militia, once we knew in which direction they were taking them.

It wasn't long before, to our surprise, a barge floated down the river. When it reached the mouth of the harbor, the bargemen threw lines out to shore. A dozen men came from the woods and took them up and towed the barge out of the current and moored it at the wharf. Another dozen men disembarked and went into the factory.

We were astounded to see them gain entrance through a locked door. We watched while they loaded crate after crate of rifles onto the barge.

By mutual consent we crept closer, our pistols drawn, with the idea of cutting the barge adrift while they were inside. Instead we came upon the lookout for the group. As he turned, William and I were struck dumb. It was Andrew Reynolds, William's younger brother. A traitor to the northern cause! As we stared, he raised his pistol and shot William, his own brother! I killed Andrew in the next instant. He staggered back, hovered on his feet, then dropped his torch onto the barge before he fell into the river, never to be seen again.

His fellow traitors were alerted and I barely managed to throw William over my shoulder and make our escape. I heard the explosion as I rode away with William in my arms. I took him to Reynolds Place and stayed by his bed as he died. His last words to me were to never tell of the perfidy of his brother. To save his family name.

I have kept that promise, though men have reviled me. And I will take that promise to my grave. For though one Reynolds died a traitor, another died a hero.

I killed Andrew Reynolds, a traitor and a murderer. But I never killed another soul.

> *Written this day, 14 September 1868, year of our Lord.*
> *Josiah Hezekiah Excelsior.*

Julie dropped the last sheet of paper onto the table. "He didn't murder your great-great-grandfather."

Cas shook his head. "All these years, feuding over nothing."

"Except a promise."

"We're not obligated to keep that secret. The feud ends now."

"But Cas, your family."

"Every family has a rotten apple." He smiled. "So to speak. It also has its heroes. I think it's time for both Josiah and William to have their moment of glory."

"You're sure?"

"Oh yes. Come on, gather up these things. We're going to Reynolds Place."

"Not me."

"Yes, you. Because like Wes said, you are about to become a Reynolds."

Julie stared at him, while her heart skittered in her chest. "Is this a proposal?"

"Yes. What do you say?"

Julie thought a moment, looked down at the sheets of paper spread out on the table. "I say . . ." She took a deep breath. "I do."

Cas pulled her off her chair and kissed her. "I do , too."

Larue's eyes grew round when he saw Julie and Cas standing at the door. It was the first time Cas had ever seen him react to anything.

"Is my father in?"

Larue nodded then finally found his voice. "They're all in

the parlor." And he stood at the door while Cas led Julie across the foyer.

"Just hang tough," Cas said and pushed Julie into the room.

Reynolds and Marian sat by the fire, Melanie was slouched on the window seat looking bored. They all looked toward the door when it opened. Reynolds's drink sloshed out of the glass, Marian's mouth dropped open. Melanie clenched her fist, and said, "Yeah."

"What—what," sputtered Reynolds.

Cas held on to Julie and propelled her along until they were standing before his mother and father. "Sit down, Reynolds. Julie has something for you." He felt her trembling. Wes's letter to Reynolds was clenched tightly in her hand.

"Get that—"

"Sit down."

Reynolds sat down and stared, outraged at his son.

Cas pried the letter out of Julie's fingers and handed it to his father. "Read it out loud."

Out of the corner of his eye, he saw Melanie come to stand on the other side of Julie and his heart filled with joy. He had the makings of a pretty damn good family here. Reynolds opened the letter. His lips moved as he read, but he didn't read it out loud. "Never," he said when he'd finished. He let the letter drop to the floor. Cas leaned over to pick it up, but Marian beat him to it. He watched the color drain from her face as she read.

"What does it say?" whispered Julie.

Cas shrugged.

"He can't mean this," said Marian, looking from the letter to Julie to Cas. "It isn't possible."

Melanie snatched it from Marian's hand. Then she read it, too. When she finished, she grinned wickedly at Cas.

"It worked," she said. "Son of a bitch, it worked."

"Do not use that language in this house," said Reynolds.

"You lose," said Melanie and handed the letter to Cas. He and Julie read it together.

> *Reynolds. I'm dead now. Obviously, or you wouldn't be reading this. And with my passing so passes the feud. It's time to put your energies into helping this town recover instead of obsessing over the past. So these are my last words to you. As much as it pains me to let the Excelsior line die out, I relinquish it gladly. For if I'm not mistaken, the last Excelsior is about to become a Reynolds. And I expect you to welcome her into the family with open arms.*
>
> *Wes*

"The Excelsiors betrayed—"

"No they didn't," said Cas. "Josiah Excelsior left a confession. I think you will be interested in seeing it."

"He confessed?" Reynolds's eye grew interested.

"Oh, he killed a Reynolds all right, but not William. William's brother did that."

"Lies."

Cas pulled out the envelope and read Josiah Excelsior's confession. When he finished, no one moved or said a word.

"Let me see that." Reynolds lunged for the letter, dropping his drink on the carpet.

"Charles," shrieked Marian.

"It's over, Dad," said Cas as he steadied Reynolds on his feet.

"Our family name. Our pride."

"William Reynolds was a hero. He died saving the Union. That's enough to make any family proud."

Reynolds slumped down on the couch. "And are you going to marry . . ." Reynolds glanced in Julie's direction.

"Yes," said Cas. "Congratulate me."

Marian stood up. "You're getting married?"

"Yes. To Julie."

Marian cocked her perfectly coiffed head. "I'm going to be a grandmother twice?"

"Twice?" said Cas.

"Christine and Ian," said Marian, looking slightly befuddled.

"Well, we're not quite there yet." He took Julie's hand and put it to his lips. "But it shouldn't be too long."

"I'll have to plan another shower." She looked at Julie. "I think May would be nice, don't you?"

Julie stared at her until Cas nudged her with his elbow.

"May would be lovely," she answered, sounding as confused as Marian looked.

"We'll have to draw up a guest list. I'll just get a piece of paper."

"She's totally nuts," Melanie told Julie. "But harmless."

Cas and Julie left a few minutes after that. Marian was making plans. Reynolds was stunned but beginning to accept the idea. Melanie walked them outside.

"Cool . . . sis." Melanie gave them one of her rare smiles.

"So you knew all about this?" Cas asked.

"Pretty much. I didn't know he was going to leave me money. He was—" She had to stop.

Cas and Julie looked away while she fought not to cry.

Then Julie said, "He sure was." And put her arm around her soon-to-be sister's waist.

"But the thing I don't get," said Cas, "is the egg."

"What egg?"

"The answer to the riddle. In marble halls as white as milk, lined with skin as soft as silk, within a fountain crystal clear—"

"A golden apple does appear." Melanie shook her head. "I told Wes you wouldn't get it."

"I did get it. Well, Julie got it. It's an egg."

Melanie rolled her eyes. "You take everything so literally. Must be those banker genes."

"Boats," said Cas. "I build boats."

"Whatever. Anyway, it isn't an egg. It's Julie."

"What?" said Cas and Julie together.

"Hello. Skin milky and soft as silk? Golden apple is her heart. I know. It's really cornball. But that's Wes for you."

"But what about the thieves? I thought Reynolds had ripped off the Savings and Loan."

"You're kidding," said Melanie.

"No," said Cas. "And I've been worried sick."

"You are such a dickhead."

"And you are such a sister to a dickhead," replied Cas. "You could have helped out here."

"I did. I stole the chickens, didn't I?"

"You?" said Cas.

"I thought so," said Julie.

"Why?"

"To get you out to Julie's so she wouldn't have a chance to leave town without seeing you."

"What about the other chickens?"

"I kinda improvised there. It was a gas. Did you see Reynolds's face when those chickens were running all over the VFW?"

"That was a cruel thing to do to Isabelle."

"What? Candy Apple Queen? Give me a break. She doesn't care about you. Everybody was just trying to marry her off for their own reasons and none of them had anything to do with her." Melanie shrugged. "Besides, it's the most attention she's had in her whole white-bread life. She enjoyed all the pampering she got afterwards."

Cas took a deep breath. "And the stereos and televisions? Please tell me that wasn't you."

"That wasn't me. I only steal chickens."

"Well, don't steal anymore."

"Don't worry. My work is done. I gotta go apply to some colleges." She started back toward the house. At the steps she turned back to them. "Did Cas ever tell you the one about the chicken, the horse and the Harley?"

Chapter 25

She had money. Enough to start over anywhere she liked or even never have to work again. She could stay here and raise chickens. She could marry Cas. She could do anything she wanted. But what did she want?

Julie looked out of the turret window at the front yard, at her little Volkswagen, the copse of trees that surrounded the fishing pond, and thought, *I can't stay here. Not forever. And I can't really marry Cas, if he decides to stay. Seeing the Reynoldses every day.* Marian might be planning a bridal shower, but Reynolds would never let them live in peace.

Bridal shower. What had she been thinking? She wasn't exactly the bridal shower type. She was more of a Glock kind of girl. How did that fit into married life?

She thought of Tilda and how she was happy because she owned the Roadhouse and had Terrence. Was that enough for Julie Excelsior? She'd seen the real world, and for all its crime and ugliness, she had loved the challenge. She was suddenly afraid that raising chickens or children wouldn't be enough.

She shuddered. It was time to make her last stop down memory lane. She didn't want to, but she knew now that Wes was right; to get to the future, she had to revisit the past.

Smitty wanted to go with her, and though she would have appreciated the company, this was something that she had to do alone. She drove down the hill and cut through town until she was at the bridge that led to the mill. She pulled to the side of the road and just looked across the river, suddenly nervous. She didn't want to remember growing up there.

While she was contemplating turning and running, the passenger door opened. Melanie threw her backpack on the floor and got in.

Melanie scowled at her. "You aren't leaving, are you?"

Julie didn't answer. She didn't know the answer herself. "How do you manage to be everywhere at once?"

"I owe it to Wes."

Julie looked at her, and saw what she had only glimpsed before. A girl on the verge of adulthood, trying to make a place for herself. And feeling the kind of aloneness that came from being cut adrift just when you needed someone to show you the way.

"For now, I'm going to visit my old home." Julie lifted her chin toward the opposite shore of the river.

"I'll go, too," said Melanie and buckled her seat belt.

"Afraid I'll run away?" asked Julie, only half joking.

"Yes."

Okay. Julie shifted into first and thought, *Did you send her, Wes, this guardian in Goth clothes, to help me through this and make sure I didn't chicken out?*

She drove across the river. The bridge and the road that lead to the mill had been plowed, but the side roads were still covered in snow, which meant a trek on foot if Julie were to complete this last task. She pulled the Volkswagen into a narrow opening where the plow had dumped a mountain of snow into the harbor. Melting snow banks rose up above the car on both sides.

Wordlessly, she and Melanie got out of the car, walked back to the road and looked down it to where the old brick factory seemed to totter on its foundations. It had been closed for Julie's entire life and she'd never paid it much attention before. Now, she tried to imagine Josiah and William, crouched in hiding, watching the traitors load rifles onto the barge. Andrew

Reynolds seeing them, aiming his rifle, shooting his brother dead. And Josiah killing him in turn. The barge catching fire. The long hopeless ride to Reynolds Place where William died. Josiah reviled by the town, despised by the Reynoldses because he had kept his promise to his friend. You wouldn't see that kind of loyalty these days.

And for the first time in days, Julie thought about Donald, the bribe taker. He was sort of like Andrew Reynolds. An unregenerate man who had to be stopped. And Julie felt a sudden affinity with her ancestor, Josiah. They had both done the right thing.

"Stupid," said Melanie, breaking the silence. It took Julie a moment to realize that Melanie wasn't commenting on her, but had been thinking about the same event. "So what if they saved New York? They left our families broken forever."

"Until now," said Julie.

"Yeah, sure."

Yeah, sure, echoed Julie's mind. Would any of them ever really be free of the feud? Christine's children would be. And Melanie's, someday. And what about her? Would she ever be free from the feud or from doing her duty as she saw it? She shook the thought away, turned from the mill and began looking for the beginning of the street that ran past her old house.

Melanie returned to the car and Julie thought she would be making this trip by herself after all, but then Melanie was walking beside her, zipping up a down parka.

Julie smiled, but didn't let Melanie see.

They waded through heavy wet snow, leaving holes every time they took a step. It would have been smarter to wait a few days until it melted, except then she would be wading through mud. Even so, she wasn't prepared when she looked up and saw the place where she had grown up. The patch of yard was covered with drifted snow. The wooden front porch floor had completely collapsed. The window panes were all missing, and the roof sagged beneath a blanket of snow.

"There's no place like home," said Julie.

"Cool," said Melanie with no inflection and walked toward it.

Julie followed her, wondering how Melanie could find this anything but tragic. "Maybe to you. But it wasn't so great living here."

"Then why did you?"

Julie shrugged. "Because we were poor, I guess. And don't ask me why. I don't know. Though I've often wondered."

"Maybe your dad was a history buff."

"I don't think so."

"These cottages are two hundred years old."

Julie looked at her in surprise. "Are you a history buff?"

"History sucks."

Taking that as a yes, Julie said, "It's a shame how everything has been forgotten. This was a really important part of the nation's past."

"I guess. They teach all that shit in school."

"Right, I remember. Junior year. American history. Pretty boring."

"Yeah."

"Well, I've had enough of my family history. I'm for lunch."

They retraced their steps back to the street and Julie took a last look. Tried to see the old house as a historical site instead of just the other side of the river. It didn't work.

She started off back toward the main road, Melanie a few steps behind. They'd made it half way there, when they heard a car engine. Then a gray van sped past, headed toward the mill.

"Hey," said Julie. "That's the van that was used to kidnap me." She tried to move faster, but by the time she'd reached the cleared section of road, the van was gone.

"What are they up to?" she said.

"To no good," said Melanie. "That's Henley's van."

Julie looked at her, then fumbled in her pocket for her car keys. "Go get Cas or Terrence. I think we might have found some kidnappers and some thieves."

Melanie hesitated. "What are you going to do?"

"Hide and watch, just like our great-great-grandfathers."

"Do you have your gun?"

Jeez, thought Julie. Did the whole town know about her Glock? "No. So hurry."

Melanie took off toward the car, moving faster than Julie had ever seen her move. Julie began walking down the road toward the mill.

She stayed close to the snow banks, taking what cover she could. The van was parked in the front of the mill. She jumped back as Henley and Bo came out of the door, carrying stereo equipment.

Julie reevaluated her opinion of their stupidity. They must have learned something in school, like a little local Civil War history. She watched as they loaded the contraband into the van and went back inside.

She was torn between keeping an eye on them and going back down the road to warn Cas or Terrence when they arrived. She was pretty sure Henley and Bo would have to go back the way they came. Unless the road had been cleared all the way out to the old state highway on the other side of the mill.

Too late, she saw a shadow spread across the snow bank. She started to turn but felt something poke her in the ribs.

"Don't get any ideas, Ms. Excelsior. Now, put your hands up. I've got a rifle."

Damn, she hadn't expected another accomplice. Slowly she raised her hands. The rifle poked her again. "Move."

She began to walk toward the van.

Henley and Bo came out of the mill, stopped and stared.

"Where did she come from?" asked Henley.

"Found her hiding back in the snow, watching you, you dumb shit. I told you to be careful."

"Dammit, Dad, I *was* careful. She's a sneaky one."

Arnold Baxter. Of course. Julie knew Henley and Bo would need help to figure out anything more complicated than lifting a beer bottle to their mouths. She just hoped Cas had the good sense to bring Terrence and not walk into a trap.

"I suggest you boys hurry and get out," said Julie. "Somebody might see you."

"Yeah, like you?" Henley laughed. "Too bad you won't be around to tell."

Julie went still. "It will be my word against yours. Won't hold up in court." Of course, it would, but she bet they didn't know that.

"Sure won't if you're dead," said Arnold. "Now shut up."

Bo stared at Arnold. "You're not gonna kill her. That's murder. I'm not gonna be part of any murder."

"Shut up, Bo," said Henley and Arnold together.

"No, I mean it. They can send you away for murder. I'm getting out." Bo dumped his load of equipment on the van floor and straightened up.

"Hold it right there unless you want to join her," said Arnold.

Julie rolled her eyes. She didn't really think Arnold would shoot her. Nobody could be that dumb, not even the Baxters.

Then she heard a faint sound. A car. Far away, but coming toward them. The others didn't seem to notice.

"I'm not kidding. I'm not going down the road for a few stereos."

"You dumb fuck, just load the stuff," said Henley.

"First you tell me you aren't gonna kill her."

Henley shoved Bo. Bo stumbled back, then lunged for Henley. They both fell to the ground and started pummeling each other.

"Stop it," yelled Arnold. Julie felt the rifle move against her back. Now was the time to move.

"Freeze," yelled a new voice.

Oh no, thought Julie. *Please say he isn't waving that unloaded .38 at them.*

"Drop the rifle."

Slowly Arnold moved the rifle away.

Julie readied herself to grab it. Everyone in town, including Arnold must know that Cas couldn't shoot worth shit. Julie turned her head enough to see that Arnold was still holding the rifle and that Cas was walking toward him, the .38 aimed at Arnold's chest.

Damn it. If Arnold didn't kill him she would, for being such an idiot.

Julie spun around intending to knock the rifle away. At the same moment, Arnold turned, raised the rifle and aimed.

She bit back a scream, but Cas wasn't where he had been a moment before.

Arnold pointed the rifle indiscriminately, looking for him. Cas was closing in on him from the left; he dove at Arnold's legs. Arnold jerked back from the force of Cas's body; the rifle fired into the air, then fell to the ground. Arnold fought to keep his balance, but Cas just kept pushing him back. Julie snatched the rifle away as the two men fell to the ground.

Bo and Henley stopped fighting to watch Arnold and Cas roll across the pavement, fists flying.

Julie aimed the rifle at Bo and Henley. "Get up. Slowly," she said just as another car screeched to a stop. *It's a party*, she thought and motioned Henley and Bo into the open van.

Julie's VW drove right up beside her. Terrence and Melanie jumped out. Terrence ran over to where Cas was hauling Arnold Baxter to his feet.

In minutes, the three culprits were handcuffed and pushed into the back seat of Cas's police car.

Cas turned to Julie, a huge grin on his face and another black eye rapidly forming.

Julie narrowed her eyes at him. "Just what do you think you were doing?"

Cas's grin disappeared. "I was saving you. I'm the sheriff."

She stepped toward him, grabbed him by his jacket and shook him. "Don't ever do something that stupid again."

Cas frowned, then looked hurt. "I was just—"

"Trying to be a hero," put in Melanie.

"Hey," said Cas.

"I don't want a hero," said Julie, accenting each word with a shake of his lapels.

"You don't?" asked Cas, sounding bewildered.

"Arrgh." Julie pulled him into her until they were inches apart. "I just want you to keep giving me the best sex of my life, not get your balls blown off."

"The best?" Cas's frown slowly changed back to a smile. "Works for me." And he kissed her.

Julie heard someone snort. Melanie. And someone rumble. Terrence. She pulled away. "We have an audience."

"I can fix that." Cas tossed his keys to Terrence. Then held out his hand to Melanie. She dropped Julie's keys into it. "Take Mel back to the station with you. I'll be there . . . soon."

A minute later, Julie and Cas heard the police car back up and drive away, but all they saw was each other.

The following Friday afternoon, Cas and Julie were standing inside the Roadhouse with the rest of the habitués for Tilda's Grand Opening of the Old Roadhouse Inn. The original stone building had been converted to the front entrance and the clapboard addition was slated to undergo improvements in the spring. Tilda had just unveiled a new bronze sign that read *The tavern that saved New York.*

"A bit over the top," said Maude, standing in the midst of the Hellzapoppin gang.

"Not at all," said Tilda, looking proudly at her sign. "I'm having the whole history of the plot printed on the placemats and napkins, and Old Roadhouse Inn embossed on the new coasters.

"We're a historic site. I'm gonna be ready for all the tourists," she raised her voice and proclaimed, "who'll come to see where Josiah Excelsior and William Reynolds thwarted the plot to capture New York."

"I'll drink to that," said Terrence and drained his mug.

The door banged open and Larry, the biker, ran into the bar. "Wall down at the bridge broke."

"Oh, shit," said Cas.

"Anybody hurt?" asked Terrence.

"No, but—but you better come see. There's something in the water."

Julie, Cas, and Terrence exchanged glances.

"We'd better go see," said Cas.

"You ladies better stay here," said Dan Pliney and followed them out the door.

"Damn if I will,' said Maude and hurried after him.

Soon the entire patronage of the Roadhouse was walking down Old Mill Road to the bridge. Cas and Terrence were looking across the river where water was gushing out of the ruptured wall.

"Would you look at that," said Tilda.

"Damn, it looks like Niagara Falls," said Dan.

Pretty close, thought Julie.

They all watched the water churn into the river.

"Do you think the bridge is safe?" someone asked.

"Sure, it's broken through downstream."

"Hey, look over there."

Everyone turned toward the old harbor whose water level was rapidly dropping. There was something there. Big wooden beams began to stick obliquely out of the water.

It can't be, thought Julie. But it was. As the water continued to drain, the deck of what had once been a river barge came into view.

Terrence and Cas immediately cordoned off the bridge with yellow crime tape.

"Historic site," said Terrence. "No trespassing."

"Let's call the newspapers," said Dan Pliney. "We've got us a major historical find here."

"This might just put us back on the map," said Henry Goethe.

"Well, no one touches it until we get some experts up here to look at it," said Cas.

"Good idea, sheriff,' said Elton Dinwiddie. "We'll form a historic site watch, take turns guarding the place."

"That's a great idea, Elton," said Cas. "Why don't you organize it?"

Elton saluted and began making a list of volunteers.

"I see a bright future for old Ex Falls," said Julie.

"Maybe they can find a real sheriff now," said Cas.

Julie's stomach fluttered. "You're leaving?"

"We're leaving."

"We are?"

"Yep. Since we're down here, I have something to show you." He took her hand and led her through the crowd. At his cottage, he stopped and unlocked the door to the machine shop. "Close your eyes."

"Okay," said Julie, feeling wary.

He led her inside, turned her to the right and said, "Okay, open them."

She did. She was standing in front of a shiny white boat hull. Along its prow, black letters spelled out *Julie E.*

"Oh, Cas, it's beautiful."

"She. She's beautiful and so are you. Sail away with me, Julie."

Julie turned. "Aye, aye, Captain. My pleasure."

"Always," said Cas and kissed her.

The entire town came out for the bon voyage of the Excelsior-Reynolds. Even Marian and Reynolds, who'd taken a long lunch hour from his new job as assistant manager of the Henryville Mercantile Bank.

"Take care of Ernie," said Julie.

"Don't worry," said Maude.

"And Bill and Hillary and little Chelsea."

"I will," said Maude.

"And the Beetle."

Melanie waved the keys at her. "And you take care of my dickhead brother."

"I will."

"We'll have that shower when you come back for Tilda and Terrence's wedding," said Marian and dabbed at her eyes with a white hankie.

"Humph," said Reynolds. "Drive safely."

"I will," said Cas and winked at Julie.

They got into the green truck.

"Are you ever going to tell me about the chicken, the horse and the Harley?"

Cas smiled. "Once there was a chicken and a horse . . ." He started the engine.

The town waved good-bye, and Julie and Cas drove away, the *Julie E.* hooked to the bumper and Smitty smiling at everyone through the back window.

Don't miss Dianne Castell's
'TIL THERE WAS U,
available now from Brava!
Here's a first look . . .

A woman in shorts, white blouse, blond ponytail, barefoot and with a big purse slung over her shoulder was pulling something from the backseat. "The car's my rental, but I don't know who . . . Holy cow! Effie?"

"Who's Effie?"

"I . . . I'm not sure," he said to Rory as much as to himself as he took her in. Golden hair hanging free instead of bound up in some business do, a flimsy little blouse and bare legs . . . lots and lots of bare tan legs. No wonder she didn't want to lose her tan. Ryan ran his hand around the back of his neck. "I'm not sure at all and that's not good."

"I don't know who you're looking at, boy, but that gal is mighty fine."

California Effie he could handle, but this? Who the hell was this? She gave a final tug, the suitcase sliding all the way out, making her stumble backwards and fall on the ground, the luggage landing on top of her.

Ryan rushed across the grass and picked up the luggage. Rory took Effie's arm and helped her up. "Are you okay, little lady? You should have waited for someone to help you with that thing. Could have squashed you flatter than a frog on the freeway."

"I'm fine, thank you," she said to Rory with a genuine smile, making Ryan suddenly want her to smile at him like that. "The porter at the airport must have jammed that suit-case in the back. Like a size twelve foot in a size nine shoe."

Rory's eyes twinkled. "Well, I'll be. Haven't heard that expression in a coon's age. A real country girl."

Effie laughed, and Ryan's insides did a little flip. She'd never laughed open and carefree like that before either. She said, "Born and raised in San Diego, but my grandparents lived on a farm. This place reminds me of it, sort of brings out that country girl you mentioned."

Ryan nudged the suitcase. "What the hell's in this thing? And where'd you get those clothes? You never dress like this."

She turned his way. "I only packed slacks. I hadn't planned on the blast furnace you all call the weather around here and being out in it. Thelma lent me clothes." Effie smoothed the blouse and shorts. "Wasn't that nice of her?"

"Thelma does not own short-shorts." Did she just say 'you all'?

"Rolled them up. And as for the luggage, I packed a fax machine and printer along with toner and paper so I can set up an office in the dining room. Thelma said it was okay with her and—"

"You packed office equipment?" Ryan watched a hint of breeze tease the wisps of blond hair curling in the humidity at her temples.

"You're the one who said the Landing was nothing like our office, that this place was rural."

"I didn't say they used stone tablets and smoke signals."

"Well, that's what you implied. All I know about Tennessee is that it has mountains and they filter whiskey through ten feet of sugar-maple charcoal." Effie shrugged. "One of my old boy-friends was a whiskey snob."

"I'm Rory O'Fallon," Rory said on a chuckle as he nodded at Ryan. "His daddy and happy as all get-out to meet you. The two of you together is damn interesting, I'll tell you that." He held out his hand to Effie.

Ryan felt as if he were seeing Effie for the first time, like when she'd come into his office all those months ago and knocked him on his ear. Trouble was, she was more beautiful now than then. He was certainly seeing parts of her he'd never seen before. Bare legs, bare arms, buttons open down the front of her blouse hinting at delectable cleavage where he suddenly wanted to bury his face. Shit!

Why couldn't he work with the big fat guy down the hall and have him along now? Because the big fat guy wasn't half the architect Effie Wilson was.

Rory hitched his chin toward the river. "We've got whatever office equipment you need right down at the landing. Help yourself anytime, though cell phones don't work for spit in these parts." He grinned. "The crew will sure appreciate having you around, give them something nice and pretty to look at and brighten their day. Hope you don't mind a wolf whistle or two. They don't mean nothing by it, just a little appreciation for the finer things in life."

Did Effie blush? Ryan had never seen her do that. Made her eyes greener, her hair blonder, her skin shimmer. No way was he letting her go to any damn docks.

Okay, this great idea to bring her along so they could work together was not his best lifetime idea. In fact, it sucked. He'd thought things would be the same as in the office; he could handle Effie in a suit and buttoned up. Except she sure as hell wasn't buttoned up now. He had to get rid of her, just like he told Rory he would. "Afraid she won't get that far, Dad. Effie's leaving in the morning."

"I am?"

"There's no need for you to be here. I've reconsidered."

She folded her arms and glared at him. "Well, bully for you."

"I can take care of everything."

"Like designing the mall by yourself." She toed the luggage

by his feet. Cute toes with dark red painted toenails. "I don't think so, and I didn't haul all this crap across the continent to just pack it up again and leave without using it."

She tied together her shirttails with a decisive yank, showing her narrow waist and giving Ryan a quick peek at her navel—her navel pierced by a little gold ring—as she made the knot.

His mouth went dry; his head wobbled on his neck. He had to swallow before he could speak. How could she make a baggy shirt of Thelma's look like this? "What happened to 'I'm a businesswoman, a California girl?' What about your cat and sushi?"

"What happened to me owing you for the shoes and the mall plans?"

Rory's eyes widened a fraction. "Ryan, this Ryan, bought you shoes?"

Effie nodded and did a mischievous wiggle with her eyebrows. "And they're Italian."

Thank God she didn't wiggle anything else.

Here's a sizzling teaser from
BAYOU BAD BOYS,
featuring JoAnn Ross and "Cajun Heat,"
coming next month from Brava . . .

It was funny how life turned out. Who'd have thought that a girl who'd been forced to buy her clothes in the Chubbettes department of the Tots to Teens Emporium, the very same girl who'd been a wallflower at her senior prom, would grow up to have men pay to get naked with her?

It just went to show, Emma Quinlan considered, as she ran her hands down her third bare male back of the day, that the American dream was alive and well and living in Blue Bayou, Louisiana.

Not that she'd dreamed that much of naked men back when she'd been growing up.

She'd been too sheltered, too shy, and far too inhibited. Then there'd been the weight issue. Photographs showed that she'd been a cherubic infant, the very same type celebrated on greeting cards and baby food commercials.

Then she'd gone through a "baby fat" stage. Which, when she was in the fourth grade, resulted her being sent off to a fat camp where calorie cops monitored every bite that went into her mouth and did surprise inspections of the cabins, searching out contraband. One poor calorie criminal had been caught with packages of gummy bears hidden beneath a loose floor board beneath his bunk. Years later, the memory of his frightened eyes as he struggled to plod his way through a punishment lap of the track was vividly etched in her mind.

The camps became a yearly ritual, as predictable as the return of swallows to the Louisiana Gulf coast every August on their fall migration.

For six weeks during July and August, every bite Emma put in her mouth was monitored. Her days were spent doing calisthenics and running around the oval track and soccer field; her nights were spent dreaming of crawfish jambalaya, chicken gumbo, and bread pudding.

There were rumors of girls who'd trade sex for food, but Emma had never met a camper who'd actually admitted to sinking that low, and since she wasn't the kind of girl any of the counselors would've hit on, she'd never had to face such a moral dilemma.

By the time she was fourteen, Emma realized that she was destined to go through life as a "large girl." That was also the year that her mother—a petite blonde, whose crowning achievement in life seemed to be that she could still fit into her size zero wedding dress fifteen years after the ceremony—informed Emma that she was now old enough to shop for back-to-school clothes by herself.

"You are so lucky!" Emma's best friend, Roxi Dupree, had declared that memorable Saturday afternoon. "My mother is so old fashioned. If she had her way, I'd be wearing calico like Half-Pint in *Little House on the Prairie*!"

Roxi might have envied what she viewed as Emma's shopping freedom, but she hadn't seen the disappointment in Angela Dupree's judicious gaze when Emma had gotten off the bus from the fat gulag, a mere two pounds thinner than when she'd been sent away.

It hadn't taken a mind reader to grasp the truth—that Emma's former beauty queen mother was ashamed to go clothes shopping with her fat teenage daughter.

"Uh, sugar?"

The deep male voice shattered the unhappy memory. *Bygones*, Emma told herself firmly.

"Yes?"

"I don't want to be tellin' you how to do your business, but maybe you're rubbing just a touch hard?"

Damn. She glanced down at the deeply tanned skin. She had such a death grip on his shoulders.

"I'm so sorry, Nate."

"No harm done," he said, the south Louisiana drawl blending appealingly with his Cajun French accent. "Though maybe you could use a bit of your own medicine. You seem a tad tense."

"It's just been a busy week, what with the Jean Lafitte weekend coming up."

Liar. The reason she was tense was not due to her days, but her recent sleepless nights.

She danced her fingers down his bare spine. And felt the muscles of his back clench.

"I'm sorry," she repeated, spreading her palms outward.

"No need to apologize. That felt real good. I was going to ask you a favor, but since you're already having a tough few days—"

"Don't be silly. We're friends, Nate. Ask away."

She could feel his chuckle beneath her hands. "That's what I love about you, chere. You agree without even hearing what the favor is."

He turned his head and looked up at her, affection warming his Paul Newman blue eyes. "I was supposed to pick someone up at the airport this afternoon, but I got a call that these old windows I've been trying to find for a remodel job are goin' on auction in Houma this afternoon, and—"

"I'll be glad to go to the airport. Besides, I owe you for getting your brother to help me out."

If it hadn't been for Finn Callahan's detective skills, Emma's louse of an ex-husband would've gotten away with absconding with all their joint funds. Including the money she'd socked away in order to open her Every Body's Beautiful day spa. Not only had Finn—a former FBI agent—not charged her his going rate, Nate insisted on paying for the weekly massage the doctor had prescribed after he'd broken his shoulder falling off a scaffolding.

"You don't owe me a thing. Your ex is pond scum. I was glad to help put him away."

Having never been one to hold grudges, Emma had tried not to feel gleeful when the news bulletin about her former husband's arrest for embezzlement and tax fraud had come over her car radio.

"So, what time is the flight, and who's coming in?"

"It gets in at five thirty-five at Concourse D. It's a Delta flight from LA."

"Oh?" Her heart hitched. Oh, please. She cast a quick, desperate look into the adjoining room at the voodoo altar, draped in Barbie-pink tulle, that Roxi had set up as packaging for her "hex appeal" love spell business. Don't let it be—

"It's Gabe."

Damn. Where the hell was voodoo power when you needed it?

"Well." She blew out a breath. "That's certainly a surprise."

That was an understatement. Gabriel Broussard had been so eager to escape Blue Bayou, he'd hightailed it out of town without so much as a goodbye.

Not that he'd owed Emma one.

The hell he didn't. Okay. Maybe she did hold a grudge. But only against men who'd kissed her silly, felt her up until she'd melted into a puddle of hot, desperate need, then disappeared from her life.

Unfortunately, Gabriel hadn't disappeared from the planet. In fact it was impossible to go into a grocery store without seeing his midnight blue eyes smoldering from the cover of some sleazy tabloid. There was usually some barely clad female plastered to him.

Just last month, an enterprising photographer with a telescopic lens had captured him supposedly making love to his co-star on the deck of some Greek shipping tycoon's yacht. The day after that photo hit the newsstands, splashed all over the front of the *Enquirer*, the actress's producer husband had filed for divorce.

Then there'd been this latest scandal with Tamara the prairie princess . . .

"Guess you've heard what happened," Nate said.

Emma shrugged. "I may have caught something on *Entertainment Tonight* about it." And had lost sleep for the past three nights imagining what, exactly, constituted kinky sex.

"Gabe says it'll blow over."

"Most things do, I suppose." It's what people said about Hurricane Ivan. Which had left a trail of destruction in its wake.

"Meanwhile, he figured Blue Bayou would be a good place to lie low."

"How lucky for all of us," she said through gritted teeth.

"You sure nothing's wrong, chere?"

"Positive." She forced a smile. It wasn't his fault that his best friend had the sexual morals of an alley cat. "All done."

"And feeling like a new man." He rolled his head onto his shoulders. Then he retrieved his wallet from his back pocket and handed her his Amex card. "You definitely have magic hands, Emma, darlin'."

"Thank you." Those hands were not as steady as they should have been as she ran the card. "I guess Gabe's staying at your house, then?"

"I offered. But he said he'd rather stay out at the camp."

Terrific. Not only would she be stuck in a car with the man during rush hour traffic, she was also going to have to return to the scene of the crime.

"You sure it's no problem? He can always rent a car, but bein' a star and all, as soon as he shows up at the Hertz counter, his cover'll probably be blown."

She forced a smile she was a very long way from feeling. "Of course it's no problem."

"Then why are you frowning?"

"I've got a headache coming on." A two-hundred-and-and-ten pound Cajun one. "I'll take a couple aspirin and I'll be fine."

"You're always a damn sight better than fine, chere." His grin was quick and sexy, without the seductive overtones that had always made his friend's smile so dangerous.

She could handle this, Emma assured herself as she locked up the spa for the day. An uncharacteristic forty-five minutes early, which had Cal Marchand, proprietor of Cal's Cajun Café across the street, checking his watch in surprise.

The thing to do was to just pull on her big girl underpants, drive into New Orleans and get it over with. Gabriel Broussard might be *People* magazine's sexiest man alive. He might have seduced scores of women all over the world, but the man *Cosmo* readers had voted the pirate they'd most like to be held prisoner on a desert island with was, after all, just a man. Not that different from any other.

Besides, she wasn't the same shy, tongue-tied small-town bayou girl she'd been six years ago. She'd lived in the city; she'd gotten married only to end up publicly humiliated by a man who turned out to be slimier than swamp scum.

It hadn't been easy, but she'd picked herself up, dusted herself off, divorced the Dickhead, as Roxi loyally referred to him, started her own business and was a dues paying member of Blue Bayou's Chamber of Commerce.

She'd even been elected vice mayor, which was, admittedly an unpaid position, but it did come with the perk of riding in a snazzy convertible in the Jean Lafitte Day parade. Roxi, a former Miss Blue Bayou, had even taught her a beauty queen wave.

She'd been fired in the crucible of life. She was intelligent, tough, and had tossed off her nice girl Catholic upbringing after the Dickhead dumped her for another woman. A bimbo who'd applied for a loan to buy a pair of D cup boobs so she could win a job as a cocktail waitress at New Orlean's Coyote Ugly Saloon.

Emma might not be a tomb raider like Lara Croft, or an international spy with a to-kill-for wardrobe and trunkful of glamorous wigs like *Alias*'s Sydney Bristow, but this new, improved Emma Quinlan could take names and kick butt right along with the rest of those fictional take-charge females.

And if she were the type of woman to hold a grudge, which she wasn't, she assured herself yet again, the butt she'd most like to kick belonged to Blue Bayou bad boy Gabriel Broussard.

Please turn the page for a funny
sneak peek at Susanna Carr's
LIP LOCK,
coming next month from Brava . . .

She scurried back into the closet, begging—absolutely begging—for him to not to enter the closet. It was midnight, after all. On a Saturday.

But time meant nothing to Kyle.

She heard him enter the bathroom and hit the lights. Molly dove for the very back rack in the closet and squatted down.

Her heart pounded. Her tongue felt huge and she couldn't swallow. She kept her eyes glued on the door, but she didn't want to look.

This is why she could never play hide-and-seek as a kid. she couldn't handle the idea of being found. Couldn't tolerate the wait.

She knew she was going to get caught. She couldn't shake off the feeling. Or bravely meet the inevitable.

No, instead she was huddling in the corner, images of work record flashing in he head. *Terminated because she was hiding in her boss's closet.*

Yeah, let's see how long it'll take her to get another job with that kid of reference.

She drew in a shaky breath, ready to have that door swing open. For Kyle to find her. The interrogation that would follow. She'll have come up with a good reason why she was here. Something brilliant. Irrefutable. Logical.

So far, she had nothing.

And why wasn't he opening the door? She couldn't take much more of this.

Molly craned her neck and cocked her head to the side. All she heard was the shower.

The shower! Molly sat up straight as a plan began to form. The bathroom would get all hot and steamy. The glass would fog and she could sneak out. Perfect!

But that would mean getting out of her hiding place. Maybe she should wait until he left.

So that he could what? Go to his desk and spend the rest of the night working on the computer? Leaving her stuck here?

This was her only chance to escape. She needed to take advantage of it. Now.

Molly reluctantly crept to the door. She winced and cringed as she slowly opened it a crack. She was so nervous that Kyle might see the movement. Or that he would spot her. Look right at her. Eye to eye.

Instead she got an eyeful.

Kyle grabbed the collar of his white rugby shirt and pulled it over his head. The bright lights bounced against the dips and swells of his toned arms.

Molly ignored the tingle deep in her belly as she stared. She already knew that guy was fit, but oh . . . my . . . *goodness.* . . .

Kyle's lean body rippled with strength. He was solid muscle. Defined and restrained.

She memorized everything from the whorls of dark hair that dusted his tanned chest to the jutting hip bone. Her heart skittered to a stop as his hands went to the snap at his waistband.

Oh . . . The tingling grew hotter. Brighter. She shouldn't look. No. She really shouldn't. Not even a peek.

He drew the zipper down.

She should turn her head away.

Her neck muscles weren't cooperating as the zipper parted.

Okay, at least close your eyes! She forced herself to obey and her eyelids started to lower.

Until the jeans dropped to his ankles.

Molly's eyes widened. *Oh . . . wow.*

He was long, thick and heavy. There was nothing elegant or refined about his penis. It looked rough. Wild. And this was before he was aroused?

She could imagine how it would feel to have him inside her. Before he even thrust. Molly pressed her legs together as the tingling blazed into an all-out ache.

Kyle turned around and she stared at his tight buttocks. *Oh, yeah.* She could go for one of those, too. She could imagine exactly how it would feel to hold onto him as he claimed her.

He stepped out of her field of vision. A shot of panic cleared her head. Where did he go? She caught a movement in the mirror and saw Kyle step into that sinfully decadent shower. She watched the reflection as he stepped under the water.

Great. Just what she needed. A hot, naked and *wet* Kyle Ashton.

The shower stall didn't hide a thing from her. Water pulsed against body. It sluiced down his chest and ran down Kyle's powerful thighs. She wanted to lick every droplet from his sculpted muscle.

Molly pulled at the neck of her sweat shirt. How hot was that shower? It was getting really warm in here.

The scent of Kyle's soap invaded her senses. Sophisticated. Expensive. It usually made her knees knock on everyday occasions, but this was concentrated stuff. It knocked her off her feet.

The steam wafted from the shower stall and began to cloud the glass. Molly had to squint as the fog slowly streaked across the shower glass. She was half-tempted to wipe the condensation from her view when she remembered this was what she was waiting for.

Sure she was.

She glanced at the door. It was closed, but not all the way. That was her escape. She'd better get moving before he was finished. Molly glanced back at the mirror.

His head was tilted back and water streamed down the

harsh angles of his face. She fought the fierce urge to join him and press her mouth against the strong column of his neck. Of running her hands along his body as his hands remained in his drenched hair.

That was never going to happen. She could fantasize about that later. Right now, she had to get away from Kyle.

She slowly opened the closet door, thankful it didn't creak. Hoping Kyle was like the rest of the world and closed his eyes when rinsing out the shampoo, Molly got on her hands and knees. She gathered up the last of her courage and began crawling along the bathroom floor.

Her heart was banging against her chest. Nerves bounced around inside her. She couldn't breathe. When she had to pass by the shower, she got down on her elbows and shimmied her way to the door.

Almost there . . . She wasn't going to look at Kyle, no matter how tempting. Her focus was solely on the door, and once she got it open, she was making a run for it.

Molly reached out and grabbed the edge of the door and slowly, oh-so-slowly opened it enough that she could squeeze through. She could feel the cool air wafting in from the other room.

Home free! Molly exhaled shakily.

"Hey, Molly," Kyle called out from the shower. "Could you grab me a towel while you're at it?"